RUTHLESS ROYALS

The Completed Duet

AMANDA RICHARDSON

Ruthless Royals
Amanda Richardson
Published by Amanda Richardson
© Copyright 2021 Amanda Richardson
Special Edition Paperback v.2, 2022
www.authoramandarichardson.com

Editing by Traci Finlay

AUTHOR'S NOTE

This is a special edition paperback of the Ruthless Royals duet (Ruthless Crown and Ruthless Queen) version 2.0. It is a high-school bully reverse harem romance. All characters are 18+.

Please note the trigger warnings in the blurb, which is located on the next page.

BLURB

Please note: This is a special Edition paperback of Ruthless Crown and Ruthless Queen (the completed duet)

Plus, a bonus epilogue exclusive to this paperback!

Their names are whispers in the hallways.
Hunter, Ash, Ledger, and Samson.
The Kings.
Four of the most beautiful men I've ever seen,
with cruel agendas and an even crueler reign over Ravenwood
Academy.

Wreaking havoc in our small, New England town, no one asks
questions.
For the most part, people ignore or avoid them.
After all, they're royalty here.
Because one of them—the cruelest one—is the headmaster's
son.
And my new stepbrother.

They can try to torment me.
They can try to break me.
But they have no idea what I've endured.
They're used to getting whatever their ruthless, little hearts desire.

Maybe I should keep my mouth shut.
Maybe I should let them win.
But I'm not afraid of getting my hands dirty.
Lord knows I'm used to it by now.

My name is Briar Monroe, and these Kings are about to find out just how fucked up this Queen can be.

*Please note that this is a special edition paperback of the Ruthless Royals duet. The duet is a high-school, bully reverse harem romance and contains explicit language, bullying, violence, and flashbacks of abuse/trauma. This edition also includes an extended, bonus epilogue.

For all of the ladies who wished Buffy, Feyre, Peyton, Katniss, Aelin, Rachel, Bella, Rory and Sookie never had to choose...

❦ I ❦
RUTHLESS CROWN

BRIAR

"He must have a big ol' you know what," I mumble as the movers finish bringing our boxes inside the large estate. There seemed to be so many more boxes when we packed up our small two-bedroom condo, but here in the grand foyer, the actual number before us looks so pitiful. I swallow as I look around, putting on a brave face. As my therapist would tell me: *I can do hard things.* And moving across the country to a gigantic house I've never seen, complete with a new stepfather and stepbrother? Yeah. That's hard—though I'd never admit it out loud.

"What's that, hon?" my mom asks, a clipboard in her left hand. She's perfectly put together despite the hectic morning, her athleisure wear snug against her toned body, and her blonde hair pulled into a tight ponytail. One of the movers not-so-discretely checks her ass out as he moves a dolly back outside, and I roll my eyes. She had me at eighteen—the age I am right now, which is crazy to think about—so I'm used to people openly hitting on her and thinking we're sisters.

"Nothing," I answer, smirking as I run my finger along the dark wood of the staircase. The house—if you can even call the grand estate a mere *house*—is way nicer than I expected. *Go, Mom. Way to score that rich peen.* "Where's Andrew? I thought he'd be here to welcome us."

My mom shakes her head as she checks things off her to-do list. "Nope. He's in Saint Tropez until Sunday."

"How rude of him not to invite us," I joke, and she chuckles.

"It's for business, Briar. I wouldn't want to go anyway. I have so much to do around here." She looks around, and her eyes have that excited gleam she always gets when she has a new project in front of her. To me, this is a house—to her, this is her newest endeavor. By Thanksgiving, this house will be scrubbed from top to bottom, artwork hung, rugs placed down, candles set up on every surface imaginable...

"Mmm."

I look around. It seems pretty put together to me, but I know she intends to make it ours. Right now, anyone could live here, and the furniture and decorations are generic and dated. The foyer, which is where we're standing, opens up so that the formal living room is to our right, a formal dining room to our left, and straight ahead is the casual breakfast room, a library, an *informal* living room, an office, a kitchen, a wine cellar, and a conservatory that leads into the expansive garden out back, flanked by an Olympic-sized pool and tennis court.

And that's just this floor. Up the wide staircase by the front door are *eleven* bedrooms. Downstairs, there's a large basement lounge area with a wet bar, a game room, a theater to watch television, another office, and an ensuite guest room, as if the eleven upstairs don't cut it. Who even needs that many bedrooms, anyway?

"Have you had a chance to look around?" Mom asks, pulling her credit card out of her wallet and handing it to one of the movers. They must be done. It didn't take as long as I thought, given the amount of time we spent packing up, but I guess any number of personal items in a place like this would feel meager.

"Briefly."

"Which room would you like? Andrew said to take any of them except the two at the end of the hallway."

I nod. "There are a few upstairs with a bathroom." Little does she know, I've already claimed the biggest room.

She mumbles something unintelligible. "Sure, hon. He made me promise to tell you that *mi casa es su casa*." She looks up from signing the receipt and gives me a soft smile. "He wants us to make ourselves at home, whatever that entails."

I put my hands in the pockets of my ripped, black jeans. "That won't be a problem," I quip, looking around. "The second bedroom is his son's?"

"Yes. But I get the feeling Hunter isn't here very often." She puts her card away and we both wave the movers off. Shutting the door, she turns to me and squeals. "Isn't this amazing?"

Amazing? Sure. My mom eloping with an older, rich guy? Great. After what happened, she deserves to be with someone stable. And being able to attend one of the most renowned private schools in Massachusetts because he's the headmaster is a convenient benefit. I think of what my life could be a year from now—living in Paris, attending university, eating croissants, outdoor cafés... *if* all goes according to plan, that is. I'm also glad to be as far away from California as possible. But I can't help the nagging, anxious feeling of being in a new place, when Marin City was the only town I've ever known.

"It's massive," I declare, looking around.

She walks over and puts an arm around my shoulders. Giving me a quick squeeze, she steps away and reaches down for a box. Relaxation is not in Mom's vocabulary. Doesn't matter that we've been driving for three days—now that we're here, there's work to be done. She's a bottomless pit of energy.

"Okay, time to unpack," she chirps, handing it to me. "Take this up to your room, please."

"Fine," I sigh, feigning annoyance.

I take the box from her and haul it up the sprawling staircase to the room I've already claimed as my own. It's the biggest one available, and it has its own bathroom, so those two things are a win-win for me. I push the door open and set it down. I have five boxes to my name, two of which are clothes. It felt really, really good to think about starting over here, so I didn't bring much.

I go downstairs and bring the other four boxes up, and I'm unpacked in a matter of thirty minutes. Mom promised a shopping trip soon, so aside from clothes, I have everything I need here. Photo albums, books, a blanket from my grandmother, a couple of sentimental knick-knacks, and then practical things like toiletries and accessories. I ignore the lump in my throat when I think of our condo, my friends, the fog of the bay area... it was my home for eighteen years. As I look around, I pull my arms around myself.

I guess this is my home now.

As I sit on the edge of the bed, I admire the shabby chic décor. There's a four-poster bed, chest of drawers, wardrobe, desk, and matching side tables. The window looks out onto the garden, and there's even a small balcony with a small table and two chairs. I envision sitting out there with some coffee, listening to music, reading, or just enjoying the changing seasons. I'm looking forward to experiencing a true fall, winter, and spring.

There's a knock at my door, and a second later, my mom walks in.

"Oh, this one's nice!" She walks over, sits on the edge of the bed, and puts an arm around my shoulders. "How are you doing, Briar?"

I let out a loud sigh. "Oh, you know." I nuzzle my head on her shoulder. "I think I'm fine."

She nods. "It's a fresh start. For both of us."

I close my eyes. "Thank god."

I love my mom, and she means well. We're super close, though I do often wonder if I was adopted. We're two entirely different people. Since she had me so young, and my father was never in the picture, we grew up together, in a way. Figured life out together. At thirty-six, she's still young and spry, and most of her friends are just now starting to have kids. She's the strongest person I know because of it, and still somehow manages to look like a model every freaking day. Blonde, athletic, a former cheerleader, she's perky and happy and is the first person to volunteer to help you out. It's no wonder she's a professional wedding planner.

I, on the other hand, have long, dark auburn hair, grey-blue eyes, and in the mornings before I've had my coffee, I resemble the girl from The Ring. I'm naturally pessimistic, sarcastic, and I've never done a sport in my life—I even failed out of physical education at my last school. I don't know my dad, but I assume I get all these lovely, cumbersome traits from him.

Despite our differences, I would be lost without my mom, and I know half the reason she moved us across the country right before my senior year was for my benefit. She saw me struggling with what happened, got me to see a wonderful psychologist, and when she met and married my new stepfather, the opportunity to move here presented itself. It seemed like a welcome change.

She stands. "I need to run a few errands, get the house in tip-top shape before Andrew returns on Sunday. Need anything while I'm out?"

"Maybe a cheeseburger?"

She snorts. "Two cheeseburgers it is." Bending down, she kisses me on the head. "Be good. Don't snoop around too much."

And then she's gone, leaving me to explore the house by myself.

BRIAR

While Mom is out, I do exactly what she asked me not to do, which is par for the course. Quietly stepping foot into the hallway, I explore the other rooms, most of which are just for guests. When I reach the last two rooms, I look around before opening the one I suspect is Hunter's room.

I've never met Hunter, nor do I even know what he looks like. When mom and Andrew eloped in Vegas after dating for six months, I wasn't surprised. I'd never seen her so giddy about a guy before, and it seemed he was smitten with her as well. Because of them being long distance, I'd only met Andrew a handful of times when he was visiting mom, and he'd mentioned Hunter in passing. I knew Hunter was my age, and that he was also a senior at Ravenwood Academy. But that was the extent of my knowledge.

We'd planned our inevitable move to Greythorn after they'd eloped, waiting until the end of summer to give her time to wrap up her existing wedding jobs in California. It made the most sense for us to move here since mom can plan weddings anywhere, and we were excited at the prospect of a fresh start. Andrew had offered to move him and Hunter to Marin City, but when we talked about it—and there were lots of discussions, because my mom wanted to be *sure* this was all okay with me—we'd both decided we'd needed a change of scenery.

I like Andrew. I don't know him very well since they've been long distance most of their relationship, but he's stable and boring, so that's good, I guess. Mom adores him for reasons I can't understand, but they seem like they're truly in love—*the real deal*—despite their fifteen-year age gap and glaring lifestyle differences.

Hunter's door creaks when I open it, and the bedroom inside surprises me. Black satin sheets, full bookcases made from black, ornate wood, a leather chair, a wooden desk, and a white shag rug on the floor. There isn't any art on the walls —just tons of small postcards pinned to the wall above his large bed. *Rio, Madrid, Copenhagen, Lima, Melbourne...*

I raise my eyebrows. I wasn't expecting a cool space like this, and I certainly wasn't expecting to like it as much as I do. I had no reason to dislike Hunter, but I couldn't help but form assumptions about him—like that he was a soulless, rich boy. I'd Googled Greythorn, MA, as well as Ravenwood Academy, so I had an inkling of the kinds of people who lived here. I'd already resigned myself to the fact that we'd have nothing in common. I mean, we obviously grew up *so* differently.

But... I would totally live in this room, and I'm officially intrigued.

I step into his bedroom and walk to the ensuite bathroom. Cologne and an electric toothbrush sit on the counter, and a luxurious black robe hangs over the towel rack haphazardly. I open the medicine cabinet, and several orange prescription bottles stare back at me. I pull one off the shelf and look at the label. *Lexapro.* Just as I'm about to check out the others, the front door slams from downstairs.

I rush out of Hunter's room and pretend like I'm just walking down the hallway casually. I cross my arms and glance downstairs from the railing, which overlooks the foyer perfectly. I'm just about to call out to my mom when four guys quickly jog back to the front door. They're all wearing black, hooded sweatshirts, and the one at the back has a bottle of alcohol in his arms. Though they seem distracted, I pull back a bit so that none of them see me. My pulse speeds up at the notion of being alone in an unfamiliar house with four strange men, and I wipe my clammy hands on my shirt.

"Let's get the fuck out of here," one of them says, his voice low. Another one laughs. Before I can digest their words, they're gone, and the sound of the door slamming again reverberates through me.

Maybe Hunter Ravenwood is *not* the unremarkable prep I thought he'd be as the headmaster's son.

I glance over to Andrew's room at the end of the hall. I walk over and quickly pop my head in, taking in the large master suite. My mom's boxes are sitting on the tufted bench at the end of the bed frame, and her suitcase is already half unpacked on the bed. When I walk into the bathroom, I see she's already placed her toothbrush next to Andrew's, and her favorite vase is on one of the shelves above the toilet. Smirking, I shake my head as I make my way back to my room.

I decide to go on a walk and stretch my legs after the long car ride, maybe check out the neighborhood... though something tells me it's just copies of this McMansion for miles on end. To say we're out of our element here is an understatement. I feel like I'm on a movie set. Everything is so clean, and the houses are all so stately. Even the cars are shiny and new. I didn't necessarily grow up poor—Mom's business brings in a decent amount of money—but Marin City is rustic, middle-class, and while it can be beautiful, it's also quite basic. I grab my Air Pods and phone, skipping down the stairs and grabbing one of the spare keys the housekeeper left for us. I lock the door behind me and head out, pulling up directions to the town center.

The sun is still high for being late afternoon, so I walk on the shady side of the street since my skin is vampire pale. I pass enormous houses with aging trees, and every few minutes, someone jogs by with a high-end stroller. At the end of the street, I follow the directions and turn right.

Of course, I researched our new hometown, so I know a little about Greythorn. It's a suburb of Boston so small that most people just pass through it on their way to nearby Salem. It sits between two large forests, so the town is surrounded by trees, making it feel way more nature-y than it is. It's also ripe with cemeteries and historic homes, which fascinates and intrigues me. Going from an overpopulated, California public school to a New England prep academy is going to be interesting. I know Mom is excited. She has high hopes for me since she never got to go to college, and she loves the idea of visiting me in Paris.

I round the corner and enter the main square, which has a large, tree-laden park in the heart of Greythorn with a thicket of trees in the middle. Shops and storefronts all face the park, and in the very center of it all is a large gazebo and lake. I walk along the perimeter, passing people out shopping and enjoying the weather before the darkness descends. There's a bite to the air now, and I suspect in an hour, it won't be warm anymore. I turn left and cross the main street, entering the expansive park. It's darker in here with the trees, and I hesitate at first. But then I remember Mom bragging about the practically non-existent crime rate in Greythorn, and I shake my head. I'm just being ridiculous...

I follow the dirt path deeper into the park, and even a few feet in, I can see the other side of town a couple thousand feet away. I'm safe here. But...

I look around, my spider-senses perking up. Someone laughs—a deep, cruel laugh.

I pull my Air Pods out and stop walking, listening. *I should be running.* I can't see anyone near me, but the eerie feeling of being closed in, being *watched,* makes me catch my breath. *I'm safe,* I tell myself. *I'm safe.* It's something Sonya, my therapist and I, have been working on.

Evaluate my surroundings. *A public park.*

Listen to my gut. *It's dark, but I'm okay.*

Apply common sense. *Just walk to the other side. Don't dawdle.*

I squint deeper into the thick forest surrounding me, and just as I'm about to continue walking ahead, a voice sends chills spider walking down my spine.

"Hey little lamb, come out and play."

The voice is male, reverberating through my core. I spin around, and my heart jumps out of my chest when I see four figures standing near the mausoleum in the middle of the park a couple hundred feet away. It's dark enough that I can't make out their faces—the sun behind them and the hoods shield that from me, and I clench my fists. Something tells me one of those figures is Hunter Ravenwood.

I ignore them and keep walking, my feet moving me quicker than before, and soon I'm on the other side. I look behind me, but no one is there, and I shake off the goose-bumps at the sight of the four of them—lurking, watching me from the dark.

I finish my walk and get back to the McMansion just as my mom pulls into the driveway with cheeseburgers, fries, and shakes. I help her inside, chuckling as I spy decorative throw pillows and other miscellaneous items to make the home a bit more personalized. I'm sure Mom will bring it up to speed soon since the decor really could use a makeover.

We're both starving, having not eaten since we stopped for lunch earlier today, so we plop down on the nearest couch and devour our food. I manage to spill ketchup all over my grey sweatshirt, and I'm in the middle of dabbing it with a napkin when the front door opens across the foyer. I look up just as dark eyes find mine.

Hunter.

Some sort of quick recognition passes over his face. His eyes travel down my body briefly before he cocks his head, like an animal studying their prey. He's carrying the black sweatshirt from before, revealing a tight, white T-shirt that clings to his abdomen. He's tall and muscular in a subtle way —honed, but not outrageous. Dark, messy, wavy hair, and a face with a shadow of stubble and dimples. And his lips? They're full, tilted up on the sides, and cherry red.

I swallow. He doesn't break eye contact with me, smirking as he closes the door with one of his boots. The dimples in his cheeks are so much more pronounced when he smiles. He takes a few steps into the house, the muscles in his abdomen contracting with every step.

Lord. That is one fine specimen.

My mom jumps up and walks over to him. "Hunter! So good to see you." She gives him a quick hug.

"Hello, Aubrey," he says, his voice low and smooth. His eyes flick to mine over her shoulder, something akin to amusement flickering in his dark irises. "This must be your daughter." His words are dripping with something disingenuous, and my hackles rise instantly.

They pull apart, and my mom gestures to me. "Yes, this is Briar. Did your dad tell you that you'll both be seniors at Ravenwood Academy?"

His pupils darken as he watches me with cruel amusement, and I stop chewing. What the hell is his deal?

"Yes, he did." The tone of his voice is pompous, and his intonation is that of someone with a well-rounded education. *A rich boy.* How much does he know about *me*?

"Maybe you could show her around the school next week? Introduce her to your friends? Your dad says you're a straight-A student. Briar was in all AP classes back in California."

Please, Mom. Just stop talking.

"Is that so?" Hunter asks, smirking. "I'd be delighted to show her around, give her a taste of true Ravenwood Academy spirit." I scowl at him as he moves to the stairs, but I don't answer. I won't give him the time of day. "Please, make yourselves at home." He turns to leave, winking at me before jogging up the stairs two at a time.

"Such a nice boy," my mom says as she sits back down, finishing her meal.

For some reason, I doubt that, because my gut is telling me otherwise.

$\mathcal{H}$ 3 $\partial\!\!\!S$

BRIAR

I look up from my phone. *You've got to fucking be kidding me.*
Sighing, I climb out of the Subaru and look up at the ivy-
covered, brick edifice. Students in blue and green uniforms
identical to mine file through the iron gate, clumped together
in groups I can only assume are as ruthless as they were at my
last high school. Luckily, I haven't seen Hunter since Thursday, when we moved in—apart from a very vivid sexual dream
that left me all sorts of confused about my new stepbrother,
but I digress.

I close my door and grab my backpack from the back
seat, throwing it on as I lock my car with the fob. As I walk
past luxury vehicles and fellow students with gold watches,
designer bags, and diamonds, I keep my head up and eyes on
the prize.

One year. I can handle this place for one year, and then I'm
off to college. *Hopefully* in Paris.

I walk through the gate, ignoring the looks from other

students, the curious gazes. My eyes take in the massive structure. This place is big enough to be a university. Four brick buildings surround the green quad, ancient maple trees scattered every few feet. My backpack thumps against my back as I walk to the administrative office. I glare at a group of girls as they snicker at me, but I hold my head high.

Picking up the requisite school laptop and a printed copy of my schedule, I head to the largest building—which I presume to be the library. I've never gone to a school that just gives its students computers, but then again, I've never gone to a school like Ravenwood Academy before. I have a few minutes to kill, and I might as well learn my schedule and see if I can orient myself.

I push the heavy, wooden doors open, and when they close behind me, I soak up the quiet and emptiness of the library. Inhaling contentedly, I stalk toward the back where several couches lie sprawling between two large bookcases. Just as I'm about to sit down, someone taps me on the shoulder. I twirl around.

"Hey, new human," a girl says, smiling up at me. She has short, black hair and golden skin. Like me, she's in uniform— white shirt, green plaid skirt, navy sweater with the white emblem on the top left collar. It's a crest with an 'R' in the middle, and wings on either side. According to Google, the symbol dates to Andrew's grandfather, who started Ravenwood Academy in the early 1900s.

I set my backpack on one of the couches. "Hi," I answer, somewhat surprised that she's being so friendly. "I'm Briar."

She shakes my hand. "Scarlett. And this is Jack." She gestures to the guy behind her who is typing maniacally on his computer. "We're the nice ones," she whispers.

"How do you know I'm new?" I ask.

She laughs and points to my shirt. "Uniform rule number one: tuck in your shirt."

I set my computer down. "Shit," I chuckle, quickly tucking my shirt in. That explains the laughs. "My mom and I just moved here from California."

Her eyes flick up and down my body. "Okurr, I can sense that vibe now that you mention it."

Laughing, I shake my head. "I hope it's not that obvious."

She smirks. "No, it's not. Don't worry. You got that Cleopatra vibe going with your dark hair, but you also seem chill as fuck." Her eyes peruse my face once more. "They're going to eat you up," she mutters, looking me up and down. "I assume you're straight, which is too bad for me."

"Scar, are you seriously hitting on the newbie?" The guy behind Scarlett shuts his computer and stands. Walking over, he holds out a hand. He's tall and handsome, with red hair and thick, black glasses. "Hi, I'm Jack." He turns to Scarlett. "You're relentless."

I chuckle. "I'm Briar." As we shake hands, he wiggles his eyebrows. "She's not wrong. You come in here with your Xena the Warrior Princess vibes..." He eyes my combat boots. "Those are most definitely not adhering to the dress code, and I love you for it."

I look down. "What's wrong with the boots?"

"Oh, I'm sure you'll get reprimanded by Mr. Ravenwood. He's the headmaster."

I swallow. "I know who he is."

Before I can elaborate, Jack pulls out his phone. "Scar and I usually meet at the coffee shop in town on Tuesday mornings. You should join us tomorrow. Here, program your number."

I add myself as a contact and hand it back. "Mmm, coffee."

"Oh good, I've found another addict," he retorts, smiling. "This one's no fun."

"Hey," Scarlett whines, hitting his arm. "I like caffeine, too."

"Green tea doesn't count, sweetie," he jokes, shaking his head.

"Foul," I mutter, making a face, and Scarlett laughs, throwing her arms up. I point to my backpack. "I actually came in here to figure out where the hell I'm going for first period," I add.

"We'll show you," Scarlett offers, and I gratefully hand her my schedule.

"Ugh, history," she mutters, glancing at the sheet of paper.

"That's right by my first class. We can walk you over," Jack declares. Before I can thank him, he changes the subject. "So where in California did you come from?"

"Marin City." They both stare blankly at me. "It's the town on the other side of the Golden Gate Bridge, near San Francisco," I add, my words practiced.

They both *ahh* at my answer, and we continue chatting for a few minutes. Luckily, the reason for me being in Massachusetts doesn't come up during our conversation. I'm not sure how Andrew and Hunter are perceived here, and I want to get the lay of the land before I go telling people the head-master is my new stepfather.

Just as I'm about to ask which classes they each have first, a loud bell sounds. I tug my backpack over one shoulder. They pull me along with them, through the door of the library and out into the quad.

"Just follow us," Jack offers.

"I'll give you a quick rundown," Scarlett starts as we make our way across the quad. "Don't make eye contact with anyone. Just focus on your own work." I swallow, but she continues. "Don't be intimidated. Most of them are just your typical rich kids, you know? Nothing special."

"Well, except..." Jack trails off. We enter the building to the right.

"Except who?"

They both halt in front of the first door.

"Okay, here's your classroom, bye!" Jack screeches, and then they're gone.

I sigh, looking into the large room where a few students are already seated.

Here goes nothing.

❦   4   ❧

BRIAR

During my first class, I keep my wits about me, only looking up as the teacher goes through the slides. Lucky for me, being the first day of school, no one notices that I'm the new *new* girl. It's a big enough student population that I don't think any of them really pay much attention to me, anyway. There are a few snickers when I wander around the hallway trying to find my second class, but it doesn't bother me. It's going to take a lot more than that to break me. If the students here think I'm an easy kill, I prove them wrong with every glare I send back in their direction.

I didn't endure the worst nine months of my life for nothing—I was hardened now, safe from ridicule. These were kids, and I knew now that high school drama was nothing compared to the monstrous things adults were capable of.

Even though it's early September, the weather has turned cool, with mist and fog clinging to the brick buildings even though it's after ten in the morning. In a way, the fog is comforting, since my hometown is known for the beautiful fog. I stumble into one of the other buildings, tripping over the ledge of the door and catching myself before I fall face first onto the floor.

"Woah, there," Scarlett chirps, and I breathe a sigh of relief. She helps steady me. "Sorry, we tried texting you," she says quickly, and Jack comes up behind her. "We were going to show you to your second class."

"Thank you," I say, smiling as I pull my phone out of my backpack. "It's nice to know someone has my back. Literally."

"A lot of the kids here can be dicks. We're just trying to do our part," she replies.

Before I can respond, Jack grabs both of our hands. "Fuck. Here they come."

I look up, and it's as if the cluster of students normally crowding the halls has parted like the Red Sea. Four guys walk slowly down the hall, and everyone goes quiet.

Of fucking course Hunter is one of them.

"The Kings," Jack whispers into my ear.

I shift my weight to my other hip. "Kings?"

Scarlett sighs, whispering. "The Kings of Ravenwood. The headmaster's son and his three cronies." I glance over at the four guys. The hallway is silent now, and I have to try not to roll my eyes. "There are four names you need to remember: Hunter Ravenwood, Ash Greythorn, Ledger Huxley, and Samson Hall. The four Kings," she adds.

I chortle. "What's wrong with them?" I hitch my backpack and take a step to walk away.

"Everything," Jack whispers frantically.

I freeze. When I look around, everyone is looking down or away, averting their gaze like this is some animal kingdom bullshit.

I hold my place at the other end of the hallway, but Scarlett pulls me closer to her to make room for them to pass.

The other students don't seem *scared*, per se—just aware of them. I study them, my eyes landing on Hunter first.

He's wearing the requisite uniform. Navy slacks, white collared shirt... except instead of a green blazer, he's wearing a fitted leather jacket with ribbed arms. It accentuates the muscles that somehow still poke through the thick material. His dark eyes find mine immediately, and something passes over his face—something dark and amused—as he, too, recognizes me.

I swallow and flit my eyes to the next guy. He's just as tall as Hunter, but leaner somehow, with short black hair and ice blue eyes. *Stunning yet cunning.* The uniform is perfectly fitted to his toned body, blazer and all. He's glaring at everyone he passes, throwing intimidating glances like he owns the place. A girl accidentally brushes against his arm, and he turns to face her while everyone quiets further, waiting for him to speak.

"Sorry," she squeaks out, backing up until she's against the metal lockers.

He just watches her and gives her a lecherous smile before slipping his tongue between his two fingers in a vulgar gesture.

Prick.

As they keep walking, I study the third guy. Long-ish blonde hair, edgier than the others, with tattoos peeking through the collar of his slightly unbuttoned shirt. He glares at everyone, an athletic jacket in his arms. As he walks, I see a flash of metal in his mouth. He's the only one not smiling and seems genuinely dissatisfied to be here. *Interesting.*

The fourth guy is different. Dark hair, fair skin, with glasses that perfectly frame his beautiful face. He doesn't seem as brutal as the others—like he's softer, somehow—or maybe it's because he's the only one not brooding. He's carrying a stack of books. When his eyes find mine, he stares at me for a beat and nudges the blonde guy. *Fuck.* They're both staring at me now, and Scarlett tugs me closer to her protectively—which causes my phone to clatter to the ground.

Before I have a chance to grab it and slide back into anonymity, Hunter squats down and hands it to me, the other three guys behind him. I take it from him, but I don't back up. They may have a bad rap, but I'm not afraid of them. The four of them falter slightly when they see me staring them down, and a few people whisper excitedly.

"Briar," he says, his voice like velvet.

"Hunter," I answer, tucking my phone in my backpack.

I'm just about to let him by when he takes a step forward, reaches out, and plucks a stray hair from my sweater—studying it for a moment before discarding it. Cocking his head, he doesn't move away—giving my body a slow sweep with his brown eyes. When they reach mine again, there's nothing nice in his expression. I swallow, and my heart races in my chest. He takes another intimidating step forward, and Jack gasps from behind me. I'm about to back up, but he grabs my shirt and tugs me impossibly close. Being this close to a guy, him *touching me* without my consent—

My head roars as I reach up and shove him backward. Just enough to show him that he can't touch me, can't *do* shit like that to me. He doesn't expect that because he stumbles backward ever so slightly. He narrows his eyes at the same time his lips quirk upwards, like this is a game.

"Don't touch me," I hiss.

He smiles and tilts his head, a piece of dark, curly hair falling in front of his face.

"What's wrong, *sister?*" The way he enunciates *sister,* the way it cuts through me like ice, *taunting* me... he's not going to make this easy, is he?

Scarlett audibly gasps. "Sister?!"

Rage fills me then, and I ignore the shocked squeaks from the other students. Heat flares across my skin, and my cheeks tingle.

"Screw you," I hiss, pushing past him. Scarlett and Jack follow me, and with flaming cheeks, I walk to my next class with them at my heels, ignoring the stares of every single student who witnessed our new sibling dynamic.

5

Briar

"I don't think anyone's ever talked to Hunter like that." Scarlett laughs as I link arms with her and Jack. We're back out in the quad. I'm thankful that they're in my second class with me, because right now I want to cry and punch something simultaneously. I'm going to need their support if these small interactions with my stepbrother continue to sucker-punch me. I ball my fists a couple of times to get the shaking to subside.

"Are we going to talk about how he called you his stepsister, or should we just ignore that fun tidbit of information?" She pauses and turns to face me with an expectant expression.

I sigh. "Fine. It's not gossip-worthy, though. My mom married Andrew Ravenwood." I pause and look at them, but they're waiting for me to continue. "It hasn't been so bad. Andrew is fine, and my mom adores him." I look back at the building we just exited. "I don't really know Hunter."

I think of his room—of the postcards, and the anxiety medication that made him seem like a real human for an hour —until he and his creepy ass friends catcalled me in the park. I don't know what I expected. Of course the headmaster's son is the leader, and of course he's kind of a bully. It's disappointing, but not surprising. He's a walking cliche.

Scarlett stares at me and twiddles her lips with her finger. "Rumor has it that Mr. Ravenwood threatened to kick Hunter out last year. But you didn't hear that from me."

I look between her and Jack. "So, he knows about Hunter and his..." I trail off. What, his *reign?* It sounds so silly.

Jack nods. "He's the eyes and ears of this school, Briar. Nothing happens without Andrew Ravenwood knowing. But technically, they never break the rules. They're just assholes."

"So, you *live* with Hunter?" Scarlett asks as we begin walking again, changing the subject.

"I guess so," I shrug. "He hasn't really been around much, though. He's out with his friends a lot."

"They go everywhere together," Jack whispers as we pass a group of students. "It's *kind of* weird. So that doesn't surprise me."

"I've known him his whole life," Scarlett adds. "He changed after his mom died."

I don't know much about Hunter's mother—just that she died a few years ago. I remember Mom vaguely mentioning at one point that while Andrew did well for himself, seeing as Ravenwood is a few generations old, his mother was the one who came from old money. Hence the McMansion.

"Well, considering I live with him, maybe he'll leave us alone now."

Scarlett's smile drops from her face. "There's no chance in hell, Briar. You awakened the beast. He's never going to leave you alone."

I swallow. "They don't scare me."

Scarlett throws Jack a look, but I ignore them.

As we walk through the door to one of the other buildings, a few people glance in my direction. I adjust my backpack as we reach our pre-calculus class. I find us three seats in the back, and the final bell rings, signaling the start of class. I prepare to endure the class in all its boring glory, sighing and attempting to forget my run in with the Kings.

An hour later, I'm still in the what-the-fuck-did-I-just-learn mindset as we walk out. They agree to show me to my locker, even though they're not really utilized now because of the laptops. Still, it'll be good to have a place to store things. On our way to the other building, Scarlett begins to talk to Jack about something animatedly, and I'm barely paying attention. I stop only when Jack and Scarlett stop walking.

"Shit," Jack whispers, glancing at the row of lockers in front of us. "We have company."

I look up and notice Hunter leaning against a locker, glaring at me. *How did he know I'd be here?*

Something fiery shoots through me at that gaze, and I notice Ash, Ledger, and Samson standing near the other wall of lockers.

"Let me guess," I murmur to Jack. "That's my locker?"

"I told you," Scarlett hisses. "They're not going to leave you alone."

I grind my teeth together and clench my fists. "This is ridiculous," I whisper. "I'm putting my foot down."

I stalk over to where Hunter is standing, arms crossed. "Excuse me," I order, not breaking eye contact. There's nothing kind in his expression, and his jaw ticks ever so slightly. A few people stop to watch us, their expressions stunned.

"You're excused," he muses, his face dripping with disdain.

My pulse speeds up, and anger flares through me. "This is my locker."

He tilts his head, and his eyes flash with amusement for a split second. "Yeah. I thought that was obvious."

Looking over his shoulder, I notice his friends watching me haughtily. *Okay, so they truly think of themselves as the rulers here, then? They sure have the arrogance to match it.*

"What do you want, Hunter?" I sigh, crossing my arms.

He chuckles, and the sound is both terrifying and thrilling. He reaches into his back pocket, pulling out a few folded pieces of paper. Handing them to me, he gives me a savage smile before I look down and take them. Willing my hands not to shake, I open the paper. My heart thumps against my ribs, and a flush works its way up my neck.

Snapping my eyes up to him, I pin him beneath an angry gaze. "You went through my diary?"

My diary—detailing the inappropriate dream I had about him the other night.

He crosses his arms and shrugs. "If you wanted me so badly, why didn't you just ask?"

Oh, the nerve...

"You wish," I growl, getting ready to turn and walk away.

Just as I move, he grabs the hand with the papers and tugs me into his hard body. Leaning down, his breath fans against my forehead.

"Tell me, just how wet did you get for me in that dream of yours?" To my horror, he raises his other hand, and a pink, lacy thong—*my* thong—dangles from his fingers.

My mouth goes dry, and my heart wallops against my chest as I close my eyes.

No. No, no, no.

Grabbing my underwear, I twist away from him and turn to walk away. Tears prick at my eyes, but I take a deep breath. I refuse to give them the satisfaction of knowing they got to me. Scarlett and Jack usher me out of the hallway, but before I get to the door, I feel a presence behind me.

"I told him not to do it."

I turn. One of the Kings—the one with the glasses—walks up to me. *Samson Hall*.

"He's lashing out. Give it a few days."

"You can tell him I won't tolerate this shit for a few more days."

"He won't listen."

I clench my teeth. "Why? Just leave me alone."

Samson laughs and shakes his head. "The more you resist, the more interesting you are to him, little lamb."

Hey little lamb, come out and play.

And then he turns around and walks back toward where Hunter is still watching me, and the four of them head off in the other direction.

Was he talking about Hunter, or himself? I certainly don't trust any of them.

I glare in their direction, and Scarlett and Jack tug me toward the entrance of the hallway. I'm still fuming as I shove my underwear into my backpack. When I finally look at Scarlett and Jack, my pulse has slowed and I take a deep, calming breath.

"This is war," I declare, ignoring the look Jack and Scarlett share.

I have a really sickening feeling that this is going to be a long year.

Andrew Ravenwood calls me into his office during my next class, which happens to be my favorite subject—French. We're just going over the syllabus, detailing the class trip to Paris later this year, when I'm called into the headmaster's office. Scarlett and Jack aren't in this class with me since they're taking Mandarin, but I scoff at having to leave, none-theless. I sulk the whole way to the main building.

I'd talked with Andrew last night briefly at dinner, and he was cordial, as he always is. I think he enjoys having my mom around, and he seemed excited at the prospect of doing family things together. I'd ignored the nervous pang when I'd realized he was referencing my darling, new stepbrother. I guess after three years of it just being him and Hunter, he was craving the true family dynamic again. I couldn't fault him for it.

I push the wooden door open, and he smiles as I walk in. Now that I've met Hunter, I can see where he gets his looks from. Andrew is older, obviously—over fifty, though I'm not sure of his exact age. He has dark, wavy hair like Hunter, but he keeps his trimmed short. It's flecked with silver, and his skin is a shade darker than Hunter's—tanned from his trip to St. Tropez last week. His eyes are green, and his smile is just like his sons.

"Briar, so good to see you." He's perched behind his large desk, and I nod at him.

"Hi, Mr. Ravenwood." *Mr. Ravenwood?* I've never called him that, but seeing him behind his desk, in a suit...

"Please, honey. You can call me Andrew. I heard there was an incident earlier today?"

Nothing happens without Andrew Ravenwood knowing.

I don't know what to say. For one, as much as I like him, I still don't completely trust men. After everything that happened, I just assume they have bad blood until they prove otherwise. Two, and maybe I'm just imagining it, but his voice almost sounds pitying. I assume he knows about what happened, and being a cognizant human, might realize my encounters with his son have been anything but pleasant. Still, I'm furious about what Hunter did. It was a violation of my privacy. So, I decide to go for the jugular.

"Yeah, there was. I think you might want to have a conversation with your son about going through my private diary." I stare at him, and he shifts uncomfortably in his seat.

"Right. My thoughts exactly. I will talk to Hunter tonight. We have a zero-tolerance policy when it comes to bullying here at Ravenwood, but besides that, he needs to learn to get along with you. You should feel safe in your own home."

I nod. "Thank you."

He leans back and watches me contemplatively. "Other than that, how is your first day going? Your mother and I were worried, after everything that happened..."

And there it is.

I sit up straighter and look at the clock behind him. *Tick, tick, tick.* "It's going well, thank you."

He waits for me to elaborate on that, but I don't. Like I said, I'm not sure I trust him yet.

After all, I trusted Cam, too.

"Good, good. I'm glad to hear it." He stands. "If you need anything—and I mean anything—let me know. We're all a family now, and I hope you know that you can talk to me."

Yeah—one big, happy family.

He gives me a genuine smile, and the ice inside of my heart melts just a tiny bit. I know he means well, and this is his way of connecting with me.

"Thanks, Andrew. I will."

I head back to French, attempting to fly under the radar until it's time to go home.

❧ 6 ❧

BRIAR

After my last class, I walk to my car with Scarlett and Jack, ignoring the four luxury vehicles parked up by the front gate. *Assholes.*

After the underwear incident, the energy at Ravenwood was different somehow—more frenetic. Like ravens waiting for the kill, the other students circled me, watching, and everyone we encountered whispered amongst themselves. I guess word had spread even though no one else could hear our conversation. They just knew shit went down. *Twice.* But I haven't encountered the Kings again, and by the time I unlock my car, I'm ready to go home, relax in front of the TV, and eat some chocolate. I quickly say goodbye to Scarlett and Jack, telling them I'll meet them for coffee tomorrow morning. It's nice to head home in the Subaru after what feels like an eternally long day, and I smile when I see Mom's car in the driveway.

"Hello!" I shout, waltzing through the door.

"Oh good, you're home," my mom yells back. "I'm in the kitchen." I walk to the back of the house, and my mom is sitting on the floor surrounded by plastic containers. "I'm trying—and failing—to bring a little organization to this household," she grumbles as she pours some rice into the container in her lap. "I'm pretty sure there were cans of soup that expired ten years ago in there," she mumbles, gesturing to the expansive pantry.

I laugh and sit down next to her, grabbing the pasta and beginning to organize it by type. I should've known she'd come in here and completely overhaul everything. While she gets her business up and running on this side of the country, I predict she'll be spending a lot of time bringing the house up to shape, too.

"You can definitely tell two men lived here by themselves for three years," she mutters, handing me the lentils next. I swallow at the thought of one of those men being Hunter. "How was your first day?"

I shrug. "You know. Same shit, different school."

She nods. "Yeah. Sounds about right." She turns to face me. "Did Hunter show you around?"

I stop what I'm doing and look down, wondering how to broach the subject. She obviously thinks Hunter walks on water and has no idea what kind of reputation he has. Sighing, I prepare myself to disappoint her about another man in her life, as if Cam weren't enough.

"Mom, how well do you know Hunter?"

She frowns. "Not well, I guess, but he's always been such a gentleman to me. Why?" I look away, and she nudges me. "Briar, what happened?"

I look down at my nails. "He's kind of a bully at school."

"Really? That's too bad. He's always so sweet to me," she laments, sighing. "Well, what do we always say?"

"It's always the nice ones," I answer, smiling.

That was our mantra this past year—the thing that justi-fied Cam's behavior. The thing that brought us closer, like hey, *girl power* and all that bullshit. But it did help me open up to her, and as horrible as the situation was, it somehow brought us closer.

"I'll talk to Andrew about it later. Maybe he can talk to Hunter, really enforce some house rules about acceptable behavior outside of the house."

Pretty sure acceptable behavior was not *humiliating your new stepsister and asking how wet she got for you.*

I nod. "Andrew called me into his office to talk about it," I add, shrugging. "At least he's trying."

"Good. Do you want to talk about what happened?"

I shrug. "Hunter just needs to learn that I have boundaries."

Sonya would be so proud that I referenced boundaries.

"Okay. I'm always here if you want to talk."

I load the lentils into the container, closing the airtight top and handing it to her. "I know, mom. Good luck with this. I'm going to eat some candy and watch some TV."

"Okay, sweetie. I'll promise to talk to Hunter later."

I smile. "Thanks, Mom."

I grab a chocolate bar and my phone, heading up to my room to change out of the itchy uniform. Dropping the chocolate on my bed, I pull off my clothes, quickly walking into my bathroom to tie my long hair up. As I head back into my bedroom and reach down for the candy, it's gone.

"What the hell?" I ask, looking around. My skin begins to tingle with dread. Groaning, I pull on a pair of baggy sweat-pants and an oversized T-shirt and stomp down the hall to Hunter's room. As I get closer, I notice music playing. I don't bother to knock—instead, I throw the door open and cross my arms.

Hunter, Ash, Ledger, and Samson are all here. Hunter is leaning back in a chair at his desk, his hair disheveled, his eyes on mine—smirking with delight. Ash is behind him, looking like an arrogant twat. Ledger is sitting on Hunter's bed with his phone, and Samson is reading a book on the floor.

"What the fuck," I declare, walking over to Hunter. He brings his hand up and pops a piece of chocolate into his mouth.

My chocolate.

"Sorry, did you want some of my chocolate?" he asks, his voice low.

I glare at him and contemplate swatting it out of his hand, but then think better of it. Why fuel the fire? I flip him off and glare at all of them before walking out. Just as I reach my room, there are footsteps behind me.

"Briar, wait," Samson begs, grabbing my arm and turning me to face him.

I pull out of his grasp. "What do you all want from me? Tease me at school, sure, but let me have some fucking peace at home," I begin, tears beginning to prick at the corners of my eyes.

I will not fucking cry in front of them.

I take a deep breath and stand up straighter.

"I just wanted to say, we're not bad people. Hunter's just acting... ornery." His golden eyes watch me, and those dark lashes are captivating.

I cross my arms. "Why do you keep acting like his protector?"

Samson swallows, and I admire the way his throat moves. He's a beautiful asshole. *Why God, why?* In fact, they're all beautiful. It's just their souls that are rotting.

He doesn't answer me, so I continue. "I just want to graduate and move on with my life."

He steps closer, and I get a whiff of something minty. "Fight back," he murmurs, sending goosebumps down my arms and spine.

Without another word, he walks away, leaving me hot and conflicted.

7

HUNTER

Samson walks back into my room and closes the door. I glare up at him.

"Why bother?" I ask, my voice dripping with disdain.

Samson shrugs. "You're being kind of a dick."

Irritation rolls through me, and something else, too—some sort of possessiveness that I know is misplaced. Samson is the nicest one out of all of us.

Ledger laughs. "And that's surprising, why?"

I clench my jaw, but then Ash nudges my shoulder. "Come on. We all know I'm the real prick."

That causes me to smile just a tiny bit.

"Did you get the stuff?" Ash asks Ledger, who is still on his fucking phone.

Ledger nods. "It's in my car."

"Maybe we should stop messing with her," Samson suggests, shrugging, obviously still on the subject of my new stepsister. "Considering she lives here now and everything."

I look down and pick at a thread on my button-up. "But that would be so boring," I muse.

Something in my chest tightens at the thought of Briar and her mother being here. This is my house. Where my mother used to live. And they've just... taken it over.

Ledger laughs and shakes his head. "You're ruthless, dude."

I smirk. "You should know how much I like fucking with people."

There's a knock at my door, and then my dad walks in.

"Hunter? A moment, please." His face is serious and weary, and for a second, I feel bad for causing him to worry. He took my mom's death hard, and it was only after he met Aubrey that he started to feel like the father I had growing up. Still, if you'd asked me, meeting and marrying a woman he barely knew after only dating six months... I was skeptical. And bitter.

Ash, Ledger, and Samson are all quiet as I get up and walk out into the hallway with him. I cross my arms and lean against the wall, playing it cool.

"What's up?" I ask, playing dumb. It's not that we don't get along. If anything, he's a great dad. But he's strict, and I know I push his buttons often.

His jaw hardens as he loosens his tie. "I heard there was an incident with Briar at school today?"

I give him a dumbfounded look. "There was?"

He narrows his eyes. "Don't play dumb with me, Hunter. I know you're acting out because her mother and I..." He looks away. "I know you're acting out because of your mother, and the fact that Aubrey has taken her place."

I frown. "I was just teasing her."

"Reading her diary is more than teasing, son. It's unacceptable. She is your stepsister," he adds, his voice a little louder with frustration. He sighs and shakes his head. "No more hazing Briar. No more underwear," he commands, shaking his head. *How the hell did he know about that? Did Briar tell him?* "What were you thinking? I raised you better than that."

Yeah, until you forced me to cohabitate with the hot-as-sin stepsister.

Maybe if I taunt and intimidate her enough, she'll leave.

I don't say that, though.

Ignoring the pang of disappointment at the thought of her leaving, I swallow. It's been so much fun having someone to taunt, someone to take my frustration out on. I was so irritated at the thought of her and her mother moving in all summer, and then when I finally met her—when I saw her that day, out and about in Greythorn...

She wasn't what I was expecting.

Something inside of me twisted around that day.

Some deep, dark part of me was exposed.

"You may think that as my son, you get special privileges at school, but my threat still stands. We will re-evaluate your performance at the end of the semester, and if there's no improvement, I won't hesitate to send you to Jefferson," he adds, referencing the local public high school.

He'd given me an ultimatum last year. I was to do better this year, be nicer, or he would uproot my life and send me to that shithole.

But then she showed up, and I felt... off kilter. I wasn't sure I could keep my promise to my dad before, but now I was more than skeptical with Briar around.

I look down at my shoes. "Fine, okay."

He jabs a finger into my chest. "She's your sister now, so start treating her like family."

I swallow, trying to dislodge the lump in my throat. The notion of Briar being my sister feels all sorts of wrong, but I suppose that's what we are now.

"I will try my best," I answer, giving him a winning smile.

"That's my boy." He pulls me in for a quick hug, kisses me on the forehead, and then walks off. "Oh, and you're grounded. I turned the Wi-Fi off for the night, so send the boys home."

I don't go back into my room just yet. Instead, I clench and unclench my fists, take a deep breath, and clear my throat before shaking the whole day off of my tense shoulders.

8

BRIAR

A couple of hours later, I head downstairs for dinner. I hadn't wanted to run into the guys again, so I'd stayed in my room and sulked, reading one of the books I had on my Kindle app. Crossing my arms, I walk into the casual dining area, and my stomach sinks when I see Hunter sitting there, chatting with Andrew and my mom. If they hadn't already seen me, I would've turned around and walked back to my room.

I'd rather starve than deal with Hunter again.

Glowering, I sit down next to my mom, helping myself to the chicken dish on the table. I ignore Hunter's gaze, though I can see him studying me from my peripheral. I begin to eat, and my mom clears her throat.

"I am very sorry for my actions today, Briar," Hunter grits out. "It was wrong of me, and I promise it won't happen again."

Anyone with ears can hear the sarcasm in his tone—the

disingenuousness. He gives me a diabolical grin and tips his head in an apology.

I look over at my mom, and then Andrew, and they're both quiet and preening. It's obvious that Hunter got reprimanded and they ordered him to apologize, because when I look back at him, he looks like he's in pain.

"Okay," I retort, nearly rolling my eyes. Does he expect that a forced apology means I'll forgive him?

"How was the rest of your day, Briar?" Andrew asks, chewing his food. He's in jogging pants and a t-shirt—the neck damp with sweat. Does everyone in this household exercise regularly besides me?

I shrug, eating quickly so that I can leave to go somewhere else. *Anywhere else.* "Fine. I really like my French teacher," I offer, my cheeks heating. I don't like that Hunter is here—that he will know more than he needs to about me.

"That's wonderful!" my mom croons. "Briar wants to study in France next year," she adds, looking at Hunter.

His expression doesn't change—in fact, it doesn't seem like he heard her at all.

Or he doesn't care.

I take a couple more bites as my mom and Andrew discuss coming to visit me in Paris—anecdotes about turning it into a European honeymoon—when Hunter bolts upright, startling all of us.

"Goodnight, everyone."

He's gone before I can register his rudeness, and I swallow thickly before standing.

"I should go to bed, too."

"Night, hon," my mom chirps.

I wave before heading to the staircase, looking up toward my bedroom. I'm not tired—it's barely after seven. But hopefully Hunter is in his room for the night, so I can hang out in the basement until I get sleepy, which won't happen for several more hours.

Curse of the night owl.

The basement has been converted into a cozy, casual living room. It's unlike the rest of the palatial house, opting for comfort rather than style, with mismatched, oversized sofas, thick throw blankets, and the biggest TV I've ever seen.

I settle into the couch, practically melting into the soft, tufted fabric, when footsteps thud on the carpet. My skin erupts in goosebumps. I sit up straighter, and I don't look up as a figure in my peripheral watches me from the other side of the room.

I know it's Hunter without having to look. Only he can have such a melancholy presence.

I don't say anything. I just cross my arms and flick through the channel guide, trying to find something benign to watch. My whole body erupts in goosebumps as Hunter wanders over to where I'm sitting. Finally, I allow myself to look up at him. He's in grey sweatpants and a black T-shirt, and he looks angry that I'm here. My eyes rove down to his bare feet.

"Hello," I grumble, glaring at him. "Can I help you" I ask.

He laughs and rubs his lips with his thumb. "You're in my room." I open my mouth to protest, but he interrupts me. "I think we need to set some ground rules for the house, Briar." His voice is clipped, precise. Why does he sound so pompous all the time? "For example, this room. It's mine, and you don't belong here," he says slowly. I *really* try to ignore the way the sweatpants hang on his hips, how if I look close enough, I can see just what my stepbrother is packing. My mouth goes dry as I shake my head. "You can arrange to have a tv sent up to your room."

I frown. "Oh, I can? How sweet. Thank you. I'll arrange

to have the butler bring it up," I retort sarcastically. He's so accustomed to this life that he thinks he can just flick his wrist, and things will appear.

His jaw ticks, and he takes a step forward. Just as I'm about to ask him to leave again, he sits down on the ottoman opposite from me, leaning forward so that his knees just barely touch mine.

"This is not up for debate," he growls, scowling. "You're in my space." He's trying to intimidate me, but it's not working.

I frown. "I'll leave, but I'll be back tomorrow."

I begin to stand, but he reaches out and tugs my hands down so that I fall back into the couch. Leaning forward, he gives me a tight, cruel smile.

"Second, the next time you tattle, I promise it will be much more than your wet panties in my pocket," he says, his voice foreboding.

I glower at him. He's a rich, arrogant prick used to getting his way, apparently. But tonight, I'm too tired to duel. Standing abruptly, I kick the blanket off me and march to the door.

"I don't want to catch you down here again," he adds, and when I turn around, he's leaning forward and watching me with darkened eyes.

"You're an ass, do you know that?" I throw back, narrowing my eyes. "You think I'll fold, surrender, give up— but it just shows that you don't know me at all."

He smiles then, and fury rolls through me. "I think I know you better than you think."

I clench my jaw and take a step toward him. "You know nothing about me," I hiss. "Or what I've been through."

My words cause his haughty expression to falter for a split second, catching him off guard. I wonder if he knows what happened to me.

I doubt it...

"Sweet dreams," he croons, winking.

He definitely doesn't know about Cam.

I twist around and stomp up the stairs before he can fire me up even more.

~~~
~~~

9

BRIAR

Scarlett, Jack, and I meet at Romancing the Bean just before eight, which gives us twenty minutes to socialize before we have to head to Ravenwood. The small cafe is idyllic, situated right on the outskirts of the park with outdoor seating and lots of plants. Scarlett's parents own it, and they're both behind the coffee machines when they introduce themselves. It's nice to meet them—to know that there's at least one other family in Greythorn who appears to be normal. Since it's cold out, we opt to sit inside, and I fill Scarlett and Jack in on my night with Hunter.

I swirl the liquid around and take a quick sip. "What exactly is their problem?" I ask. "The Kings?" Scarlett looks at Jack, and their smiles drop off their faces. "What?" I ask, frowning.

"You really want to know?" she asks. I nod, and she lets out a resigned sigh. "There's a rumor that they were the reason someone killed themselves last year."

The words slam into me, and I think back to how they acted in school yesterday—like they were Gods who kept to themselves, who taunted anyone who dared enter or breach that fortress of power. Is it possible their behavior caused someone to end their life? Sure, they were mean—but were they capable of something that horrible?

"Who?" I whisper.

"Micah Smith. He was our friend," Scarlett starts slowly. "He was kind of like you—gave zero fucks, didn't care who knew it, and wasn't about the high-school drama and bullshit."

I let her words roll through me for a few seconds. "So, what happened?"

Jack shrugs, sipping his coffee. "No one knows for sure. But he started dating Samson Hall, and rumors starting swirling about a sex tape, and next thing we knew..." he trails off, looking morose.

Scarlett chews on a pastry as she chimes in. "Micah was already having a hard time in his personal life—his parents had just gotten divorced, and they lost a lot of their money..." She looks away, brushing a tear off her cheek. "He fucking hung himself, Briar."

"Were they ever found to be accountable?"

Jack bursts out laughing. "No, absolutely not. Micah's mental health history was a known fact, so blame could never be placed. But we know them—and we know what they're capable of. And the worst part is, they used it to their advantage." Jack looks at Scarlett. "They went from popular to royalty overnight. People bowed to them, scared of what they'd do if they retaliated or became their next source of entertainment. Over the course of a few days, people began to worship them—dressed like them, ran errands for them... We all knew the power they now held, and even worse, they knew it too."

"But they're just bullies," I grind out, fuming. "Nothing more."

Jack sighs. "You forget how impressionable we all can be. It's why we made it our mission to protect others. To take them under our wing and keep them safe. When you showed up—"

Scarlett nudges him.

I look between them. "When I showed up, what?"

"We knew you'd be bait, which is why we came on so strong."

I ignore the pang in my chest. "So, you faked being nice to me?"

"No, not at all!" Scarlett says, scooting closer. "But we knew if we didn't get to you first, that... Look, you're not the first new girl at Ravenwood, and you're certainly not the only one this year. But you're pretty, and interesting, and Hunter Ravenwood enjoys playing with pretty things." She looks at me with wide eyes. "I was just trying to protect you."

I look between them. "I appreciate you both looking out for me, but I promise, I'm okay. I've been through a hell of a lot worse, trust me."

They nod, and soon, we finish our coffees and head to Ravenwood. The rest of the day is surprisingly uneventful—and I only run into the Kings once, just before the second bell rings, so I'm gone before they can acknowledge my presence. Scarlett seems pleased that the bullying has stopped, at least for now, but I'm not convinced. The energy on campus still seems fraught with tension, still waiting for the ball to drop somehow.

It's the calm before the storm, and I'd be an idiot to believe they're going to leave me alone from now on.

I am sure the worst is yet to come, and I need to prepare for battle.

10

BRIAR

My mom is out when I get home, so I spend the afternoon in my room doing homework. We were given a reprieve yesterday, being the first day of school, but all my teachers had assignments for us today. Once I'm done, I take a quick shower before deciding what to make for dinner. I dry my hair quickly, pull on leggings and a sweatshirt, and grab my phone before exiting my bedroom. I'm about to pull the door closed when voices sound from downstairs.

Creeping to the railing, I peer down and see Hunter, Ash, Ledger, and Samson huddled near the front door, whispering animatedly. Narrowing my eyes, I try to decipher what they're saying, but it's futile. I creep down the stairs as silently as possible, and once I get to the landing, I peek around.

"...gasoline, it'll be too obvious." *Hunter*.

"No shit, Sherlock." *Ash*.

"What's wrong with a good old match or lighter?" Ledger drawls.

"We can't leave any evidence," Samson interjects, shaking his head.

They continue whispering, and I continue eavesdropping. *What are they up to?* Just as I'm about to make my presence known, they head out, slamming the door behind them.

I climb down the rest of the stairs and look at the front door. My eyes dart to my purse and shoes near the door, and for a second, I shake off the curious thoughts. Do I *really* want to see what the Kings get up to in their free time? And then...

What if I could gather evidence to take them down?

Maybe it's revenge for the journal, or maybe it's Scarlett's tear-stained face when she told me about Micah. If Hunter can't grant me privacy privileges, maybe he doesn't deserve those same privileges, either.

Either way, I feel compelled to see what they're up to.

If not for me, then for Micah.

I pull on my boots, grab my purse, and head out. Opening and closing the heavy door behind me, I slowly walk to the driveway just as Hunter's car drives away.

Not on my watch, assholes.

I start the Subaru and reverse out of the driveway as quickly as I can while still being subtle. I can see Hunter's black Range Rover at the end of the street, so I slow down until he turns. I need to put some distance between us, or he'll get suspicious. He drives out of town, toward the edge of the forest. I'm three cars behind him, and we weave down the single-lane road, through the thick trees of Greythorn.

Where the fuck are they going?

The car in front of me turns left, holding me up for a solid twenty seconds. I almost lose sight of Hunter's car, but then it turns right into one of the natural preserve areas. Slowing, I pass the entrance so I'm not *too* obvious. Hunter's car is in the parking lot, and all four doors open just as I pass.

Wonderful.

I make a U-turn up ahead and drive into the parking lot of the preserve, parking on the other side of the lot. The Kings are nowhere to be seen, but there's only one path into the preserve. It won't be hard to find them. As I exit the car, I grab my black windbreaker from the trunk. It's cold now, and the sky is light pink, nearly sunset. I shoot a quick text to my mom, sharing my location and telling her that I'm on a quick hike in the preserve. I put my phone on silent and tuck it into my pocket before starting the hike into the wooded, dusky preserve.

The air is cool and damp, moisture sticking to the ends of my hair. It's not raining, but the forest is dense, and the weather is humid enough that even in the cold, it feels misty. I slow my breathing and listen for them as my feet crunch on the dirt. I wish other people were around, but we seem to be the only ones.

My breathing turns ragged as the path starts to incline slightly. *Fuck this.* Why am I even following them? *Because maybe they're going to hurt someone or do something stupid.* I slow and look around. I contemplate going back home, snuggling up under my covers...

But then I remember Hunter's rules last night. How, even in my home, I am relegated to my room. How he thinks he can boss me around. How he *touches* me, despite me asking him to stop.

They deserve to go down.

And I need to be the one to do it.

I continue up the path a good fifteen minutes, breaking into a light sweat and removing my windbreaker. The thought of turning around is appealing, and I contemplate it again as I squint against the impending darkness.

Then, I hear a faraway male laugh.

The scent of burning wood wafts through the air, and I

swallow, tiptoeing to the edge of the path. They're in the forest—talking, laughing, breaking bottles. I step into the woods, following the sounds and the smell of fire. Swallowing thickly, I pull my windbreaker back on, so I blend in better with the trees. A howling breeze has picked up, giving the forest an eerie, supernatural vibe.

After a minute or two into the woods, I see them. Four figures in black hooded sweatshirts... and the burning house behind them.

ASH

I grin as Ledger takes a step back, howling into the dark abyss of the forest like a feral wolf. When my eyes find Hunter's, they're alight with mischievous glee.

Good.

If anything deserves to burn in Greythorn—and I should know, being the mayor's son—it's this fucking house.

Burn it to the ground.

"I'm going to feel really guilty if the forest catches on fire," Samson muses, laughing. He takes a swig from a bottle of whiskey before handing it to me.

I sip the fiery liquid, trying to pace myself. There will be repercussions if I come home drunk again.

"The forest won't catch on fire," Hunter muses. "We took precautions."

It's true. As much as we wanted to do this, we were also careful about it. We may be dicks, but at least we were safe. We waited for a cooler day, we waited for evening, low wind, and lots of moisture. I yelp and throw the nearly empty bottle into the fire, and it causes a small uproar of flames.

"Fuck this house." I dig in my pocket for a cigarette. I don't smoke that often anymore, but tonight feels like the perfect occasion. Samson walks over and lights it for me, his eyes on mine for a second too long as I inhale the heady smoke. "Let's fuck this shit up."

"Fuck this house," Samson echoes.

"Fuck this fucking house," Ledger chimes in, taking an empty beer bottle and throwing it into the flames.

We turn to Hunter, who walks up to the billowing smoke, the flames nearly licking the skin of his arms. For a second, we remember—the body, haphazardly dumped here, the way the town grieved, the way people expected Hunter, then a gangly fifteen-year-old, to cope with the gruesome death of his mother. His best friend.

He was never the same.

Taking something metal from his pocket, he kisses it before throwing it into the fire, and I realize it's his mother's locket.

We may think we're up here drinking, having a good time, but for him?

This is a goddamned funeral.

12

BRIAR

My pulse quickens as I walk up to the clearing, the scene coming into view before me. Drinking, lighting shit on fire, throwing glass into the flames. I don't understand the reason, but then again, I don't pretend to know what they're thinking or why they act like pricks most of the time. The four *Kings*, once again pretending that the rules don't apply to them. Committing *arson*. Acting like fools. I grimace as a cloud of smoke smothers me, engulfing my throat with ashy dust. Before I can stop myself, I cough.

Ash spies me first, his head snapping toward me. My stomach clenches when his smile spreads, an evil grin on his beautiful face.

"Well, well, well," he sneers, turning and walking toward me. "Looks like the little lamb wants to come and play, after all."

The other three follow his gaze and their eyes land on me. I stand up straighter, balling my fists as I take a step forward.

"You're all idiots," I yell, looking at Ash specifically. "You guys could burn this whole forest down."

"So?" Ledger asks, taking a threatening step forward. He looks at the other guys with a wolfish grin, and they all nod. "What are you going to do about it?"

"Tell someone," I declare, crossing my arms. The crinkling of the windbreaker is drowned out by the roaring of flames. *Jesus, I hope they can put it out safely.*

"Are you sure you want to find out what would happen if you tattled?" Ash leers, baring his teeth as he saunters up to me. "Again?" He reaches out and plays with my zipper.

I jump back. "Don't touch me," I growl.

"Leave her alone," Hunter says from behind them all. His voice is calm, eerie—*practiced.* While the other guys are immature and callous, Hunter is smooth-talking, and his heart as dark as they come.

Like a psychopath.

Ash takes a few steps back as Hunter comes into view. My god—even as criminals, even as the assholes that they are, they're gorgeous. Hunter with his dark, mysterious swagger. Ash with his confident arrogance. Ledger with his brooding, bad boy vibes. And Samson—the quiet, hot nerd. Apart, they'd stand out in a crowd. But together? They're a force to be reckoned with, and for a second, my confidence wavers. The *Kings* of Ravenwood Academy. Royal, feared, powerful. I can feel it rolling off them, too. The internal light within them, the way they *know* they can get away with anything, *do* anything.

Gods. They're gods in human bodies. Omnipotent. Invincible.

To think I could take them down alone...

"You won't tattle, little lamb," Hunter muses, rolling his tongue along the inside of his cheek. "You forget that I know where you sleep. The things I could do would rival your worst nightmares."

The words cause my legs to wobble a bit, my core to clench. I glare at him, tamping down the small inkling of fear spider-walking up my spine. I want to say he could never do the monstrous things I'd experienced before, but as I look at them all, their eyes gleaming... I wouldn't put it past them. Men are men, and except for a few of them, they're all the same.

"Why the fuck do you all keep calling me a little lamb?" I ask, zipping my jacket up again as a cool breeze blows the smoke away.

"St. Augustine's sermon," he answers. "I knew public schools in California were abysmal, but I had no idea they didn't teach you basic history," he mocks, and the other guys laugh.

My cheeks flame. "I know who St. Augustine is, you idiot," I retort.

Hunter takes another couple of steps forward until he's standing right in front of me. "The lion is Christ resurrected, and the lamb is his sacrifice." He brushes a stray hair out of my face, his fingers grazing my jawline. Instead of immediately slapping his hand away, I stare up into his dark, soulful eyes. The flames dance in his dark irises, and I'm mesmerized. *"He endured death as a lamb; he devoured it as a lion."*

I close my eyes for a second—just a mere second—and I hate myself for faltering. Hunter notices, chuckling. I take a step back.

"Talk to me like a normal person, not like the rich snob that you are. Explain why I'm the lamb."

"Don't you get it?" he murmurs, backing me up against a tree. His hard body presses into mine, and I inhale the scent of vetiver—from the fancy cologne he wears.

Run. I should run. Nothing good can come from taunting them like this.

"Get what?" I ask, my voice harsh and impatient.

"You're all talk, Briar. We are the lions, and you are the lamb. And we're going to tear you apart, piece by piece. People want to believe the lion will lie with the lamb, but that's not realistic," he murmurs, his face inches from mine. I want to push him away, hit him, put him in his place—but I'm frozen. "We are not of the same breed," he adds, and then his nose grazes mine. My eyes flutter closed. "And we never will be."

Before I even open my eyes, he's gone.

I blink a few times and look around, and Hunter is walking backward, an irritated expression on his face.

"Go home, Briar. And don't even think of telling anyone what you saw tonight."

This time, I don't protest.

I make it home just before Mom, but since I still feel rattled, confused, conflicted... I head straight to my room. Around midnight, the front door slams, and I hold my breath as Hunter's heavy footsteps walk down the hallway. I wait to see if they pause at my door, but they don't falter in their cadence. His door closes and I exhale, relief rolling through my body.

13

BRIAR

By the time I park at Ravenwood Academy the next morning, my mind is fuzzy with exhaustion. I slept like shit last night, tossing and turning, eventually dreaming about how Hunter's body collided with mine. I woke up frenzied and irritable, and the double shot latte my mom made me with Andrew's fancy espresso machine did nothing to cure my bad mood. I saunter up to Scarlett, and she can immediately tell that something's wrong.

"Spill," Scarlett demands as we sit at one of the tables in the quad. It's surprisingly warm today, and the sun is already out. She hands me a croissant, and I swear, if pastries could turn moods around, this would do the trick.

"You are a goddess," I croon, squeezing her hand. "Thank you."

"You're welcome," she smiles, chewing on her own croissant.

I lean back and let the rare warmth shine down on my

face and neck. "I would love to open up my own café one day. In Paris. Maybe sell macarons and croissants like this, make fancy coffee... I'm applying to the Sorbonne in Paris for college," I admit.

She punches my shoulder gently. "Shut. Up!"

I nod and giggle. "Yeah. Who knows if I'll get in? I speak French conversationally, but being fluent enough to take classes in French..." I look down. "And then being able to afford it..."

She groans. "I feel you on that. I think we may be the only ones here *not* getting a full ride to college on Mommy and Daddy's dime."

I crumple the pastry paper and shrug. "Yeah, but that means we will actually enjoy college. Because we'll have earned it. Where do you want to go?"

She shrugs. "Boston University is the only way I can save money by living at home," she says glumly. "I'd love to go to Paris, though. Or New York. Or London..."

"That would be incredible."

We're both quiet as we watch the other students stand around, clutching their Louis Vuitton's and showing off their Rolexes. Scarlett and I seem to be on the same wavelength, because she laughs.

"Jack is filthy rich," she adds, nudging my shoulder as he approaches. "But he doesn't like to talk about it. He says he'd rather pretend to be poor."

We dissolve into a fit of laughter as he sits across from us, and we chat for a few minutes before the bell rings.

I manage to circumvent Hunter and the gang for most of the morning. I change for gym and walk out of the locker room, dreading the fact that I must attempt athleticism. We're outside in the state-of-the-art track that looks nicer than most professional football fields you see on television. The other girls look cute and stylish in their gym shorts. I just look like a bridge troll. Rolling my eyes, I walk over to where the coach is beginning to instruct us on how to run a mile.

Sure. Let me just casually run *a freaking MILE.*

I grimace as he blows the whistle, wishing more than anything that I had Jack or Scarlett here to help me through this. I can't afford to fail out of gym—which I almost did in California. I need straight As for the Sorbonne. Sucking it up, I start slowly, building my pace bit by bit, my feet pounding on the firm ground of the track. A couple of seconds later, Ledger wanders up to me, looking like a dark, tortured god with tan, well-muscled legs.

"Didn't realize you were in this class," I say glumly, and even barking out that sentence is an effort. I begin to breathe heavier, and I'm barely one-hundred meters into the run.

"It's your lucky day," he says, keeping his pace with mine. His tongue ring slides around inside his mouth, glinting in the sunlight.

I ignore him and try to focus on *not dying.* We jog side by side the entirety of a lap, and I try not to let him see just how out of breath I am.

Is it possible to die of a heart attack if you run too hard? Because that's where I'm at.

"You know, some people just aren't built for running," he muses as we pass the marker.

I stop and glare at him, my chest rising and falling quickly. "Screw you, Ledger." Sweat is dripping down the back of my neck. God, how can anyone possibly enjoy this?

"Just a word of advice... you're running with your toes up," he says, pausing next to me and pulling his shirt off. *Holy mother of...*

I look up at his face, trying not to stare at his sculpted-like-a-statue abdomen with dark whirls of ink that creep up to his chest and neck.

I'm practically wheezing as I respond. "What?"

He walks up to me, his lopsided smile taking me by surprise. "You're running with your toes up when you should be running on the middle of your foot." He bends down and takes my sneaker, tapping the middle of my arch. "You're going to injure yourself if you keep landing on your heel. Midfoot will absorb most of the shock." He sets my foot down and stands. "You want to land completely flat."

I wipe the sweat from my brow. I don't know why he's being nice to me. "Thanks."

He winks. "And maybe consider swimming or something instead."

Ah, there it is.

My cheeks flame as he jogs off effortlessly.

࿎

I get back to the locker room and grab a towel, taking my clothes off and *still* trying to catch my breath. Of course coach was timing us, and *of course* I was last, but at least I finished. Fifteen minutes and twelve seconds. I walk over to the showers, washing my hair and body quickly before heading to the area with blow dryers. At my last school, we had sturdy wooden benches to get ready. Ravenwood Academy has a state-of-the-art gym—with a sauna, steam room, and a locker room equipped with blow dryers, deodorant, dry shampoo, straighteners, curling irons, and face wipes... you name it. I sit down and dry my hair, running a straightener through it.

I feel great—maybe running *does* have its perks. The exhaustion from earlier is gone, replaced by some sort of euphoria I can only assume are the endorphins everyone talks about.

My mom—Athletic Barbie herself—is going to be so proud.

When I get back to my locker, I pull my clothes on, searching for my sweater and my blouse. I pause. Checking that I have the right aisle, I look again, my heart beating faster as I realize my tops are gone. My heart thumps in my throat, and I look around to see if there's an easy explanation, but I already know who did it. There are a few other girls hanging around, getting ready in front of the mirrors, but it wasn't them.

Shaking my head slowly, I walk through the locker room in my skirt and my bra, holding my head up high, nonplussed. Seems as though Ledger's friendliness on the track today was fueled by an ulterior motive, or perhaps a distraction. I let my guard down just a tiny bit—assuming the *women's* locker room would be safe.

But I forgot who they are.

What they are.

I grind my teeth as I walk toward campus, hoping I can find Scarlett and Jack easily. I know once I find them, I'll be fine, and Scarlett will get me sorted. I can't afford to miss my next class and get a truancy.

I don't have time for this bullshit.

The eyes of the other students are on me. People stare at me with mouths agape, eyebrows raised, and a few of them even laugh out loud. My cheeks are burning, and for a second I want to run and hide and never come back.

But if I did that, they would win.

They don't deserve to see me rattled, and they don't deserve my compliance and my silence.

They can try to break me.

They can keep tormenting me.

I know this certainly won't be the last time.

But as I walk through the halls in just my bra, I vow to never give them the satisfaction of feeling like they won.

I've been through too much, endured enough bullshit. It's quite comical how much effort they're going through just to get me to bend to their will.

It's never going to happen.

My bare feet slap against the linoleum, and I stare at anyone who dares to snicker or giggle at my expense. I push the door open to the quad, and within seconds, I spy the Kings walking in my direction. Hunter stops and stares at me, his eyes roving over the bare skin of my stomach and chest like a predator assessing its bait. Ash whistles through his fingers and unabashedly checks me out. Ledger gives me a small smile and winks, and then he holds his other hand out with my shirt and sweater in his hand. *Fucking bastard.* Samson is the only one who seems a little concerned.

I am out of fucks to give.

Hunter chuckles. "Did you lose your shirt, sister?"

My throat constricts. Ash and Ledger are smirking at me. Samson's expression is unreadable, but he doesn't look happy to see me without a shirt.

Ledger walks up to me and discards my shirt and sweater onto the concrete. It lays in a heap on the ground, and I clench my fists as fiery rage burns through me. A group of people begin circling us, watching, and I snap.

I take a step forward and shove Hunter backward as hard as I can. "You think you can break me?" I taunt, baring my teeth. "That forcing me to walk out of the locker room in my bra will cause me to bend to your will and submit?"

"Briar," Samson warns.

I turn to face him. "Stop acting like the nice one, Samson. You're just as bad as them. Maybe even worse, because people want to let their guard down around you."

He goes quiet, looking down at the ground, his jaw ticking.

"Is that all you've got?" Hunter muses, his arms crossed. His lips quirk to one side and he raises his eyebrows, an amused expression on his face.

I hate them.

I reach down and grab my shirt, pulling it on and buttoning it quickly. When I'm done, I look up at Hunter.

"Keep pushing me, I dare you."

"Yeah? What are you going to do? Tell our parents?"

I swallow. "You're all the same, aren't you?" My voice is quieter than I expected, edged with emotion. "Men. Men who hurt women." Like last night, his expression falls for a second. *Good.* I keep pushing. "You rape us," I growl, and his eyebrows fly up. "Defiling us, teasing us, invading our space, ensuring even our *home* doesn't feel safe," I add, my lips trembling slightly.

I stand up taller and look at Ledger. "If you ever touch my things again, I will report you."

My eyes flick to Hunter again, and I swear some sort of mercifulness—understanding—appears on his face.

I twist around and walk back to my locker, my whole body shaking.

A few people clap, but the murmurs soon die down.

People are still terrified of the Kings, but I'm about to pull a checkmate.

Hunter, Ash, Ledger, and Samson are about to witness how this Queen attacks—slow, premeditated, and lethal.

❦ 14 ❦

SAMSON

Something about her makes me want to protect her from the guys—makes me want her all to myself. Sometimes they go a step too far, and today is one of those days. I know Hunter has mixed feelings because of his mom, but his feelings for Briar are starting to cloud his vision.

I know because I was the exact same way once with Micah.

Thinking of Micah—of *us*—is really fucking hard. I close my eyes briefly and will the memory of the man I used to love —the man who's gone now—out of my mind.

"She likes to play the victim, but secretly she enjoys it," Ash murmurs as we walk through the hallways to our next class. "Did you see the tramp stamp?" he adds, nudging my side.

I nod, shoving my hands in my pockets. "Yeah."

"Slut," he murmurs.

Before I can respond, Hunter shoves Ash against the

locker. "Don't call her that," he growls, walking away to his next class.

I look at Ash, displeased. Sometimes his vulgarity gets annoying. None of us are really like that. We may be dicks, but we're not going to go around slut shaming women.

Briar intrigues me, baffles me, surprises me. I can see the strength shining behind her eyes, the tenacity and resoluteness.

You're all the same, aren't you?

Briar is a fucking badass—a survivor.

Why the fuck are we trying to torment her when we should be trying to recruit her?

As Ledger, Ash, and I walk to our next class together, I think about how we became the *Kings* of Ravenwood—a title I *still* don't deserve. Mob mentality is a funny thing, and it just sort of happened after Micah. None of us bothered to correct them—not with who our families were. It was so much easier to fit into the mold everyone had already created for you.

Hunter was the original *King*. His dad being the headmaster meant he was automatically the leader of our class. He's a free spirit, eclectic, and intelligent—when he's not being an ass. In fact, he's my favorite person to talk to. His dad is a world traveler, and they've been to some cool places. People misunderstand him.

Ash came second. As the mayor's son, his position as Hunter's beta formed naturally. He hides behind his vulgarity and comes off as a total dick to most people, but I know the truth. The Greythorn family has more secrets than anyone I know, and Ash bears the brunt of it all as the only child.

And Ledger, the all-star athlete with a future in track and field. He goes against the grain to spite his parents, but it doesn't matter, because despite the piercings, the tattoos, the defiance... he can do no wrong, and his family connections have saved him on numerous occasions. Life comes easy to

Ledger Huxley. His *I-walk-on-water* attitude gets on my nerves, but he's loyal as fuck, and a good friend.

And me? I don't quite know where or how I fit in, but Ash befriended me freshman year, and I've been here ever since.

As we sit down in economics, Hunter scans the classroom for Briar, who has this class with us. Again, that overprotectiveness reverberates through my body, and I shove the feeling away.

Just as the second bell rings, Briar slips into the room, glaring at each of us before taking a seat, completely put together and composed.

Badass.

Ledger quirks an eyebrow as he flips his computer open to the virtual textbook, and Ash thumbs his lower lip suggestively as his eyes rove over Briar's legs. Hunter just stares straight ahead with furrowed brows, his arms crossed, trying to ignore her.

She's an enigma, and we all seem to want a piece of her.

❦ 15 ❦

BRIAR

Scarlett texted me she's convinced that everyone is now just as wary of me as they are of the *Kings* after this most recent showdown, and that I now have my own bad rap as the person dumb enough to defy the Kings. I meant it when I said I wasn't here to deal with this bullshit. I am here to get through the year, to add it to my resume, and to get into the Sorbonne in Paris. I didn't ask for any of this.

Except, maybe I did when I fought back that first day...

I'm still fuming after economics class. I swallow as I walk out of the classroom after the bell rings. I didn't look back at the boys the entire class—which took a lot of self-control. When I walk up to where Scarlett and Jack are already eating lunch, they both whoop and holler as I blush and sit down.

"Oh, please. They need to be taken down a peg," I explain, holding my hands out.

"Yeah, but you just like... stood there all Xena-like, your

hair flowing, your bra showing..." Jack trails off, his voice high-pitched and excited. "It's like one big alpha show." He shakes his head and takes a sip of his iced coffee.

I raise my eyebrows. "What's an alpha show?"

"Jack reads a lot of wolf shifter novels," Scarlett explains.

Jack places his palms flat on the table and grins like I just asked his favorite question. "Okay, so every pack has an alpha wolf. Obviously, that's always been Hunter. But then you showed up, and it's like you're trying to get him to kneel *to you*—like you refuse to submit."

"I do refuse to submit," I answer, taking a bite of my sandwich.

Scarlett laughs. "See?" She looks at Jack. "We were so worried when we saw her, but look at how she's holding up." She smiles at me. "I'm proud of you."

I shrug. "Really though, they're just guys. Rich, snobby guys who are used to getting their way. I see right through them."

I don't admit to the fear lurking underneath my courage—the small, nagging feeling that they are still men.

Men who could hurt me.

"It'll be interesting to see who wins," Jack adds, cocking his head. "Truthfully, I just want to see Ash cry," he confesses.

"Why Ash?" I ask, laughing.

Scarlett and Jack look at each other briefly. "As much as we hate him, it's not our story to tell. But let's just say that Ash and Jack had a thing the summer before freshman year."

"What?" I screech, grinning. "Ash? The douche?"

Jack rolls his shoulders as if he's trying to repel the memory. "We were young, and he wasn't always such a douche."

"Ash broke his heart," Scarlett declares, chewing her salad loudly. "Jack is always looking for ways to get back at him."

I chuckle as I sip my water. "Everyone sleeps with everyone here," I mumble.

"If you ever want to kiss a girl," Scarlett starts, and we all laugh.

"You'll be the first person I proposition," I answer.

☙❧

Fortunately, the *Kings* give me the space I need to recalibrate, and I don't see them the rest of the day. *Dumb move on their part because this Queen is always thinking one step ahead.* I head home, finish homework, and then spend the rest of the late afternoon watching TV. Mom and I eat dinner together— some pasta recipe she learned from a yoga friend. It's delicious, and I go back for seconds just as Hunter walks into the dining room, grabbing a plate.

Oh, hell no.

"Smells delicious, Aubrey," he purrs. I hate the way he says her name. I hate the way he says everyone's name. Like he loves to hear himself talk.

He's wearing a thin, worn white T-shirt and black jeans that fit his sculpted legs without being too tight. Button-up boots complete the look, and I wonder, as I study his tan forearms, why he has to be so good-looking while also being such an ass. To my chagrin, he sits down right next to me.

"Briar," he says slowly, twirling his pasta. "How lovely to see you."

I narrow my eyes at him. "Hello," I answer, pushing my plate away. I cross my arms, and the gesture exaggerates my cleavage.

Hunter's eyes flick to my chest and then back up to my eyes, slightly darker than they were a second ago. Then he shakes his head and looks away, running a hand through his hair.

"How's school going?" my mom asks, taking a large bite and chewing loudly.

Oh, the innocence. She has no idea what school is like for us.

Her eyes flit between us, and I have to wonder if she suspects there's something more going on. She has that curious, bright look in her eyes, and when she meets my gaze, a knowing smile forms on her lips.

Great.

"I think Briar is fitting in quite well," Hunter muses. Even the way he eats—the way he chews—is perfect, coordinated, elite. He holds his utensils like someone who's used to eating in fine dining establishments.

God, I hate him.

"That's great!" my mom chirps, facing Hunter. "She was worried about Ravenwood being a private preparatory school and all. It's so different from the school she left..."

Hunter's lips twitch as he takes a sip of water. I watch the way his throat bobs, the golden skin there flawless except for the day-old dark stubble. I like how he doesn't shave—just a close trim, leaving a thin, dark layer that gives him an edge. Shaking the thought away, my eyes find his, and he smirks as if he knows I was checking him out.

"I assume that means you've both decided to get along?" she adds, her expression hopeful. She *so badly* wants us to get along—*so badly* wants me to find my place here in Greythorn, and ultimately Ravenwood. A place to shuck my trauma. A fresh start. And I know that getting along with my dear step-brother is one way to do that.

As I look at Hunter—the way his calloused hands grip the drinking glass roughly, the tips of his fingers white as his eyes find mine again—I know we'll probably never have that. There's too much of something I can't quite put my finger on.

Tension.

Competition.

Aggression.

Abhorrence.

"We have," I answer, giving Hunter a sweet smile. I swear, he's seconds away from shattering the glass in his hands. "And his friends have been nothing but kind to me, too."

Hunter's brows furrow ever so slightly, but before he can respond, Andrew walks into the dining room. He smiles and throws his arms wide, clad in jogging pants and a T-shirt. He bends down and gives my mom a long kiss on the lips. I avert my eyes and focus on the pasta, feeling Hunter's eyes on me.

"Well, well, well," he muses, grinning as he sits. Scooting closer to my mom, he looks at Hunter and me. "Isn't this nice? Sitting down to eat as a family again. I say we make this a weekly thing," he suggests.

My mom nods, grinning. "Or daily! We have all of this space, and a beautiful room to eat in," she adds, looking at me. "What do you think, Briar?"

I shrug. "Sure," I reply, refusing to look at Hunter.

Annoyance rolls through me as his arm snakes around the back of my chair. "I think it would be wonderful to sit down as a family," he agrees, smiling. Andrew and my mom smile and kiss again, nuzzling noses. They can't hear the bite—the *threat* in Hunter's words.

I slide my eyes to his and narrow them, frowning.

"Don't you think that'd be nice, Briar?" he taunts, leaning back and smiling at me salaciously. His shirt clings to the muscles of his abdomen, not an ounce of fat on him. Just strong, honed muscle everywhere. "Maybe Ash, Ledger, and Samson can join us every now and then," he suggests.

Andrew nods. "We'd love to have them," he says cheerfully. He smiles and helps himself to a heaping pile of pasta. "They're welcome anytime."

I'd rather die.

Hunter chuckles. "I know they'd love that," he quips, his eyes sliding to mine. He winks, and I look away.

I want to slap the cocky smile off his face.

❧ 16 ❧

BRIAR

After dinner, I retreat to my room with every intention of flipping through channels on the TV in my delegated area—according to Hunter's house rules. The prick had the audacity to install a flatscreen above my dresser after our argument the other night. The more I think about it, the angrier I get, especially when I try to get comfortable in bed against the hard, wooden frame. A couch would be so much easier.

Why am *I* the one who must sanction myself to my bedroom? I know this was his house first, but there are no posted signs that said the basement was for Hunter Ravenwood's use only. As far as I'm concerned, this is just as much my house as it is his, now that our parents are married, and my mom and I are fully moved in. I have no doubt that our parents would back me up if push came to shove.

Throwing the covers off and climbing out of my bed, I stomp down the hallway and then down the stairs. It's nearly ten, and I know my mind won't let me sleep until I've zoned out for a bit. He might not even be in there. He could be sleeping.

But something tells me the devil doesn't sleep.

I glance into the library for a second as I pass it. I stop abruptly when my eyes adjust to the scene before me. The motion must catch Hunter's eye, because his eyes snap to mine. He's sitting at the desk, a typewriter in front of him, and it looks as though he's writing. A *typewriter.* Who even uses a typewriter anymore? His fingers were flying over the round keys effortlessly until I interrupted him, and now he's leaning back and watching me with irritation, his arms crossed.

"Hello, Briar," he says, my name on his lips somehow sensual and smooth.

"You're a writer?" I ask, because I can't think of what else to say—I'm completely caught off guard.

"I'm not a writer," he starts, sighing. "But I do dabble in writing from time to time, yes."

Can't he ever just speak normally?

I walk into the library and lean against the door. The mood in here is dark, old-school—unlike the rest of the house, which is a bit airier. The shelves lining the paneled-wood walls are stuffed full of books. There's a leather Chesterfield sofa, and the desk where Hunter sits next to the grand window is large and ornate. He's watching me impatiently.

"So, what do you write?" I ask casually.

He pushes out from behind the desk and stands next to me. My pulse spikes, but I hold myself tall and ready myself for a fight.

There's a gleam in his eyes as he leans against the opposite door frame, inches from me. I back up a step, but he reaches out and tugs me forward by my wrist.

"I don't show anyone my writing," he says, his voice

rough. His warm hand wraps all the way around my wrist, holding me still. "What makes you think you're special?"

His words clobber me, and my cheeks heat. I try pulling away from him again, but his grip on my wrist tightens. Not enough to hurt—just enough to show how powerful he is. I start to pull away, instinct telling me to fight back, but something about his expression makes me stay. It's unguarded in a way I've never seen before. The way his eyes lock onto mine, the vulnerability somewhere deep within those dark irises... like I caught him doing the one thing he truly enjoys.

I smirk. "It's just a question, Hunter. Not everyone has an ulterior motive."

"I don't trust you," he says slowly, narrowing his eyes. "You're not like the rest of the girls at Ravenwood. You don't bow to anyone, do you?"

I smile and tilt my head. "Absolutely not."

"Well, then it looks like we're at a stalemate."

"I guess we are," I muse, quirking my lips to the side.

"Don't do that," he commands, his brows furrowed.

"Do what?"

"That thing with your lips." His words cause my heart to pound in my chest, and I blink a few times as I digest them. "Why did you move here, Briar?" he asks, leaning forward just enough for me to get a whiff of the vetiver. I open my mouth to state the obvious, but he puts a finger on my lips. "Not your mom's reason. Yours." He pauses. "What happened to you in California?"

A sudden coldness hits me in my core. "What?"

The lines in his forehead deepen as he studies me, something akin to concern passing over his face.

"Did someone hurt you?" His scowl falters for just a second, and I swallow.

"Why would I ever tell you that? After what you did?" I pull out of his grip. "Just leave me alone," I add, my voice sharp and venomous. I twist around and begin to walk away, but his voice stops me in my tracks.

"I didn't know." He sounds almost... anguished. "I had no idea that you would be like..." he trails off, and I turn to face him.

"Like what?" I whisper.

He sighs, trying to find the words. His hand at his mouth, brushing against his full lips, causes me to stare.

"I expected a little girl. Not you." His eyes narrow ever so slightly, and he pushes me against the door frame. *Should I be worried right now? Because I'm not...* He has hands on both shoulders now, pinning me beneath him. Sighing, I look him straight in the eye as I tell him.

"I was raped. He's in prison. End of story."

His eyes bore into mine—the dark brown irises rich and beautiful. *Cunning.* And yet... they soften as my words plow through him. He releases his grip slightly, licking his lips as a flash of anger crosses his face.

"I'm sorry that happened to you," he growls.

I shrug. "It's in the past now. I'm working through it." Furrowing my brows, I stare at him. "Which is why I might've overreacted to you touching me." Understanding passes over his face. I continue. "I'm still not sure why you felt the need to be mean, anyway," I confess. "I never did anything to you, and yet you humiliated me."

And there it is. One of my most vulnerable thoughts.

"I was annoyed," he starts, the corners of his lips quirking upwards. "I was acting out. The two of you moved in and I sort of lost it," he says slowly. "It's been my dad and I for years. And then you showed up, and I was conflicted. I know it's not an excuse, but at least now you know where my head was at," he adds, smirking.

"Okay, but today—"

"Will not happen again," he growls, pushing against me. I

gasp as his body collides with mine. "I made damn sure the guys knew they were not to touch you ever again. And that was before I knew what *actually* happened. I'm sorry, Briar. Truly."

His words cause my body to heat, my knees to weaken. He... he asked them to leave me alone? He's apologizing?

His words awaken some sort of primal beast inside of me —something fervent and impatient, hot, needy... I lick my lips. I don't know what to say to that. He must realize my hesitation because he presses against me again.

"Now that we're at a stalemate, don't you think we should join forces? Combine our efforts?"

I look away, my cheeks flaming. My core is throbbing, and I squeeze my legs together.

"Your friends would never agree to it," I answer. "They love tormenting people."

He chuckles. "Do they? Are you sure?"

I snap my eyes to his. "Yes, they—"

"Have you seen it with your own eyes?"

His words roll through me, and it takes me a minute to digest them. "You're bullies," I state.

"Are we? Or do we just have a reputation?"

I swallow. *What about Micah?*

I'm about to ask when he thrusts into me, his hips rocking into mine, and I have to stifle my moan. Words have escaped me. I close my eyes for a second before opening them and looking into his brown ones.

Only then do I let myself imagine it—sharing a reign with them. Being *friends* with them—with all of them. Trusting men again—allowing Hunter's protection to shield me, to help me. And then my mind wanders, and I imagine *being* with each of them. Shared among Hunter—the powerful alpha— and Ash, Ledger, and Samson, who all get pieces of me in different ways. The thought causes the space between my legs to throb, causes my throat to constrict. His hooded eyes drink me in, his smile lopsided, like he knows what I'm thinking.

I pull away, trying to forget the ridiculous thoughts running through my mind. Just because he's being *sort of* nice to me, doesn't mean I should be imagining what it would be like to sleep with all of them. It's just so easy to imagine— they're so close, always together... like they come as a packaged deal. I squeeze my eyes shut briefly before taking a step away.

This is a game.

This is all just a game to him.

Another move on the chessboard.

"This is silly. The only thing we need to do is to make a truce. Stop bullying me, and maybe we can be cordial."

"Cordial?" he mocks, a feline smile on his face. He takes a step forward. "Don't you feel it?" he asks, his face not even an inch away from mine. His breath is on my lips, the sweet scent of it turning my core to liquid. He cocks his head and scans my face, the angled jaw defined in the low light of the room. "This thing, between us?"

"Your mom married my dad—"

"So?" he asks, reaching out and running a finger along my jaw.

"So? Even if I did feel it, which I don't, we couldn't."

He smirks, licking his lips. His tongue is long, elegant. I squirm beneath him.

"We don't share blood, Briar. We are not a true brother and sister."

"Still—"

"Why are you fighting it?" he asks softly. "Think about how good we could be. Together." I fight the urge to nod, to agree wholeheartedly, but my mind is screaming at me. "Truth be told, I haven't been able to concentrate since you arrived in Greythorn."

My body heats, and I wonder where my mother is—where Andrew is... and what they'd think if they walked in right now and saw us like this.

"That's your problem," I start, feeling my resolve crumble. "Not mine."

I can't tell if he's playing me—if this is all just one, big prank. But then he pushes me gently against the door frame again, thrusting against me—*God, I wish he'd stop doing that*—and I realize he's not playing. He's very, very serious, and it's evident by the way he presses his thick erection against my stomach.

"Admit it," he whispers, his mouth an inch from mine. My eyelids flutter closed, and my hands press firmly against his hard chest. My nipples peak beneath the t-shirt I'm wearing. As if Hunter can sense it, he lowers his gaze to my chest, and his dark eyes come back up to mine. His dilated pupils are anything but playful—they're enigmatic, ruthless, animalistic. He lowers a hand from next to my head and twists my nipple firmly between his thumb and forefinger.

I cry out, arching my back. I can't help it—it feels *so* good. That fact surprises me more than anything.

"Or maybe you don't need to. Your body responds to me like a marionette, doing whatever I want it to. Your mind may be fighting it, but your body? It wants me."

I can't even argue with him, can't think of an excuse for the way I'm arching into him and breathing heavily.

"The lion and the lamb," he whispers, sending shivers down my spine as he licks my neck. My pulse thumps against the delicate skin there, and I know he can feel how it's beating erratically. He groans as he devours my skin, and his hips buck against me.

I'm just about to tilt my head up—just about to let him

kiss me, and who knows what else, when the front door slams.

We jump apart, and I touch my lips with my fingers.

What the hell just happened?

Did I let him kiss my neck?

Did I feel his hard length against the band of my sweatpants?

Did he confess he's attracted to me?

My head is spinning, and Hunter takes a few steps back just as my mom walks past us, and she smiles as she continues into the kitchen. As if us chatting against a door frame—being *cordial*—is normal. Instinctively, I follow her, and when I look back, Hunter is watching me with a darkened, feral expression, and then he turns back into the library.

"Where did you go?" I ask as I walk into the kitchen, still breathless and slightly dazed.

"Late night Target run. I had this great idea for how to organize the upstairs linen closet."

I nod, and as I begin to turn away, she hands me a chocolate bar.

"Thanks, Mom," I say, my voice catching as I take it. I'm not sure why I'm emotional. The new house, new city, new friends, new problems... It's a lot.

But she's here.

She's always been here.

For that, I will forever be thankful.

"So nice that you and Hunter are hanging out." Her voice is distracted as she pulls clear, plastic bins out of the white bags. Even in jeans and a sweatshirt, she looks so put together. I realize, with horror, that I'm wearing my favorite stained T-shirt. Hunter cornered me and kissed my neck in my schlubby pajamas. I make a mental note to buy some nicer ones.

For *me*, not for him.

"Mmm hmm," I mumble, unsure of how else to respond. "I should go to bed. Night, Mom." I give her a quick peck.

I walk back to the library, and Hunter's eyebrows rise with amusement as he watches me walk toward him. I set the candy bar down and slide it to him.

"A peace offering," I explain, giving him a small smile.

Before he can respond, I walk out and to my room, closing the door and trying to calm my racing heart.

17

LEDGER

I bend down and tie my sneakers, looking up just as Briar comes onto the track. I stifle a laugh as she glowers at everyone, her expression sour and displeased.

My dark, little rain cloud.

I jog over to her.

"Listen," I start, putting my hands on my hips. "I'm sorry about yesterday."

She glares up at me. "I honestly don't care."

I reach out and grab her hand, but she pulls away, as if I've burned her.

"Don't touch me," she hisses.

I hold my hands out. "I'm not going to hurt you, Briar. I'm just trying to apologize."

She scowls, looking down at the track. I've noticed her nose wrinkles whenever she's upset, and I hide my smile because it makes her seem so innocent.

"I don't understand why you continue to taunt me," she starts, looking up at me. Her eyes are wide, open.

"I didn't know," I explain, running a hand through my hair. "None of us knew about..."

"Hunter told you."

Her words are resigned, and I swear I hear a hint of relief, too.

"He said we shouldn't fuck with you anymore." She looks at me and doesn't say anything, though I can tell the wheels are churning. "I'm not a bad guy, Briar. People think I'm this tough jock, but that's their assumption, and I never bothered to correct it."

She looks up at me through her lashes. "Why steal my shirt then?"

I shrug. "I was just teasing you."

"I'm waiting for an apology," she quips.

I smile. "I'm sorry."

"Thank you." She gives me a small smile in return, and then she begins to stretch, lifting her arms over her head. I catch her starting to open and close her mouth a few times, like she wants to say more, but she must decide against it because she bends forward.

I don't mind the view...

"What do your tattoos mean?" she asks suddenly as she snaps up.

I smirk. "That's second date territory, so you'll have to wait and see."

A flush creeps up her neck as my words sink in. "You're so full of shit, do you know that?"

I begin to walk backward, throwing my arms wide and cocking my head. "One day, little lamb."

I'm ready for the chase.

18

BRIAR

For all intents and purposes, Hunter, Ash, Ledger, and Samson all leave me alone the next day at school. I don't know if it's because of what happened yesterday, or my conversation with Ledger during P.E., but there are no more affronts by the Kings. Scarlett is right though—people watch me differently now. The ones who witnessed my shirtless show yesterday must've spread the word that I wasn't going to lie down and take the bullying. A few students look at me with admiration, but also reverence, anticipation... and maybe a bit of fear. I try to smile at everyone I notice glancing in my direction. I want to shout from the rooftops that I'm nothing like them—nothing like the Kings. I am just trying to get through the school year intact, just like the rest of the seniors.

As Scarlett, Jack and I are walking out of the school at the end of the day, Ash saunters up to us. I try not to roll my eyes as we continue to our cars. I suppose Hunter told him to play nice, too.

"Can I help you?" I ask, quirking an eyebrow up.

"Calm your tits, I just want to invite you guys to my party tomorrow night," he says, his voice polite.

"A party? The omnipotent Kings throw parties?" For a second, confusion flashes across his face, but it's gone just as quickly as it appears.

He looks at Jack. "Tell her I always throw parties." I notice the way his eyes linger on Jack for a second too long, and again, something flashes in his expression.

"It's true. We don't usually go, though," Jack answers, crossing his arms. His response says everything I need to know.

Ash sighs and turns to me. "Please come. I promise we don't bite." His eyes flick to Jack. "Except in certain situations."

Jack chokes, covering it with a cough.

"What time?" I ask, crossing my arms.

He grins, his light blue eyes twinkling. If he wasn't such an ass, his smile might make me blush.

"For you, anytime."

"Jackass," Scarlett mumbles. If Ash hears, he doesn't say anything.

"I think we already have plans but thank you." I push past him.

"Hunter really wants you to go," he says, pleading.

Jesus.

First Ledger, and now Ash?

"Hunter can ask me himself, then." I grab Scarlett's and Jack's hands, pulling them behind me as we leave Ash by the gate of the school.

"What was that all about?" Scarlett asks, and we stop in front of my car.

I shrug. "Hunter and I have come to a sort of... ceasefire," I explain, feeling immediately guilty that I didn't tell her or Jack what happened last night. "After everything happened yesterday, he told the guys to leave me alone. I think we're... cordial now?"

"Cordial? With the Kings?" Scarlett quips, her voice hesitant. "They are *jerks,* Briar. They don't know how to be friends with anyone else. Trust me, other people have tried to breach the ironclad wall they have around themselves."

I don't know what to say to that. On the one hand, it's kind of true. But on the other hand, I don't think Hunter acquiring a new stepsister was in their grand plan, so sometimes things change.

"We're both tired of clashing. So, we agreed to a peace offering. We're *not* friends," I clarify. I think about the chocolate bar—about the way my coffee was ready and waiting for me this morning. Sure, it could've been my mom. She was up early for a meeting with a potential client. But something told me it was one of the other occupants of my new home.

"Be careful, Briar," Scarlett warns. "I don't trust them."

I laugh. "*They* shouldn't trust *me.*"

🌣

I text Sonya—my therapist in California who is paid for 24/7 text access, thanks to my mom—and update her on everything that's happened. She doesn't respond right away, but when she does, her blunt answer surprises me.

You've been through the ringer, Briar. And we've been working on letting the trauma go, learning how to feel good again. Learning what feels good. I need you to listen to your body, your intuition. After all, one of them is family...

I stare at my phone for a few minutes after reading her text.

One of them is family...

But it's sort of true. After last night, something about Hunter changed. He went from irritated at having to share his space—the space his mother once occupied—to protective of me.

Maybe... maybe they're not as bad as everyone makes them out to be.

I'm in the middle of a shower a few minutes later, just before dinner, when the power goes out. Groaning, I step out and feel for my towel, and then I carefully search for the door handle. I left my phone on my bed, but since it's dark out already, I can't see a damn thing. I finally make my way back into the bedroom when someone pounds on my door.

"Mom?" I ask, turning on the flashlight setting on my phone.

"No," a voice says, and goosebumps rise on my wet skin.

I throw the door open. "Hi?" I pull the towel tighter.

"They went to grab dinner," he says, running his hands through his hair. "Just wanted to make sure you were all right."

Okay, so maybe having a stepbrother isn't so bad.

Ignoring the warm feeling spreading throughout my chest, I tilt my head as water continues to drop onto the carpet. His words from last night enter my mind as his brows knit together ever so slightly with concern.

Are we bullies? Or do we just have a reputation?

"I'm fine," I answer. He nods, and just as he turns to walk away, "Thank you for checking on me."

He gives me a small smile, his eyes rolling over every exposed inch of my body.

"I like your tramp stamp, by the way. I forgot to tell you yesterday."

I blush. "*That* was a drunken, spur-of-the-moment mistake when I was fifteen," I laugh, referencing the Magic 8-Ball on my lower back. "I had a fake ID, got plastered, and then got a tattoo."

He smirks. "Well, it suits you."

As he walks away, I want to ask him to stay—want to see more of *this* side of Hunter Ravenwood. The nice one—the one who comes to check on me.

But I don't.

Because though we're at a stalemate now, I have no idea how long it'll stay that way.

After all, only one alpha wins the final battle.

When the lights come back on a minute later, Hunter walks past my door. I notice his shadow pause for a second, but then he continues to his room without knocking.

One of them is family...

BRIAR

"No," I declare, turning to look at myself in my mirror. When I'd convinced Scarlett and Jack to go to Ash's party, I did not expect Scarlett to go full-on makeover mode on me.

"Oh, come on," Scarlett whines. "You look fucking hot."

"Speak for yourself," I murmur, my eyes taking in Scarlett and all her glory.

She opted for a silver, metallic suit with a black tie, and she finished the look off with her platform Docs. Her short, dark hair is slicked back, and her heavy makeup looks amazing.

I glance back at my reflection. A lacey, short, skin-tight dress clings to my body. The arms are see-through, and I feel like a sexy Morticia Addams with my loose waves and red lipstick.

"Please," she begs. "Pretty please?"

Jack makes an annoyed sound from my bed as he scrolls

on his phone. He's not really paying attention since he's already dressed in a black shirt, black jeans, and a silver tie that perfectly matches Scarlett's suit.

I look back at myself. For one, my ass is nearly hanging out. Two, this is not really my style. I'm all about function and comfort over style. If I had my way, I'd be wearing my jeans, Converse, and a tank top, but Scarlett seemed completely appalled by that idea.

"You are the Queen of Ravenwood. You need a show-stopping dress. Not some jeans and a tank from American Eagle."

I frown at her. "Fine. But I'm not wearing heels." I instead opt for my Docs, lacing them up as we get ready to head out. I turn to Jack, studying him. "What exactly happened between you and Ash?" I ask. It just seems like such an unlikely pairing. Sweet, sarcastic Jack, with his ginger hair and thick glasses... and Ash. The most overconfident guy at Ravenwood.

He sighs. "We were young and stupid. That's all I'm going to admit."

"Even *I* don't know what really happened," Scarlett muses, walking over to Jack and giving him a soft smile.

Jack frowns. "I really liked him, and he really liked me, but he got scared and pulled away." He shrugs. "It was nearly three years ago."

"So, when Micah started dating Samson," Scarlett starts, her voice uneven, "we knew what they were about. And we tried to warn him."

"But he didn't listen," Jack finishes.

I look between them, swallowing. "I'm sorry Ash broke your heart," I say, tugging my purse over my shoulder.

He gives me a warm smile. "Thanks."

"Anyway, shall we go?" Scarlett asks.

We head out of my room. My mom is sitting on the couch with her computer on her lap. After the three of us came home earlier, I could tell mom was happy I'd found friends so quickly. And she seemed to like Scarlett and Jack.

"Oh, you guys look great!" she exclaims. "Have a good time." She turns to me. "If you drink, *please* call me and I will pick you up, no questions asked." Turning to my friends, she tilts her head. "Same applies to you two."

"Thanks, Mom," I say as I bend down to give her a hug.

"Thanks, Aubrey," Jack and Scarlett echo.

We say goodbye, climbing into my Subaru.

"Your mom is so cool," Scarlett states as I back us out of the driveway.

"Yeah, having a baby at eighteen will do that to you."

We drive in silence to Ash Greythorn's house. I expect another McMansion, being the mayor's house, but as we weave through the forest, I realize I'm in for a surprise.

The Greythorn's house is not large, but it's the sleekest house I've ever seen—angular, modern, with floor-to-ceiling windows. Surrounded by miles of forest, it's small compared to its surroundings and the houses I'm used to seeing around here. I park behind a string of cars, and even though we're technically on time, the house is already bursting with people.

"I like the house," I muse, tucking my phone in my bra and handing my keys to Scarlett, who agreed to stay sober tonight.

"You wouldn't if you knew the mayor," Jack answers.

I cock my head as we trek through the grass to the front door, which is propped open.

"Is the mayor a jerk or something?" I ask, pushing the heavy door open all the way.

"You could say that," Scarlett answers.

A shiver works down my spine as music blares through the speakers.

"We'll tell you about it another time," Jack shouts. "I'll get us drinks."

Scarlett and I push our way through the mass of bodies writhing to the music. If I thought I would be overdressed, I was wrong. Greythorn—and Ravenwood in particular—once again proves that most of the people who live here have money. The girls are dressed in stylish clothes and spiked heels. They have perfect hair and makeup. It feels like prom, but with shorter dresses. The guys are all dressed sharply, too. *This is nothing like the laid-back California parties I've been to*, I think, as two girls snort a line of coke next to us.

"Welcome to a Greythorn party," Scarlett yells into my ears. "Where the shoes and watches are designer, the consequences are nonexistent, and the expensive drugs are passed around like candy."

I look around, admiring the stylish furniture, the large, built-in bookcases made of dark wood, and how minimally decorated it is. It's clean and mindful. My mom would love the style of this house—especially the dark green velvet sofa. Someone's set up a state-of-the-art stereo system with a live DJ, the music thumping and vibrating through me. Instead of red solo cups, actual champagne flutes and glass tumblers are being used.

"Where is the mayor? I assume he doesn't approve of these parties..."

"He's probably in Boston or New York for the weekend."

I look around. "What about Ash's mom?"

Scarlett swallows. "She doesn't live here. She's in a psychiatric facility."

Yikes.

I want to ask more, but I know it's too loud and crazy right now. I casually glance around for Hunter, Ash, Ledger, and Samson, but I don't see them. Instead, Scarlett and I make our way to the backyard, intercepting Jack on our way.

He slides the door open, and several people are standing around, vaping. The backyard is amazing, with fairy lights lining the tree branches, and no fence—so the forest goes on endlessly behind the house. It's gorgeous. A couple of stylish outdoor furniture sets are placed around the pool, which is lit up with a green pool light. We head to an empty bench near the jacuzzi since it's much quieter there. A few people glance in our direction. As we sit, the closest group gets up and leaves, scurrying off quickly.

"See?" Scarlett asks, sipping her soda.

I take a couple sips of my drink, which tastes like Kool-Aid mixed with vodka—heavy on the vodka. I set it down and look around, frowning.

"See what?" I ask, even though I already know what she's going to say.

"They saw you and left. You have *power* now."

Or a reputation.

Jack and Scarlett chuckle, and we chat for a few minutes until I get up to use the restroom. It's an excuse, of course. After sipping the rest of my drink, I'm starting to feel sexy in my dress, and as people watch me with reverence, I do feel kind of formidable—but in the friendliest way possible. Like I won't take any shit from bullies, but I also have no plans to torment people the way the Kings do.

Mostly, it feels good to know that the Kings have been knocked down a peg.

As I wait in line for the restroom, I try not to act completely distracted as my eyes scan the crowded house. I use the restroom and walk out, heading to the kitchen for another drink. One of the senior guys—Darian—offers to get it for me, but I refuse. I've watched too many Dateline episodes. He's cute—tall, muscular, with dark hair and bronze skin. We chat for a minute or two, mostly about our French class.

As we're talking, my mind keeps going back to the notion that *this* is how high school is supposed to be. See the cute guy from class, have a nice, innocent conversation... maybe make out after a few drinks. No hierarchy, no caste system. Just innocent teenage drama.

But I know that's not my destiny, and as his arm goes around my shoulders casually, my skin begins to tingle, as if someone's watching us—watching *me*.

I'm laughing at one of Darian's jokes when I see them, and my smile drops from my face immediately.

All four of them are watching me from the other side of the kitchen. They're hidden in the shadow, leaning against the wet bar, and each one is dressed in dark jeans and a black hoodie. I can only see their eyes—Hunter's in particular boring into mine with displeasure. I'm just about to excuse myself from Darian when they turn and walk out the front door.

Stunned, I stammer an apology to Darian and set my drink down. They invited *me*. And yet, as soon as they saw me, they left. What gives? The thought stings as I make my way to the front door.

I wanted to make an impression, wanted to show them I could level up. Until this point, I hadn't realized that this dress was for them. I wasn't sure which of them I was trying to impress the most. I just knew I wanted them all to kneel at my feet and apologize for how they treated me—like maybe tonight could've been the turning point, and we could've been civil to each other from here on out.

Shooting Jack and Scarlett a quick text update that I'm with Hunter and to drive my car home—since they have my keys—I throw the door open and look for them. I rub my arms, the cool air beginning to settle in my bones in this skimpy dress. I shake my head and turn around. As my hands touch the door handle, a car horn beeps a few feet away. The brake lights are on, and I recognize the black Range Rover as Hunter's car.

Smiling, I step off the concrete and make my way to the sleek SUV, my heart thumping nervously in my throat.

HUNTER

Fuck.

Me.

I never thought a dress could undo me, but I was wrong.

So utterly, gravely wrong.

Ash's party got out of control, and because I know Ash, I suggested we leave in favor of a more interesting activity. He doesn't give two shits if people wreck his house, and I don't blame him—his dad is the world's biggest ass. But I didn't want him to do something stupid.

Briar walks toward my car, a smirk on her red-as-sin lips. I watch her in my rearview mirror, my cock instantly hardening as I drink in her long, pale legs, and the way the dress rides up slightly with each step forward. I remember the feel of her skin, the way it tasted like honey. The way my initial hatred turned to lust. The primal, feral need to have her. I adjust my pants just as she climbs into the back with the guys, since the front seat is filled with trash bags of materials for tonight, and the trunk space is nonexistent thanks to the boxes of books I picked up last week—books I probably won't read but will add to the library, nonetheless.

"I assume this means you'll be giving me a ride home," she says, her voice low. It hits me then—this dress, the way her eyes land on mine—it was for me. *For us.* I saw her looking, saw her long neck crane above the crowd, her grey eyes scanning, hoping to land on one of us.

Come out and play, little lamb.

"If you're good," I answer, and when our eyes meet in the rearview mirror, something darkens in her pupils.

I'm not going to be able to think of anything else until I'm inside of her.

Ash's arms slide around her stomach as she sits on his lap, and I smile.

These guys are my best friends. My soulmates. There is no jealousy. As her stepbrother, I don't care who she chooses to be with, if they treat her right. I'm slowly starting to learn that her presence is shaking up everything I once knew, everything I once thought. I find myself thinking about my friends in ways I never did before, *sharing* her, knowing they're happy, knowing they like her just as much as I do.

Seeing her through their eyes is exhilarating, and something savage burns through me when I think about watching her... with them.

We used to be the *Kings* of Ravenwood.

I guess I never realized until Briar Monroe showed up that we needed a *Queen*.

21

BRIAR

Ash's arms linger a little too long on my stomach, his fingers grazing the delicate skin there. When I twist around, I look into his hooded eyes—the light, ice blue of his pupils that are now a deep, denim blue in the darkness of the back seat. My skin heats as his hardness presses against me, and he squirms almost uncomfortably.

"Look what you do to me, little lamb," he murmurs into my neck.

God, why are they all so beautiful?

The vulnerability on his face right now is stunning. The arrogance is gone, and for the first time, I see him as a human being. His sharp jawline, pronounced cheekbones, and short, black hair can make him seem evil—like a thing of the night. But then I remember what Scarlett said about his mom, about the mayor. We both have a past that haunts us, don't we?

I need you to listen to your body, your intuition.

Suddenly, I find myself leaning back against him, and his hand wraps around me again. This time, he claws at my dress, and my body sparks to life for the first time in a long time.

And it feels really fucking good to be wanted like this.

My intuition is screaming *yes*.

"Where are we going?" I ask, trying to ignore the goose-bumps erupting along my skin at Ash's touch.

"You'll see," Ledger answers from next to me. His hood is still on, and he's watching me raptly.

I turn to Samson, who gives me a small smile before turning to face the window.

It hits me then—that I'm in a car with four men who don't have a good reputation. Four men that everyone fears, that control the students at Ravenwood with one look, one word. They have no obligation to keep me safe, other than their word, and history has shown me that I can't always trust men at their word. They can do anything they want to me, and they will probably end up getting away with it, thanks to their family statuses.

Maybe they're still messing with me.

Maybe this is all just a game for them.

But... *maybe it's a game I want to play, too.*

Since day one, they've intrigued me. And something tells me they aren't as mean as everyone seems to think they are. In fact, as I look at each of them, including Hunter in the rearview mirror, I can see how they might be misunderstood —their families essentially run Greythorn, and the other students know it.

But they don't care if people hate them—don't care to correct the assumptions about them. And there's something commendable about that.

I close my eyes and go through the checklist.

Evaluate my surroundings. *In a car with four guys—one of which is my stepbrother.*

Listen to my gut. *They will take care of me.*

Apply common sense. *Scarlett knows I'm with Hunter, and my mom can track my phone.*

I'm okay.

I'm safe.

I swallow as Ash's other arm loops around my waist. We bounce along the dirt driveway in front of the Greythorn property until we get to the road, and I feel slightly guilty for leaving Scarlett and Jack at the party. I pull my phone out and see a text from Scarlett.

For real? Okay... be safe. We'll take good care of the Soob.

I smile at her nickname for my car, promising myself that I will tell her and Jack everything soon.

Hunter turns on some music when we pull up to a stop sign, and I squirm in Ash's lap.

"What's wrong, little lamb?" Ash whispers, his breath hot on my neck. "You're so tense." He grazes a finger down the side of my body and trails it down my leg. I shudder at his touch, and he chuckles. "You have no idea, do you?" he murmurs.

"What?" I ask, my voice rough, gravelly. My eyes flutter as his hand runs back up my leg, and my skin pebbles beneath his touch.

"How much we already possess you, body and mind." The answer sends a shock wave of pleasure through me. His hand moves to my inner thigh. "Do I make you wet?" he asks, and I close my eyes.

Filthy. He has a filthy mouth, and my body is betraying me by reacting this way.

"You wish," I answer, finding the tiniest bit of resolve.

"Liar," he whispers, his breath fanning out across my neck. "Why are you denying it?"

"I'm not, I just—"

"You wouldn't fight it, would you? If I could make you come so hard that you saw stars?"

I let out a tiny gasp. *Holy fuck.*

"Admit it," he murmurs, his fingers finding my panties. I let my legs part just slightly, granting him access. It's been so long since I've known pleasure like this. And I've never been with a guy—with *guys*—who knew what they were doing, who knew just the right words to make me part my legs for them. It was always sex, sure, but it was awkward and stilted. And this? This feels so damn natural, so good. "Admit that you would scream if I was deep inside of you, fucking you senseless."

Jesus.

His dirty talk doesn't surprise me. I twist around to face him and place an arm around his shoulders. I open my mouth to say something, but his hand moves my panties to the side, and he takes a ragged breath.

"I was right, Briar. You're already soaking wet for me," he mutters, and I see it then—the hunger in his expression—the moment of being a real fucking human. His reputation prevents him from dropping his guard with anyone else but us—anyone else but *me.*

"Who says it's for you?" I ask, my voice low.

He opens his mouth to retort, but instead, he punishes me by slipping a calloused finger into my wet slit.

I arch my back against him, thankful for the music, thankful for the fact that Ledger is looking at his phone, Samson is looking out the window, and Hunter is driving. *Thankful for the darkness.*

"Stop fighting it," he whispers into my ear and pulls me closer. He thrusts his hard cock against my ass, and though I don't hear it, his voice hums in pleasure, his body vibrating with need. I'm about to move his hand when he slips his middle finger into my pussy, his thumb working my clit.

"Let me own you," he growls, nibbling my neck.

"Yes," I whisper, my voice barely audible.

And then he inserts another finger into my pussy. My dress hides what he's doing—it just looks like his hand is between my thighs. Only his fingers curve and flick against the sensitive spot, his thumb pressing down on my clit. There's no outward friction, but whatever he's doing with his fingers, whatever angle he has them in...

I arch my back further, throwing my head back as heat courses through me. I pleasure myself, of course, but this is the first time I've let someone touch me since Cam. I haven't wanted to until now.

We've been working on letting the trauma go, learning how to feel good again. Learning what feels good.

"Good girl," he says, his voice breaking. He's subtly moving his cock against my ass at the same time, and the thought of him coming undone—of Ash Greythorn coming undone because of *me*—sends me over the edge.

I manage to hold myself as still as possible, and when I look up into the rearview mirror, Hunter's dark eyes bore into mine, as if he can sense I'm coming. I grip Ash's forearm tightly as wave upon wave of my climax rips through me, the feeling clawing out from inside and spreading along my limbs in a hot, fiery tempest of pleasure. My eyes never leave Hunter's, and something must pass over my face because he grips the wheel tightly, his fingers white against the firm leather.

"What did I tell you?" Ash asks, removing his hand and licking his fingers. "Wet as a whistle. Did you know that you taste like vanilla ice cream?" he whispers into my neck, gently placing a kiss against the hot skin there.

"Fuck off," I whisper, my voice shaky.

He just chuckles, and when I look back into the rearview mirror, Hunter is watching me with fervor.

22

BRIAR

About five minutes later, we pull up to a large building with a wrought-iron gate guarding the entrance. The gate is open, and Hunter pulls up to the front of the building. It's dark, and obviously not open or inhabited—if the shuttered windows and lack of lighting are any indication. Once we park, Samson opens the door and hops out. I follow, ignoring the way Ash's hand grazes my upper thigh. Hunter and Ledger walk around the car, and Ledger throws his jacket over me. Each guy is holding a flashlight, and Ledger hands one to me.

"Thanks." I give him a small smile. "Where are we?"

"Medford Asylum," Hunter answers. "An abandoned psychiatric hospital. One of the most haunted places in Massachusetts."

My skin breaks out in goosebumps. "Why are we here?" I ask, looking around. A sign hangs precariously over the large gate, and it creaks as it swings in the cool night breeze. "Shouldn't Ash be monitoring the party at his house?"

Ash laughs, and it's not a nice laugh. "I don't give a flying fuck if they burn the place down."

Hunter's eyes scan my bare legs. "Let's go," he commands, handing each of us a backpack filled with what sounds like soda cans, if the heavy clacking of aluminum is any indication.

The five of us walk to the front of the hospital. I follow Hunter, practically on his heels as we climb the short staircase to the front door. Hunter tries the door, and it doesn't budge, so he takes a step back and kicks it open with such force that it startles me. I follow him inside, with Ash, Ledger, and Samson behind me. Our flashlights illuminate a few feet in front of us, but beyond that, it's all black. Thank God for my boots, because the floor is littered with dirt, broken glass, and trash.

"This is so fucked," Ash says, walking ahead of me. I swallow, thinking of his mother and what he must be thinking to be walking through a place like this. He kicks a piece of trash and walks ahead of all of us.

I walk up to Hunter. "Is he okay?" I whisper, stepping over a large pile of dirt. What Scarlett told me earlier—paired with his response to leaving the party...

His father must be a terrible person.

"We all have our demons, right?"

His lips tick upwards ever so slightly. The hardness in his expression—the crease between his brows that usually runs so deep—softens slightly as he watches me. It's not full-blown vulnerability, but it's a small token of friendliness—of camaraderie.

So different from the first few days we knew each other, when it was mean and cruel... it's as if the roles of the Kings were created for them, and they never bothered to correct anyone.

"Yo, check this out," Ledger calls, walking into a room off

what must've been the admissions desk. My flashlight illumi-nates several overturned chairs on the floor, and a large desk under a shattered, protective window sits in front of us.

I turn right and follow Ledger into the mystery room. It's deathly quiet in here, away from the other guys. The moon shines through a large, barred window. I shine my light on the metal wall to my right, and then with a sinking, sick feeling, I see the autopsy table in the middle of the room, the metal dented and scratched with a layer of dust atop it.

"This is wild," I murmur, walking around the table and then up to the body shelves. I pull one open and slide the table out, which makes Ledger jump back.

He chuckles. "This doesn't scare you?"

I shake my head. "Why would it?" *I've seen far, far scarier things in my eighteen years, Ledger Huxley.*

"I just assumed…" He puts his hands in his pockets.

"Does it scare *you*?" I smirk.

He leers down at me, the flashlight giving his face a ghoulish look. "No." He smiles. "The living scare me way more than the dead."

I cock my head. "The living? Like whom?"

He smiles, taking another step closer. "My parents. Their friends." He rolls his eyes. "Religion can do a number on vulnerable people—can turn them into monsters."

"Your parents are religious?" I ask, crossing my arms.

He chuckles. "You could say that."

I look at him—*really* look at him. "But you're not like that," I muse, narrowing my eyes.

"Definitely not," he murmurs, his voice low. "I like fuck-ing, and drinking, and debauchery too much," he growls.

My pulse speeds up as his eyes flit down my body once. I try not to notice the way his tongue moves with the stud, or the way his pouty lips look pillowy and butter soft. His blue eyes find mine again, and his blonde, disheveled hair gives him an unhinged look—especially with the moonlight pouring through the window.

He reaches out and slips the backpack off my back, and it falls to the floor with a loud, metallic thud. A hand curls around the hair at the back of my neck, and I gasp just as his coat—the one over my shoulders—falls to the floor.

"You're not like the other girls, Briar. You give zero fucks, and you're the only person who's not afraid of us." He bends down, his breath on my cheek. Pressing his hard body against my back. "I thought you'd run away screaming by now, but here you are."

"You don't scare me. None of you do."

With his hand fisted around my hair, he yanks me backward ever so slightly, his mouth near my ear. "Is that why you let Ash finger fuck you in the car just now?"

His words turn my core molten, and I inhale sharply. "So what? Are you jealous?"

He laughs, the sound dark and unhinged. "What do you want, Briar?"

"You tell me," I say, trying to pull out of his grip, but he just tightens his hold. "You're all so hot and cold. I can never tell if you... if you want me, or if you're messing with me."

He pulls me backward again, and this time the entire back of my body collides with the front of his—including the bulge in his pants.

"I think you have your answer, yes?"

I inhale sharply. "Yes," I whisper. "But—"

"Do you want me?" he asks, fingering my hair. I moan in response, his touch causing a spark of pleasure to work its way down my neck and spine. "Good. Have you thought about how it would feel to fuck each of us? To see how we're all different..." One hand reaches around, grazing my taut nipples beneath the fabric of the dress. "Or perhaps how we're the same?"

Breathless, I shake my head. "I haven't thought about it."

He chuckles. "You're such a fucking liar, little lamb. Are you trying to convince me that you're not wet for me, too? Minutes after Ash fucked you with his fingers?"

I gasp again as he grinds into me. "I'm not—"

"Let me ask you again. Does your pussy get wet whenever I pull your hair?" He tightens his grip on my strands, making my scalp sting and tingle in the best way possible.

Pain and pleasure.

"You wish," I growl, my voice fractured. But despite my best efforts to resist, I push my ass against him, wanting more.

His mouth is on my neck as he whispers, "Maybe I should check."

I clench my legs together, and he must know, must assume I'm bursting for his touch, because he trails a hand down to my legs and lifts my dress up to my waist. I arch into him, waiting...

"What the hell is going on?"

Ledger and I jump, and a second later, my stepbrother comes into view, his dark eyes finding mine. His expression is veiled and unreadable—and he looks down at my dress gathered at my waist. When his eyes snap back to mine, his expression is lecherous, with a lopsided smile forming on his lips.

"Seems as though my sister can't get enough of my friends," he says slowly, circling us. "First Ash, now Ledger... Should I call Samson now, or will you wait to fuck him on the drive home?"

"Maybe she wants all of us at once," Ledger teases, his voice dark.

The words heat me from the inside out, and even though the thought of being with all of them intrigues me, I pull away from Ledger's grip and pull my dress down. I grab

Ledger's jacket and my backpack. Hunter's eyes don't leave mine the entire time, but he doesn't answer Ledger, doesn't acknowledge what happened between us in the library at home last night. The notion stings a bit—that maybe he doesn't want me after all of that. Embarrassment floods through me.

"I didn't realize it was a crime to enjoy casual sex," I answer, glaring at Hunter.

"It's certainly *not* a crime. You may enjoy as much dick as you want," he adds, his face hard. "But maybe try not to fuck all of my friends in one night."

Ledger laughs. "Sounds like someone's jealous of his sister's sexual exploits."

Hunter runs a hand through his dark hair. "I promise you, I'm not."

And then he turns and walks out, leaving me stunned.

For some reason, his rejection erases the experiences with Ash and Ledger. I am getting carried away, falling for their titles and their power, opening my legs for them...

And the one I want the most doesn't want me back.

23

ASH

I'm still high as a kite from the smell of Briar's pussy—which is saying a lot, because I was in a pretty messed up place when we left my house. Something about watching other people destroy my dad's house spurs me on, causes the adrenaline to pump. Hunter noticed, and now, here we are—even though we weren't supposed to fuck Medford up for a few more weeks. I smile and pull my fingers to my nose, inhaling the sweet smell. Hunter catches me once or twice, giving me an annoyed look. Technically, I finger fucked his sister.

And I know it bothers him that he wasn't the first to do it.

Briar and Ledger walk out of one of the front rooms, and I attempt to hide my smile. I don't blame her for wanting to fuck all of us. I've never been one for polyamory, but I don't think any of us are willing to give her up, so it may just be where we're all headed. I mean, we're closer than most blood brothers. I'd be more worried if she *didn't* want to fuck all of us. I can appreciate the sexual appeal of my best friends. Hunter's bewildering energy, the frenetic, artistic passion that he exudes. Ledger's bad boy vibes—he may look like the meanest one, but deep down, he has a heart of gold, and I know for a fact that a tongue stud can be life changing in bed. And Samson...

I clench my fists as I watch Samson Hall walk ahead of me, careful not to step on the trash littering the floor. He's a smartass—and because of our history, I have a soft spot for him. I shake my head and look away.

It was a long time ago.

"So, are we ready?" Ledger asks, throwing an arm around me.

I nod. "Fuck yes, we're ready." I quickly glance around for cameras. I wouldn't put it past my father to install cameras in a place like this, but luckily, I don't see any.

Samson walks up to me, shrugging his backpack off. He unzips it and holds it out.

"You go first, Ash," he says, his face serious and solemn. Out of all of them, he understands the most—knows the most. He's seen the most—every morbid detail. The others have a vague idea, but I gave Samson the full truth.

I reach in and grab a can of spray paint. "Which room should I do first?" I ask, looking at my friends. I feel oddly nervous, my hands shaking slightly when I pull the cap off.

"What are we doing?" Briar asks, looking around.

"Sending a message to my father," I sneer. "A loud one."

She must've heard about what happened to my mom, because some sort of understanding passes across her face. Without another word, she grabs a can and then cocks her head, smiling.

"Let's fuck some shit up," she says, using the words I uttered at the burning house a few days ago. My eyes find hers, and my throat bobs.

The guys reach into the backpack and grab a can, and the four of them wait for me to take the lead.

"The more destruction, the better," I snarl, gripping the aluminum tightly. And then I turn, walking into the depths of the asylum—a place that will surely strike a chord with my father once he sees what we're going to do to this place.

24

BRIAR

Hunter drops Ash back at his house around midnight, and the party is still going strong. I'm sleepy, my head lolling against the passenger seat. I'm glad the front seat was empty when we got back to Hunter's car, since we'd used up all the cans. It saved me from deciding which lap to sit on, and Hunter's words still eat at me. I didn't expect to enjoy being with Ash like that—or Ledger.

On the same night.

Still, it's not a crime. Sonya was right. I need to start... exploring what feels good. And truthfully, these last couple of days, being with the guys feels good. Maybe it's because I'm starting to get to know Hunter more, and I know he'll look out for me, but the other guys haven't done anything to lose my trust since the shirt incident.

Since I let it slip about what happened in California.

And I appreciate that they never asked questions—that they knew to stop heckling me.

Because there was once a man who didn't know how to stop.

They make me feel... *alive. Worthy. Sexy.*

And I won't apologize for that.

The guys are still on an adrenaline high as we pull back into the main part of Greythorn. To say we fucked Medford Asylum up would be an understatement. The outside is nearly unrecognizable, and Ash's hope is that it will call for a special election that ousts his father from mayorship. Since Medford is still within the city limits of Greythorn, the news will spread quickly.

I didn't get the full story, but between the bits and pieces Scarlett and Jack told me, as well as the things the guys wrote on the walls... Mayor Greythorn, who's been mayor for twenty years, deserves to go to prison—both for what he did to Ash, and what he did to Ash's mother. Apparently, Christopher Greythorn committed his wife to a psychiatric hospital. Because of his status, she's locked away with around-the-clock security.

Because of him and his lies, she's wasting away in a padded room.

I shake my head. I can't imagine being in a prison like that—unable to leave or go home.

Or see her child.

Ash is stuck living with a monster, so I don't blame him for throwing parties that trash the house—or vandalizing something so personal and metaphorical for Christopher.

I'm starting to realize that the Kings don't cause destruction for no reason.

They cause destruction to get *revenge*.

Samson gets dropped off next, and though I don't know his story at all, I can tell he also comes from money, because his house is just as ornate as the rest of them.

"His parents are doctors, and surprisingly normal,"

Hunter muses. Ledger makes a sound of affirmation from behind me.

"That explains a lot," I joke.

We drop Ledger off next. He lives in a gated house—like ours. When he closes the door and gestures goodbye, winking at me, Hunter sighs.

"He's old money—related to the writer Aldous Huxley. The Huxley's have lived in the Boston area since before America was founded," he says casually. "His parents are religious and super freaky. They have a wall of crosses and a chapel in their house, if that tells you anything."

I shudder. "That *also* explains a lot," I quip, referring to the piercing and tattoos. We both laugh. "What about you?" I ask, my curiosity piqued. "Are you and Andrew old money?"

He thumbs his lip as we stop at a light. His face is illuminated in red, and he turns to face me.

"My mom was. Some branch of a Brahmin."

I wrinkle my nose. "Brahmin?"

"Descended from pilgrims, similar to Ledger," he muses, and his lips twitch upward. "You really don't know the name Brahmin? It's everywhere in Boston."

I shrug. "California girl." I look out the window, wondering what kind of power trip I've gotten myself mixed up in. These guys aren't your ordinary popular guys—the notoriety goes back generations. These families have been established for *centuries*. I wonder if that's one of the reasons people fear them.

Perhaps the fear, the *reputation* they all have goes back generations—Hunter and the Brahmins. Ledger and the Huxley's. Ash and the Greythorn's...

"Do you like them?" Hunter asks, changing the subject. His voice is gruff, strained.

"Who?" I ask.

"Ash and Ledger."

I let out an exhausted, soft laugh. "No. I mean, maybe? I don't know, Hunter. I like sex. Well, I did." I pause, closing my eyes. "My therapist is helping me to enjoy it again, to listen to my body." I shake the memories of Cam and California away. "So, while it may have seemed like I was whoring it up tonight, it was really nice to just... have fun."

Hunter's throat bobs as he rests his hand under his chin. The gesture makes him seem older, more distinguished—and more arrogant that he already is, if that's even possible.

"I understand, Briar. I'm not jealous, if that's what you think."

I look away and watch as we pass one McMansion after the other. "Okay. It just seemed like you were mad earlier—"

"Mad?" He laughs. "You thought I was *mad?*"

I shrug and turn to face him. "Yeah. When you walked in on Ledger and me, you were acting angry. Like you didn't want your friends to..." *To what?* Touch me? I mean, yes. Ash did pull an orgasm out of me, but in that dark back seat, against his hard on, knowing how *filthy* he was, how daring with his friends surrounding us—I got turned on. But I didn't do that much. It wasn't like I'd fucked all of them tonight.

Once again, the thought of that scenario pierces through me, and I have to bite my lower lip so hard that it nearly bleeds.

"I don't care who you *fuck*, Briar. Fuck one of us, fuck all of us, it doesn't matter to me."

And you? I want to ask. He seems to sense the question on the tip of my tongue.

"You turned me the fuck on. Watching you in the back seat, knowing Ash was being his normal, charming self and probably messing around with you, and then when you looked at me in the rearview mirror..." He parks in our driveway, cutting the ignition. "In the mortuary with Ledger, your ass was pressed into his cock, and you looked so... *happy*..."

I wring my hands and swallow nervously, my face hot. I can't look at him—can't see how his face will be illuminated by the motion sensor near the front door, how his eyes will look darker somehow, like they did last night.

"I'm not blind. I can see how beautiful you are, how defiant you are, how *strong* you are." He pauses. "I want you, Briar." His words are a growl—a confession. Whatever game we started earlier this week is turning very real, very quickly.

I look down, playing with the two rings on my fingers. "We probably shouldn't. If my mom or your dad found out—"

"What do *you* want, Briar?" he asks, his voice edged with something... emotional? I can't really decipher his tone.

I look up then, breaking the spell. And the expression on his face is that of someone being deprived of a meal after starving. He licks his lips and leans back, spreading his legs.

"Fuck me," he murmurs, narrowing his eyes. His low voice lands in my core, sinking like molten lava. "I dare you. And I want to be the first." He pauses. "You want it, too."

I shift, squeezing my legs together, trying to dispel the throbbing arousal between my legs.

"When did you get so conceited?" I huff and look away. He infuriates me sometimes, but something about him makes me want to rip his clothes off.

A warm, calloused hand lands on my thigh, and it makes me jump. "Take your dress off, Briar."

I wonder if these are lines he practices—if he often sleeps with other girls. I've only been at Ravenwood Academy for a week, so I'm unsure if he or the other Kings sleep around a lot. For all I know, I'm one of many.

The thought should repulse me. I hated guys like him at my last school. The ones who thought they walked on water. I was always immune, always able to pry myself away from their cocky attitudes while every other girl kneeled for them.

But Hunter is different.

Hunter isn't like those high school boys.

As he watches me with amusement, his eyes hooded, I realize he's *nothing* like them. They were boys. They had no worldly experience, no passion, no personality. But Hunter? He's traveled the world. He's a tortured writer. He's witty, and arrogant as all get out because he knows all of this about himself. He's been through some shit—they all have.

Maybe that's why I feel some sort of connection to them.

Because we're not all normal seniors. We all have stories, and pasts, and demons.

We all have our demons, right?

"Do I have to ask twice?" he says, tilting his head and frowning.

I let out a surprised laugh. "You're ruthless."

He just smiles and watches me as I lift the tight, lace dress over my head, practically peeling it off my arms. Then I lean back and smile, crossing my arms as I kick my boots off.

"Move your arms and let me see you," he says slowly, leaning forward ever so slightly.

What are you doing, Briar? He's your stepbrother...

I move my arms and my body heats under his gaze. His expression is serious. Gone is the pompous prick. In his place is an artist studying a piece of art. His jaw ticks as his eyes drink me in. I feel exposed even though I'm in a high-waisted lingerie set with a matching bra. It's my *one* nice pair of undies —and I wore it for them.

He reaches out and moves my hair off my shoulder, exposing my bare neck, my chest. His eyes grow dark, his expression hardening into something wild.

"Get over here," he commands, his voice husky.

I climb over the center console, placing my knees on either side of the seat so that I'm straddling him. I've never been this close to him—not even the other night—and his warm hands pull me impossibly closer.

"Fuck, Briar," he whispers hoarsely. His hand trails over my thigh to the top of my underwear. Following the seam, he moves it to the side, exposing my pussy. "You're soaked," he adds. "I'm not sure if it's from me or from my friends, but both scenarios turn me the fuck on, and my cock might explode soon if I don't fill you to the brim."

I gasp, panting. "All of you make me wet as fuck," I whisper, throwing my head back. "But you..."

He groans and thrusts up into me. I rock my hips against his pants, his rock hard shaft hitting me perfectly. I'm just about to ask him to unzip when he pulls at my panties and rips the delicate lace off of me in one swift motion.

"Hey!" I cry, my voice shrill. "That was my favorite pair."

He laughs, casting them off somewhere behind him. "I'll buy you new ones." *Stupid, fucking rich boy.* His hand trails to my pussy again, and he brushes my landing strip. "I really love this," he rasps, moving his hand down and inserting two fingers with zero fanfare. I gasp, my body exploding into a fiery tempest. His fingers perform a flurry of curved movements that perfectly hit the right spot.

"Fuck," I cry, rocking against him, my body shaking already. He unzips his pants and pulls them down slightly. I barely notice when he reaches up and unclasps my bra, letting the purple material fall to the floor.

"And these are fucking perfect," Hunter whispers, and I look down just as he takes one of my nipples into his mouth, sucking.

"Oh, fuck," I cry, shamelessly riding his hand now. His fingers are still curved inside of me, still doing some sort of dance I've never experienced before—sort of like a light fluttering. Just enough to keep me going, but not enough to push me over the edge.

Teasing me.

"Tell me you want my cock," he says roughly. I can tell he's aroused by the cadence of his voice—uneven and breathless.

"I want your cock inside of me," I beg, all dignity lost.

"Why?" he asks as his length nudges my opening, the skin warm and wet from pre-cum.

"I want to feel you explode," I confess.

"Are you clean?" he asks, kissing my other nipple gently and removing his fingers.

"Yes. And I have an IUD," I answer impatiently.

He purrs. "Good." He pushes against me, his head thick. It stings slightly, because of his size. "Now," he hisses, thrusting upwards in one single motion, claiming me as he enters me to the hilt.

I break against him, bucking my hips and holding onto his shoulders as he slams into me again. A moan rips through me, and one of his hands comes around to the back of my neck, grabbing a handful of hair. The other hand moves my hips against him, directs me, controlling the tempo. The sound of our wetness permeates the air, and the *wrongness* of it all, the fact that we're parked in front of our house, spurs me on further.

He grabs the flesh at my hips and moves me quickly, sliding me back and forth against his rock-hard cock. When he's satisfied with the tempo, he moves a thumb to my clit, pressing down and using his pre-cum as lubricant as he works me slowly at first, but then it gets rougher, quicker, grittier. He strums faster as he gets closer.

I bare my teeth as my climax begins, the dizzying pleasure pulsing through me. My pussy grips his cock, milking him, feeling the way he inhales sharply as his own orgasm starts because of it, finding his eyes as it rips through him like a hurricane, too. I grip his arm, nearly drawing blood, and we both cry out in unison—but I don't close my eyes.

I can't miss it.

I can't miss Hunter Ravenwood coming undone at the seams.

For me.

We're both convulsing as the last of it leaves our bodies, our skin slick with sweat, the windows fogged up, breathing heavily... I collapse against him, my breathing heavy.

He slowly slides out and reaches over to the glove compartment, grabbing a handkerchief.

I look at him skeptically. "Because why wouldn't you have a cleanup rag in your car?" I ask, raising my eyebrows.

He cleans me up without answering, but his mirthful smile tells me everything I need to know. I'm just about to climb back to my seat when his arm holds me to his lap.

"Tonight changed everything," he murmurs. "You're ours now. You realize that, right?"

I laugh. "You can't stake ownership over me."

"I don't mean we own you like a slave," he muses. "But at least for me, now that I've had a taste of you, I don't think I can go back. And I think I can speak for all of my friends."

I pull out of his grip and climb back to my seat, quickly throwing my dress on before opening the door, sliding out, and slamming it shut. When I glance back at him a few feet from the front door, he's watching me with a triumphant smile.

He may think he won—he may think the war is over, that this Queen will bow down to him and the others like all the other students do.

But it's only just begun because I bow to no one.

25

SAMSON

I am just finishing up breakfast when my mom gasps, her eyes on her phone.

"Oh my god, Paul, look at this." She hands the phone to my dad, who scowls at her large screen.

"Who would do such a thing?" he asks, shaking his head.

"What happened?" I ask innocently, my voice feigned with indifference.

Of course I know what happened, because I did it.

"Medford Asylum was vandalized," my mother answers, her voice fraught with displeasure. She clucks her tongue once. "Kathy just texted me, and she heard from Christopher. The things these thugs wrote..." she trails off. "He was only doing what was best for Hannah. That poor woman needed help, and the park incident—"

"How did they vandalize it?" I interrupt, changing the subject. I don't need a recounting of Hannah Greythorn's mental breakdown. It felt way too close to home.

My mom and dad debate whether they should show me the pictures. In the end, my dad nods, handing me the phone gently, as if that'll help buffer the words on the screen. Someone took the pictures—one of Christopher's employees, or maybe the devil himself.

The words are splashed against the grey stone, haphazard and uneven, large and obvious. We covered most of the front, and a lot of the rooms. I think we all felt like we were avenging our friend and everything he'd gone through. My eyes scan the words—the words we all wrote.

Christopher Greythorn is a monster.

Fuck Chris Greythorn.

Free Hannah.

Greythorn has its own Blanche Monnier.

That last one was my creation. Blanche Monnier was a woman who was locked up for twenty-five years in France in the late 1800s. Her mother, an aristocrat, kept her in one of the many rooms of their manor.

She hadn't seen sunlight for twenty-five years.

Hannah hadn't seen it in five.

Despite her mental illness, Hannah didn't deserve the life her husband sanctioned her to, locked away like a menace to society.

Christopher was the real menace to Greythorn.

"That's awful," I say, eating my eggs and toast in silence for the rest of the meal.

It's truly difficult to conceal my smile.

26

BRIAR

I spend most of Saturday morning in bed, regretting my actions and anticipating seeing Ash, Ledger, and Hunter next. Would it be awkward in the light of day? Does last night mean I'm one of them—that we're friends? I don't know if we are still competing, or if fucking Hunter's brains out counts as a ceasefire.

Around noon, I finally throw my covers off and shower, taking my time as I shave my legs and wash the smell of *three* guys off me. I don't feel ashamed, exactly—but society is so adamant about choosing one love interest, and the truth is, they all interest me in different ways. I am young—we all are —and I crave adventure. Plus, like Sonya suggested, I need to start exploring what feels good, what feels *right*. It's important to follow my gut, and my gut wants to see where this will lead me.

Everyone is gone as I make a late breakfast. Hunter's car isn't in the driveway, and my mom had texted earlier that she and Andrew were out picking up some furniture. I shoot a quick text to Scarlett and Jack, and when they respond a few minutes later asking for deets about why I left early last night, I just send the nauseous emoji, hoping that'll explain my abrupt departure. It's not something I want to confess via text.

I catch myself smiling as I make my eggs. I haven't felt this happy in... months. Not since California, not since before Cam and everything that happened.

Shivers crawl down my spine as I think about that afternoon—how I ran away so fearful, so angry. How I knew my life would never be the same, because of one man—and I was right.

I remember how the officers asked me about what happened.

And I told them.

About the rape.

About the knife, and the blood.

About *everything*.

And I knew, in that moment, that I would never be the same.

☙❧

I'm watching TV in the basement an hour later when the doorbell rings. Or rather, an alert pops up on my phone, since Andrew set up the smart doorbell for me. I look down and see Samson on my screen. Hopping up, I climb the stairs and walk to the front door, throwing it open.

"Hey," Samson says, waving.

"Hi," I answer. I cross my arms since I'm not wearing a bra. "Hunter isn't here."

"That's okay. You were with us, so you should know." He gives me a crooked smile that makes my heart flutter a bit. "A reporter is digging into Hannah's story. Someone leaked some photos of what happened last night, and people are beginning to ask questions."

I raise my eyebrows. "Someone?"

He just gives me a small, knowing smile. Something flutters in my abdomen at that look—at the way his eyes find mine, the way his chiseled jaw holds a smirk.

"Here, come in." I step aside so he can enter. "I'll get you a drink."

"Okay, thanks."

We walk into the kitchen, and I move around, trying to find where my mom put the drinking glasses. I find them after opening and closing nearly every cabinet.

"Is water okay?" I ask, setting a glass in front of him. "My mom also has soda, juice, milk..." I look around. "I can find some wine or beer?"

He laughs. "I'm fine with water."

I pour us both a glass of water and sit next to him at the breakfast bar. "Will they release Hannah if they find Christopher at fault?"

Samson shrugs, playing with his glass. I study his profile as he does—his handsome, strong face. The square glasses that perfectly frame his strong brow bones and aquiline nose. His lips are cherry red, making him look sultry and beautiful. And his body? It's strong, large—muscles cut from stone underneath his black shirt and fitted, dark green pants.

"I have no idea, but people are talking, so that's always a good thing." I'm quiet as I think about Ash—about everything he's endured. Samson continues.

"Christopher is abusive—he always has been," he starts, grimacing, as if it pains Samson to talk about. "I remember freshman year, seeing the bruises..." He looks away. "My whole life, people suspected something was off with the Greythorn's, but no one was willing to do anything about it.

When Ash was thirteen, his mother had sort of a breakdown and started wandering around town in her nightdress. She suffered from postpartum psychosis and PTSD. Christopher involuntarily committed her to a psychiatric hospital, and she's been there ever since."

"Jesus. Postpartum psychosis?" I ask.

"She had a late-term miscarriage a few months prior."

My heart sinks. "That's horrible."

"Rumor has it that it wasn't Christopher's."

I swallow. "Wow." When I look at Samson, he's watching me with a funny expression. "What?"

He shakes his head and narrows his eyes. "Are you and Ash an item now?"

I scowl. "No. Did he tell you we were?"

"Not exactly. I was just wondering because of what happened in the car."

I thought we'd been so slick.

"No one has claimed me," I joke, taking a sip of water. "If that's what you mean."

Not exactly.

He angles his head and smiles, his light brown eyes playful and amused. I can't help but smile when Samson smiles. I can tell he has a good soul. He's young and impressionable, like we all are, but one day, Samson Hall is going to rule the fucking world with his charm.

"Would you go on a date with me, then?" he asks.

I rear my head back in shock. "A date?" I ask, shifting in my seat.

He shrugs. "Why not? How about tonight?"

I pull my lower lip between my teeth. "Sure. But you should know that Hunter and I..."

Understanding registers on his face.

"I'm just asking you on a date," he answers, giving me a wicked smile. "I'm not asking you to marry me."

I twist my lips to the side, thinking it over for a few seconds. "Okay. Doe seven work?"

He helps me up as we stand. When his hand touches mine, an electric current zaps down my arm, and he must notice too, because he smiles and kisses my hand. My eyes flutter closed at the contact.

"Perfect. I'll pick you up. Goodbye, Briar." He walks out of the kitchen.

I'm still blushing when the front door closes behind him, and I can't help but smile. They're all so different—and they all bring something different out in *me*. It would be impossible to find a guy with all their good traits—mysterious, filthy talker, bad boy, romantic—and I feel lucky that I get to see what it's like with each of them.

27

LEDGER

I take a quick jog around the perimeter of Greythorn Park, my legs moving me quickly and perfectly on track to beat my record five minute, fifteen second mile time. It's fucking cold out for September. I'm immersed in one of the songs on my playlist, so I don't see them immediately—Briar and Samson.

I slow, watching as they're escorted into *Enclave,* the nicest restaurant in Greythorn. Watching as Samson's hand lightly brushes the back of her red dress and *fuck me* if she doesn't look gorgeous. I continue running, adrenaline coursing through me. I've never felt this rattled by a woman —never this off-kilter. From the moment I saw her, I couldn't focus, couldn't think straight.

And last night? Feeling the way she wanted me, the way her ass rubbed against my cock...

I stop and bend over, pretending to catch my breath. I run twelve miles on the weekends—I don't ever need to catch my breath. But I do need to hide my growing erection from the people walking around town.

Jesus.

What the hell is wrong with me?

I'm not religious, but she makes me want to kneel before an altar and confess the downright filthy things that run through my mind when I think of her.

I quickly make my way back home, saying a quick hello to Gloria, our house cleaner, before climbing the marble stairs two at a time. Once inside my room, I rip my clothes off and lean against the door, grabbing my throbbing cock and spreading my legs. I bend over myself, stroking fast, hard —*quick and dirty*.

I moan, imagining those red lips from last night around my cock, imagining myself thrusting into her throat, claiming her... My cock twitches in my hand, and I growl, stroking faster, needing release as soon as possible.

My legs begin to shake as I imagine how wet she was for me, how her breathing quickened when I moved her dress up over her waist. Imagine how it would feel to bend her over that table and fuck her brains out.

"Fuck," I rasp, my climax close.

I think about how her skin smelled like honey, how soft and pale she was, how she'd look underneath me as I'd squeeze her large breasts, filling her to the brim with my come...

I cry out as my orgasm rips through me, the pleasure coursing down my legs, more intense than it's ever been. Trembling, I stroke my cock slowly, continuing to pour out onto my floor.

"Fuck," I whisper, closing my eyes.

It takes me a few minutes to be able to even walk to the bathroom to clean up. And as I stare at my reflection—the long, blonde hair, the tongue stud glinting every time I smile, the tattoos on my bare, tanned chest—I imagine how we'd look together.

And it's then that I realize, I'll do anything for just a piece of her.

Even if I must share.

28

BRIAR

Samson takes us to one of the restaurants on the perimeter of the park, and as I glance down at my table setting, I realize this place must be fancy, since there are not two, but *three* forks.

"Shall I order us some wine?" he asks, the corners of his lips tilting upwards, like he has a secret.

"How?" I laugh, resting my elbows on the table and leaning forward. The dress I'm wearing is new—red, silk, form-fitting. I feel like Jessica Rabbit.

He shrugs, his smile real and infectious. "I can make it happen. My uncle owns this place."

I quirk an eyebrow. "I'll have a glass of whatever you're having."

Before I can even ask him about this place—about his uncle, or anything about his life—the server is upon us, and we are showered with not only champagne, but a breadbasket, appetizers, and a salad. It's a flurry of motion that makes me dizzy, and since I haven't eaten in a few hours, I'm ravenous.

"Oh my god," I mumble, my mouth full of delicious, oil-soaked focaccia.

"It's good, right?" He bites off a piece and chews, and we both laugh.

This is so *fun*. With the other guys, it feels sort of... melo-dramatic. *Angsty*. But with Samson, I kind of feel like a normal eighteen-year-old. Samson orders us dinner, making sure I don't have any allergies, and I let him take the lead. He knows the menu and the food better than I do.

"So, your uncle owns this place?" I ask, sipping my bubbly wine.

He nods, mimicking me, and I remember something I read in one of those magazines—that if your date copies your body language, they're interested in you. Well, considering I'm leaning forward on my elbows and Samson is doing the same, I'd say he's interested... especially since his eyes keep flitting down to my lips.

"Yeah, this place and a few others, mostly in the city," he answers.

"And your parents are doctors, right?"

"Yes. Pediatricians, actually."

I nod slowly, my lips quirking up. "That makes total sense now. All of you—and what your parents do... it all makes sense."

He leans back and laces his hands behind his head, the white fabric of his shirt taut and clinging to the corded muscles in his arms. "How so?"

I laugh. "Yours have normal jobs, and by proxy, you seem like the least fucked up of the bunch. Ash is... well... Ash. He has his own issues thanks to the mayor. Ledger is like a walking *fuck you* to his devout parents, and Hunter is the misjudged, angsty son of the headmaster." I sit back, satisfied with my observations.

He smirks. "You think you have us all figured out, but my life has been far from perfect."

I don't have a chance to ask him what he means, because the server brings our food out. Neither of us speaks for a few minutes, inhaling the fresh pasta, the tender steak, and the incredible fish. It's way too much food, but I manage to eat most of it while Samson watches me.

"What's your story, Briar?" he asks, placing his napkin on the table.

I lean back and groan, rubbing my stomach. "I ate too much, if that's what you mean."

He laughs. "No. I mean... before. In California."

I swallow. "Right. California."

He reaches out and takes my hand in his—the soft warmth is comforting, and when his thumb grazes my palm, my skin erupts in goosebumps.

"I know what happened—you don't have to talk about it if you don't want to." I'm about to pull my hand away when he tugs me closer, bringing my hand to his lips again. "I'm sorry for their actions when you first got here. I tried to get them to stop," he explains, his eyes wide and solemn. "And then that day in the quad, when we realized..." He looks down, and when his eyes find mine again, they're swimming with emotion. "He threatened us that day," he laughs. "Said if we messed with you again, that he'd fuck us up," he adds, chuckling.

I ignore the way my throat constricts, how my pulse speeds up at the notion of them all agreeing to at least that. The taunting, the diary, the underwear, the shirt... sure. Those were classic bully moves. But Samson was right—after that day, none of them tried anything questionable.

I lean back and study him, and he watches me with a serious expression.

"Tell me about Micah."

The words must shock him—either he was unaware that I knew, or he wasn't expecting me to ask outright.

"Micah?" he asks, his voice rough. His face is harder now, and the playfulness is gone. "What about him?"

I shrug. "You were dating him when he committed suicide."

Samson grinds his jaw, and his disposition completely changes. "Yeah, and?"

"And there are rumors that you—"

Samson slams his hands on the table, startling me. "Exactly. They're rumors."

I study him, and I notice the flared nostrils, the flushed neck, the furrowed brows.

"You loved him, didn't you?" I ask, leaning forward.

Samson frowns while he picks at a loose thread on his shirt cuff. "Of course I loved him. I'm not a monster."

"Then why does everyone think you bullied him to death?"

This causes him to break, and he sags a bit as he lets out an exasperated breath. "Because, Briar. It's easy to place blame when you know nothing about the situation. When you don't know the people involved. We're human, but we're held up to this standard..." He looks down at his hands and unclenches his fists. "Hunter especially, but us, too, since we're his friends." He pauses, his lips thin. "Micah was sick. And I didn't see the signs until it was too late."

"The sex tape?"

He stares at me. "How do you know about that?"

I shrug. "Scarlett told me."

He looks over my shoulder, his eyes fogging over with

nostalgia. "There was a sex tape, yes. I was not the one who released it."

"Who did?"

He shrugs. "We never figured it out, but I suspect it was Micah."

I nod, and we're both quiet for a minute. "Thank you for telling me."

He thumbs his lips, watching me. "It's so much easier to keep people afraid of you—to keep people hating you—than it is to be vulnerable. It's easier to continue the charade. We never corrected people when they made assumptions and look where that got us."

His words are like a dagger to the chest. I reach for his hand, and he lets me take it, giving me a small smile.

"For what it's worth, I don't think you're a monster."

He grins. "Thank you."

He orders us dessert, and then he pays for dinner, like a true gentleman. I can't remember the last time I enjoyed myself on a date. Maybe never. We talk about Paris as we drive to my house, the Sorbonne, and I teach him how to say *fuck you* in French. It's so easy talking to him—and I can be myself completely. When he drops me off, I wait for a second, thinking that maybe he'll kiss me on the doorstep.

But he just grazes my cheek with his lips, gives me a real smile as he walks backward to his car.

"Hey!" I yell, grinning, touching the place on my cheek. "Where's my goodnight kiss?"

He tips his head and smirks as he opens his door. "I never kiss on the first date, Briar."

"But—"

"Trust me," he adds, his eyes darkening. "I won't be so nice next time."

🥀 29 🥀

BRIAR

I wake up the next morning to the sound of my phone ringing. Rolling over in bed, I glance at the screen and see an unknown number—and the fact that it's barely six in the morning. Groaning, I sit up and press the green button.

"Hello?" I answer, my voice a croak.

"I'm outside."

Ash.

My pulse quickens. "It's early," I whine.

He sniffs, and something uncomfortable slithers down my spine. The asylum—what Samson told me about the Greythorn's...

"I had to get out of the house," he adds.

I jump out of bed, the phone still attached to my ear. "Are you okay?" He doesn't answer, but I know he heard me, because I hear him breathing. "I'll be right down," I add, hanging up and throwing on a pair of leggings. I grab a sweat-shirt and my boots, phone, and keys. Once I'm dressed, I quickly brush my teeth and slink down the marble stairs, careful not to wake anyone—though the house is so big that waking someone would probably take a lot more than footsteps on the stairs.

I close the front door behind me and walk to his car—a silver Mercedes G-class. When I climb in and shut the door, I look over at him and my throat constricts.

"Did he do this to you?" I whisper, running my finger over his split lip and black eye.

Ash nods, but he doesn't pull away or flinch at my touch like I expected him to.

"We got in a fight as I was getting ready to go on a run," he explains, and my eyes glide over the jogging pants and long-sleeve athletic shirt that clings to him. "He punched me twice and then stormed out."

I frown. "He's a monster."

Ash shrugs. "I can guarantee I'm not the only child with a monster as a parent."

I shake my head. "I'm sorry."

He wipes his nose and turns to look at me. The light blue of his eyes stands out against the purple of the bruise, and my heart clenches.

"I'm sorry I woke you up," he explains, shifting into drive and pulling out onto the street. "I didn't really want to call any of the guys, you know?"

"I understand. But Hunter should know," I respond, looking out the window.

"I'll tell him later. I didn't—" He pauses, and his fingertips turn white as he grips the steering wheel. "I didn't know who else to call."

He doesn't have to say it. Even the ruthless Kings have feelings. They are human after all, despite being treated like gods. And for someone who is so hated, conflict and turmoil must be isolating with no one to turn to.

"I wish there was something I could do," I say, flicking my eyes to his face.

He looks at me for half a second and smirks. "I can think of something." He puts two fingers in his mouth and licks them vulgarly.

I swat his arm. "Not that."

He shrugs. "I just want to break shit. I'm so sick of playing nice. I want to show him this time, you know? *Really* hurt him."

I run my finger along my lips. "What's his favorite thing?" I ask, pulling a knee into my chest as we head out of town and into the forest.

"His expensive whiskey. His crystal. Anything in his bar— he was a bartender once upon a time, and his status allows him to collect one-of-a-kind pieces..." He stares straight ahead, his eyebrows furrowed.

"I think you just answered your own question," I say, smiling.

He grins and turns us around, skidding on the damp pavement as we pull an illegal U-turn. I screech and grab onto the door handle until we straighten out, and he speeds through the thicket of trees to the outskirts of town.

I'm quiet as he pulls up to his house. It's still early, and fog clings to the mid-century home, so different from the debauchery spilling out of it on Friday night. No lights, no music, no people. It's eerie and beautiful at the same time. He jumps out of the car and comes around to my side, opening the door for me and helping me out. He looks down at my boots and raises an eyebrow.

Pulling me into him, he whispers, "I want to fuck you in those boots one day."

I let out a breathy gasp, but quickly recover. "If you're lucky."

Sonya's words reverberate through my mind.

Find what feels good...

Even a week ago, those words would've stunned me to the point of wanting to leave. But now? They excite me.

I push away from him and walk away as I smile, hearing him come up behind me. He unlocks the door and lets us inside, and there's no pomp and circumstance—no warning—before he takes a large, crystal decanter and smashes it against the wall.

I cover my ears at the sound, but then adrenaline begins to course through me. Grabbing a bottle of liquor, I pour it out on the large shag rug, and then Ash takes the bottle from me, swigging the last little bit before tossing it at the window.

Both the glass—and the window—shatter completely.

I open my mouth in shock, and I can't help the smile on my lips as he hands me another.

And another.

After a minute, I pause, turning to face Ash—who is red-faced and breathing heavily. This is good for him. I know violence can be an unhealthy outlet, and there are probably other ways to channel his rage that aren't so destructive, but I can't help but support him in this.

For him.

For his mom.

"Are you going to get in trouble?" I ask softly, looking around at the damage. We've destroyed the bar area, and considering we've broken windows, it's going to be a hefty sum to repair.

"I might have," he says slowly, his long fingers curling around the neck of a vodka bottle. "Except I saved the camera footage from our fight earlier on my phone. No one will tolerate seeing the mayor beat the shit out of his son," he adds, watching me with a burning expression.

I give him a wicked smile, and then I pick up another bottle. I can tell by the heaviness and the old, fraying label that this whiskey is old—and probably very expensive. I toss it across the room and yelp as it collides with the television.

Ash chuckles, stepping on glass as he saunters over slowly.

"Good girl." Brushing the tangled hair out of my face, he cocks his head. My breathing halts as he smiles down at me, his lips twisting to the side slightly. "This is so fucking hot."

My breath quickens, my chest rising and falling rapidly, and before I can respond, he pulls me into him and smashes his mouth against mine, hissing briefly and pulling back, touching his cut lip. He must decide it's worth the pain because his lips are back on mine in an instant. My core clenches, and I fist the material of his running shirt, pulling the stretchy fabric until he's flush with my body. It's a flurry of hands, teeth, lips, and nails as I scrape the back of his neck.

He moans, and my body liquifies in his arms. As he moves against me, his hardness pushing against my stomach, my clit pulses with need. I don't wait—reaching up and pulling his shirt off, running my hands over the lean muscles of his abdomen. He may not be as muscular as the others, but he's still fit, still sculpted and easy on the eyes. I groan and pull my sweatshirt off, but he twists me around and presses me against the granite countertop of the bar.

"Briar," he warns, his voice rough and broken.

"Let me make you feel better," I whisper, frantic. I can't tell if I'm being completely selfish or completely *selfless*.

He doesn't wait—just pulls my pants down to my ankles. I step out of my boots and then my pants. I shriek when a palm comes between my legs, spreading me and forcing me apart. I'm panting as he tears into a condom wrapper.

"I have an IUD," I say quickly, backing into him. "Are you clean?"

"Yes," he answers. "You?"

I laugh. "Of course."

"Thank fuck," he whispers. His cock presses against my opening. Using his thick head, he spreads my wetness everywhere, sliding between my slit a couple of times without penetrating me. I arch my back and give him better access, and he presses my abdomen and chest flat against the counter, his hand on the back of my neck so I can't move. I turn my head to the side, my cheek cool against the black granite. "Will you admit it now?" he asks, circling his hips so that his length teases me.

"Admit what?" I breathe, my hands on the edge of the counter, gripping tightly.

"How fucking wet your pussy is for us," he murmurs, his voice so low that I barely hear him.

"I think it's pretty obvious," I chide, and before he can answer, he slams into me, completely bottoming out inside of me.

I cry out, my body sliding on the hardness of the granite as he pulls out slowly and thrusts into me again.

"Oh fuck," I whimper, my hands coming up to the counter, my fingers splayed on the cool stone to give myself some semblance of control. He tightens his grip around my neck, holding me in place as he continues. My body rocks back and forth with every movement.

"You like it when we tease you," he grits, his breathing heavy. It's a statement, not a question—one I'm beginning to wonder myself. "Your mind may protest, but your body is ours. Admit it."

I keep my mouth closed. I won't surrender to the notion of being *theirs*, but what else could I be? Each of them now has a part of me—two of them have been inside of me. And he's right. I am Play-Doh in their arms.

"Just keep fucking me," I order, grinding my jaw.

He chuckles, loosening his grip on the back of my neck

ever so slightly, and I take a deep breath. I wish I could see him—what his face looks like as he pounds into me amidst the broken glass. The look in his eyes, the way his mouth is probably slightly open. I moan, rocking backward so that I can control the tempo. He lets me, and his free hand comes around my stomach. Two fingers begin to work my clit. The smell of it—of my arousal mixed with alcohol—swirls around me. I arch my back into him as he removes his hand from my neck.

"I knew you'd be soaked, but this is a whole new experience," he mutters, the sound of him strumming me getting louder. I fist my hands as my climax draws closer. He's right—I'm so fucking wet. It's dripping down my legs.

The hand that was on my neck slides down to my ass, and his warm, calloused fingers edge closer to my entrance there.

"Ash," I warn, his palm spreading my cheeks.

He spits into his hand, and my body tenses.

"Relax, Briar," he murmurs, his voice low and crooning. "Do you trust me?"

I do. I do trust him. "Yes."

He swirls a finger around and around my ass, and I hold my breath.

"Relax," he commands, circling his hips ever so slightly so that his cock hits the perfect spot inside of me. His other hand continues to strum my clit.

"Oh my god," I cry, closing my eyes. He presses a finger against my ass, not penetrating—just enough pressure to send me over the edge, electrifying parts of me that have never been touched by another human. "Oh my god," I repeat, my pussy grabbing onto his cock as the waves of my orgasm power through me. He inserts a finger into my ass, and I cry out, feeling it against the thin barrier, feeling it everywhere and nowhere at the same time.

Everything intensifies, and my legs shake as another orgasm rips through me, stronger than the last.

"Oh fuck," Ash breathes, inserting another finger into my ass. The feeling of both fingers inside of me is exquisite—to be filled both ways, at the same time, to have his other hand stroking my cunt... "You're making me come, Briar." His voice is undone—raw, ragged, hoarse.

I feel a gush of fluid stream down my legs as I tremble against him, my whole body pulsing with each electric current. Thank God for the counter holding me up. Ash empties into me, stilling as he pulls his hands away and collapses on top of me, his arms forming a cage around me.

"Shit," he whispers, moving the hair off the back of my neck and delicately placing a few kisses along the sensitive spot near the back of my ear.

I can't even speak—I'm still twitching. We push ourselves up, and he quickly bends down and cleans me up. I don't look at him until I've pulled my pants back on. When I do, he's watching me raptly.

"What?" I ask, stepping into my boots.

He walks over to me, erect cock hanging slightly—and *holy fuck*. I scrunch my eyebrows together, confused.

"Did you enjoy it?" There's a bite to his words, and I cock my head.

"Do you really need validation, Ash?" I laugh, crossing my arms. "I thought it was very evident that I did enjoy it."

His eyes sweep down to the puddle where I'd been standing and then they trail back up to my eyes. Something passes over his face—concern or worry of some sort. My eyes fixate on the bruises. And it hits me—he *does* need validation. Today, at least.

I smile and pull him into me. "Yes. That was the best sex I've ever had."

He gives me a cocky grin, reaching around and slapping my ass. "Good. Because I was just warming you up."

My eyebrows shoot up. "How so?"

He tilts his head and walks backward, pulling his pants up quickly.

"You'll see."

Hunter

I'm making myself an Americano when Briar walks into the kitchen. Her wet hair is pulled over one shoulder, and she's wearing a skimpy, silk pajama set that borders on indecent. Averting my eyes and smiling, I hand her a vanilla latte, and she looks down, surprised.

"For me?" she asks, reaching out and taking it.

I nod. "You had an early morning."

She visibly stiffens, her eyes widening just a tiny bit before her stubborn resolve takes over. I literally see the emotions pass over her face—shock that I know, fear that I'm mad, and then regret... as if her fucking my best friend will deter me from pursuing her at all. And then the mask she loves to wear —the ruthless persona she's adopted to protect herself from men like the scum in California who hurt her.

But I see right through it.

Chuckling, I take a couple of steps forward, close enough so that our bodies are touching.

"Do you think I care if you fucked Ash?" I murmur, my lips feathering against her neck. Her eyes flutter closed. "I told you before, fuck one of us, or all of us. They're like my brothers. As long as you're mine when you're with me," I finish, kissing the pale, delicate skin behind her ear.

She looks up at me, her eyes hooded and dark—my hungry, little tempestuous Queen—and smiles. The way her full, pink lips curl up in the corners, the way her face is completely bare of makeup, a light smattering of the palest freckles along the bridge of her nose... I swallow. Why our parents thought we could pretend to be stepsiblings is beyond me.

She's my kryptonite, and I knew the instant we met that staying away from her was never going to be an option.

She's breaking down every barrier I worked hard to build over the last three years, every defense mechanism I've had in place since my mom died. At first, this was all fun and games. Dropping a gorgeous woman into my house, calling her my stepsister, watching as she walked around with such an attitude... It left me intrigued.

Annoyed.

Aroused.

And now that I had a taste of her, now that I know what it feels like to be inside of her, I want more.

I'm just about to kiss her when bare footsteps sound on the wood, and I jump away just as my dad pads into the kitchen.

"Morning, kids," he starts, refilling his mug. He turns to Briar, chuckling. "Your mom is still asleep."

Briar cocks her head and narrows her eyes. "Really? She never sleeps in."

Andrew shrugs. "She was up late organizing our closet. Pretty sure she found clothes in there I haven't worn since the nineties." He turns to face me, and I lean against the counter, crossing my arms. "I thought it would be fun to go apple picking today," he muses, smiling. "As a family."

A small part of me wonders if he knows about Briar and me—if he can sense it. He hasn't been this family friendly since... well, before Mom died.

"Apple picking?" Briar watches Dad with amusement, her eyes twinkling. "How quaint."

I shake my head. Briar obviously loves the idea. I can tell by the way she's impatiently hopping from foot to foot.

"Sure. Fine," I agree.

Briar turns to me. "Apple picking."

I laugh. "That's what he said."

She swats my arm, and my dad mumbles something about waking Aubrey up. When I turn to face Briar, she's watching me behind her large mug of coffee.

"See you in a bit," she says, smirking. "Brother."

BRIAR

I dry my hair, run a straightener through it, and then I pull on an oversized sweater and ripped jeans. Tugging my Docs on, I grab my phone and head downstairs, where everyone but my mom is waiting. Andrew is dressed in jeans and a fleece jacket, while Hunter is wearing faded jeans, boots, and a white T-shirt. He has his black leather jacket in his hands—the same one he wore that first day at school, with the ribbed material on the arms. I'm just about to ask where my mom is when she comes up behind me, smiling at everyone.

"This is so exciting," she beams, throwing an arm around my shoulders. "Our first family outing." She's wearing an outfit like mine; except she has on skinny jeans and sneakers with her sweater. She looks over at me and grins. "You look nice, sweetheart." Something about the way she says it, and the way her eyes flit between Hunter and me, like she's in on our secret...

I plaster on a fake smile for her, and then I look at Hunter, who is trying so hard not to laugh.

He thinks this is hilarious, doesn't he? Brother and sister out for a day of apple picking and family fun... except the brother and the sister fucked like rabbits on Friday night.

Except he isn't my brother, is he? We didn't even know each other before ten days ago, so I feel like we deserve some credit for that.

"We can't forget to take a picture for our Christmas card," my mom croons, unlocking the Subaru as we all climb in.

Yeah, this isn't going to be awkward *at all*.

I climb into the back seat as Hunter drops into the other side, that cocky smile still pasted on his lips. I glare at him again, and he just shakes with laughter. I'm so glad my discomfort brings him amusement.

"What should we listen to?" my mom asks, her hand resting gently on Andrew's as he navigates us out of the driveway.

Hunter and I both mumble something unintelligible, and just as I click into the seatbelt, Hunter's hand slips onto my thigh.

I widen my eyes. How dare he? I flick my eyes to the front seat quickly, shoving his hand off of me. He just chuckles, and I spend the next thirty minutes uncomfortable and acutely aware of the guy next to me, who's face as we came together is burned into my memory.

"Briar?" my mom asks from up front. "Can you hear us?"

I snap out of my daydream and clear my throat. "Sorry, what?"

"One of Hunter's short stories was accepted by the *New Yorker*," Andrew answers proudly.

I look at Hunter, who is gazing out the window. "What? It was? When?"

"This morning," he answers, turning to face me.

"You didn't say anything earlier," I add, flushed. "Congratulations!"

"Thanks." He shrugs and tilts his head, smiling. "Sis," he adds.

"It's very commendable," my mom continues, looking back at us. "Have you thought about moving to New York for college? Maybe one of those small, liberal arts schools would really nurture your writing."

He shrugs again, and I have to laugh. He's so broody, like he enjoys being melancholy even though his life is very, very comfortable. Even so, The *New Yorker* is a huge deal. I don't know anything about writing, and even I know of the *New Yorker*.

"I've thought about it. I kind of want to take a year off and write a book," he explains, clearing his throat.

"We have time to talk about it," Andrew interjects, and the two of them begin chatting as we pull onto a dirt driveway leading into a cute-as-hell orchard.

After we park, I get out and look around as Mom, Andrew, and Hunter begin walking to the ticket counter. Andrew pays, purchasing the large buckets for picking, and then he tells us to team up. Taking my mom's hand, they walk away excitedly, leaving Hunter and me alone at the entrance.

Hundreds of large apple trees are lined up in perfect rows. The sun is strong, but it's not hot at all. In fact, the air has that potent *autumn* smell to it today—a little bit of burning wood, cinnamon, and crisp air. Add in the scent of sweet apples, and this is a *fall-gasm* if I ever saw one. Our falls were mild in California, but every few years, we were blessed with a decent autumn.

"So, the *New Yorker,*" I say as we walk deeper into the orchard. There aren't very many people here, and the people we see are all preoccupied with filling up their buckets.

Hunter groans. "It's not that big of a deal. It's just a small piece I wrote over the summer."

"Can I read it sometime?" I ask, shielding my face from the sun.

Hunter stops walking, turning to face me with a frown. "You really want to?"

I laugh. "Of course. Why would I ask if I didn't really want to read it?"

I'm about to apologize for being so pushy when he reaches down and pries the bucket from my hand, setting it down. He gently pushes me up against one of the trees, hiding us from view. I open my mouth in surprise, but he bends down and his lips crash against mine, his breath sweet, his lips velvety soft. He pulls away a few inches, breathing heavily.

"It's like you're a zipper," he says slowly, running a finger down the middle of my chest, mimicking the movement. "You go your whole life zipped up, and then someone comes along and starts to tug. Inevitably, you'll be unzipped—and you won't be prepared for what spills out. That's how I feel when I'm around you."

I quirk my lips up slightly. "Yeah, I can definitely tell you're a writer."

He laughs and kisses me again, our bodies rocking against each other, our tongues sliding, our hands fisting. I moan when he bends down and grabs my ass cheeks, pulling my core into his hard length poking through his jeans.

"We shouldn't... Not here."

"What, you don't want Mom and Dad to see us kissing?" he jokes, and I shove him away.

Walking back to my bucket, I pick it up and continue down the lane of trees. We're quiet as we pick, with Hunter helping me grab the higher fruit I can't quite reach. After we've filled our buckets, we set them down and sit under the shade of one of the larger trees, each eating a sweet yet slightly sour apple. I must say, fresh apples are *so* much better than store bought—the tangy acidity compliments the sweetness, and it's so crisp that the flesh cleaves away cleanly with each bite.

"So how will this work?" I ask, curiosity eating at me.

He must understand what I'm asking—how I'm going to come to terms with the fact that I'm essentially dating all of them at once—because he smiles and shrugs.

"We each get our share of you," he muses. "We protect you. Show you that sex can feel good again. Date you, fuck you, worship you..."

My body heats. I can't justify cutting any of them loose— can't fathom *not* seeing where it goes with each of them. And none of them seem to be jealous. Sonya's words really resonated with me. I need to listen to my intuition. I need to follow my heart, and right now, my heart cannot possibly choose.

He chuckles, the sound low and throaty. "Do I get jealous? Maybe a little. But not enough for me to ask you to stop," he answers, looking at me with furrowed brows. "I don't expect you to be beholden to me and only me, Briar."

"Yeah, but—"

"Listen," he says, his eyes dark as he leans in closer. I get a whiff of vetiver, the wind carrying it over to me. "You're allowed to date or fuck whoever you want. Well, that's not true—I prefer it was one of the guys, since I can vouch for every single one of them, and I know they'll take care of you."

So, the devil has a heart after all.

"And if I hadn't told you about my past?" I ask, my voice quiet.

He looks down at his hands. "I don't know, honestly. I think we were scared. No one—and I mean no one—had ever challenged us like you did. I can't say for sure, but I do know that all of us felt something the first time we saw you. And I think we assumed you'd label us monsters, so why bother acting nice, you know?"

"I was angry when my father told me you and your mom were moving in. That first day in the park, when we called you our little lamb? We were drinking, being idiots, and I wanted to push you away. I wanted you to leave. Except, I didn't expect what you did. Most women would've run away or called the cops after seeing four guys in hoods in the dark... but not you. You stayed, and then you kept walking, like it was nothing. It was like watching a car wreck. You don't necessarily *want* to look, but you do it anyways, because you want to see what happens when you do. That's what it was like for us those first few days."

I shrug. "Well, none of you ever scared me. You all wore your attitudes on your shoulder, so I knew what I was getting myself into from the get-go. I'm way more terrified of men who hide their monstrosities."

Hunter's eyes slide to mine, and he reaches for my hand. "I'm here if you ever want to talk about it. But I also don't expect a recounting of what happened. It's your story to tell."

I swallow thickly, trying not to cry. My hands are shaking as I place them on my thighs, turning to face Hunter again.

"My—my mom's ex raped me," I whisper, my voice uneven. "And then I stabbed him with a kitchen knife."

Hunter's mouth twitches, and he nods. "I truly hope you killed him," he muses.

No one besides my mom ever made me feel like I did the right thing, but Hunter... I am grateful for him.

My lips tilt up into a smile. "Not quite. They revived him, and he's in jail."

I think back to that night, as painful as it is. He raped me, and while he was inside of me, while his hand was over my mouth, I'd reached around and grabbed the kitchen knife I'd been using to chop vegetables. I'd stabbed him in the neck, and he'd fallen onto the floor. I can still see the puddle of blood soaking through his light blue shirt.

And then I ran.

A few hours later, the doctor interrogated me. They did a rape kit, and confirmed it was Cam.

But the police—his friends? They never believed me. They said it was consensual. And then the rumors started, saying I'd lied.

Saying *I'd* done something wrong by tempting him.

My mom had gotten us out of there as quickly as possible. There was a trial, and he was sentenced to thirteen years since I was a minor at the time.

It didn't stop the rumors, though.

I kept my head down, my mom lost customers, and then we left everything behind.

She met Andrew at the perfect time.

"He was so nice to me," I continue, pulling my knees up into my chest. "He'd been dating my mom for a few months. I'd never gotten a bad vibe from him. He was funny, kind, and he cooked us dinner every weekend." Hunter is watching me with careful concern. His eyes are harder now—darker, somehow. "We were hanging out in our apartment. My mom was gone—coordinating a wedding in Utah—and he texted me about coming over. I didn't think anything of it. I never met my father, and I liked the idea of hanging out with Cam... like a father/daughter thing, you know?" My voice breaks, and I look away.

I shake my head. When I look back at Hunter, his jaw is clenched, but he doesn't say anything. He just listens.

"He'd been acting sort of weird—touchy-feely, and he offered me wine, but again, I thought that maybe this was normal. I had no precedent, nothing to compare what a normal relationship like that was like. I thought maybe he was attempting to be cool."

"It's not normal," Hunter growls. "He is a predator."

"I was in the kitchen chopping zucchini when he came up behind me. I was wearing a dress—something I now regret. Pants would've been a better barrier—"

"Don't you dare blame your *outfit*, Briar," Hunter fumes, his nostrils flaring.

I tilt my head and rest my cheek on my knee. "I was surprised. He'd never shown that kind of interest in me. And I thought perhaps it was a misunderstanding. So, I asked him to stop. But he held me against the counter and things got out of control."

"You asked him to stop, and he didn't. That's rape," Hunter growls. "He's lucky he's behind bars." His jaw is taut, and he releases his fisted hands a few times, splaying them over his pants like he doesn't trust himself not to punch something.

I smile, lifting my head and pulling his hand to my chest.

"Anyway, he... raped me. I tried fighting, but he was strong. As he... finished... I reached over and grabbed the knife. He almost slapped it out of my hand, but he was distracted—his phone was ringing—so I was able to twist around and stab him."

"I thought I killed him. It wasn't until later that night, after my stint in the hospital, that I found out. They couldn't get him to wake up. He'd lost forty percent of his blood, and his body was in shock. But after a couple of hours of being in a coma, he woke up. The trial was a couple of months later, and because of the evidence, he was sentenced to thirteen years."

Hunter shakes his head. "He deserves to be dead."

I nod. "I know."

He stands, pulling me up the next second. I brush myself

off and reach down for my apple bucket. When I straighten, he's watching me with a dark, concerned expression.

I sigh. "I promise, I'm okay."

"I was a little rough with you—"

"Stop," I murmur. "I liked it, Hunter. Cam didn't ruin sex for me. I'm strong as fuck. My mom sent me to the best psychologist in the bay area. I feel... okay. Sonya taught me how to claim my sexuality, how to take my pleasure back. Through healing, I've learned what I like and what I don't like. And I can assure you, I like you—all of you."

He smiles, grabbing my bucket and placing it on top of his.

"Good. Because now that I've tasted you..." he gives me a long, heated look before walking away, carrying both buckets. His muscles strain against the leather, but it doesn't faze him that he's carrying at least forty pounds of apples.

I cock my head and watch him walk away, admiring the way his jeans sculpt the back of his thighs. Sighing, I follow.

❧ 32 ❧

BRIAR

After spending nearly two hours getting caught up on homework—Ravenwood Academy's college prep curriculum is no joke—I spend the rest of the evening with my mom. Andrew is working, and Hunter is out with Ledger, but I feel like vegging out in front of the TV. We watch Friends down in the basement, since Hunter and I resolved our territorial issues, and I tell her about the other guys. I don't go into detail, obviously, but I think she suspects something's going on with Hunter. We talk about my classes, and she tells me about the new couch she ordered for the living room. It's nice to just hang out with her away from Andrew and Hunter.

Around ten, she heads up to bed, kissing me on the top of the head before retreating. I continue watching season seven alone with some of Hunter's chocolate.

I shoot Ash a quick text asking how he is, and he responds almost immediately.

I'm staying at Samson's. Haven't heard from my

father, so either he's still not home, or he got the hint with the video surveillance footage I sent him from our fight.

I hit the call button, and he answers straight away. "Hey," he says, his voice gravelly. I hear Samson murmur something in the background. "What are you doing right now?"

I pause, looking down at myself. I'm clad in my new pajamas from earlier—a silk camisole and shorts.

"Nothing, just watching TV. I wanted to check on you."

He's quiet for a beat, and I can tell my question catches him off guard. "I'm fine," he answers quickly. "You should come over," he adds, his voice low.

I sigh. "It's a school night."

I hear him hand the phone to Samson. "Come on, Briar," Samson begs. "We have brownies. Fresh baked."

Dammit. These guys have only known me for a week, and it seems they've already discovered my weakness.

"Fine."

I hang up, and Samson texts me his address. I hop up and turn the TV off, heading upstairs and changing into jogger pants and a sweatshirt. I pull a pair of sneakers on before shooting a quick text to my mom that I'm heading to Samson's with the guys for a bit. I know it's late, but I don't have a curfew. When I turned eighteen over the summer, we agreed that if I was transparent about where I was and who I was with, I could go anywhere, anytime.

I'm sure if Samson and Ash weren't Hunter's best friends, she might have more of a problem with it. But I think she trusts Hunter—trusts that he and his friends will keep me safe. After all, her own brother took care of her when she got pregnant

She texts me back.

Be safe. I love you.

I set my phone down and look in the mirror, tilting my

head as I study myself. *What am I doing?* It's a school night. I think I know these guys, but do I *really* know them? Sitting on the edge of my bed, I shoot Sonya a quick text, even though it's late, asking her how I'll know if its intuition driving me, or something silly, like lust. Relief washes through me when she responds.

You'll know it's intuition when you feel relief at having made that choice. For example, you say you're not sure if you should go to Samson's house. Why? Do you trust them? Have they ever given you a reason not to trust them? Think about calling back and saying no. Would you be relieved? Or disappointed? I don't want you to feel like you're being forced to hang out with two guys from school, but there will come a day when you'll have to relinquish control a little. Sometimes the best memories are made with sporadic decisions. Follow your gut, Briar. I won't be around forever, so you're going to need to fine tune your instincts, you know? Evaluate your surroundings. Listen to your gut. Apply common sense.

I smile as I head downstairs and get into my car. She's right. The second Ash asked me to come over, I was *excited*. I've never feared them—not even that first day in the park.

I drive the two miles to Samson's house, which I'd been to briefly after Hunter and I dropped him off the night of Ash's party. His house sits at a slightly higher elevation in the hills surrounding the main part of town. Ornate, large, ostentatious. Parking in the circular driveway, I walk up to the door, and it opens just as I walk up the steps.

Ash smiles at me and lets me through, closing the door behind me. My eyes flit across the house. Do all rich people have the same decorators? My mom would have a field day remodeling this basic, beige mess. I look at Ash, wincing when I realize his bruises are so much worse than they were this morning. His cut lip is more pronounced, too. He's in sweats and a T-shirt.

"Ash," I chide, reaching up to his face. "You should be icing that."

He takes my hand and kisses it. "I'm fine. I promise."

"There she is," Samson says, sauntering up to us. He's wearing plaid pajama pants, and it startles me to see both of them so casual. "Who's up for the hot tub?" he smirks, crossing his arms. The biceps are pushed up with his hands, and I swallow.

"I didn't bring a suit," I huff. They look at each other and smile. "Hell no," I whine, frowning.

"We promise to behave," Samson says, gesturing for me to follow him.

"I can make no such promises," Ash muses, and we all walk through the living area, back to the kitchen, and then out to the back yard. "Besides, I've been inside of you," he murmurs, his voice low enough so that only I hear.

"So that's why you invited me over?" I ask them both, crossing my arms.

"No. I invited you over to show you this," Samson answers, and I gasp when he moves out of the way, showing me the view.

An infinity pool decked out in rainbow lights sits before us. And above it, a jacuzzi cut into the stone, with a waterfall cascading into it. The cityscape before us is incredible—we can see all of Greythorn, including some of the forest and the other parts of Massachusetts beyond it. I take a step forward, my mouth hanging open.

"Holy shit," I whisper, looking at Samson. "I love it." I turn to Ash. "You're both assholes who knew I couldn't say no." I pin him with a serious expression. "And I expect brownies as a reward later."

Samson snorts. "You got it." He gestures to the pool. "Come on. Let's go. You only live once, right?"

Fucking right.

"Where are your parents?" I ask, looking at the house behind me.

"They're not here," Samson answers cryptically, smirking.

Sometimes the best memories are made with sporadic decisions.

I sigh and walk over to one of the chairs, disposing of my purse and stepping out of my shoes. Samson and Ash follow me, and soon we're all naked.

I'm too distracted by the pool to pay attention—and I've already seen Ash naked from the waist down—but Samson surprises me.

He has a cock piercing, and the guy is *hung*.

He must see me admiring his package, and he gives me a shy smile before running and jumping into the pool. I put my hands on my hips, waiting for Ash to do the same.

"You first," he says, his voice low, eyeing my peaked, hard nipples. It's not exactly warm tonight, which doesn't help the situation.

I flip him off before jumping in, the cold water shocking me at first. When I surface, Samson is placing his glasses on the side of the pool. Without them, he looks less innocent—and more like the other guys. Darker, edgier—like a whole new person. He swims over to me as I wipe my face with my hand.

"Are you having fun yet?" he asks, his voice low.

Ash jumps into the pool, but I don't look up. Samson is watching me like a vulture—a look I've never seen on his face before.

"You promised to be good," I murmur, treading water and giggling.

"I know. And I'll keep that promise as long as you want me to."

Forever the gentleman.

"This water is fucking cold," Ash barks, swimming over.

"You'll get used to it," Samson jokes, splashing him.

"Dude, fuck off," Ash growls, wiping his face. "Let's go in the jacuzzi."

I watch as he exits the pool, admiring the sculpted muscles of his ass. His legs are long and lean, and the muscles in his back contract with every step. I look at Samson, and it appears I'm not the only one admiring Ash's backside.

"How can you see without your glasses?" I ask, splashing him playfully.

He chuckles. "I'm far-sighted. I can see things far away, just not up close."

I smirk. "But you *were* admiring his ass," I tease.

He cocks his head. "And? I'm not ashamed that I find him attractive, and he knows it."

Heat flares through me. "You and Ash?" I ask, glancing up at the jacuzzi. Ash is sitting in the water with his head back and eyes closed.

Samson smiles—his teeth are so white, so straight. He's beautiful—the way the water drips off his pale skin, the way his coppery eyes look gold from the pool lights.

"You guys have…"

Samson nods. "A few times. He's not quite out of the closet though. Whereas I'm proudly bi."

I pull my lip between my teeth, imagining the two of them. I squeeze my legs together—something that's not so easy to do while trying to stay afloat.

"Love is love," I concede, grinning.

"It's definitely not love with Ash. Just fun. Though I do love him as a friend."

"And what about me?" I ask, swimming a little farther away.

Samson's lips twitch slightly. "What about you, Briar?"

"Could you see yourself loving me? Or am I just a fun time?"

His eyes darken slightly, his face turning serious. My breathing hitches at that look, and I can't take my eyes off him.

"You're both. Neither. I don't know how to explain it. I feel like..." He shakes his head.

"What?" I ask, changing my mind and swimming closer. He inhales sharply when my hand brushes his abdomen.

"I feel like an animal around you," he says, his voice gravelly. "I am a feminist, I believe in women's rights, and consent, and all of that..." He swallows, and I admire the way his throat bobs. "But you make me wild. *Feral*," he growls.

I smile, reaching down and gripping his firm length.

He hisses, surprised. And he's rock hard.

"Are you guys coming in or what?" Ash yells from across the pool.

"Yeah," I answer, letting go of Samson and swimming to the stairs.

Walking out, I saunter to the jacuzzi, sitting across from Ash. He gives me a closed-mouthed, lecherous smile. I'm about to make a snide remark when Samson climbs in.

Holy...

Ash must notice Samson's hard on too because his eyes flit from me to him, and something akin to lust passes over his face. Samson sits next to Ash, and even though I'm in a jacuzzi, my entire body tingles as they stare at each other.

"Is that for me or for her?" Ash asks, swallowing.

Samson smiles and looks between us. "Both, I think."

A tremor of excitement runs through me when Ash reaches out and brushes a piece of wet hair off Samson's forehead. And then he pins his eyes on me.

"Get over here," he commands.

Fuck.

33

BRIAR

I slowly drift over, bracing myself. I sit next to Ash, and he quickly pulls me into his lap. His hard length presses into my ass cheek.

"Didn't I tell you earlier that I was warming you up?"

My heart pounds against my ribs. "Yes," I breathe.

"Well, this is the real deal. You ready?"

I nod a little too vigorously. Just as I'm about to ask how something like this starts, Samson brushes my nipple as he moves to a spot in front of me.

"Which one of us do you want where, Briar?" Ash asks.

I look between them. How can I possibly choose something like that? Who has to make that kind of decision in real life?

Is this real life?

Before I can answer, Samson takes my hands and presses himself against me, placing his lips on mine. They're buttery soft, and his tongue nudges my lips apart, asking for access. I groan when he bites my lower lip, and his hands come to my face as he continues to kiss me. I stand, and Ash follows suit, coming up behind me and rocking his cock up into me, moving my hair off my neck and kissing me there. His body is firm behind me, and Samson pushes himself against the front of me, his hard abdomen against mine.

Holy shit.

"Briar," Ash purrs. "Where do you want me?"

I pull away from Samson, tipping my head back as Ash kisses my neck from behind.

"I want to see you two together first."

Samson slowly moves away from me, backing up against the other wall of the jacuzzi. He's smiling at Ash.

"Well? Let's show her how we do this. Unless you're scared."

Fire ravages my body as Ash swims over, gripping the back of Samson's hair and pulling it backward.

"You don't fucking scare me, Hall," Ash growls. And then he smashes his lips against Samson's, and I have to squeeze my legs together as I watch them writhe against each other—hard muscle, smooth skin, wet hair. Ash pulls away, breathing heavily. "Stand on the step."

Glad I'm not the only one he loves to boss around.

Samson's eyes are darker now, his face serious. He stands up, his erection taught, causing the cock piercing to stick out slightly. I lean back in my seat and spread my legs, my fingers drifting downwards to the slick wetness between them. I begin to circle my clit with two fingers as Ash grips Samson's ass and places his mouth around Samson's cock.

Samson groans, throwing his head back and grabbing Ash's hair as Ash slides his lips down to the base of his cock.

Shit.

My hands move faster as Ash ups his tempo, his hand coming underneath Samson's balls, stroking him there.

Samson cries out, putting his hands behind his head. And then he looks at me.

"You like this?" he bites out, thrusting slightly into Ash's mouth. "Seeing Ash on his knees with my dick in his mouth?"

I nod, biting my lower lip as I arch my back and close my eyes.

"Stop."

My eyes fly open, and Ash is next to me now. Samson is stroking his cock, watching us. "Do you really think we're going to let you come by yourself? Or without you?"

I open my mouth to respond, but he stands up and gestures for me to follow him out of the jacuzzi. I look at Samson, who just nods.

We all walk over to the large lounge set, decked out with an outdoor daybed made of thick, white linen. Ash stops and points to it, so I climb onto my back and wait.

"I'll be right back."

He walks away, and I turn to find Samson standing next to me.

"That was the single hottest thing I've ever seen," I laugh, suddenly feeling very exposed. Samson must notice because he climbs into the bed and hovers above me.

"Just wait," he whispers, bending down and kissing my neck. I tilt my head backward and give him access, moving underneath him and closing my eyes. I can feel his firmness, feel it touching the side of my hip, so I buck them upwards and spread my legs, waiting.

"Please," I whisper.

His warm hand slides down, gripping the flesh on my side. His lips graze mine, and I gasp when his hand spreads me farther.

"What did Ash mean earlier?" he mumbles, planting kisses along my jawline. "About warming you up?"

"I'm back," Ash says, a few feet away. He places a bottle of lubricant on the table.

"Ah," Samson purrs, knocking my legs apart with his knee. "I should've known." He's breathing heavily, and out of the corner of my eye, I see Ash douse his cock in lube, the sound exhilarating. "Watch us," Samson whispers, pushing the thick head of his length against me. "Watch as I fuck you." The cool metal against my skin is electrifying, and I moan, low and deep. And then he enters me, sliding in smoothly, filling me completely.

I gasp, and he hisses—I try to accommodate his girth, but there's no point. It burns, but the burning soon gives way to immense fullness.

"Holy shit," Samson whispers, his voice husky and uneven. "You're so fucking tight."

And then pulls out, and I can feel every inch of him thanks to his piercing. It slides against the spot inside of me, the sensations new and incredible. Driving back into me, I cry out. He does this a few more times—until I begin to meet him with every thrust. And then he rolls and flips me in one swift movement, so that I'm on top of him. I place my knees on either side of him, riding his cock slowly as he throws his head back.

Ash comes up behind me, placing a warm hand on my ass. I look back, and a nervous tremor works its way down my spine.

"If you need to stop, tell us to stop," Ash murmurs, his voice thick. He spreads my cheeks with his hand. "Just like before, remember?"

I nod, looking down at Samson. He's moving underneath me, thrusting into me from below. Ash hands him something silver, and I don't register what it is until he turns it on. He gently presses the world's tiniest vibrator against my clit, and my whole body convulses on top of him.

"This will make it easier," he murmurs, rubbing it in slow circles. "Breathe, Briar."

I'm about to ask him what he means when I feel Ash's cock against my other opening, and I immediately clench up.

"Breathe," Samson repeats. When I look back down at him, I take a few steadying breaths. His bottom lip is between his teeth, and *God,* he is so beautiful. I smile and close my eyes, breathing heavily as Ash's cock presses into me again. This time, I don't protest. Because of the lube, it slides in easily, and I let out a loud breath of air as I feel him inside of me, stretching me. It stings a little, and I'm grateful that he isn't moving yet.

"Holy shit, I can fucking feel you," Samson grinds out, looking at Ash over my shoulder.

Those words reverberate through me, and I nudge Samson's hand with the vibrator. He chuckles as he moves it quicker, and then I hear a click right before it gets stronger.

"Oh fuck, yes," I moan, propping myself up on my elbows over Samson as he moves slowly inside of me. Ash grunts, and I rock my hips just slightly. Ash begins to move, and Samson ups the vibration one more time.

I think I'll probably shoot straight up into the sky when I come.

"You good?" Ash asks, a hand on my ass again. He moves into me slowly, but it doesn't hurt anymore. Now... now it just feels so full, *so* good...

"Yeah," I whisper. "God, yeah."

Samson swirls the vibrator against my clit, moving it to where we're joined and back up to my hood again, sliding between my swollen vulva.

"Oh my god," I cry, my hands turning into fists.

"This is incredible," Ash murmurs. "I can feel both of you at the same time."

"You're going to make me come," Samson growls, speeding up and working into me harder now.

Ash does the same—so that they're both slamming into me at the same time. The friction from the vibrator builds my climax so high, it's almost painful. I can't speak, can't move, as Samson rubs me with the silver bullet. I've never felt this much—the piercing, both cocks inside of me, the vibrator—and my legs begin to quake violently. The intensity builds, and I cry out loudly now, clawing at the fabric, at Samson's arms, trying to hold on to something before I go flying off the rails.

"I'm going to come," Samson says, his voice throaty. "Oh fuck, I'm going to come," he says again, baring his teeth.

"Me too," Ash growls, placing another hand on my other ass cheek and plowing into me with zero abandon now. I look back at him, his face blazing. They both groan, the sound causing me to convulse with pleasure, and then—

"Me three," I cry, the climax spilling over and running through each muscle, contracting and pulsing, my one giant muscle releasing all tension in a long, intense seism. I feel a gush of liquid rush between my legs, my body still gripping their rock-hard cocks firmly as the pulsing stops. I look down to see Samson watching me raptly, his chest wet.

"Holy fuck," he whispers, sweating and panting. "You came all over me, little lamb."

"Breathe," Ash commands, pulling out of me slowly.

Now *that* is the weirdest feeling ever.

Samson helps me sit up, pulling out and cleaning me with a washcloth Ash must've grabbed when he got the lube and vibrator.

"That was..."

Ash comes to lie next to me, so that I'm in the middle.

"Incredible," Samson answers.

"Fucking hot," Ash adds, and we all laugh. "Are you okay?"

I pause before answering. Not because I'm unsure, but because I've never been surer about anything in my life.

Whatever happened that first day in Ravenwood Academy tethered them to me—all four of them, all at once. And oddly, it's comforting to know that I have four guys who seem to want to take care of me, to give me pleasure, to ensure I am safe and comfortable and happy.

For the first time, I have no doubts that I am okay.

As long as I am with them.

"Yeah," I answer. "I'm more than okay."

34

BRIAR

The next day at school, I brace myself for the onslaught of questions from Scarlett and Jack. I don't want to be dishonest with them, but I also know the situation I'm in is... unconventional. Then again, they're both open-minded, so it's possible that they won't even care, especially if I explain the change in attitude with regards to the Kings. I pull up to the parking lot and find a space in the back row, and just as I put the car in park, I hear tapping on the glass of the passenger side.

I roll my window down and stare at Ledger.

"Hi?"

He leans on my door, the sleeves of his button-up rolled up to his elbows, showing off his tan, corded forearms that are scattered with various tattoos.

"This isn't your spot anymore," he says, looking at me like I just committed a faux pas.

"What do you mean?" I ask, looking around. "We don't

have assigned spots."

He gives me a lopsided smile. "You do now. Follow me."

I start my engine and pull out, and when I loop around the parking lot, he directs me to a spot between the four cars.

Sighing, I pull in between Ash and Hunter's car,

I turn the engine off and climb out, grabbing my backpack. When I pivot to face the school after locking up, I'm met with stares from everyone still mingling in the lot.

Great.

"Come on," Ledger says, guiding me to the gate with a gentle hand on my back.

"I don't need to be chaperoned through campus," I joke, rolling my eyes.

Turning to face me, he smirks down at me. "Is that what you think I'm doing?" His blonde hair is hanging down one side of his face, and his navy pants cling to the thick muscles in his legs. He doesn't look eighteen. He looks twenty-five—especially with the ink. I ignore the way everyone has quieted, watching us as we interact, but I don't think any of them will be able to hear what we're saying.

"I don't know. I just don't want to be treated differently."

He shrugs. "You're one of us now. It would be strange if you didn't park with us. I figured you'd enjoy being near the front gate."

That is true.

I shift my weight from one hip to the other. "Fine."

He smirks, rubbing his bottom lip with his thumb as his blue eyes find mine. "You're not beholden to us just because you park with us. Go be with your friends," he says, smiling. And then he turns and walks away, and I'm left to ignore the lingering gazes as I make my way to the quad.

Scarlett is sitting with Jack when I walk up, and as I do, Jack lets out a whistle.

"Someone was busy this weekend," he jokes.

I shrug. "I have to tell you something," I start, looking between them. Just as I open my mouth, the bell rings. "At lunch, okay?"

"Fine," Jack whines, standing. "But I want all the deets."

The fifty minutes spent in pre-calculus go by so slowly, and I don't notice the way every seat surrounding me is empty until I get up to leave as the bell rings. Swallowing, I look around at my classmates, and sure enough, none of them meets my eye. I quickly gather my things and leave, shaking my head.

In French class, it's the same thing. No one wants to sit next to me, and no one makes eye contact. It's like I'm invisible. I'm walking through the hallways toward lunch when people start whispering, parting the walkway down the middle for me to pass.

Is this what it's like for the guys? Do they just play into the stereotype everyone has them in? Because even as my eyes land on another student, they must mistake my confusion for intimidation. They look down—and they look...

Just like they do when Hunter and the guys walk by.

The Kings aren't bullies. Not really. But people presume they are, and that's where their reputation comes into play.

It's so much easier to keep people afraid of you—to keep people hating you—than it is to be vulnerable. It's easier to continue the charade. We never corrected people when they made assumptions and look where that got us.

"I'm not contagious," I mutter, rolling my eyes.

A girl with thick, black curls and a pretty face shakes her head as she leans against the lockers. "You're their property now."

I whirl to face her. "I'm no one's property," I reply, cocking my head. "They don't own me."

She matches my stance, pushing off the locker and standing in front of me. "That's what you think."

Her words rattle me, but I continue out of the building toward the quad. When I spot Jack sitting with Scarlett, I perk up, skipping over to them. But as I approach, Jack looks over his shoulder and glares at me.

"What?" I ask innocently.

Scarlett crosses her arms. "We know what you did."

My heart leaps into my throat. "How?"

Jack laughs. "She's not even trying to deny it." Then he turns to me. "It's your funeral, not mine, so you do you, boo."

"What are you talking about?" I beg, sitting next to them.

Scarlett looks at me, her expression pained. "I don't think you should sit here with us today."

My body turns to ice, and my eyes flit between them. "I don't really understand why you're mad at me. Out of everyone, I thought you'd both understand."

Is it the fact that I slept with them? Or is it something else?

"You're new, Briar," Jack grits out. "You have no idea what they're capable of. You've only been here a week. I've known them my whole life."

My eyes sting with tears. "I'm really confused. Are we talking about how I slept with them?"

"*Them?*" Jack asks, eyeing me suspiciously.

"It doesn't matter who you fuck. Personally, I don't care as long as it's consensual," Scarlett hisses, looking around at the people staring at us. "But Greythorn is a small town. Micah was our best friend. We can never forgive Samson for what he did to Micah, but apparently that doesn't matter to you. I think you're making a mistake. I mean, there are rumors that you vandalized Medford Asylum. You've got balls, considering Christopher Greythorn is certifiably insane. Oh, and by the way, we didn't want to go to that stupid party on Friday. But we did—for you."

It's like cold water spills over my body, and I stare at Scarlett. "How did you know about Medford—"

"Have you checked your phone, Briar?" Jack asks, his voice quiet.

I quickly pull my phone out. It's been on silent since I left the house, but he's right. I have texts from my mom, from Andrew, from Hunter...

"I don't understand," I mumble, feeling my vision tilt a bit.

"The police arrested Ash a few minutes ago. Took him straight from class. I guess his father figured out what happened."

Fury burns through me, hot and potent. "Do the police also know that Christopher Greythorn beats his son?"

Also, why wasn't anyone else caught? We were all there...

"He's the mayor, Briar—he has the potential to ruin my family's business, and we need all the business we can get," she adds, referring to Romancing the Bean. A small pang of guilt runs through me. I didn't even think about that. "Look, I really don't care if you want to sow your wild oats with all of them. But Samson Hall is dangerous." She pauses. "If I'm caught associating with Greythorn's newest criminal... I guess I just thought you were smarter than that."

Jack nods, and his eyes flit to something over my shoulder. "Your keepers are here. See you later, Briar." He and Scarlett get up and walk away, and I hate the way his voice sounds so disappointed—how they both sound disappointed.

Maybe I should've been smarter. Maybe I should've said no to vandalizing Medford, to smashing Christopher's nice things at the house.

I twist around as Hunter, Ledger, and Samson stroll toward me, their expressions hard.

"They arrested Ash?" I ask, crossing my arms.

"Let's go," Hunter growls. He doesn't answer my question

—just grabs my hand and pulls me toward the gate. Everyone is staring—all their eyes are on us. When I look at Samson, his lips are a tight line. Ledger, too—they're all expressionless, but I can see the minute details that tell me they're beyond pissed off.

The security guard doesn't even balk as we approach the gate. He just lets us through.

The Kings, always getting what they want.

I glance at Hunter, and he looks down at me, blazing fury written all over his face. I pull away from him and stop a few feet from our cars.

"What happened?" I ask, glancing between their three faces. "I thought we made sure there were no security cameras at Medford?"

Hunter's lips quirk just slightly, but then the anger reappears, causing his brows to furrow together.

"Ash will be fine," he says, and the other guys let out exasperated sighs. "Christopher is in deep shit, considering Ash sent the police department footage of their fight. He got his dad in full view, beating the shit out of him. No matter what happens with Medford, the fact that the mayor is on video abusing his child will never be forgiven. Mission accomplished," he murmurs. "Ash was the only one identified. I guess we missed a camera somewhere. They might not have identified us yet, but everyone knows we were there too."

Dread fills me, and I swallow thickly. "It's only a matter of time before they do," I murmur, crossing my arms.

Will this jeopardize my future? The Sorbonne?

I'm about to ask when Hunter starts to talk. "Do you ever check your phone?" he chides, his voice cold. "Do you have any idea why your mom has been trying to contact you?"

I stop short. "I had it on silent for class," I mutter, looking down at the screen. "I just assumed it was because of Medford—"

"Cameron Young escaped from prison today."

Cam.

For the third time today, it feels as though someone is pouring ice cold water over my head. My hands begin to shake as I look down at my phone, opening my texts. I have nine from my mom—long, block-like messages. One from Hunter that just asks where I am, and one from Andrew, asking to see me in his office.

Great.

I scan my mom's texts quickly. *Escaped, his friends in the department, not answering your phone, Medford...*

I swallow. "How?" I ask, looking up at Hunter.

Dark fury burns behind his eyes as he rolls his tongue around the inside of his cheek.

"Fuck if I know how the asshole did it." He inhales deeply. "I'm going to kill him, Briar."

I look down at the ground as my vision begins to tilt again. Ledger steps forward, showing me a news article from my old hometown on his phone—a mugshot of Cam below it.

Cameron Young, a former police officer in Marin County who was charged with rape earlier this year, escaped from San Quentin State Prison yesterday. The details of the escape are still under investigation. There is a $5,000 reward for anyone who finds him.

With shaky hands, I rub my eyes and sigh. "Fuck," I whisper, looking around nervously.

"Hey," Samson says, stepping forward. "We are going to keep you safe."

I look up at Hunter, and he nods. My eyes flick to Ledger, who just scowls, and then he pockets his phone.

Something comes over me then—something dark and menacing. I turn to Hunter again, clenching my fists.

"We have to find him." His eyes burn into mine, and Ledger and Samson stand next to Hunter, their arms crossed.

"What's the alternative? We wait for the authorities to do their job? What if he..." I look down as tears prick at my eyes. "What if he finds us first?"

Ledger is the first to pull me into him, and his warm arms calm my racing heart.

"We'll find him," he murmurs into my hair, kissing the top of my head.

"But what if he hurts you?" I ask, my voice small against Ledger's broad chest. "I couldn't possibly ask you to help me with this. It's my mess," I finish.

They have futures—college applications, writing publications, school, notoriety, and familial reputations to uphold. I am a nobody. If anyone is going to put themselves at risk to find him, it should be me.

"There's no question that we're going to help you," Ledger answers, fisting my shirt and squeezing me tight. "All of us. We vowed to protect you, so we will do just that."

"Your ours to protect," Hunter agrees, smirking.

I pull away from Ledger, looking behind him at Samson—whose eyes bore into mine with fiery intensity.

"I will owe you my life," I whisper, looking at them.

"You," Hunter growls. "We just want you."

"You have all of me."

I make eye contact with each of them, so they know I mean all of us. Nine months ago, I had no one to turn to except my mom. I was called names and my story wasn't believed. But when I look into Ledger's blue eyes, when I see the fury roiling underneath the surface of his cruel smile, I know I'm safe. I can take care of myself but fighting against a crazed rapist will be a hell of a lot easier with four guys willing to risk everything for me—four guys willing to help me.

I've gone my entire life on my own. Fighting for peace after my trauma, fighting to fit in, fighting to be strong. I always had my boxing gloves on, always ready and on the defensive.

But as I look at the guys, I realize, they can help me take the gloves off. They can help me learn to depend on others again. They can help me—with their connections, their money, their reputation.

They can *help* me.

And I'm going to need all the help I can get taking Cam down.

❧ 35 ❧

ASH

I sigh, running my hands through my short hair. *This is such utter bullshit.* I glance at the guard pacing outside my cell. I know the chief received my video—one of the sergeants mentioned it in the interrogation. *So why am I still here?*

I stand and walk to the door, waiting for the guard to head back this way. I wish I could text Briar, the guys— update them. I didn't expect two officers to barge into my physics class, and I sure as hell didn't expect them to ask me to follow them outside. I didn't want to cause a scene, so I followed them—where they proceeded to arrest me on the hood of their car. Third period was in session, so only a couple of freshman girls on their way to the office saw me.

No doubt word will be out by now.

The guard walks up to the door and shakes his head. "It's for your own safety, Ash."

I glower at him, eventually kicking the bars, and he

doesn't even flinch as he walks back toward the other end of the path.

Fuck this—fuck my dad.

According to the sheriff, I'm in deep shit for Medford—but my father is in deeper shit for punching me, and for the new investigation into my mom.

I swallow and look down at the cement, breathing heavily.

My mother and I are both prisoners in his world, and he wouldn't have it any other way.

I'm just about to ask to make a call when he wanders back over to the door, unlocking it.

"I guess it's your lucky day, Mr. Greythorn. We found your father, and he's in custody." He swings the door open, and I pause.

"What next?"

He shrugs. "Your bail has been paid. You just have to await a trial. Because your father is a danger to you, and because you're still in school, you can either arrange to stay with a family member or a friend, or we can contact social services."

I frown. "I'll figure it out."

He leads me out, and we stop by the property room to grab my cell phone, wallet, and keys. I sign some papers, including a requisite form showing where I'll be staying for the time being. I scribble down Hunter's address. He directs me to the exit.

"Who paid my bail?" I ask, pushing the door open as I unlock my phone.

He nudges his jaw to the black Range Rover waiting out front.

I smile as I walk over, and when I get closer, Briar throws the passenger door open.

"Let's fuck some shit up," she purrs, grinning.

36

BRIAR

Hunter drives us all back to our house, and fortunately, my mom's car is gone, which means both she and Andrew are out. He cuts the engine, and we exit. I unlock the door and look over at Hunter as he smirks.

It's still strange to know that we share a house together.

That this is *our* home.

We walk to the kitchen, and Ash grabs a beer from the fridge before we sit at the table.

I like this—that I'm a part of their exploitations. That they're including me in their plans.

"So, what are we going to do?" Samson asks, licking his lips. He has his hands clasped together, and he's watching us expectantly.

I shrug. "I don't know. Ash was the only one identified, so—"

"Briar," Ledger growls, his eyes fixed on my face. "He's not talking about Medford. He's talking about you."

My body goes cold. "That's why we're here? We're not making sure our stories about Medford are tight, that they align in case we're interrogated?"

Hunter turns in his chair and bends forward, placing his large, warm hands on my bare thighs. My body explodes with electricity.

"None of us give two shits about Medford, baby."

I swallow. "Oh. I just thought—"

"I'm going to fucking kill him," Ash declares, his voice edged with anger. He looks at me as he takes a swig of beer. "Skin him alive and make him eat his own flesh." His light blue eyes grow darker by the second as he sneers. "For what he did to you, he deserves much worse."

Shivers claw down my spine, one vertebra at a time. My breathing hitches. They're all looking at me, waiting.

Plotting.

I think of the guys I saw that first night in the park.

The guys who lit the house in the preserve on fire.

The guys everyone at Ravenwood Academy feared.

My heart pounds against my ribs as I realize they're waiting, ready to pounce.

For me.

I'm just about to ask what our options are when the front door closes. Hunter and I both hop up, and I breathe a sigh of relief when my mom walks through the arched doorway of the kitchen. She looks between Hunter and me, a bag of food in one hand, and a fountain soda in the other. I don't think I've ever seen her drink soda.

"Hi, honey," she says solemnly, setting her cup down and sighing. She flicks her eyes to Hunter. "Can you please give us a minute?"

The guys stand up and walk out of the kitchen. Ash's eyes find mine just before he turns the corner. The rage is still blazing, and I realize with a start that Ash *will* kill Cam if given the chance.

I sit down and sigh. "Do they know the motive?" I ask, crossing my arms and leaning back.

She slides in next to me, putting an arm around my shoulders. "No, but it's not hard to guess," she starts, her voice low. When I look at her, tears begin to well in her eyes.

"I'm so, so sorry, Briar," she says, sniffling and pulling me into her. "I'm your mother. I was supposed to protect you."

I stiffen. "Mom, this wasn't your fault."

"He was my boyfriend. I thought—I thought he was safe," she whispers, swiping the tears that have begun to run down her face. "And I thought this mess was behind us."

I nod. "Me too."

"I can't believe he escaped San Quentin," she adds, her voice hard. "Someone must've helped him." She sighs. "But I want you to know that we're safe here, Briar."

I loosen in her arms, closing my eyes. "I know, Mom." *I have four guys willing to take a bullet for me...* "And I'm sorry about Medford."

I'd seen her ask about it in one of her texts this morning.

"One thing at a time," she murmurs, chuckling.

My eyes snap open and I pull away. "Why are you drinking soda?"

She waves my question away. "I don't know. I heard about Cam, and then Medford... stress eating," she laughs, shaking her head.

I rear my head back suspiciously, but before I can ask any more questions, the front door slams again.

"That's Andrew." We stand, and Andrew comes stalking into the kitchen. He's in his suit, having come straight from school. He walks right up to me.

"Briar," he says, relieved. He pulls me into a hug, and my throat constricts. Despite everything—despite not knowing me that well—I can tell he really cares about me. "I've spoken to my lawyers. I think we should hire our own investigators to find him."

"I agree," my mom chimes in, turning to me. "But it's up to you, hon."

I nod. "Yeah. Let's do it."

Let's take that motherfucker down.

◈

After Andrew, my mom, and I talk logistics and they head out to run some errands, I walk down to the basement, where I suspect the guys have been hanging out. As I land on the last stair and look into the room, I see only Hunter sitting on the couch. He's watching TV, but his eyes are unfocused.

Distracted.

They snap to mine as I walk over. Standing in front of him, I grab the remote from the couch, and he smirks.

"Rule number one," I murmur, turning the TV off. "No more wearing that uniform around me when you're at home." My eyes trail across the tight, white button-up he has rolled up to his elbows, and the navy slacks that fit his thighs like gloves. He's kicked his boots off, but it doesn't matter. He looks unkempt, yet...

Godly.

He smiles, spreading his legs and leaning forward, his hands clasped together as he rests his elbows on his knees.

"I suppose that should be a household rule," he utters, looking directly at me. He brushes his hand across my bare leg, his thumb trailing up the inside of my thigh. I shudder.

"Rule number two," I say, faltering slightly as his fingers move upwards and flick against the wetness pooling in my panties. "Help me get my revenge, and you can have me in whatever way you want."

It feels good to say it out loud. Because while a legal trial is fine, my idea of revenge is so, so much worse. I probably wasn't the first girl he raped. And I certainly won't be the last if he finds a way to remain under the radar.

We have to find him.

"That's far too tempting," he murmurs, pulling my thong to the side. "I can't decide if we're doing you a favor, or if you're doing us a favor."

"Neither," I whisper. "We're helping each other."

"You are ours," he says again, his other hand coming to the back of my skirt and lifting the material. He grips the flesh on my bare ass, squeezing. I let out a loud moan. "And we are yours. I think it's time the *Kings* of Ravenwood appoint a *Queen*."

My stomach lurches. "What?"

He bites his lower lip as he pulls me down onto his lap. I place both knees on either side of him so that I'm straddling him. I can feel his erratic heartbeat, and his throat bobs as he swallows. He unzips his pants and positions himself below me, moving the material of my undies to the side.

"Your ours now, Briar Monroe. Body, mind... and soul."

And then he thrusts into me, and I gasp, arching my back. "Oh, fuck," I whimper, shuddering. He fills me completely to the hilt, and my eyes flutter closed.

Yes. If this is what making a deal with the devil is like, I will sign everything I am—everything I ever was or will be—over to them.

They can have me.

I surrender.

"Say it, little lamb," Hunter commands, his hand on my shoulder, holding me low as he drives into me, his length as deep as it will go. "Say you're ours."

"I'm yours," I whisper without even thinking. "I've always been yours."

He groans and moves faster, his thick, hard cock hitting my cervix with every thrust. There's a deep ache—but it also feels incredible.

"Good girl," he grumbles, a thin sheen of sweat on his face as he works himself underneath me, holding me down.

Heat courses through me, and I move my hips to try to ride him, but his grip on my shoulders is strong.

He wants control.

I stay still as the pace quickens, breathing heavily and meeting Hunter's eyes as they blaze with lust and fury. He bares his teeth as he works harder, and the feeling of him so deep, of taking me fully, makes me delirious with pleasure. Our breathing quickens, and he begins to pump faster, nearing his climax.

"Come with me," he demands, squeezing my nipple between the material of my shirt.

Fuck.

I lean forward and kiss him, claiming him as much as he's claiming me. I may be theirs—but that means they are mine, too. Our lips work each other, slow and smooth, and he moans into my mouth, biting my lower lip as he begins to tremble.

It sends sparks through my body—feeling him harden, feeling him pulse inside of me. I fly over the edge with him.

"Oh, fuck," he says, his forehead touching mine as he empties into me, and I quiver in his arms as the last of it leaves my body. He's panting, and he holds my wrists down at my side as we both take steadying breaths.

I climb off him and hold my skirt up as he reaches into his pocket, cleaning me up with a handkerchief. We both stand, and he zips himself back up. I smooth my hair out, and once we're both presentable again, he takes my hand.

"Come on."

I grab my phone and let him pull me out of the room. "Where are we going?"

He chuckles, making sure we grab our things before we close the house up and head back to his car.

"Let's go make a spectacle out of you and introduce Ravenwood Academy to their new Queen."

37

LEDGER

It's like she's made for this, like she's always been the fifth element to our group. I think of Plato, and how he came up with the notion of the rare fifth element—or what's known as an aether.

Rare.

Unknown.

Celestial.

Pure—purer than the other four elements.

The next day, exactly ten days after showing up at Ravenwood Academy, Briar parks next to us and unabashedly secures her position as the Queen of Ravenwood. And she does it so naturally, with a calm demeanor and a ruthless expression on her face as she positions herself directly in the middle of the four of us.

I know people expected it. I could tell she was already making a name for herself. But just how natural it feels, how she fits right into the lockstep, like our missing puzzle piece —*that* was unexpected on my part.

Our little lamb.

I find myself distracted most of the morning, zoning out and thinking about Medford, about how pliable she was in my arms. How I was ready to make her *feel something good,* how I wanted to fuck her senseless to get rid of the death permeating the surrounding air.

I walk into the locker room and change into my gym clothes, running my hands through my hair and grabbing a towel. It's sprint day, and though I love running, today I don't feel like withholding myself from Briar for fifty minutes while Coach screams at me. He seems to push me and ride me harder than the other students. Maybe because he knows I have a future in track.

Briar walks over to where the students are all grouped together, waiting for the coach to instruct them. I shield my face from the sun, wanting to be inside of her, and only her. He tells us to run sprints—100 meters, grouped by last name. I smile, knowing that means Briar will probably be with me. I saunter up to her as the first group begins.

"Remember to warm up," I instruct her, bouncing and running in place. Her hair is pulled back into a tight ponytail, and I like seeing her face bare of makeup like this.

She mimics me, jumping up and down as we jog in place together. As her tits bounce, my cock swells in my shorts.

"Want to race?" she says playfully, tilting her head.

Fuck me.

"You're going to lose," I chide, grinning.

"We'll see," she responds, furrowing her brows as we walk up to our place on the start lines. I was right—it's Briar, me, and two other guys.

"And if I win?" I ask, bending over and getting ready for Coach's whistle.

Her eyes drift down to my shorts, and her eyebrows shoot up as she bites her lower lip and looks back up at me.

"Remember to warm up," she purrs, her voice low so that no one else can hear her.

My cock hardens, and I groan as Coach's whistle sounds.

I'm too distracted—and my dick doesn't allow me to move as quickly as I know I can. Briar sprints past me, and I push myself to catch up. The problem with 100 meters is that you don't have very long to redeem yourself, unless you want to work two, three, or even ten times harder to overpower the others.

She finishes just before I do.

"Fuck," I whisper, smiling.

She whoops her fist in the air, and then she walks up to me, her face flushed. "I won."

"Yeah, no shit," I mutter, adjusting my cock. "You had an unfair advantage."

She grins before flicking her eyes down to my shorts. "Did I?"

And then she walks away.

The rest of the class goes slower than molasses. By the time Coach dismisses us, I'm sweaty, rock hard, and fidgety. I try to calm down for a few minutes, waiting until the other guys are done showering, so they don't see my hard on while I rinse off.

When the shower room is finally empty, I strip and grab a towel, wrapping it around my waist as I walk to the small, tiled room with four showerheads.

"I'd give it a nine," a voice sounds from behind me just as I let the first drops of hot water run down my body.

I'd know that low, light timber anywhere. I glance over my shoulder, smiling, and see Briar standing at the other end of the shower room.

Naked.

38

BRIAR

It was advantageous of me to even attempt to beat Ledger at the sprint. But did I expect to beat him? Absolutely not. And I couldn't help but sneak into the boy's locker room to see if he was still there—and he was.

Alone, naked, and *mine*.

I admire the way the water runs down his tanned, naked body. His back is to me, and his ass is chiseled and firm, with little dips on the top of his hips that accentuate his muscular back. I don't think he has an ounce of fat on him. Just muscles wrapped in thick, black ink. It runs down his arms, forming two half-sleeves, and inward onto his back and chest. His hair is slicked back and wet, and he grins at me with that perfectly straight, white smile as he finishes rinsing his body off. When he turns around, my mouth goes dry. His cock is already hard, tilted upward and thick against his stomach.

"Are you coming in here, or do I have to throw you over my shoulder and drag you in?"

There's no doubt that he could—he is tall, nearly a foot taller than me, and his muscle mass alone makes him twice my size. I slowly walk over, and his eyes rake over my body once—twice. His eyes narrow as he turns to face me fully.

"Aren't you the little daredevil," he purrs, and as he reaches out for me, I drop to my knees. "Well, well, well," he adds, smirking.

"Shut up," I counter, and then I take his length and stroke it with my hand. He moans, unconsciously thrusting into my hand as water runs down his body. I smile up at him. "Out of all the things that happened to me since being here, you stealing my clothes was the most mortifying. Maybe that's why I made you wait—why you're the last one I'm going to fuck."

He chuckles. "I was just teasing you," he replies, and before he can say anything else, I open my mouth and take him in as deep as I can. "Holy shit," Ledger growls, his voice hoarse as I work my lips along his veiny shaft, allowing his thick head to hit the back of my throat with every thrust.

I use one hand to stroke him and the other to play with his balls. Sweating from the steam, I moan as his dick twitches, and he grabs my wet hair and forces himself deeper. I gag but I don't show it.

"Deeper," he grunts, panting. "You look so fucking good sucking my cock, little lamb."

I moan into him, quickening my pace and taking him as deep as physically possible. My eyes water, but the notion of nearly swallowing him whole makes me wet. I take the hand on his balls and move it between my legs, circling my clit with two fingers as I work him, squeezing my eyes shut.

"I want to come all over your tits," he murmurs, groaning as he squeezes my hair. "I'm getting close. I've been thinking of your tight, little pussy all week long."

I moan and quicken the pace on myself. Sparks fly down

my limbs, and wetness drips down my legs as I listen to him breathe fast and loud. My core tightens as my climax begins to build, and just as I'm about to come, he cries out.

"Fuck, I'm going to come so soon," he hisses.

I look up at him through my wet lashes, and his cock hardens further. He's so close to exploding in my mouth. Which is why the next thing I do is so fun. I pull off quickly and stand, wiping my mouth before I cross my arms. "I lied. You're like a six."

If I could bottle up the startled expression on his pretty face, I would. I just smile and turn to walk away.

"You think I'm going to let you walk away after that?" he growls, and before I can brace myself, he's behind me, his wet, hot body against my back and dragging me back to the shower.

I'm laughing as he drops down to his knees and pulls my hips to his mouth roughly.

"You sure you don't want to run away screaming?" he murmurs, referencing the night at Medford. His chin is on my stomach, and my heart leaps into my throat. He grips my bare ass with his rough fingers.

"No," I whisper, fisting his hair and pulling his head back a little. "But like I said before, you don't scare me."

He hums in satisfaction before bending down and *feasting.* Because that's what he does—he flicks his tongue between my slit, devouring me. And holy fuck. I'd forgotten about the tongue ring until now. It knocks against my clit, causing my hips to buck and my legs to quake from the intensity. I cry out loudly as the warm metal slides against my nub, and his tongue tries to swallow me whole.

"God, you taste like fucking honey," he growls, inserting two fingers as he slides back and forth against my clit forcefully.

"Oh, fuck!" I cry, throwing my head back as my knees

wobble. I grip the shower control—something to hold on to —and fiery sparks begin to go off in my core and run down my arms and legs. My hair is matted to my face, the stream of the shower making his hands slip and slide between my legs. I look up for just a second, and I still, my heart leaping into my throat.

Hunter is leaning against the shower room entrance, watching with dark amusement. His lips quirk up in the corners when he sees me notice him, and he nods once. I look down at Ledger, but he doesn't notice his friend. As I look back up at Hunter, he just holds a finger in front of his mouth as he unbuckles his pants.

Holy shit.

I fist Ledger's hair harder, and he moans into me, causing the vibrations to roll through me. Hunter whips his cock out, stroking it quickly as he watches Ledger go down on me.

"Fuck," I whisper, my whole body tingling and on fire.

"Come for me, Briar," Ledger demands, thrusting his tongue against me. He pulls back for a second. "I need you to come for me now. The next class will be in here any minute."

He's right—though the shower room is separate from the main locker room, *anyone* could walk in and see us. Just like Hunter did.

My eyes snap to my stepbrother, and he has a serious, concentrated look on his face as he thrusts his hips into his hand rhythmically. I remember how he felt underneath me, how his face contorted ever so slightly as he came, as he let me ride him until I was full...

I fall over the edge quickly, my legs shaking as Ledger grabs both ass cheeks and dips his tongue ever so deeply. I groan and shatter on top of his face, watching Hunter as he sprays the floor with come, twitching as the last of it leaves his body. He winks and zips his pants up before turning to go.

Ledger slaps my ass, standing and kissing me intensely on the lips. Pulling away, he smiles.

"Get to class, little lamb," he murmurs, handing me a towel and pushing me away gently.

I wrap myself up and he does the same, but it barely disguises the hard erection poking through the thin material.

"You don't want to..." I look around.

He laughs and runs a hand through his wet hair. "Despite what my friends might consider a good shag, I know better, and your time is coming," he adds, his eyes hooded as he bends down and gives me a gentle kiss on the lips. "The first time I fuck you will not be in a school locker room."

I blush and grab my clothes as we exit the shower room. To my horror, several guys are standing around and talking before P.E. They go silent as Ledger and I walk through, and one of them looks particularly surprised, so I wink at him. He blushes, and I smile as Ledger leads me to the girls' locker room. Once we're about to go our separate ways, he tilts his head and dips his fingers in his mouth, walking backward. Slowly licking them, he grins.

"Like honey."

39

BRIAR

That night, after I spend three hours catching up on homework, I find my mom furiously scrubbing the kitchen sink. I wrap my arms around her. She pivots and pulls me into a tight hug, kissing my forehead.

"Everything's going to be okay, you know that, right?"

I nod, suddenly *so* exhausted.

It's been *go, go, go* since my first day at Ravenwood. I haven't had a chance to process or even catch my breath. The drama is high, and the sex is... tiring.

I sigh as she brushes a strand of hair out of my face. As I open my mouth to say something, I realize up close that she's not wearing makeup. She doesn't necessarily wear a lot, but she has an everyday look that consists of mascara and blush, at least. She hardly ever starts her day without it.

"Are you okay?" I ask, pulling away.

Her eyes widen, and she puts a hand on her hip. "Of

course." She's in sweatpants and a loose T-shirt. She never stays this casual—usually only on Christmas, or if she's sick...

Something's going on.

"Are you sick?" I ask, crossing my arms. "The sleeping in, the soda, no makeup, *sweatpants*," I screech, laughing. "What's going on?"

I see it then—her giving in to whatever is ailing her. She looks *exhausted*. Running a hand through her hair, she sighs, giving me a small smile.

"I'm pregnant."

My vision tilts slightly, and I grab on to the counter. "What?"

"I found out the week before we moved. I didn't say anything, because I wanted to give you time to settle in, but..." She puts a hand over her mouth. "I am having the *worst* morning sickness, and it's getting to be impossible to hide," she confesses.

I laugh and pull her into a hug, making sure I'm gentle. "This is amazing news! I'm going to have a brother or a sister?"

She nods, and then she starts to cry. "I'm sorry, I'm just an emotional mess," she sobs, wiping her cheeks. "You and Hunter are going to have a little brother or sister."

Her words bolt through me, and I frown.

Oh, fuck.

The thought of sharing a sibling with Hunter—despite us not sharing blood—somehow makes what we're doing so much worse. I hug my mom again, squeezing my eyes shut. I think of earlier, in the shower room—watching him stroke himself, making eye contact as Ledger devoured me—and I suddenly feel so guilty.

"This is really exciting," I manage to say. "Can I help with anything?" I shoo her away from the sink. "You shouldn't be using all of these chemicals," I chide, shaking my head at the bleach she's using the scour the porcelain sink.

She laughs. "I cleaned with you, and you turned out fine, hon."

Did I?

"Andrew knows, right?" I ask, putting the gloves on and rinsing off the white foam.

"Yep. We weren't trying, but I guess life's funny like that."

It sure is.

We chat for a few more minutes before she excuses herself to go take a nap. *Pregnant.* My mom is pregnant, and that baby will be related to both Hunter and me. Before, we had no blood connection, so we could justify what we were doing. But now? We'll be tethered together by a sibling forever. And if things don't work out with him...

I finish cleaning the kitchen, and then I pull my phone out of my hoodie pocket. I want to tell my friends, but instead, I shoot a quick text to Sonya. She doesn't respond, and I chew on the inside of my cheek as I draft a text to Scarlett and Jack. I didn't see them at school the second half of yesterday, and they made themselves scarce today. A pang of guilt rolls through me when I think of them, how they took me under their wings on my very first day without question. And what did I do? Make a fool of myself? I know I wasn't identified on camera at Medford, but the rumor is already out.

They know I was there because they know I left the party with them.

I delete the long text I have drafted, instead dialing Scarlett's number. She picks up on the fourth ring.

"I almost didn't pick up," she mumbles.

I smile. "Thank you for changing your mind."

"What do you want, Briar?"

"I just want to apologize," I answer, chewing on a hangnail. "I didn't mean for you guys to find out the way you did, and I know how stupid it was to vandalize Medford Asylum. I just... got caught up in the moment, I guess."

She's quiet for a few seconds, and then she sighs. "They have questionable morals. And truthfully, I feel like they're taking advantage of you. Like maybe you have Stockholm Syndrome."

I try not to snort. "Scarlett, it's not like that at all, I promise. I think their reputation precedes them." I pause. "Something... terrible happened to me in California. They've been nothing but helpful since finding out. They talk the talk, but they're mostly harmless."

"Yeah, well, Micah said the exact same thing."

Goosebumps rise on my skin, making the hairs stand up on my arms. "His situation was different," I mutter.

"Was it? Because I'm trying to find the differences and I can't. Except you now have four guys sharing you... Mind you, I am all for polyamory, but you really think they won't fight to the death for you? If you're going to be in a relationship with multiple guys, at least make sure they're decent human beings."

I swallow. "No, they're not like that. I promise. The situation with Micah was—"

"Whatever, Briar. Honestly, I just need a few days to cool down. I really like you. I don't want to lose you as a friend. But it's hard watching a friend go down this path, with seemingly no care in the world. I did it once, and I won't do it again."

And then she hangs up, leaving me to feel like the most worthless pile of shit ever.

Hunter doesn't come home until after midnight, just as I'm climbing into bed. He knocks on my door gently, and I smile as he walks in.

His eyes rove over my body, scantily clad in my new silk pajamas, and he leans against the door frame. He's in jogging pants and a sweatshirt.

"Out with the guys?" I ask, fluffing my pillow.

He shakes his head. "I went on a run."

I smirk. "All night?"

He stares at me. "Yes. I had a lot on my mind. Cam, Medford, you, our new sibling..." He sighs. So, Andrew told him about the baby... "I can't seem to let you go, Briar. You're infiltrating every aspect of my life. And now our parents are having a baby, and that ties us together forever."

I cross my arms. "Does that scare you?"

He watches me for a beat before walking in, shutting the door behind him. My pulse quickens as he makes his way over to my bed.

"No, it doesn't scare me," he murmurs, sitting down next to me. "I'm not afraid of having you in my life forever. I'm afraid of losing you." I swallow as he moves closer. "Lie down," he commands, nudging his jaw toward the bed.

"Are you going to tuck me in?" I tease, climbing underneath the covers.

His expression is dead serious as he answers, "Yes."

And then he does—wrapping the thick duvet around me, kissing me on the lips for a split second, and then turning the light out. Walking to the door, he pauses.

"Goodnight, Briar."

I smile into the duvet. "Goodnight, Hunter."

40

SAMSON

There's nothing I hate more than waiting in line at the grocery store. The food sitting in my basket, the ice cream thawing, the meat warming up... Frankly, it's disgusting. So, as I wait behind a burly man in a hat, his cart full to the brim, I sigh.

Of course this would be my luck.

I crane my neck and look for another available cashier, but the one in my lane seems to be the only one.

Awesome.

I pull my phone out and fidget on social media. I shoot a quick text to Briar, since she's coming over for dinner later. That's why I'm here. My parents have been out of town at a doctor's conference, so I have the house—and Briar—to myself.

I accidentally drop the pack of Skittles I'm holding, and it smacks against the linoleum loudly.

The man in front of me turns and smiles, reaching down and picking them up.

"Here," he whispers, handing me the red bag and winking.

I don't—can't—say thank you.

It registers slowly at first because I can't think of how I know him. Then, the recognition slams into me—I must be dreaming. *Cam.* I stared at his mugshot for far too long not to recognize him. I will my face into neutrality, giving him a small smile before he turns back around.

There's only one reason he's here—and all that food is not for a quick trip across the county.

He's here—and it looks like he's here to stay.

I mutter an excuse about feeling sick, abandoning my cart completely as I exit the store.

❧ 41 ❧

BRIAR

I pace around the basement as Samson wrings his hands together.

"He was just... buying food?" I ask for the millionth time.

My mom and Andrew don't know yet. They're at some sort of private ultrasound place, and I don't want to ruin their exciting day. They have the future to look forward to—a new baby, a new life, a new city...

And yet, my past is haunting me as we speak.

"He's obviously here because of you," Samson says, checking his phone for the hundredth time. He called the guys right after he told me in person. They're on their way. "I should've killed him, right then and there," Samson mutters, leaning back and shaking his head.

"That would be murder," I joke.

He leans forward and watches me through his glasses, his eyes twinkling. "I think you should do it."

I still. "Do what? Kill him?"

Before he can answer, I hear a stampede on the stairs, and a second later, Hunter, Ash, and Ledger are all before me.

Waiting.

"So, what's the plan?" Hunter asks, sitting down in front of me. "As much as I want to kill him, I think we should notify the police. Soon, before he runs."

I shrug. Ash and Ledger sit next to him, and they're all watching me.

"If he's here, he obviously doesn't want me to know right away," I start. "That gives me an advantage." I swallow. "I don't think he's going to run. He's not here by some coincidence."

Ash sneers. "I think you should kill him. Gut him from end to end."

"Jesus," Ledger says, laughing. "Calm down, Hannibal Lecter." He turns to face me. "What if we fuck with him a bit first?"

Samson tilts his head. "I don't hate that idea, either. You could trick him. Lure him into a trap, and then you'd be five grand richer."

"I'd rather not go near him in any way," I respond, my body rejecting the idea of ever getting that physically close to Cam again.

"Briar," Hunter murmurs, standing behind me. "What do *you* want to do?" he mutters, brushing the hair off my neck before kissing me there. I think of the house in the preserve —of Medford.

Of that itch to get revenge.

I shiver as his lips caress my skin. Ash stands next and stops right in front of me. "Let us help you," he murmurs, dropping to his knees.

I gasp as he licks the bare skin between my shorts and shirt.

Ledger walks over and stands next to Ash, running his

hands through my hair before trailing a calloused thumb along my jaw.

Samson is last—taking his time as he stands on the other side of Ash. He brings his lips down to my ear. "I think we all want to see you mess with him—see you show him just how strong you are, despite what the motherfucker did to you."

I begin to tremble uncontrollably, and I'm not sure if it's because they're all here, all touching me somehow, or if it's the thought—the fear—of possibly seeing Cam again.

"Our brave, little lamb," Hunter adds. "He thinks he can get away with ambushing you," he growls, and the others chime in. "But he has no idea how formidable you really are."

Me.

I'm *formidable*.

But that's how they think—that's how they treat me. Like I'm strong, like I can do this, like I'm something to be revered.

Like a Queen.

I throw my head back as hands work my body, and after a few seconds, I'm not sure who is who, but my body is on fire.

No.

I can't get carried away.

My eyes snap open. "We have to make a plan. A smart one. Something he won't see coming."

It makes me sick that Cam is here. Whatever ulterior motive he has can't be good.

"Briar," Hunter purrs from behind me. "Just tell us what to do."

My eyes flutter closed briefly as Ash's tongue flicks against the skin on my stomach.

"Help me," I whisper. "I can't do it alone."

"Yes, you can," Samson whispers, his breath on my neck. "You can do it alone. But you don't have to."

I pull my lower lip into my mouth, humming. They are

here. They are going to help me. I feel my chest constrict at the thought—at how they started as my worst nightmare but will ultimately be my saving grace. My worst enemies will become my biggest support system. But that means I am indebted to them.

"I owe you," I say, my voice uneven. "All of you."

Ash stands, reaching into his pocket for something. I still when I see it's a knife.

"An oath," he murmurs, slicing his palm. "To protect you."

"Jesus," Hunter mutters. "What the fuck, man?"

Ash grins. "Blood for blood," he muses.

Hunter, Ledger, and Samson all hold their hands out reluctantly, and Ash slices their flesh a little too easily for my liking. Then, he turns to me.

"You are ours. Body and soul. Whenever we want you, *however* we want you."

My throat goes dry. "And you are mine," I purr.

I hold my hand out, palm up, and he cuts me. I grit my teeth as the blood pools, and then I shake each of their hands.

Making a deal with the devil is one thing.

But making a deal with four?

I smile.

What the hell have I gotten myself into?

❧　II　❧

RUTHLESS QUEEN

PROLOGUE

The knife slices through the zucchini with ease, and I accidentally nick the tip of my left index finger.

"Shit," I whisper, setting the knife down and sucking on the cut. After pulling it out, the blood pools on my skin in a thick droplet, and I reach over for a paper towel. Just as I tear a piece off, a warm hand settles on my back.

"I'm fine," I tell Cam, shaking my finger. "Just a tiny cut." I twist around and look up at him, holding it up. "See?"

His face is oddly serious—his eyes narrowed.

"What?" I ask, turning back to dinner, but his other hand grips my wrist and tugs me into his body. I gasp. "What are you—"

"Shh," he whispers, his other hand reaching under my dress to caress my thigh.

Pure ice skims along the nape of my neck, and shivers claw down my spine, one vertebra at a time. My legs tremble as his hand does little circles on my skin, and then he sniffs my hair.

"Cam?" I ask, choking out a sob. His hand moves between my legs. I try to push him away, but he's so much stronger than me. "What—what are you doing?"

"I said be quiet," he snaps, bending down. His breath—hot and smelling of beer—churns my stomach. I tamp down the bile rising in my throat. "You think I don't know you wore this dress for me, pretty girl?"

I swallow, shaking. It's just a simple sundress—one I wear often.

I'm seventeen.

And you're dating my mom.

"No," I whisper, shaking my head vehemently. "No, I thought—"

"You want me," he growls, moving my underwear to the side. I stiffen when I hear him unzip his pants. "Be a good little girl and bend over."

I begin to cry. "No. Stop, please," I beg, squeezing my eyes closed as he turns me around and shoves me against the counter. I try to resist, but he has me pinned beneath him, his front to my back. The stone cuts into my stomach, and then I feel him push into me.

"Ow," I cry, tears leaking down my cheeks. "Please, stop."

You were supposed to be my friend. All these months, and you were supposed to be my friend. None of my mom's other boyfriends did this—and none of our interactions ever gave me any idea of what was to come.

Of what's happening now.

A monster—he's a monster.

"Don't be stupid, pretty girl," he rasps.

I try twisting out of his grip, but he has both hands behind my back, and his large body has me pinned underneath him. I scream, but his hand comes to my mouth.

I try biting him, but his other hand slaps my face. His breathing quickens, and my stomach roils with nausea.

"You have such a tight, little pussy," he says, his voice menacing and cruel.

How can this be the same guy who taught me how to drive? How can this be the guy everyone loves, the one who wins good Samaritan awards, who everyone respects? Is it because he's been drinking? Is he on drugs?

"Cam," I cry, my voice breaking as I sob. "Why are you doing this?"

"You want me. You've always wanted me. You think I haven't noticed the way you wear those tight, little outfits around me? Always asking me if I want a beer? Inviting me over the minute your mom goes out of town?"

No. He has it all wrong. None of that was for him. And as for tonight, *he* asked what I was doing. I had no idea.

I thought we were friends.

I was trying to imagine what it would be like to have a father figure in my life—someone to protect me, someone to watch out for me, to eat dinner and watch a movie with me.

I scream again, and this time, he shoves my face into the counter. I feel blood trickling out of my nose as I try to move out of his grip.

He grunts, panting, and I know he's almost finished. I look to my right, at the kitchen knife lying on its side. I just need one free hand, one second to grab the handle...

"I'm coming," he whispers, and the revulsion powers through me.

I hate him.

For ruining his relationship with my mom—with me.

For *raping* me.

For reading everything all wrong, for assuming a teenager would be attracted to someone almost forty.

I grind my teeth as he finishes, and then a loud, shrill ring pierces through the air.

His phone.

He loosens his grip on my arms ever so slightly—enough for me to twist around and grab the knife off the counter, and suddenly the knife is an inch from his neck.

He gives me a cruel smile and slaps my hand away. It almost works.

Almost.

I bring my hand up again and plunge it into the side of his neck.

His eyes widen, and he screams as blood spurts out of his body. The ringing phone stops suddenly. Moving his hand to the injury, he stumbles backwards.

But it's too much blood.

He sways, looking at me with a stunned expression.

I fall back against the counter, the knife clattering to the ground as Cam drops to his knees.

His eyes pin me in place, a look of hatred on his face as they flutter closed and he falls over. The blood is beginning to seep through his T-shirt, forming a small pool beneath his body...

I killed him.

I killed him.

I killed him.

With the sliver of dignity that I have left, I pick up my phone and dial 9-1-1. I could leave him here to rot, but I'm not a monster like him. That would be too easy. When the operator answers, I quickly tell her that a man has been stabbed, and that he's losing a lot of blood.

Maybe he doesn't deserve it.

Maybe I should leave him to die.

Frowning, I step over his body, my legs still shaky and wobbly.

I open the sliding door to the back patio, opening the gate and weaving through the parking lot, to the edge of the forest.

I don't know where I'm going.

I just know I need to run.

42

BRIAR

Pretty girl...

I gasp as I sit up, the darkness of my bedroom surrounding me. Cam's voice is still ringing in my ears as I look around, my heart thumping against my chest heavily.

Still breathless, I close my eyes and place my hand on my neck, willing myself to get control of my breathing. The sheets are twisted around my body, so it takes a second to untangle myself. I throw my legs over the side of the bed and lean forward, resting my elbows on my bare thighs, breathing in deeply, exhaling slowly...

My throat feels like sandpaper—I need water.

I exit my room, padding down the stairs to the kitchen. Opening a cupboard, I pull a glass out and fill it up at the sink, which is quicker than using the fancy spout we have on the island sink.

Gulping deeply, I finish the glass and refill it, drinking that one, too.

It's been two weeks since Samson spotted Cam in the grocery store—two weeks since my stepbrother and his three friends became my biggest protectors.

Two weeks since we decided not to tell anyone he was in Greythorn.

Closing my eyes, I set the glass on the counter.

These two weeks feel like an eternity. I haven't had a restful night of sleep since before everything happened.

It's not a coincidence that he's here, but the fact that I have no idea what he's planning? It's terrifying, and those morbid thoughts keep me up most nights.

And we haven't been able to track him down.

He could be *anywhere*.

I walk back to my room, closing the door. When I turn around, I scream.

Someone is sitting in the chair, hidden in the shadows.

Waiting.

43

Hunter

"Sorry, didn't mean to scare you," I mutter, standing. "I heard you go downstairs, and I couldn't sleep."

She takes a deep breath, her hand coming up to her neck as she shakes her head.

"Fuck. I thought you were—"

"Briar." My voice is hard. "He can't get to you here." What I don't say is that this place is a fortress. After my dad found out about Cam escaping from San Quentin, he had more cameras installed outside the house, and a 24/7 security guard that roams the front of the house. No one is getting in here. We made sure of that.

"I don't trust him," she breaths. "He was a cop. He might know how to get around the alarm—"

"Briar," I mutter, walking over to her. She looks up at me, her grey eyes visible in the light of the window. There's a full moon tonight, and I know that has something to do with how spooked she is lately—especially given that Greythorn is in full-blown Halloween mode.

"He'll kill me," she whispers. "I know that's why he's here."

"Briar," I repeat, my voice soothing as I pull her into a tight hug. She relaxes instantly, exhaling loudly as I rub her back. "There's no point in worrying about this right now. You need to sleep."

I remember her first day at Ravenwood Academy—how her face had shown true fear when I grabbed her wrist. But this? This is different. This is her worst nightmare come alive, and I don't know what else I can do to reassure her, to make her feel safe.

Trying to find Cam—trying to hang around the store where Samson noticed him, asking around, keeping an eye out in town, stalking the local hotel, wandering around in hopes of running into him—has all led to nothing. Samson recounted his story a hundred times, trying desperately to hone in on any clues, but nothing ever came to fruition. We hit dead ends at every turn.

He'd seemingly disappeared overnight.

I know it bothers Briar that she has no idea if he went back to California, or if he's just biding his time and making plans. We don't know when or how he'll make himself known. It gives him an unfair advantage, and I know Briar feels like a caged animal because of it.

"I won't let anyone touch you," I murmur, tugging her into me. God, she's so warm and soft. And she smells so fucking good.

She nuzzles her face into my chest, and I take a steadying breath.

"I know."

She has me—she has *us*. Four of us, sworn to protect her.

Her body sags sleepily against mine, and I help her into

bed, tucking the sheets around her body and then placing the thick duvet over her. She turns onto her side and curls into a ball, closing her eyes. All of this is getting to her—plus the fact that her friends aren't talking to her, and her mom is pregnant... It's a lot.

I sigh. "Cameron Young may think he's getting revenge on you, but we have the upper hand of knowing he's here. We can brace ourselves and plan to deploy our attack first," I murmur into her ear. "*We* have the control this time. And you have *all of us*."

"I just want it done already," she mumbles. "I want to move on."

"I know. It will be. Soon."

❧ 44 ❧

BRIAR

Scarlett and Jack walk right past me on the quad. Just as I'm about to call out to them, they disappear into the thick, grey fog, which settles over the entire campus at Ravenwood Academy. I watch as it slowly descends upon me, and as I turn around to walk back to the car, I suddenly can't breathe. I'm gasping for air, and one of my hands goes over my mouth as I try to outrun the heavy mist pressing down on my chest. Coughing, I look down at my hand, noticing the bright, red blood. As my pulse speeds up, I touch my neck and feel wetness. Thick blood is soaking my white button-up...

I scream, sitting up in bed. The early morning light is just beginning to peak through my curtains. Breathing heavily, I throw the covers off and stomp to the shower, turning it on and sitting on the toilet as I let it heat up.

I haven't had nightmares like this since I was a kid. Even when everything happened with Cam, I didn't have a single nightmare. I think knowing he had been arrested and couldn't get to me—couldn't seek revenge for what I did to him—was a comfort. As horrible as it all was, at least he was arrested and put in jail. At least he was contained, with security.

Or so I thought...

I step into the large, marble shower. Turning the brass fixture so that the water is scalding hot, I tilt my head back and get my hair wet, trying to dislodge the horror of my nightmare from my mind. I know I'm still processing everything—still coming to terms with Cam being in Greythorn. Even in sleep, I can't seem to find true peace.

Even in sleep, he haunts me.

And now he's here.

Waiting.

The thought sends shivers clawing down my spine, despite the warmth of the shower. I can't even call Sonya— and I really wish I could, because I need her more than ever right now—because I don't want anyone else to know that he's been spotted. Besides, she's only going to tell me it's an irrational fear—that just because he escaped prison on the other side of the country doesn't mean he's going to show up at my doorstep. *Oh, how wrong she would be.*

All the progress I've made these last nine months is falling to pieces, and the one person who helped me through my trauma can't even help me with this.

I wash and dry my hair, and then I get ready for the day. Zipping my skirt up, I pull on a pair of sheer black tights and step into my boots, the latter of which are against dress code.

Andrew, my stepfather and the headmaster of Ravenwood Academy, feels terrible about Cam escaping prison. He's not going to say anything, even if he did care. In the grand scheme of things, it's such a small matter.

I tuck my white button-up into my skirt and place my hair into a high ponytail before heading downstairs. I smile when I hear voices, and as I round the corner of the staircase, I see Hunter, Ash, Ledger, and Samson all sitting with my mom and Andrew in the formal dining room.

"Morning, sweetie," my mom chirps, despite the decaf she's now drinking. I don't know how Aubrey Monroe gave up caffeine. She is way more of a coffee fiend than I am, and that's saying a lot. I guess pregnancy really does change your priorities.

"Hi," I answer, walking past them to the kitchen to make myself a latte. Just as I pull the espresso off the shelf, a warm hand settles on my back.

"I'll get it," Hunter mumbles, smiling down at me. His eyes darken as he takes in my outfit, and his hand reaches up to my ponytail, yanking ever so gently. "I like this. A lot," he growls.

My knees buckle and I swallow, pulling away. "Thanks," I say, nodding to the coffee he's making me.

He does this every morning. I slept in yesterday, and I was sure he was gone when I woke up past eleven, but just as I stepped into the kitchen, I heard him sauntering over from the library where he'd been writing. It's like he has antennas attached to his head that alert him whenever I need coffee.

We don't talk as the espresso sputters out. He foams my milk, and I pull my lower lip into my mouth as I look up at him, and he glances down at me with a lopsided smile.

"You naughty girl," he whispers, smirking.

Pouring the milk into my mug, he adds a couple pumps of vanilla—just the way I like it. Stirring gently, he hands it to me. "Voila," he jokes, ushering me back to the formal dining room.

I take a seat next to Ledger, and he winks at me. "Good morning, Briar," he purrs, placing some eggs, toast with butter, and bacon on my plate. "Would you like some sausage?" he asks, his eyes twinkling at the double entendre.

I wasn't prepared for these boys—wasn't prepared for how they'd all look in their uniforms, how the white button-ups would make them seem older, somehow. How Ledger's tongue ring catches the morning light, and I remember how it felt between my legs. As I glance around the table, I have to think of something else as I cross my ankles together— something to tamp down the potent need for them. They each unravel me in a distinctive way, each offering me something different. Once again, I'm baffled as to why they want to protect me when Cam is not their problem.

"How'd you sleep, Briar?" Andrew asks, smiling and handing me the jam.

Terrible.

I want to tell him—and my mom—about Cam. That he's here. But I don't. I'm not even sure the authorities could get to him. Where would they even begin to look? If he drove here from California and used cash, like I suspect...he's untraceable. And since he used to be a cop, I have a feeling he did everything in his power to stay under the radar.

No, it's better if my mom and Andrew don't know.

"Very well, thank you," I answer politely.

I can feel all their eyes on me—and then a hand on my knee. I jerk my head to the left, and Ash's lips twitch as his calloused fingers circle my kneecap, causing me to clench my legs together.

"I'm just so glad you've found a wonderful group of friends," my mom adds, smirking. She *must* have some idea. She hasn't said anything, but then again, she's in bed at seven most nights because of the pregnancy fatigue. "How are Scarlett and Jack doing?"

My mom doesn't know that either, of course. How could I explain that they're not speaking to me because I slept with three of the Kings, and fooled around with the fourth?

"They're good. Busy," I lie.

She smiles and shifts her gaze to my left. "And you're finding your room here to be okay, Ash?"

He nods. "Yes, ma'am."

Oh, he's good.

I sometimes forget that Ash lives here now, that we've sort of taken him under our wing because his father is in jail for child abuse. He gives her a charming smile and takes a sip of his black coffee, his teeth straight and white, with a dimple in one cheek that sort of takes the edge off his harsh and brutal demeanor. It was like the universe decided one hot housemate wasn't enough—now I have two.

"Samson was just telling us that he got early admittance to MIT," Andrew says proudly, clapping Samson on the back. I swear I see his cheeks redden slightly at the attention.

"Yeah," Samson says slowly, shrugging. "I found out this weekend."

"That's amazing news," I exclaim, grinning.

"Ash and Ledger both got letters from Harvard and Yale as well," Andrew continues. "Early conditional acceptances," he adds, beaming. When I look at the two of them, neither of them seems very excited. I wonder if this is their dream, or the expectation of attending a school like Ravenwood? "Ravenwood Academy truly is the best preparatory school around." Looking at me, he smiles even broader. "You'll have no problem attending any school in Paris, Briar."

Nervous, excited butterflies bounce through me. "I'm very excited to begin the application process," I answer, sipping my coffee as I ignore the guilt working through me.

Everything happening with Cam really throws a wrench into their futures, doesn't it? I feel like I can't ask for their help without returning the favor somehow, even though returning the favor isn't or wasn't ever expected of me. But Hunter is well on his way to becoming America's next greatest writer, and now Samson, Ash, and Ledger have early acceptances to world renowned universities. They have futures to protect, reputations, money...

Them getting mixed up with me—and everything from my past—could jeopardize everything they've worked their whole lives toward.

"I think this move, aside being good for Briar's future, was good for many reasons," mom muses, giving me a knowing smile with one hand on her growing belly. "Also, Hunter was just talking about the annual camping trip coming up this weekend," she muses, looking at all of them. "Maybe you could take Briar this year."

No.

I swallow. Just what I need—alone, in the woods, with the four of them.

"I'm not really into camping—"

"Oh, come on," Ash pleads, gripping my knee tightly. "We have a big tent and an extra sleeping bag," he adds, his implication clear.

His hand slides from my knee up to my thigh to prove his point, but I brush it off and stand. "I need to get to school," I lie, grabbing my plate full of mostly uneaten food and heading to the kitchen. I feel someone behind me, and when I turn around, Samson is watching me with a frown. His arms are crossed, and he's leaning against the island. I'd almost forgotten he was here, too. He's always so quiet.

"You okay?" he asks, keeping his distance. "You hardly ate a thing."

"Yeah," I mumble, mimicking his stance and leaning against the sink. "I'm not that hungry. It's just...a lot. All of it. You guys, and Cam, and my mom, and Scarlett, and Jack..." I swallow, despite my constricting throat. "What if something happens to my mom? Or Hunter? Or Andrew?"

The thought has crossed my mind. If that night was any indication, Cam could be cruel and possessive, even though he knows how to hide it most of the time. And escaping prison just proved the fact that he has questionable morals. And now that my mom is pregnant...if he found out...

I'm worried something is going to swoop in and ruin this wonderful life we carved out for ourselves here—just when I'm beginning to call this place *home*.

Samson's jaw ticks as he takes a step toward me. "Cam is going to have to fight each of us to the death before he gets to you," he growls. "I should've talked to him when I saw him weeks ago," he adds with a hint of regret as he looks away. "I should've waited in my car, should've tried following him to see where he's staying..." He sighs, running a hand through his straight, dark brown hair.

"You were in shock," I answer, looking down at my boots. "I think we're all still in shock."

"We're going to find him, okay?"

I nod. "Okay."

Hopefully before he finds us.

A few minutes later, Hunter, Ash, and I climb into Hunter's car and head to school. We recently stopped driving separately, and they now wait for me every morning so that we can all drive together. It's sweet—and it makes me feel like a true part of their friend group. I smile as we pull up next to Ledger and Samson at school. Hopping out and throwing my backpack over my shoulder, I glance around quickly.

Everyone is watching us.

The attention I attract as one of *them* is startling. I don't really care about high school hierarchies or what any of the other students think. Knowing the Kings have my back makes the fact that Cam is wandering around Greythorn a little more tolerable, and it makes me feel...safe. Wanted.

Cherished. As I walk in with them, I try to give everyone we pass a warm smile, but they all avert their eyes.

I'm not a monster, and neither are the Kings, but I understand now how reputations start—how rumors unfold.

It's unfortunate, but I vow to show everyone that there's nothing to fear.

45

BRIAR

I'm trying not to fall asleep in my pre-calculus class when there's a knock at the door. A younger guy walks up to the teacher, a stack of papers in his hand. Once he drops them off, the teacher distributes them to every desk, and my heart sinks when I look down at what it is.

Vote for homecoming King and Queen!

There's a space for nominating both King and Queen, and my pen hovers over the spaces. I can feel eyes on the back of my neck, and Scarlett and Jack are both watching me with wide eyes from a few seats up. They haven't spoken to me at all, so I'm not surprised when they begin whispering and looking away.

"Alright, guys," the teacher drawls. He's an older man in his fifties, balding, and extremely monotone. "Let's get back to learning."

I look down at the paper again. It's not due until next Friday—and there's a drop box in the quad for people to insert their votes.

Someone laughs behind me. I turn around. A girl I don't know rolls her eyes.

"Don't think for a second that you or the Kings will win," she accuses snidely, gesturing to me. "It's usually one of the football players and his girlfriend. People actually *like* them."

My cheeks burn, but something fiery fills my chest. Some urge to prove to them that I'm not a monster, not someone to be feared or hated.

And neither are the guys—my *friends*.

Suddenly, I know what I have to do. Smiling, I fold my paper and put it in my backpack, and watch as others do the same. The dance is next Saturday—meaning I have exactly twelve days to get the entirety of the senior class to like me.

To like *us*.

They're going to vote for us, and we're going to win.

◈❦◈

At lunch, I sit with the guys in the middle of the quad. They've all purchased their gourmet lunch from the cafeteria, and I'm just about to go buy a sandwich and a cookie when Hunter sets a plate of food down for me.

"Eat," he commands.

I eye the delicious-looking, fire-roasted pizza that only a place like this would serve their students. "You bought me lunch?"

"Ash did," he murmurs.

I turn to face Ash. "Thank you."

"The line was really long." He shrugs. "I figured you wouldn't want to wait."

We eat as people make giant circles around us, ensuring they don't get too close. People aren't just scared of them— they *loathe* them. I know they've all done things to deserve

AMANDA RICHARDSON

that hate. To say they were completely innocent would be a lie, but I know now that these roles, these stereotypes they fall into were crafted without their consent. They fit the mold—the pigeonhole that someone, somewhere created.

It's so much easier to hate what you don't understand.

To outsiders, they're hard, unimpressed, cold. But I know them all to be warm, funny, and caring.

"I'm going to be homecoming queen," I state, smiling.

Samson clears his throat. "What do you mean? Don't you have to vote?"

I smirk. "Yes. But I'm on a mission to get people to like me." Hunter's lips twitch, and Ash and Ledger laugh. "What's so funny?" I ask.

Samson shakes his head. "Nothing. I just didn't think you'd care about something like that."

I shrug, looking around at everyone—everyone who is watching us, everyone with narrowed eyes and frowns on their faces. Everyone who hopes we *won't* win. People who are curious enough about us to attend the parties, whisper in the hallways... but would never admit to that curiosity.

"I don't. Not really. I just want to prove to everyone that you—that *we*—are not bad people. That maybe they might like us if they got to know us."

"Yeah, right," Ash huffs, biting into his sandwich.

"Not after Micah," Ledger adds, unsmiling.

"I don't think you get it," Hunter says slowly, frowning. "I appreciate the optimism. I really do. But these people would rather burn us alive than appoint one of us as homecoming King." His eyes rove over my body, hesitating on my bare thighs for a split second. "And now that you're one of us..."

He doesn't have to say it. I'd been ignoring the fact that everyone now hated me since I parked next to them that day a few weeks ago. It's easier to ignore it—to pretend that I'm not detested simply by being with them. But I can't ignore the shifting gazes, the wide berths while walking, the whispers and murmurs.

"I'm going to do it," I say, my voice loud and clear. "Which one of you will be my King?"

Hunter's eyes narrow slightly, and Ash shifts uncomfortably in his seated position on the step. Ledger swallows. I look at Samson.

"Please?" I beg.

He sighs. "Fine."

"He's the nicest one," Ash mumbles. "It makes the most sense."

Samson gives Ash a soft look that I don't have time to decipher, and I take Samson's hand in mine.

"Thank you." Smiling satisfactorily, I drop his hand and take a bite of my lunch. "So, are we all going to the dance together?" I ask.

"Yeah, but we don't stay past the ceremony," Ledger adds, tilting his head. "We usually host a party at my house instead, since my parents are out of town on the weekends."

I don't know what to say to that. Out of all our parents, Andrew is the most normal, and Samson's parents are nice, yet busy. Ash's dad is...well...incapacitated, and his mother is still locked away in a psychiatric hospital. It's then that I realize I know nothing about Ledger's family, except that he comes from old money and is related to the famous author, and that his parents are very religious.

"What do they do?" I ask, taking another bite of the gooey pizza.

His eyes twinkle as he gives me a mischievous smile. "They're inspirational speakers."

I cup my mouth with my hand, trying not to laugh, but he nods.

"Oh, you're serious?"

"Very. They took my great uncle's fame and used it to

their advantage. They're super religious and travel the country—sometimes the world—preaching about God and how most things are a sin."

I open and close my mouth. "I—wow."

He chuckles. "My older brother is a tattoo artist in Boston. And I'm...me. If that gives you any indication of how we turned out."

"Now the tattoos make complete sense."

He nods, chewing. "Yeah, they definitely didn't approve of those. Silas, my brother, started inking me when I was sixteen. At first, I did it to be rebellious, a big fuck-you to my zealot parents...but I actually really enjoy it now."

"His parents are nuts," Ash laughs, shoving Ledger's shoulder gently. "They won't even let me in the house."

I narrow my eyes. "Why?"

He winks at me and nudges his jaw toward Samson. "Both of us. Because we lie with men, and that's a sin."

My face falls. "Seriously? That's horrible."

"They're bigots," Ledger adds, "but we sure do have fun messing with them."

I laugh. "How so?"

Samson interjects. "I've had Out Magazine sent to the house for years. They keep canceling, but I keep sending it. Oh, and the hefty donations I've made in their name to various LGBTQ+ organizations. Imagine the horror when people find out New England's biggest bigots donate to the Human Rights Campaign and the Transgender Law Center." He smirks.

"That's amazing, and wickedly clever."

"Anyways, our homecoming party is always lit," Ledger muses.

Just as I'm about to ask about his brother, some freshman trips and falls, spilling his soda and spraying us. All four guys jump up, and Ash takes a menacing step forward.

"Watch where you're fucking going," he growls, and the kid scrambles up and runs away.

When he sits back down, I glare at him. "No wonder everyone's terrified of you guys," I say sharply. "If Samson and I are going to be King and Queen, you need to be nicer."

Hunter's jaw ticks as he watches me. "It's easier to keep them afraid of us. Other than you, we've only ever befriended one other person."

"You mean Micah?" I ask quietly.

The four of them go still. Hunter rubs his lips with his thumb and forefinger.

"Yes. With Micah. We decided then and there that we would continue the facade until graduation. Ash and Samson...if they weren't Kings... My father. Ash's father. Greythorn isn't as progressive as you might think. And Ledger's family..." He looks away, shaking his head. "If people weren't afraid of us, Briar, they would eat us alive. It happened once—one incident—and we almost lost our footing completely. It's just easier this way, like I said."

I look around—at the students who watch us, waiting— who look away the instant any of us make eye contact.

I swallow. "You're the most vulnerable, so you stay on the offensive," I murmur.

It all makes sense now.

Hunter nods. "None of us enjoy fucking with these kids," he starts, and then he looks at Ash. "Except maybe Ash," he jokes.

Ash punches him. "Shut the fuck up, man."

"Anyways, the point is, it kind of just happened after Micah, and we never questioned it. Yeah, maybe we play into it a bit. But we're just trying to survive. Like you. Like all of them."

I nod. "I get it. But I won't play along. I can't be an asshole just to hold up the silly status quo. And by this time next week, maybe we can change their minds about you. About *us*."

When I look at Samson, he's watching me with a mix of wariness and awe.

"I'll play nice," Ash concedes, standing.

"Me too," Ledger agrees from where he's seated.

Hunter cocks his head and gives me a lopsided smile. "Just tell me what to do, little lamb."

46

BRIAR

"No way," I mutter, glancing at the tent Ledger set up for us while I was helping Samson get dinner prepped.

"Oh, come on," he exclaims, throwing his hands out to the side. He looks like a tatted-up lumberjack in his flannel shirt and tan hiking boots. His blonde hair is haphazardly coiffed to one side, and his white teeth gleam in the late afternoon sun. "Don't knock it 'til you try it."

I twist my mouth to one side and cross my arms. "I don't sleep on the floor. Scientists and engineers invented beds for a reason."

He smirks and walks over to me. "How about we snuggle up together tonight? I'll make sure you're comfy..." He brushes his finger along my arm. I shiver at his touch.

"She gets her own room in the tent, dude," Hunter growls, walking past us. He's with Ash, and they have armfuls of wood.

"Did you just chop that?" I ask, impressed.

"You bet your ass we did," Ash replies, and I laugh.

"Okay, whatever. I don't care where I sleep, as long as I have some sort of cushion."

I walk off in search of Samson, ignoring whatever it is they're mumbling.

In hindsight, agreeing to an overnight camping trip with the guys was probably stupid. I mean, what did we expect would happen? My stomach clenches every time I think about what *could* happen—not just with one or two of them, but with *all* of them. There's no buffer here, no going home tonight, no hiding. We're here together, alone, out in the open. Whatever flame has been kindling between me and all of the guys is about to combust now that we're in a place like this together. I can feel it—the tension.

Nearly tripping over a large twig, I curse and cross my arms as I head toward the picnic tables. I don't hate camping, per se, but we just never went when I was growing up. My mom isn't exactly the rugged type. We took a lot of vacations to Disneyland and stayed in hotel rooms, and we went to Portland and Seattle a couple of times. Once, we went to Hawaii and sat by the pool for five days. To my thirteen-year-old self, that was the dream, and the extent of our vacationing.

But... I also needed this. The thought of getting away for a couple of nights sounded so appealing. Everything with Cam has been weighing on my shoulders, as well as getting everyone to like us before homecoming, Scarlett and Jack, my mom... I loved the idea of relaxing with all of them off the grid.

I swallow as I crunch through the foliage, spying Samson at the grill. I tuck my hands into my puffy vest, and he smiles at me as I walk up.

"Getting hungry?" he asks. I clear my throat. "Very. I never knew that watching you all set up our camp from my place in the lounge chair would be so exhausting," I joke, cocking my head.

He laughs. "Yeah, well, someone has to do it."

Why is it so much easier to talk to him than any of the others? Maybe not Hunter, but Ash and Ledger, certainly. It's always so primal with them—physical, lusty, heady. With Samson, it feels like I'm dating my best friend most of the time.

Except for the night in his pool, when he most certainly was not *a gentleman.*

He turns the camping grill off, turning to face me. "I feel like we made a mistake bringing you up here," he murmurs, his eyes darkening ever so slightly behind his glasses. My pulse quickens as he scowls at me.

"What do you mean?" I ask, but I already know.

"Because it's wild here, and it brings out the wild in us," he starts, looking around. "There's no one around, and you're here with four guys who want to screw you every second of every day," he adds, laughing as he takes a step forward.

"I think you're exaggerating," I retort, rolling my eyes.

"Every second," he whispers, reaching up brush a strand of hair off my cheek.

"Let's eat!" Ash calls from behind me.

I spin around, and the other three guys come stomping over, and we begin our feast. Devouring my cheeseburger, I go back for seconds. I wasn't lying when I said lounging around while they set up camp was tiring. I could use a nap right about now.

The sun begins to set behind the pine trees, and the air cools significantly. Now I understand why Hunter packed extra blankets, hats, and gloves. It's the first week of October, and fall has begun in New England. In Greythorn, that means everything is Halloween themed all month long.

There's no one around.

Samson's words cause the hairs on my arms to stand on end.

They'd been here before—this was *their* spot, a place they came every year for the last four years. It wasn't a camping ground, but instead, an unrestricted area about an hour west, deep inside the dense forest. I don't even have cell service. I glare at my phone, sitting on the table with four others, useless in this damned place.

I get up and walk to Hunter's car, grabbing a blanket. When I get back, Ledger is stoking a fire.

"S'mores?" he asks, winking.

I look down longingly at the grocery bag at his feet filled with treats, but the forest is starting to get loud. I remember hearing that wild animals come out to prowl at dusk, and just then, a twig snaps in the distance.

"I think I'm going to go to bed," I whine, glancing in the direction of the noise.

"It's not even six," Ledger grumbles. "I thought we could play a game."

I blow out a loud breath of air. "There are critters out there, and I'd rather be safe in my tent when they arrive here to eat us."

Hunter hides his laugh behind his hand, but the other three guys burst out laughing.

I hate them all.

"Nothing is going to eat you," Ash chides, gesturing for me to approach. When I do, he pulls me down into his lap and moves my hair away from my ear, whispering, "Except me."

Goosebumps erupt on my skin as Ledger passes around the coat hangers and marshmallows. Ash is surprisingly calm underneath me, his hand on the flesh of my hip, but otherwise, he's distracted and talking to Hunter.

Once we've all gorged ourselves on S'mores, the campsite

gets noisier with crickets chirping all around us. Ash pulls a blanket around us, and when I look up at the guys, they're all lit up from the fire.

"What about strip poker?" I suggest, and Hunter, Ledger, and Samson all look at me with dark, hooded eyes.

Hunter tilts his head, his hand propping his chin up as he leans back in his chair.

"Fuck, yeah."

47

BRIAR

Did I really just say that out loud?

Samson puts the fire out, and we all duck into the large, two-bedroom tent. I can't help but scold myself in my mind.

Way to sound desperate, Briar.

Someone must've placed a battery-powered lantern in here at some point because it's all lit up. There's one sleeping bag on a single air mattress in the smaller bedroom, and four sleeping bags are squished together in the other, larger room, which feels silly. I'm not exactly the virgin Mary.

We all sit in the large bedroom in a circle, leaving the opening unzipped a little for fresh air. Hunter walks to his backpack, pulling out a bottle of whiskey and a deck of cards. He passes the whiskey around, and we all take a sip. I cringe as it slides down my throat, burning. Wiping my mouth, I hand it to Samson on my left while Hunter holds the cards out.

"Okay, who knows how to play?" he asks.

"I do," I murmur. "Cam taught me." I look around, and Hunter is watching me with furrowed brows. Ash is sitting cross-legged, scowling. Ledger is playing with his tongue ring —something I wish he'd stop doing—and Samson is picking a piece of lint off his shoulder. "I guess he was good for one thing," I add, my stomach churning at the happy memory— now tainted with what Cam did to me.

"So, let's erase all memories of him then," Ledger offers, his voice low and deep. "Let's have some fucking fun tonight, because fuck him."

I swallow, looking between them all, and they all have determined expressions on their faces.

"Right. So for Texas Hold'em, we each get five cards," I say quickly, nodding to Hunter. He doles out our hands, and then I get into explaining the different types of hands—royal flush, straight flush, 4 of a kind, etc. "I think it'll be easiest if we play a straight five-card draw, so from our five cards, we can take turns exchanging one or more of them from the remaining deck." I look at Hunter, and then at each of the guys. "Ready?"

"Easy enough," Ash muses from across from me. "You start, little lamb."

This place brings out the wild in us.

I can feel all of them watching me, and the hairs on the back of my neck begin to tingle.

We take turns exchanging cards until we're all satisfied with our hands. We each lay down our cards. I have a straight flush, but Ledger has a royal flush.

"I win," he smirks, nodding to my jacket. "Strip."

My eyes snap to his, and something heated looks back at me. Something, not someone—almost like he's no longer human. Not my friend—but an animal. I pull my lower lip between my teeth as I remove my jacket, and Samson begins to reshuffle the cards for the next round.

"You guys have to strip, too," I command, glaring at Hunter, Ash, and Samson.

And they do.

The air turns then—and I'm suddenly so aware of that fact that all five of us are out here together. *Alone*. Teenage hormones raging, dirty thoughts racing...it's not like there's not a precedent. Aside from Ledger, I've slept with all of them. So why are my hands shaking? Don't I trust them? Is it just being with them together—or the uncertainty of what could happen? Up here, it almost feels like there are no rules.

We continue to play. I manage to win the next round, and as the guys take off another article of clothing, my senses awaken. I can smell the cologne Hunter uses, and the laundry detergent on Samson's shirt. The light, while bright, feels artificial, and I reach over to turn it down a couple of notches so that it's dimmer in here. I can feel the body heat radiating off each of them—and my own, as my chest flushes with color at Ash's lingering gaze. The clicking of the shuffling cards reverberates down my spine as Samson shuffles, his eyes never leaving mine. I end up losing my shirt, and then my pants, and I must actively keep my gaze on the floor of the tent, the plastic sticking to the backs of my bare thighs.

Hunter bought me a few new lingerie sets, including this one—a white, lace push-up bra that does wonders for my boobs, accompanied by a high-waisted, white thong.

"You wore *that* to camp?" Samson grits out, incredulous.

"I bought it for her," Hunter mumbles.

A twig snaps outside the tent, and the adrenaline that courses through me, the way my heart pounds against my ribs, just adds to the intensity of the game. The dim light exaggerates our shadows, so that each movement causes the light in the large tent to flicker. I swallow as the only sound I hear is an owl hooting, and the cards flicking against the fabric of the tent floor. Everyone is silent, and I dig my nails into my palms nervously. Each of them still watches me like a hawk—like they want to take turns devouring me whole.

I can't help but admit to myself that I want them to.

I want all of them.

Hunter and Ledger are down to underwear and socks. Samson is mostly clothed, and Ash has pants on. My eyes find his, and I swear I see something feral moving behind them.

This place brings out the wild in us.

By the time Hunter strips completely naked two rounds later, we've all had a few more sips of whiskey, and the air inside of here is stale, warm, and blistering with tension. My clit throbs, and my stomach keeps dipping with butterflies. I lose a bra, but I wrap my arms around myself.

Ledger gets naked next, and then Samson. I lose the next round, and I peel my thong off. I can hear Samson's shallow breathing from here. Ash concedes, and then he removes his pants.

I look down at the ground, unsure of what I'll find when I look up. Four hungry beasts? Will they be nervous? Will it be gentle or rough? How does this work?

"Come here," Ash commands, leaning forward. I suck in a breath of air as his large erection stands up straight, the thick head already wet with pre-cum. His shaft is veiny, dark, and it intimidates me. "I said, come here."

"Ash—"

"Whenever we want you. However we want you," he reminds me, his eyes dark. "You took an oath. You're ours."

Hunter scowls and clears his throat. "Dude, she doesn't have—"

"I want to," I squeak, sitting up straighter. They all stare at me, and I crawl on my hands and knees over to Ash.

Kneeling next to him, I smile. "How do you want me?"

48

ASH

I reach out and grab Briar gently by the hair, pulling her onto my lap so that she's facing me. Groaning, I kiss her and use my other hand to play with her taut, pink nipple. She opens her mouth with every twist, and tiny moans come out of her throat. I thrust my heavy cock into her slit, sliding it in and out, not penetrating her yet but needing friction.

God, she smells like fucking vanilla. Always. I can't fucking get enough.

I pull away and see Hunter moving down her neck and placing a kiss on her shoulder. Samson slides one hand around my torso, and he kisses my earlobe.

I nearly explode.

It's a lot of heavy breathing, skin brushing against skin, the scent of whiskey permeating the air. Ledger moves to Briar's other side, stroking his cock and rubbing it against her leg.

This is so fucking hot.

"Who wants her first?" I ask, smiling.

Her eyes widen, and I hope she knows I'm only half-joking.

"Let her pick," Hunter growls, staring at me.

"Ledger," she whispers, rubbing her pussy on my cock now. Her pupils are darkened, and her eyelids hooded. She climbs off me and gestures to him. "Lie down." Then she looks over at Hunter. "Get behind me."

She's nervous, but the two-word commands are purely her animalistic urges coming to light.

I'm fucking here for it.

I watch in what feels like slow motion as Ledger lies down, and she straddles him, his cock bouncing every time she brushes against it. Her pussy is gleaming. Hunter comes behind her and reaches around to her front, swirling his fingers against her clit. She bucks her hips and slides against Ledger, jerking him off with her pussy. He puts his hands over his face, and I notice his toes curling. Hunter's cock teases at her ass.

"Hey," Samson whispers, pulling me backwards onto his lap. I shudder. I forget how strong he is, how completely ruthless and powerful he is in bed. It's so different from the guy everyone knows him as—the guy in glasses who is smart as hell and the nicest one of us all.

"Do you have lube?" I whisper, grinding against him as I watch my three friends before us.

"In my backpack," Samson mutters. I crawl over and find it in the front pocket. My cock is wet with pre-cum as I move back toward him, and I see Briar watching us with a mirthful smile.

Fuck yes.

I look back at Samson, on my knees before him as I cup his erection. God, I love his piercing. He groans, the sound reverberating through the air. His breath is ragged, and his throat bobs as he swallows.

"Bend over," I demand. He gets on his hands and knees, and I lube my shaft generously, tossing it to Hunter. Samson strokes his cock slowly with one hand as I press my head against his opening. Gently, I nudge myself into his ass, and he hisses.

"Fuck," he mutters, his voice frayed. "Fuck."

It's hot and *so, so* tight. He clenches against me, and I groan.

"You feel so fucking good," I mutter, looking over at Briar. She's bent over Ledger now, and he's pressing into her. Hunter is poised to fuck her ass next.

With every slow thrust into him, Samson lets out a sharp breath.

"Harder," he rasps. "I want to feel all of you."

His knuckles are white as he fists the sleeping bag underneath us. We both look over at Briar, who's mouth is open as she takes Hunter *and* Ledger in fully.

"Fuck," I whisper, my cock hardening even more at the sight of my friends, of Briar being filled just like she was with Samson and me a few weeks ago.

I let out a few sharp breaths and quicken my pace. Hunter's hands are gripping Briar's ass firmly as he pounds into her, and his face is contorted into something feral and needy. He's massaging her clit and she moves into his hand, throwing her head back so that her long hair is trailing nearly down to her ass. Ledger meets each of Hunter's thrusts so that they're diving into her rhythmically.

Underneath me, Samson quickens his pace as he jerks himself off, moaning and meeting me with every thrust. My balls tighten, and I feel my climax getting close. My head falls back as I cry out, upping my tempo and squeezing his ass cheek.

"I forget how good it feels when you fuck me," Samson growls, his hand moving quickly along his length. "So fucking good," he whispers.

"I'm going to come," I rasp, my whole body tensing as pulses of pleasure begin to coil, ready to release in a fountain of come.

"Fill me, baby," he answers, his voice hoarse. The way he says it sends me over the edge, and I spill into his ass, filling it with every pulse of my cock.

My breathing is ragged and heavy, and I'm still twitching several seconds later. When I look up at Briar, she's watching us with a darkened expression. She turns to Samson.

"I want you to come in me when these two are done."

❦ 49 ❦

BRIAR

I never knew something like this was even...possible. It's beyond what I'd ever imagined. My elbows sting from the coarse blankets as Hunter pounds into my ass from behind, and Ledger moves underneath me, their shafts filling me. Like the time with Ash and Samson, I feel *so* full, stretched to the brim, feeling like any wrong movement could tear me in half. With that pain though...comes immense pleasure. A pleasure so deep, so visceral, that my whole body craves it— my whole body responds to it.

Watching Ash and Samson together is the hottest thing I've ever witnessed. Sparks of pleasure course through me, my legs shaking as Hunter grunts from behind me. He slaps my ass, and I cry out.

"Harder," I groan, and he slaps my ass cheek again. This time, the pain lingers, and it intensifies how full I feel with both inside me.

Ledger circles his hips underneath me, his cock hitting

the perfect spot inside me and his thumb pressing against my clit, having taken over for Hunter. I buck my hips, and everything everywhere feels like it's on fire. My body begins to quake, and something fiery hot and intense as fuck shoots through me. I feel a gush of liquid underneath me.

"Holy fuck, you're soaking me," Ledger mutters. His voice is broken, edged with something like disbelief and awe. "God, you're so fucking beautiful," he growls.

When I look down at him, his face is sweaty, his eyes vulnerable and open. I can't concentrate—I'm drifting between nearly unconscious and too conscious of what's happening. I'm no longer a person—just a body, just a large muscle waiting to unfurl.

I throw my head back and ride Ledger, gliding back and forth on top of him as Hunter meets my movements. I reach back for him, and he takes my hand, squeezing it firmly.

"Come for me," Ledger demands. "I want you to soak me again." His voice is serious, concentrated. He flicks my clit hard, and I nearly tell him to stop, but when he does it again, everything springs open, and I lose control of my body completely. Waves of undulating pleasure coarse through me, and I notice another gush of liquid as my hips buck uncontrollably. I can't speak, can't move, can't do anything until it's over. With my mouth open, I collapse on top of Ledger, gasping.

His hands cup my face as he continues to fuck me. "Has that ever happened to you before?"

I shake my head. "No. I didn't think it was possible."

"Do you want me to come inside of you?" he whispers, slowing down.

I nod. "Yes."

"I'm close," Hunter growls, slapping my ass again. "Let's come together."

And then they do. It's a mix of roaring, grunting, and

throbbing—I can feel both turn to steel inside me as they empty themselves, and I sit up and watch as Ledger pulses to completion, groaning. Hunter pulls out first, and this time, I anticipate the strange feeling of that happening. Ledger pulls out next, and I fall onto my back, squeezing my legs together. I twist my face to Samson and give him a small smile.

"You next."

Who the hell am I with these guys? I feel like the confident, sexually awakened version of myself that I always hoped to be.

Samson strokes his hard cock and hovers over me. "That was so fucking hot," he murmurs, kissing my jaw. "But I want you to come with me."

Before I can stop him, he moves down and presses his face into my pussy.

"But—they—"

"It's fucking delicious," he says, licking slowly.

"Dude," Ledger says, his voice weak. "I'm straight, but that's fucking sexy as hell."

Hunter sits back and watches us, a small smile playing on his lips. "I don't know if I'm straight anymore knowing you're eating my come. I'm already hard again."

Samson chuckles, and I start to laugh, but then Samson's tongue darts into me, and he inserts two fingers, curving them so they hit my G-spot. I arch my back and cry out as his tongue slides hungrily up and down my slit, tasting me —*feasting on me.*

I feel like my body is levitating, like the pleasure is too much, and I'm ascending into the sky. It's a religious experience, and I don't know how I'll ever be able to go back to one sexual partner. Not after this—not after having three of them at the same time.

"Oh god," I whisper, my voice fraying. My legs begin to shake again, and Samson curves his fingers even more, hitting some unknown nerve that sends me skyrocketing into an orgasm and soaking his hand.

"Good little lamb," he murmurs. "At least we know you're not faking it."

My body is still jerking as he removes his fingers and slams his cock into me, and the fullness, the steely, hard warmth of having him inside me...

As my legs tremble, I grip onto his hair and wrap my legs around his torso. He sits up slightly and takes one leg, moving it over his shoulder. The angle—oh god, the angle. It clips the end of my orgasm but ensures another one immediately—something about his piercing, I think, because it feels like seven fingers at once as I spray everywhere.

"Good girl," he murmurs, slamming into me. "I'm coming."

He convulses on top of me, and I turn to look at the other guys. Hunter is jerking his cock quickly, breathing heavily, and he walks over to me on his knees, spraying my tits with come.

"Fuck," he groans, bucking his hips. "You drive me fucking wild," he rasps.

My eyes flutter closed, but a second later, I open them as Ash does the same, spilling on my torso.

"Briar," he moans, shaking. "Fuck."

I crane my neck to see Ledger stroking his shaft, and he crawls to me, giving me a cocky smile before throwing his head back and releasing on top of where Samson and I are still joined.

A wave of exhaustion slams into me, and I hear the guys muttering something about how they need to clean me up. A few seconds later, I feel a cool wipe cleaning me, from top to bottom, followed by a towel drying. Someone kisses my forehead, but I can barely keep my eyes open.

"Briar, you need to use the restroom." *Hunter.* "I'll take you."

It's an ordeal, but once I dress and pee, he brings us back to the tent. Handing me a face wipe, I shake my head. He *does* force me to drink water, and again, they murmur quietly to each other. Ash flicks the light off, and we shuffle into the large bedroom.

I feel Hunter climb in behind me, and Ash curls up on my other side.

"I knew you wouldn't need that extra sleeping bag," Ash whispers, stroking my face. "My beautiful, little lamb."

"Night, Briar," Hunter whispers in my ear. I can't see Samson or Ledger, but I know they're close by.

I fall asleep to Ash's hand grazing my jaw and Hunter's fingers caressing my back.

Yeah, I could get used to this.

50

SAMSON

I'm up before anyone else, and the light outside is still a soft pink. Yawning, I throw a hat and jacket on, finding my jeans in the corner of the tent—along with the empty whiskey bottle and pack of cards splayed out haphazardly.

Last night wasn't a surprise, and it certainly didn't feel wrong in any way. We all know Briar likes all of us, and we all like her. I mean, *fuck*, Ash and I had slept together before, so even that wasn't anything new. But the experience of being there with my friends, of somehow sharing that intimate moment... Most people might feel strange after a night like last night, but I feel euphoric. We were already close. This just brought us closer.

I walk through the woods and take a piss, and when I'm done, I find a small stream and sit on a rock, watching the water move over the smooth stones. I pick at the moss on the flat surface, and the soft, velvety feel reminds me of Briar. A few weeks ago, she wasn't a part of our life at all, and now she's such a visceral part of our everyday existence.

It reminds me of something my parents told me once. There's a specific kind of gene in a person's body—babies, specifically, because they're constantly regenerating new cells —that stays dormant as they develop in the womb. That is, until something very specific happens—an event or incident, sometimes chalked up to something as minor as a mother's diet. When this gene comes alive, it can create a miracle...or cause devastation. Briar is the special gene in our group. Until her, we stayed dormant. But then she entered our lives, and it's like she changed our brain chemistry. The question is, will she create a miracle, or cause devastation?

A couple hours later, I walk back to the campsite, and this time, Ash is working the camping stove.

"Morning," he grumbles, handing me some instant coffee.

"Morning," I reply. "Thanks for the coffee."

"It's the least I could do," he mutters, smirking. "I should probably buy you dinner first next time."

I laugh. Ash confounds me sometimes. On the one hand, he's very supportive of the fact that I'm bi, and he's confessed a couple of times while drinking that he knows he's bi, too. But his upbringing really fucked him up because he's almost ashamed to admit it out loud. Like that would make it real, instead of keeping everything behind closed doors. I know he thinks it'll ruin his reputation at Ravenwood.

"Nah. You're good. I love coffee more than food."

Something passes over his face, and he gives me a small smile. I see it then—the validation he always seems to need.

"Last night was phenomenal," I add, holding my cup out.

He clinks his cup against mine. "Yeah, she was pretty hot."

I tilt my head. "I'm not just talking about Briar."

He looks away and swallows. "Yeah man. Hey, do you want to help me with breakfast?"

When he looks at me again, he's almost pleading. *He's not ready, and that's okay.* He'll admit it out loud—he'll come out—when he's ready.

And I'll support him every step of the way.

"I'd love to."

51

BRIAR

Everything hurts.

Whoever said sex isn't a workout obviously never had a gang bang with four guys.

I laugh to myself as I pull my clothes on, grabbing my boots, my jacket, and a hat before unzipping the tent. The air is so much cooler out here than it is in Greythorn, and I shiver as I make my way to where everyone is gathered, the smell of bacon and eggs cooking on the camping stove wafting through the air. I'm the last one to wake up, rightfully so, and when I sit down at the picnic table, I expect all the guys to go quiet, or to get awkward, but they don't.

Hunter hands me a cup of coffee, and Ledger sits next to me, handing me a banana.

"Eat," he commands, raising his eyebrows.

"Yes, father," I joke.

His eyes darken ever so slightly. "Don't say shit like that," he grumbles, leaning forward. "That kink could get very out of control for me."

I nearly choke on my coffee. "Good to know," I retort, chuckling.

And then it's business as usual—the same sort of camaraderie we normally have together. Joking, laughing, flirting...

As we eat our delicious breakfast—and by eat, I mean scarf like I haven't eaten in years—I look around at each of them.

I'm starting to fall for all of them in different ways, each having their own relationship and story with me. I swallow, suddenly *so* full. How will this all play out? I'm really beginning to care for them. Will I just continue dating all of them together? Will they eventually get jealous? What happens if we break up—one of us, or all of us? I'm reminded of Scarlett's words a few weeks ago on the phone.

You really think they won't fight to the death for you?

I wipe my hands on my jeans and sit back, studying each of them. Remembering last night, how my body—and now my heart—wants all of them equally. But there's four of them, and only one of me. I couldn't ever possibly choose.

Will they eventually *make* me choose? If things were to get serious with one or more of them? When it's no longer just about hot sex and fun?

I get ready for the day, using the makeshift shower Hunter rigged up on a tree. The water is ice cold, but at least I feel clean afterwards—especially after last night. I throw my damp hair into a ponytail and pull on leggings, a wool sweater, and a jacket. The weather really took a turn last night, switching to autumn officially. My nose is numb as I pull on my hiking boots. I'm shaking as I walk up to the fire, and warming my hands next to the hot flames is a welcome reprieve.

"Jeez, it's cold," I mutter, my teeth chattering. The guys

are already in jackets and boots, forgoing a shower since we don't have much water. They're all sitting in camping chairs.

"You're *so* from California," Samson teases.

"Do you even know what snow is?" Ledger adds, leaning back and smirking.

I swat the back of his head. "Shut up."

"We have more jackets in the car," Hunter offers. "If you're cold."

I shake my head. "No. I think I'll be fine." My voice isn't as convincing as I would like, so I change the subject. "What are we doing today?" Yesterday was spent driving up here and setting up camp, and it's only nine, so I know we have all day for adventuring.

The guys all share a look, and I swallow. "Do I even want to know?"

Hunter laughs. "So, there are these caves," he starts, looking at his friends. "Supposedly, it's where the Boston Baptist got started."

I look among all of them, racking my brain. "Who?"

Ledger snorts, but it sort of sounds like *oh, boy*. I narrow my eyes at Ash, who is looking away.

"Who is the Boston Baptist?" I hiss, my hands on my hips.

"A crazy, religious zealot," Ledger chimes in. "It's who inspired my parents to become the monsters they are today."

My lips thin. "And why would we go to his cave?"

Hunter's lopsided smile widens. "Because it's sick as fuck. And there's something we've always wanted to do there."

"Something? Your version of *something* is setting fires and vandalizing buildings."

"And? You in?" Ash asks, leaning forward in his folding chair.

I cross my arms. "Do I have a choice?"

A few minutes later, we're trekking through the wilderness, a backpack of food and water at the ready on each of our backs, as well as baby wipes if anyone needs the restroom. I start to warm up as the sun begins to poke through the tall pine trees. I tie my jacket around my waist and pocket my hat, and about an hour later, we come to the side of a small hill. Sure enough, there are rock formations and an entrance to what I can only assume is the cave.

"You guys have a depraved adventurous streak," I add, panting. None of them look like they even broke a sweat, but I am damp and breathing heavily just from walking. "The house in the hills, and then Medford Asylum—"

"It's not a depraved adventurous streak," Samson interrupts, his voice ripe with warning. I glance at Hunter, but he's looking away. Ash, too—they both have haunted looks on their faces. "The house in the woods is where they found Charlotte Ravenwood's body," he murmurs. "And Medford is...well...it was a giant 'fuck you' to Christopher Greythorn."

I swallow as I look between Ash and Hunter. "I'm sorry. I didn't mean—"

"We had a bucket list of things we wanted to do our senior year. Knowing that we could probably get away with most of it, we followed through. All of us have a past that haunts us, Briar. Even you." Samson just shakes his head, and I shift my weight from one hip to the other. "If you had an opportunity to get revenge, wouldn't you?"

They all take a step toward me, and I suddenly feel like an animal being hunted.

"Isn't that what we're doing with Cam?" I ask, my voice weak.

"Why do you think we wanted to help you?" Hunter muses, his brows furrowed. "This is our year, Briar. Our year to set things right. We don't want to go off to college—or wherever the fuck we decide to go next fall—and wonder if we did enough. We have an agenda." He looks back at the cave. "The question is, are you in?"

I look at the cave, and then at each of their faces. I have no idea what the cave represents, but knowing them, they have a reason for being here.

They're helping me.

The least I can do is return the favor.

"I'm in," I retort, scowling. "I thought the blood oath was a good indication of that." I walk past all of them and into the cave first.

I don't look back to see if they're following, because I know they are.

52

LEDGER

I shift my backpack and adjust the straps as we weave through the cavern. It's fucking cold in here without the strong sun beating down on us.

Briar pulls her jacket on. "Where are we headed?" she asks, looking around.

I swing my backpack around and hand everyone a flashlight. "Straight until it forks, then go left."

I hadn't spent months researching the Boston Baptist and the layout down here for nothing. We're all quiet as we head deeper into the cave. It becomes less of a bear cave, and more of an underground, natural-wonders type cave the farther we get and the lower we descend. I once read these caves snake through the underground of most of Western Massachusetts. No one has mapped the entire thing yet. It's just too large. I ignore the cold sweat along my brow when I think of accidentally getting lost down here.

When we get to the fork, I stop and set the backpack

down. Briar sits on a large rock and winces, still sore from last night. I can't help but smile as she rolls her eyes at me. I've had my fair share of experimental sexual encounters, including three and foursomes, but last night was incredible. I swear Briar blushes as she looks away.

My little lamb.

"So, are we just waiting to get murdered, or..." she trails off and looks around. "This place is creepy."

The cave is still low and narrow here, but I see an open cavern filled with a natural spring up ahead. That's where Samuel Kent, also known as the Boston Baptist, used to hang out with his followers. He had quite a few. I know because my parents were two of them.

I start pulling supplies out of the backpack, and Briar's eyes find mine as I get the Micro-Blaster set up.

"What's that?" she asks skeptically.

I smirk. "It's called a Micro-Blaster. Uses blank cartridges and black powder to blast through rocks and other hard things—safely." I look around. "I wanted to get dynamite, but no one sells it anymore, and I didn't want us caved in from the blast."

Ash takes a swig of water. "Pussy," he mutters, and we all laugh.

Hunter points to a spot on the wall. "See that?" he asks Briar, taking a step back. "That's the rock he used as an altar. They thought Jesus would descend from the sky to this very cave," he adds, practically growling. "This wall—this rock— was mecca." He looks at the wall with repugnance. "It's been worn down with time, but it's still a place of worship for some crazy ass people." The surface is smooth, almost like a large painting, smeared with age and dirt and minerals.

She's breathing heavily as she looks among all of us. "So, what? We're going to blast it with that thing?" She looks at me with wide eyes.

Samson swings his backpack off his back. "Would being caved in with the four of us really be so bad?" he jokes, pulling a drill out of his backpack and beginning to drill the holes into the surface of the rock.

She doesn't seem to find his joke funny, because she frowns and leans forward in her seated position. "I swear to god," she mutters. "You guys are fucking nuts."

"We didn't get our reputation for nothing," I chide, smiling. I hand Hunter the detonating device. "Back up," I warn, looking down at her. She scrambles up and takes a few steps back. "It's just going to crack down the middle. And then we're hauling the rock into the spring."

She shakes her head, and Hunter nods once as we all back up several feet. The explosion isn't as loud as I thought it would be, but the entire face of the rock falls off, as if some invisible force cracked it straight down the middle. The four of us squat down to pick it up, and we hurl it into the spring a few feet away. The splash is satisfying, and when we get back, I smile.

The face of the rock is gone—in its place is a jagged, inverted wall.

We leave a few minutes later. I grab Briar's hand and pull her behind me since it's dark in here. When we get outside, she turns around to face us.

"Well, that was sort of anticlimactic," she jokes. "The fire and the spray paint were like...exhilarating, and—"

"Samuel Kent molested my brother," I interrupt. I don't mean to be rude or angry, but it's something she should know. "When we were younger, before my parents' cut ties with Samuel, he was over one evening and stayed the night. Silas was ten. I was four. I barely remember it, and to my parents' credit, they severed ties with him immediately. It doesn't absolve them of their craziness, but they did do that one thing right."

She goes completely still. Her mouth falls open and her eyes widen. "Ledger, I—"

"Not everything has to be a big production," I add, crossing my arms. "Sometimes the smallest actions can have the biggest consequences. While today might've been more satisfying with dynamite or caving the whole fucking place in, what we did will have a ripple effect. Think of doing something like that to the Western Wall. It may seem like a small infarction, but the altar is tarnished now. It's not inaccessible. It's tainted. And quite frankly, I think that's worse."

Briar looks between Hunter and me, and Hunter takes a step toward her. "Those fuckers deserve what we did. For what they did to Silas."

She shifts uncomfortably. "I get it, trust me. I want the same for Cam."

"Exactly," Samson muses, placing his hands in his pockets. "Like I said earlier... if you had an opportunity to get revenge, wouldn't you?"

53

BRIAR

Luckily, the rest of the afternoon isn't nearly as heavy as the caves. We fish in the nearby lake, catching a large trout to eat for dinner, and then we drink beer and play another round of war—except this time, we keep our clothes on. When it's time to cook dinner, Hunter grills the fish and Samson cuts some potatoes and carrots, and we all drink a little too much, indulging in a little too much food, too much beer, too much...everything. By the time I inhale my S'more, I'm ready for sleep. Being in nature is exhausting.

I head to bed alone, and tonight, there don't seem to be any shenanigans—yet. I undress and climb into one of the sleeping bags, and just as I pull it up to my chin, Samson unzips the tent and begins to undress. Without a word, he crawls in behind me, clad only in his boxers. He takes his glasses off and snuggles up against my back. It feels so good. I'm so cold that my body is shaking. His hand slides against my stomach, the warmth spreading through my core, as his chest presses against my back.

"You're freezing," he murmurs, tugging me closer. I feel his legs wrap around mine, and I stop shivering instantly, his warmth seeping into me. I run my finger along his forearm, and he shudders. "Go to sleep, Briar," he growls.

I don't obey—obviously. Especially not when I feel his hard length against my ass. Heat floods me, and I arch my back into him slightly as he hisses.

"I said, go to sleep," he chides, but there's amusement in his voice.

"I can't with that thing poking me."

He chuckles, the sound low and deep. It reverberates through me.

"I can't help but remember how good it felt to be inside of you," he mutters, sliding his hand underneath my bra, his thumb and forefinger gently twisting my peaked nipple.

"Fuck," I whisper, grinding my ass against him.

"Stop doing that unless you want me to fuck you," he growls.

I stiffen. "Then fuck me." Before he can move, I climb on top of him, throwing the sleeping bag off and trying not to balk at the cold. He pulls his boxers down, a low sound in his throat as he does. I don't even ask before I move my underwear to the side and sit on his hard shaft, slowly letting his thick head press against my opening until he slides into the hilt. *Holy shit.* His piercing really does enhance everything.

"Why do you feel so fucking good?" he groans, watching us as I move up and then down again, slamming against him —hard. Slowly. He moans. "God, I just fucked you, and I already feel like I'm about to explode."

I whimper as I drive down on him again, the sound of our joining permeating the air. My nipples are hard and sensitive from the cold, which only enhances the feel of his large cock inside me. Throwing my head back, I move my hips back and forth, but then he stops me.

"Let me," he rasps, and before I can protest, he flips me onto my back in one swift movement, slamming into me.

"Oh, god," I cry as he moves both of my legs over his shoulder. He's so impossibly deep now—I can feel it nearly at my belly button as he drives into me.

A finger comes around and works my clit, using my wetness as lube. Feverishly, he swirls two fingers against me, *almost* too rough, but the calloused skin is exquisite. I cry out as he changes his angle slightly, leaning back, and that's when I nearly lose it underneath him.

"You like that?" he murmurs, his tongue in his cheek. When I look up at him, his hair is in front of his face, and his expression is wild.

Samson Hall has come undone.

"Your piercing," I gasp, my voice uneven. "It...it..." I lose my train of thought as my eyes squeeze shut. My body tightens with every stroke of his fingers, every thrust of his cock, waiting to release like a spring that's been coiled for far too long.

"Look at us," he commands, dropping my legs and looking at where we're joined. I wrap them around his body and look down, his cock gleaming as he slowly slides in and out. "Look at us," he repeats, his voice breaking on the last word. I clench around him, the first wave of my climax tipping me over the edge. "Briar," he rasps, stilling as his shaft hardens even more.

And then he roars, sending me spiraling. I moan as he pulses into me, and I honestly don't care if the guys hear us, or if a bear eats us. Right now, all I care about is the fact that I am soaking Samson, and he's baring his teeth as his body shudders on top of me. My release slides down my spine, so potent that I know the sleeping bag is going to be soaked.

"Fuck," he whispers, collapsing on top of me.

I cover my face and laugh. "I came in here to sleep."

He chuckles, lying down next to me. "Then let's clean up and go to sleep."

A few minutes later, he's back in his position behind me. My body is heavy, and I feel so...content. Safe. Warm.

"Goodnight, Briar," Samson whispers in my ear.

I drift off before I can even reply.

54

BRIAR

The next morning, we eat a quick breakfast before packing up camp and heading out. This time around, I actively try to help break down the tent and load the car, and Hunter laughs as he watches me try to fold the tent poles so that they fit in the bag. He eventually takes them from me and packs everything up seamlessly.

It was an honorable attempt on my part.

We took two cars here, and since I rode with Ash and Ledger on the way up, I decide to ride with Hunter on the way home. Samson decides to catch a ride with the others, seeing as they're all going back to his house. Before we start our drive, Hunter turns on his playlist, and I sit back against the luxurious leather as he drives us toward home.

"Camping isn't *so* bad," I muse, twirling my hair as I look out at the two-lane road ahead. Tall pine trees surround us, like the ones in town—except here, in true nature, they're about three times taller.

He chuckles. "I told you. I knew you'd enjoy it."

I look away so that he doesn't see me blush.

"We've been going every year since my mom died," he adds, rubbing his jaw.

I play with the hem of my sweater. "When did she…"

"Freshman year. I was fifteen." I wait for him to continue, but he just clenches his jaw and looks straight ahead.

"We don't have to talk about it," I say, my voice soft.

He shrugs. "It still hurts. All these years later. It still feels like someone's jamming a knife into me whenever someone says her name."

I swallow. "Then let's change the sub—"

"But I feel like if I don't talk about her, that I'll forget all the nuanced things about her, you know?"

I nod. "I know."

He sighs and shakes his head, the indie music playing softly in the background.

"She was murdered intentionally. Because of who she was. Because of who her family was."

"The Brahmins?" I ask, remembering our conversation all those weeks ago.

He nods. "That was her maiden name. The authorities tracked her murderer down—he was a nobody, just someone obsessed with her. He's in jail now, and they traced two more bodies to him, so in a way, her death brought those two women to justice, too."

I'm quiet as I take in the information. "I'm so sorry, Hunter."

"He dumped her body right in front of that house. The one you caught us burning."

I nod. Nothing ever came of that, despite my worry that the fire would jump. I saw a small article on Twitter calling it an act of arson, but it didn't go any further than that. Ash was right that night. They'd taken precautions, and the fire remained contained to the house.

If you had an opportunity to get revenge, wouldn't you?

"Anyways, search dogs found her a day after she went missing. He'd..." He inhales sharply. "He'd *butchered* her, Briar. She was unrecognizable."

I grip the edge of the arm rest. "You saw her?"

He nods. "I was out there looking for her. So was my dad. I didn't expect..."

God.

At fifteen. Seeing your mother's mangled body at fifteen. What did that do to his mental health? How has that affected him?

"She was my best friend. The kindest, most genuine person. Happy—like all the time." He laughs, and I can tell it helps to talk about her. "Aubrey reminds me of her, actually. So do you."

I bark out a laugh. "I'm certainly not *happy* all the time. But thank you."

He smiles. "I just mean, people want to be around you. I know you think you're so different from your mom, but you both have this energy that puts people at ease."

I look down, my throat constricting. My entire life, I always felt like the runt. My mom is a goddess in every way possible. A Pinterest mom through and through, who goes to bed early and gets up at five in the morning to exercise. Who makes healthy smoothies for breakfast. Who gets all her work done before two, so that she can volunteer in the NICU two afternoons a week. She has her shit together. On top of it all, I've always felt loved. *And* she became a mother so young... I am constantly in awe of her.

It's nice to know that perhaps other people see a little bit of her in me.

"Thank you for saying that."

"I think that's why my dad was drawn to her. And why I was drawn to you."

I swallow. "Your poor dad, too," I add, thinking of Andrew and what happened to his first wife.

"He took it pretty hard. We both did. I don't think we left the house for a month. But...then we did. And somehow, our relationship got better. We started traveling, and he encouraged me to see a psychiatrist, who helped with my depression."

That explains the Lexapro in his bathroom and the postcards on his wall.

"I'm glad you had each other," I mutter, looking at him. "I know the therapy life all too well. I'm glad he got you help."

He smiles, his wavy hair falling in his face before he brushes it back.

"Yeah. My dad is cool. He's pretty strict, despite what the other students think, and he rides my ass over the important things."

I smile. "I'm sure you give him a run for his money."

He laughs, shrugging. "I don't actually know if he knows exactly what me and the guys get up to. He says he does, but if he knew, he probably wouldn't let me leave the house."

I giggle. "He must have some sort of idea. Or perhaps he just picks his battles."

"What about you?" He turns to face me for a second. "Your father?"

I frown. "I don't know. When my mom told him she was pregnant their senior year of high school, he basically ghosted her. She never saw him again. But I do know he was a football player, and he went on to play for some college team in North Carolina," I add, shrugging. "Honestly, I'm glad I never knew him. My mom and I had an incredible relationship, and I'm not sure we would have had that if he were in the picture."

"What a piece of shit," he mumbles, brushing his lip with

his finger. "To get a woman pregnant, and then not have the courage to stick around?"

I look down. "Yeah, I mean, I guess he was scared—"

"Bullshit. Every father-to-be is scared, Briar. You both deserved better."

His words eat at me, and my eyes start watering. The way he always stands up for me—how he always defends me and ensures that I know my worth...

I reach over and take his hand. "Thank you."

We're quiet most of the way back to Greythorn. I don't notice anything is amiss until I glance at Hunter, and he's scowling into the rearview mirror.

"What's wrong?" I ask, looking behind us. There's a black SUV behind us.

He shakes his head. "I don't know... I swear this guy is following me."

Chills erupt on my body, and the hair behind my neck tingles. Glancing back again, I realize with dread that the glare from the sun prohibits me from seeing the driver.

"Turn left," I instruct, pointing to a residential street just outside the main square. I twist around, my heart sinking as the black car follows.

My pulse quickens. "Again." I point to the street coming up.

Sure enough, as soon as we turn, the black car follows.

Panic floods through me. Hunter reaches for my hand. "Hey. It's probably just a coincidence."

I swallow. "No. It could be—"

Hunter lets out a breathy laugh. "No. This car has been following us since we left the road of the campsite. How the hell would Cam know we were there?"

I look behind us as Hunter continues to drive. "Okay, I read once that if this happens, keep driving and then pull into a police station."

Hunter nods. "Yeah, that makes sense." He turns right, weaving through the neighborhood quickly, barely stopping at the stop sign. I look behind us.

"Briar. don't worry. I'll get us to the station."

I wipe my palms on my pants, my heart thundering against my ribs. My feet bounce nervously as Hunter pulls into the parking lot of the Greythorn Police Station.

We both look behind us as the black car slows and then stops completely.

"Oh my god," I whisper, ducking.

Suddenly, it speeds off, plowing through a stop sign and barely missing a guy jogging in the crosswalk.

"It was just some stupid idiot," Hunter says quietly.

"He stopped—" I shake my head. "There were no license plates—"

"Briar," he purrs, taking my hand. "It's okay. We're okay."

"What if it was Cam?" I ask, my voice strained.

Hunter frowns, reversing until we're back on the main road. "If it was Cam, there's nothing we can do other than keep an eye out for black SUVs."

I nod. "Yeah."

We head home in silence, and I make the excuse of having to unpack as I walk upstairs alone. Mom and Andrew are out, but I know they'll be back soon. I bite my lower lip as I pace around my room. Was he following us? Did he—did he see us the first night?

The thought slams through me.

The tent—we left it open that night, exposed to the darkness—

No.

I'm just being paranoid.

Don't be stupid, pretty girl.

Cam's words from that night nearly ten months ago cause goosebumps to erupt on my skin, and I stalk to my dresser, pulling out the only pieces of athletic clothing I own. I have to get out—I have to move—I feel like I'm going to crawl out of my skin here. I pull on the leggings and matching top. After slipping into running shoes I've never worn, I pull my hair up and grab my phone. This is laughable—but I need to do *something*. I can't imagine just sitting around and going over the way the car slowed, the way it sped off a few seconds later...

I take a quick jog around the perimeter of the park, keeping to public places in the broad daylight. The sweat sticks to my chest and back, my hair stuck to the back of my neck. It's hard, but it feels—*good*. My phone says I ran a little over a mile, and I'm happy with that. *Progress*.

I am considerably happier and lighter at dinner with my mom, Andrew, and Hunter. He must notice my improved disposition, because he keeps looking at me with a sidewards glance, as if trying to figure out what's different.

And the best part is, after collapsing into bed with pure, utter exhaustion, I don't have a single nightmare that night.

HUNTER

I slap my mid-semester report card on my dad's desk, smiling. "Happy?" I tease, gesturing to the line of A's.

He laughs, picking the slip of paper up and studying it. "Very nice, Hunter. I'm proud of you." I'm about to make some smartass retort when he continues. "I think having Aubrey and Briar here is helping, don't you?"

He doesn't have to say it—I know exactly what he means. The dynamic in our house was very masculine for so long. Thank God for house cleaners and personal chefs—we didn't know how to do a damn thing around here. It wasn't for lack of trying—it just felt different after my mom passed. I didn't realize until recently that it's nice having someone to make you smoothies, or check on you, or organize your sock drawer...

Or to fool around with in the basement.

"Yeah, I think it is."

He leans back in his black, leather chair, putting his hands behind his head. "And you and Briar seem to be getting along *very* well," he adds, his eyes flitting up to mine.

I swallow. "She's a nice girl."

Nice?

He watches me for a second too long, his eyes narrowing slightly. If he suspects anything is going on, he doesn't say it out loud.

Sighing, he nods. "I agree," he says slowly, smiling up at me. "Well, I'm very proud of you, son. I think we can agree that Jefferson High School is now officially off the table."

An excited thrill goes through me. I would've been fine there—I would've survived. But I'm really glad I won't have to leave Briar.

"Thanks, Dad. And about the *New Yorker*," I start, running a hand through my hair. "I think I want to apply to some creative writing programs in New York. Maybe a smaller liberal arts school or something."

I brace myself for his answer. We'd never really talked about my future at college. It was always just something I was definitely going to do. He went to Yale, and my mother went to Harvard, so I think he just assumed I'd pick an ivy league and go there.

Leaning forward, he looks up at me, a twinkle in his eyes. "I think you should do whatever the hell makes you the happiest, Hunter."

I swallow the lump in my throat as he stands, coming around the other side of the desk. He gives me a tight embrace.

For the first time since my mom died, it truly feels like we're going to be okay.

56

BRIAR

I sit in front of my computer and fix my hair, waiting for Sonya, my therapist in California, to log on to our video session. We'd agreed on today a long time ago—a month after moving—thinking it would be ideal to settle in first before continuing our sessions. I'm excited to update her on everything.

The screen flickers, and Sonya smiles—looking perfect, as always. Dark ringlets, deep set eyes, full lips—she is beautiful.

"Briar," she smiles. "It's so good to see your face."

I wave at the camera. "Hi!"

"You look really good," she offers, tilting her head. "Your hair is different."

I shrug. "I have my bangs pinned back so I can run later."

Her brown eyes widen. "I didn't know you were a runner!"

I laugh. "I'm not. I actually hate it. But it really helps with...you know..."

The great thing about Sonya is that she knows what

happened, but she never, ever brings it up. She always lets me introduce my trauma. Some weeks we don't even talk about it, and I think it's that camaraderie that allows me to trust her—to open up to her.

"I heard about what happened," she says glumly, referring to Cam escaping prison. "You seem to be handling it okay..."

I nod once. "Yeah, I'm trying."

"And your stepbrother is helping you feel safe?"

I swallow. "Yeah. I know it's wrong, but—"

"Briar," she interrupts. "Why do you feel like your relationship with Hunter is wrong?"

She knows everything—maybe not the explicit details, but she knows I'm sort of dating all four of them. That they've vowed to protect me.

"I don't know. Maybe because I don't want to disappoint my mom?"

It slips out before I can even process it. Sonya's lips thin. "I understand that, but don't you think she'd be delighted to know her daughter has found a group of men who not only respect her, but act as her guardian angels, in a sense?"

"I just don't want her to think our relationship will ruin the family dynamic if it doesn't work out. She already has so much on her plate—"

"Stop. Listen to what you're saying. *Her* plate. *Hers*. What about your plate? What if she doesn't care that her plate is full? What if that's just your assumption? Focus on *your* plate. Focus on balancing your life. That balance will seep into other aspects of your life, and your mother will notice. And I promise, all mothers just want to see their children happy."

I look down, my eyes stinging with tears. "You're right."

"Now, tell me about these guys."

I laugh, and once I fill her in about the camping trip—in which I leave out the gang bang—she places her hands together.

"I already see a difference in you, Briar. I think as long as you feel safe—as long as you implement our rules—evaluate your surroundings, listen to your gut, apply common sense—you will be okay. Love like this doesn't come to those who wait around. It comes to those brave enough to go after it."

"Love?" I ask, smiling.

"Briar, I hate to break it to you, but—"

Holding a hand up, I shake my head. "I like being with them. But it's not love. Not yet, anyway."

"I see. And your friends? The ones who are mad at you?"

I swallow. "They're still mad."

She softens her expression. "I think they'll come around soon. Just be honest with them."

We chat for another thirty minutes, and I update her on mom's pregnancy, the Homecoming Queen shenanigans, and everything else—but I leave out that Samson had run into Cam. I have a feeling she'd be obligated to notify the authorities, and I don't want to do that yet.

Saying goodbye, we schedule a session for every other week until things calm down, and I sign off the video call. I head downstairs and grab some chocolate, and to my delight, Hunter is in the basement watching some travel show. I plop down next to him, handing him a piece. He just smirks.

I focus on the show, realizing with excitement that it's about Paris.

"Have you ever been?" I ask, hoping I don't sound too desperate.

He nods. "Twice."

I perk up and twist to face him. "And? Did you love it? Did you eat croissants and drink cappuccinos, and walk along the Seine? *Je voudrais me promener le long de la rivière avec toi*," I add, and his eyebrows shoot up as he smiles.

God, I love the way his smile lights up his face.

"I knew you could speak French, but I didn't know you could speak it so well. What did you say?"

I tilt my head and pop a piece of chocolate into my mouth. "It roughly translates to; I would like to stroll along the river with you."

He tugs me onto his lap, brushing a piece of hair off my face. "Briar, why do you think I'm watching this show?"

I shake my head, confused. "Because you're obsessed with berets and baroque architecture?"

A smile plays at his lips. "So that when I come visit you, we can stroll along the river together," he whispers, running a finger down my jaw, sending sparks and excited shivers down my spine.

Love like this doesn't come to those who wait around. It comes to those brave enough to go after it.

🎋 57 🎋

ASH

My shoes bounce against the linoleum as I sit at the table in the visitor's room. I cross my arms and chew on the inside of my cheek. *This is so fucked.* Glancing around nervously, I look at everyone else here waiting to see a family member or friend. Are they as nervous as me?

I'm about to see my mother for the first time in five years.

When I got the call this morning, I was unsure of how it was even possible. For five years, we've had phone calls here and there, but never in-person visits. I couldn't do it—couldn't bring myself to be here. Of course my father never pushed it. He'd gotten his way, and she was here against her will.

Involuntary commitment—that's what everyone called it.

It's been five years—five years since I've seen her golden skin, dark hair, light blue eyes...

Swallowing, I lean forward and run my hands through my hair.

Now she's waiting to be released.

Released.

They say it could be as soon as this week.

And of course there will be an investigation.

My father is in custody, and he went on record saying he wrongfully committed her, called for her release, and the doctors agreed. Two doctors were incriminated for going along with it, as well. He'd paid them off, obviously. No reputable doctor would've kept her here this long. It's completely outrageous. It wouldn't have been ethical, or legal. It just goes to show the stronghold he has over this city.

At thirteen, it wasn't the first time I'd seen my dad, the mayor, exercise his power, his family name. But it was the last time I stood on his side. For five years, it has been a battle of the wills—of me standing up for myself in exchange for a black eye.

Once, a broken arm.

I always wonder if people knew, or if they honest to God had no idea what he did to me—to us. I have to believe it's the latter. I can't fathom the idea of people looking the other way, but then again, Greythorn isn't exactly the mecca of honest, decent people. Luckily, the recent vandalization of Medford Asylum seemed to have gotten enough attention that everything is coming to light now—that enough people are beginning to ask questions, place calls, write articles...

My dad's confession cemented it.

And even though it tore me up inside to get here, even though I'm not sure what kind of person will be waiting for me, I'm here.

I don't think I've ever been this nervous about anything.

The main door swings open, and a guard lets a woman through.

A woman—my *mother*.

Some kind of warmth washes over me at the sight of her —and then my throat constricts. I stand abruptly, shaking.

My mother.

She's exactly the same as I remember—long, dark hair. Large, blue eyes. Berry pink lips. Thinner than before, and perhaps a bit older, too, but still beautiful.

Her eyes—I expected empty, vacant eyes. But they brighten when she sees me, when she takes me in, and they trail down my body once.

A boy. I was just a boy when she came here. And now?

Her cerulean irises flick back up to mine, tears welling as she smiles.

"Ash," she whispers, holding a hand out. "You're so big," she adds, her voice catching.

Her voice—the same, low, soothing voice I remember as a kid.

My mother was my best friend. My fortress against my father. My safeguard. She tried to get away a couple of times, but he always managed to drag her—*us*—back. He knew how to play her, how to perfect his words just so. And then she got pregnant, and my father...

My father lost it.

I know now that it was not his child, and to this day, I still don't know whose baby it was. As a teenager, I understood enough of the situation, and for a long time, I was angry at her. For having an affair, for getting pregnant, and then for not being strong enough to endure the hormonal shifts after the miscarriage. My father was keen to fuel my anger. The brainwashing, the gaslighting, turning me against her... it wasn't until recently that I realized how wrong he was.

How wrong I was...

How naive...

I close my eyes, thinking of Samson briefly. Of his mental

health struggles, of how he overcame them. I think of Micah and how he wasn't so lucky...

I open my eyes and walk to my mother. Without a word, she pulls me into a tight hug, and we both collapse into a fit of sobs. I clutch the material of her hospital shirt—fisting it tightly as my chest cleaves open.

There is so much she doesn't know—so much she wasn't there for.

My cowardice did this—my fear of seeing her changed. A fear that was unfounded, obviously. My mother kept herself sane here, kept her spirit alive somehow. For *five* years.

When we pull apart and wipe our faces, she smiles and touches my face.

Love. There is only love in her eyes.

"I'm sorry it took me so long," I mutter, blinking a few times and sniffing. "I wanted to come earlier, but—"

"Sweetie," she says, her voice soothing and calm. "You don't need to explain yourself." She pulls me into another hug, and I smile against her, against the smell of lilacs and lavender—a smell I'd forgotten until this very moment.

I can't remember the last time I felt this...happy.

Somehow, seeing her has given me a taste of reassurance— like everything will somehow be okay.

It will all be okay. If she could endure five years in isolation, away from me? I can do anything.

"I'm sure you have so much to tell me," she says, her voice upbeat.

How does she do it? Is she putting on a brave face? I can't even fathom the strength it must take if so. And then I think, of course she's putting on a brave face.

And the thought is so admirable, so...potent with love... I hug her again.

This time, I don't let go for a very, very long time.

BRIAR

I spend all week tirelessly introducing myself to the other students at Ravenwood. Samson comes with me, and together we attempt to appeal to the masses. The first day, I buy a bunch of cookies and hand them out. People are reluctant, of course, but soon, I get a small smile from a few people. The next day, I joke with a group of seniors about our pre-calculus teacher, and I swear I see a flicker of surprise on their faces. As we walk away, Samson squeezes my hand.

"Look at you," he muses, smiling. "A true Queen, through and through."

The third day—Wednesday—I notice several people placing their votes in the ballot box. Swallowing, I decide to make flyers after school. Ledger—who is a very talented artist, it turns out—helps me create a fun campaign slogan. *Give Me The Crown, And Together We'll Rule—Give Me The Crown, And I Won't Let Your Down. Vote Briar Monroe and Samson Hall for Homecoming Royalty!*

Ledger draws an ornate crown, and then a caricature of Samson and I that has us all howling with laughter.

But it works—because on Thursday, people are stopping to read the flyers I've placed all around the ballot boxes. I even see a few people changing their votes last minute. Only when Scarlett and Jack walk by do I second guess myself. Especially when they don't make eye contact with me.

My mom helps me bake cookies that night, and Hunter helps me decorate them. We have way too much fun, and after my mom goes to bed, he hoists me up onto the kitchen counter, screwing me senselessly—and quietly, so we don't wake our parents.

By Friday, I feel confident as I distribute the cookies with Samson, and together we make alliances with the jocks, the drama kids, the math club... People begin to wave at us, and somehow, even just for the week, the energy is different. I have to hope it's permanent—that the homecoming ceremony is just the start of people opening up to the idea of befriending the Kings.

And when I leave campus on Friday afternoon, my arm looped with Samson's, we both seem to exhale as we walk with the guys to our cars.

"Think it'll work?" he asks me, smirking.

I shrug. "I hope so."

If nothing else, this campaign was a welcome distraction, because I've hardly thought about Cam all week.

❦ 59 ❧

BRIAR

I pull the gown over my head, the white, beaded material clinging to every curve. Looking in the mirror, I swallow the lump in my throat when I remember the last time I got dressed up for something, and how I got to spend time with Scarlett and Jack. Now, it's just me—with no one to help get me ready. Because of that, I've opted for minimal makeup—just filling in my brows, adding a bit of shimmering bronzer, and a nude lipstick. I reach down and step into the silver, strappy sandals, admiring the dress and the beautiful, soft material. It's 1920s inspired, with a V-neck and a slight flare at my knees—but form-fitting everywhere else. The back is loose and hanging, leaving my back bare nearly down to my ass. My hair is simple, mostly because my mom helped me pull it into a braided crown.

"Fit for a queen," she'd said.

She'd been so excited to find out I was vying for Homecoming Queen—thanks to Andrew telling her, obviously—

because that was once her title, too. And since I was never into sports or cheerleading or anything she loved as a teenager, it made her happy to see me follow in her footsteps.

I grab my black clutch and head out of my room, closing my door behind me. I hear people downstairs, and I know the guys are all here to take me to school. In California, homecoming dances were a casual affair compared to prom. But the guys told me this would be akin to a wedding, so to dress accordingly. As I descend the stairs, everyone quiets, and my mom walks up to me, brushing a strand of hair off my face.

"You look beautiful, hon," she says, her voice fraught with emotion.

"Thanks, Mom," I say, giving her a half smile.

When I look over her shoulder, my breathing hitches as my eyes land on Hunter's. He's in a dark green dress shirt and dark grey slacks, with a black leather belt and matching boots. His leather jacket hangs over one of his arms. Ash is next to him, in a black shirt with the sleeves rolled up, and black pants. He's wearing high-top red Converse. My eyes flit to Ledger, who is in a light pink shirt and navy pants. He's also wearing Converse, but his are bright pink. I glance at Samson, and he's wearing a white shirt, black pants and dress shoes, and his tie...

Smiling, I walk up to him and reach out for his tie. It's white with the same beads as my dress.

"How did you know?" I ask, smirking.

He smiles down at me, and my heart nearly skips a beat. "I asked Hunter to do some reconnaissance for me so that we could match."

My throat constricts, but I tamp down the emotions as I turn to face the others.

"You look great, Briar," Hunter says, and then my mom's camera flash goes off.

"Sorry," she mutters, fidgeting with it. "Hunter and Briar —can I get a picture of you two first? Maybe for the mantle?"

Oh, god.

I pull my lips to one side and try not to laugh as Hunter and I stand awkwardly next to each other. His fingers barely brush mine, sending sparks flying up my arm. My nipples harden beneath the thin fabric of my dress, and I bite my lower lip as Mom takes a few different pictures from different angles. Andrew is already at homecoming, and my mom is heading over later, if she feels better—her words, not mine.

"Thank you," she says, giving us both a knowing smile. "You make a beautiful couple."

My breathing stills, and before she can say more, Ledger interrupts us.

"Okay, the bus is here. We should go."

I smile at him gratefully, and Ash walks me out the front door, his hand on my lower back. "You look positively edible tonight, Briar," he purrs, a hand moving down my exposed back.

The feel of his warm, calloused fingertips on my sensitive skin sends shivers down my limbs, and I crane my neck to look up at him. "Thank you, Ash."

We climb into the party bus, and I have to laugh when I see a disco ball and flashing lights inside. As I find a seat, Hunter approaches with two champagne glasses and hands me one, and we click glasses before taking a large sip of the bubbly, sweet liquid. The other guys take seats in the back.

The bus begins to move, and loud pop music sounds in the speakers. "Who booked this thing anyways?" I snort. "And how did you manage champagne?"

He grins and takes another sip of champagne. "We paid the driver a lot of money not to ask about the champagne bottles we provided."

Ah. That explains it.

I shrug. "I've never been to a dance before. We had them in California, but they never interested me."

"So there was no losing your virginity at prom?" he murmurs, a feline smile on his beautiful lips.

I shake my head. "No, more like joints and blankets and bonfires on the beach."

He laughs. "That sounds fun, too."

"I can't imagine anyone from Ravenwood actually enjoying the public school system," I retort. Hunter's face falls slightly, and I remember something Jack told me on my first day. "Your dad almost sent you to one, didn't he?"

He's quiet for a second, and then he looks out the window. "Last year, after Micah... After he died, my father started to get very sensitive about my reputation. For a good reason. I certainly pushed his buttons more than I should've. And one day, after he found out about me skipping class, he threatened to kick me out and send me to Jefferson High. Anyways, we've since worked through it. I can't wait to graduate, to get the fuck out of this town and see what the world has to offer."

"And write the next Great American Novel," I joke, brushing my shoulder against his.

He smiles, and I swear I see the faintest hint of a blush on his cheeks. "Perhaps."

As the bus pulls into the Ravenwood parking lot, my pulse speeds up. Climbing out, I let Samson take my arm as we walk through the gate toward the gymnasium.

"You ready?" he asks, giving me a feline smile.

I shrug and shake my head. "No. You?"

He sighs. "Same."

The cluster of people hanging out near the entrance parts down the middle as we walk up, and most of them stop talking as we walk into the gym. A few of them wave at Samson and me.

That must be a good sign.

I tighten my grip on my clutch, and my anxiety causes my nerves to fly every which way.

I spot Scarlett and Jack sitting with some juniors I don't know, and when I smile at them, they give me a small, sad smile back before turning around. I ignore the ache in my chest. I wish I could talk to them—I wish they understood.

The five of us claim a table up front, and Samson and I sit down as we look around. Hunter, Ash, and Ledger all murmur something about getting drinks and food, and Samson takes my hand and kisses it once—gently.

"Relax," he purrs. "It's a dance, and everyone is here to watch their Queen."

I roll my eyes. "A title I have not earned yet," I remind him, and we both laugh.

"Perhaps. But they'd be stupid not to see you for what you are." Looking around, he pulls a flask out from his coat pocket. "Want some liquid courage?"

I grin. "You read my mind."

When the guys return, we pour vodka into the punch, and it's not a terrible way to spend the night. After a few minutes, I feel much lighter and happier, and the impending crowning ceremony feels a lot more doable now. The guys even manage to get me onto the dance floor, and to my delight, a few students laugh at us as we flail about. Laugh—not scowl. Like maybe they don't completely hate us after all. Just as a new song starts, Darian—the guy who befriended me at Ash's party a few weeks ago—taps the microphone.

"All right, Ravenwood Academy! It's that time of the night where we announce our King and Queen." I look up at him, holding my breath. Samson takes my hand and squeezes it once.

One chance to blast apart the reputation of the Kings. One chance to show everyone that they're not brutes. The only question is, did my efforts pay off? I don't even care about winning—the crown is futile. But it would be evidence that perhaps the tides are turning.

Darian takes his place at the podium and clears his throat.

"It was really close this year, but I'm happy to announce our newest homecoming King and Queen. Please give it up for Samson Hall and Briar Monroe!"

My stomach bottoms out with relief, and I grin. There's a polite applause, and Samson takes my hand and laces his fingers with mine, squeezing me once. There's some upbeat music playing, and when I look out into the crowd, I notice that no one seems pissed off that we've been crowned. A few people clap again as we walk up, and I give them appreciative smiles.

Darian gives both of us a quick hug, and then he places two plastic crowns on our heads as we face the crowd. I feel Samson pull a sash over my head, and several people take pictures with their phones. I swallow the nerves threating to come up as bile, and my hands shake as I wave to the general student body. The shock of winning prohibits me from truly celebrating, but holy crap, we did it!

"We did it, little lamb," Samson whispers into my ear. It must look very intimate because a few people whoop.

It's hard to see with the lights shining down on us, and I hold a hand over my eyes as I smile. I look for Scarlett and Jack, but I don't see them. Maybe they'll realize that we're not so awful now—maybe they'll see that enough people voted for us, and perhaps the reputations the Kings have is old news. I continue looking for them. *We did it. Samson and I —we did it! My hard work paid off, and perhaps now we can begin dismantling the hierarchy at Ravenwood Academy.*

My eyes flit to someone leaning against the back wall, and—

No.

My blood freezes in my veins, and I suddenly can't breathe. I let out a faint gasp, reaching for Samson and squeezing his hand.

Cam.

Squinting, I watch as Cam smiles at me—dressed in a suit so that he fits in—and then he turns around and goes through one of the doors in the gym.

"Briar," Samson says, his voice concerned. "What's wrong?" The class president is talking into the microphone, and then he holds it out to me. I don't have a chance to tell Samson as I wrap my clammy hands around the black metal.

"Thank you so much, everyone," I say, clearing my throat. *He ruined this—I had so much to say to everyone, and he ruined it.* "I hope you all have a wonderful night."

There are a few snickers as I pass the mic to Samson, and he watches me with concern. I widen my eyes and gesture for him to hurry.

"Thanks, everyone!" A large group of girls in back screams, fanning themselves as they clap excitedly.

Okay, well that's new.

As the class president escorts us off the stage, I grab ahold of Samson's arm and squeeze. When we're out of earshot, he turns to me.

"What's wrong?"

My voice is shaking as I tell him. "Cam is here. He went through the back door. But he's h-here, Samson," I stammer.

How did he get through security? How did no one recognize him?

Before I can say more, he takes my hand and stalks to our table. The other guys must know something is amiss because they all jump up.

"Cam's here," Samson growls.

"He went through the back door," I explain, pointing toward the back. "Like thirty seconds ago."

Ash is the first one to bolt, and Hunter and Ledger follow.

The three of them jog to the door, and Samson turns back to me, squeezing my hand.

"You should stay—"

"Absolutely fucking not," I cry, letting go of his hand and dropping my arms to my side.

I see the resignation on his face as he nods—the surrender. "All right. Let's go get him."

60

SAMSON

Our feet slap against the linoleum of the hallway, the darkness overwhelming as we slow our pace, quieting. The only thing I hear now is our ragged breathing. Ledger and Ash check each classroom, throwing the doors open, one after the other, until we get to the end of the hallway. Hunter is hiding Briar behind him, and I almost laugh at the ridiculousness. He's gone. Why would he stick around? If someone saw him, if someone recognized him...

He'd gone back to wherever he came from—whatever shithole lair he'd been living in.

I curl my fists so hard that my nails dig into my palms.

"Let's check the parking lot," Briar says, pointing to the quad—and the parking lot beyond it.

I nod. "Yeah. Good idea."

We open the door and wander into the quad. Out of the corner of my eye, I see Hunter throw his leather jacket over Briar. An arm around her shoulder, he holds her close to him as we quickly walk to the parking lot. There are a few cars here, and some of the party buses and limos are waiting around, clustered together as if in commiseration. But I don't see anything that would indicate Cam or the car he used to get here.

I sigh and run a hand through my hair. Why did I run? I should've followed him that day in the store. If I had, we wouldn't be here now. Instead of enjoying homecoming, we're worried, on edge...and scared.

Ash sighs and sits on the curb, and Ledger and I sit on either side of him. Briar and Hunter sit on the asphalt—Briar in Hunter's lap—as we all stare out into the dark night, quiet.

Briar speaks first. "I'm not crazy. I saw him—"

"I know," I growl. "Now I don't feel so crazy. I've been going over that day in my head, and I've been questioning myself for weeks now—trying to figure out if I actually saw him, or if it was all in my head."

Her throat bobs as she nods. "You're not crazy."

"I still think we should notify the police." Hunter rubs his jaw. "Let them continue the search."

Briar shakes her head. "They'll wonder why it took us so long to say something."

"But we could say we saw him tonight—"

"Hunter." Briar's voice is sharp. "What are they going to do? They're already tracking his credit cards, his car, bank accounts, everything. He's an escaped inmate. The whole country is on alert. He's eluding the FBI, for fuck's sake—and the guy your dad hired to find him. The only thing it's going to do is make my mom more nervous. She'll never let me leave the house."

He grimaces. "I understand your reasoning, but I think it'll be a huge help to know he's been spotted here—in Greythorn. We need help now, Briar. Before, it was a shot in the dark, but now? He's hunting you. And we need as many people on our side as possible."

"I'm going to find him," Ash muses, lethal darkness passing over his face. "Even if I have to knock on every door in Greythorn."

"We'll find him." Ledger rests his chin on his hand as he blows out an exasperated breath.

Briar yelps. "Hunter...what if it *was* him following us last weekend?"

Hunter swallows, taking in her words. "Yeah...it's definitely a possibility."

We're quiet for a few minutes, the defeat permeating the air. For a second, I thought maybe we'd at least get a glimpse of his car, or some sort of clue—maybe even confront him, which might've been stupid. But it would've been something. It would've felt productive—would've been a step forward.

"Also, the suit," Briar murmurs. "He was wearing a suit." Her eyes snap to mine. "Maybe we could talk to the suit rental shop in town?"

I nod. "Yeah. We'll start there tomorrow."

Briar sighs. "You're right, though. I think we need to tell the authorities."

"Soon," Ledger insists. "He could be planning on attacking tonight."

"Yeah," Ash chimes in. "Tonight. Before the party. We go to the police station with what we know."

"And after," Ledger adds, standing and helping Ash and me up. "We can go get fucked up at my party."

I'd nearly forgotten about the party at Ledger's house.

We head back inside the gymnasium to grab Briar's purse, and then we walk out—Hunter on Briar's right side, and me on her left. I see Scarlett and Jack staring at us, and I give them both a small, reassuring smile.

61

BRIAR

It all feels too familiar—the bright lights, the cops, the interrogation room. The guys don't really have any additional information since I'm the only one who saw him. For now, we leave out that we knew he was here. I don't want to incriminate Samson or get him in trouble for not saying something earlier. But the sheriff—an older man with dark hair—looks resigned and tired by the time I'm done recounting tonight. I'm sure having one of America's most wanted in his normally safe, sleepy town is not what he signed up for.

"Thank you for telling us," he says as he walks me out of the station. The guys are waiting for me outside—the party bus still idling. "We'll find him, Ms. Monroe."

I fucking hope so.

By the time we take the party bus to Ledger's house, we've decompressed a bit, shaking the events of the night off. The two glasses of champagne the guys handed me didn't hurt. A few people are already parked outside his gate, vaping and laughing while leaning against their cars. Ledger hops out and unlocks his front door, a wicked grin on his face as he greets the early partygoers. We follow closely behind. I try not to smile as a few people smile at him—actually *smile*.

None of them make direct eye contact, but it's a start.

I walk up to the Huxley house with Samson. I get inside the ornate mansion, and I don't expect what I see.

"This is... Wow."

It's dark and moody, and the foyer is covered in crosses of all sizes. The walls are a dark grey, and as I continue farther past the entrance, my eyes take in the gothic furniture, dark walls, and religious undertones through the house. The couch is white and pristine—the desk in the office is made of clear lucite. It's strange—instead of stylish, it's...eerie. I look up and behold iron chandeliers hanging from the ceilings. It almost feels like a medieval dungeon.

"It's a lot," Samson muses. "Like we told you, his parents are freaks. Religious nuts that are so far gone down the rabbit hole, you truly wonder how they're still functioning."

I swallow, and more people file in. "So he normally hosts parties here?"

Samson nods, walking me into the kitchen. Ledger is busting out the alcohol, laying everything out on the large island. There is beer, wine, cocktails, canned drinks, you name it...

"Yeah. His parents are gone most weekends at public speaking events—mostly at religious schools—preaching about premarital sex and sin," he adds, laughing.

Hunter and Ash begin pushing all the furniture to the side, leaving large spaces in the center of each room.

"So if I remember correctly, Ledger's brother is older, twenty-four? And he's a tattoo artist in Boston?"

Samson places an arm around my shoulder, murmuring into my ear. "Yep. Both Ledger and Silas rejected this life from very early on," Samson muses, his lips brushing against my ear.

Right. I remember now. "And that's how Ledger got his ink?"

Samson nods. "His parents aren't home that often, but when they are, they don't really acknowledge Ledger, or his tattoos. They allow him to live here and pay rent, which is fucked up, but they gave up on their kids a long time ago. Silas and Ledger are close, though. So at least they have each other."

I shake my head, imagining how awkward it must be to cohabitate with people who are so unlike you—people who are supposed to be your greatest role models.

Ledger appears, handing me a water. "Thanks," I murmur, taking a sip. "Your house is a vibe," I joke, and he smiles. Samson excuses himself to help Hunter and Ash get the house ready for a rager.

"You think *this* is a vibe? I should show you the chapel."

"Chapel?" I'd completely forgotten about that.

He pins me against the kitchen island and places his hands on either side of me, gripping the counter.

"Chapel," he confirms, his eyes narrowing, focusing on my lips before flitting up to my eyes. "Come on. Let's go."

Before I can respond, he reaches for my hand and drags me to a doorway, opening it and pulling us down the dark, narrow stairway. What kind of person would put a chapel in a basement? Chills work their way down my spine the farther we descend, and then my feet hit stone, and Ledger hits a switch.

The room—the chapel—before us is plain with wood-paneled walls, a couple rows of wooden pews, an ornate runner that leads to the wooden altar. Behind the altar looms a giant cross, overshadowing the entire room. On either side of the cross, black wings carved of dark wood flare out on either side. And the lighting comes from two iron sconces on the wall, giving our shadows a moody, haunted feel.

He dims the light and walks up to the altar. There's a small podium there with a Bible, and two ornate candelabras extend on either side.

They look like devil's horns.

"We spent many days in here, punished by our parents for something any normal child would do, like fighting with my brother or taking the Lord's name in vain," Ledger starts, looking up at the cross. In his collared shirt and dress pants, he looks so...distinguished. His eyes look at me over his shoulder. "I once spent three hours down here because I didn't say 'yes, sir,' to my father. By the time I was eight, I knew I never wanted to be anything like them."

I move toward him, my heels sinking into the plush, Persian carpet leading to the altar.

"I don't blame you," I say, taking Hunter's jacket off. I cross my arms, trying not to smile as he pulls his lower lip between his teeth. "How many girls have you brought down here?" I joke, cocking my head. I run a finger along the wood of the pew.

He smirks. "You're the first," he murmurs, stepping down from the altar.

I suck in a breath as he walks over and moves his large hands to my shoulders, slipping his fingers underneath the fabric of my dress. Slowly—so, so slowly—he slips the dress down my shoulders, causing it to slip off entirely. The heavy beading falls and gathers at my feet. I step out of my dress and shoes and place my palms on his chest in nothing but a black lace bustier and a matching thong.

He growls, studying me, then grabs my waist and pulls me

into him, tipping my chin up as he places a kiss on my mouth. I melt—my body relaxing against the warmth of his body.

"Lie down," he commands, and when I look up at him, his tongue ring slips between his teeth briefly as he toys with it.

"Where?"

He nudges his jaw toward the altar, and I lie down facing the cross. This feels...*so* sacrilegious. Blasphemous. But in a way...so right. Ledger runs a hand through his blonde hair as he slowly unbuttons his shirt, one button at a time, his eyes on me.

"Last weekend was fun," he remarks, tilting his head as he studies me. "But I've been waiting to fuck you alone—all by myself—for weeks now, so I apologize in advance if you're sore tomorrow." I open my mouth to respond, but he interrupts me. "I want you to think of me—and only me—when one of the other guys fucks you tomorrow. That I got here first. Just tomorrow. And then I can be a good boy and go back to sharing."

My breathing turns heavy, my chest rising and falling rapidly. Without taking his pants off, he walks onto the altar and leans over me—his shirt unbuttoned, his hair falling in front of his face. The cross behind him makes it look as though the horizontal beam is attached to his shoulders, holding him up, the painting giving him the illusion of wings. I swallow as he removes his belt, tugging it out of his pant loops and wrapping it around the base of the podium behind me.

"Arms up, Briar," Ledger growls, and I move my arms above my head so that my fingers graze the wood of the podium. I gasp as he loops the belt around each wrist, securing my hands together above my head.

"Ledger—"

"Let me admire you," he mumbles, sitting back and drinking me in with his eyes. A sound so low I don't hear it—

instead, I *feel* it—reverberates through me as his thumb moves to the band of my thong. "These," he grumbles, looking down at me. "I love these." He slips a finger inside, the heat of his skin cool against my burning flesh. He removes my thong, and I help him by shimmying my hips. His hands move up then, unclasping my bustier at the front so that my breasts spring out. "Fuck," he rasps.

He lowers his head, and I squeeze my eyes shut and arch my back as his tongue flicks against my taut, sensitive nipples. I let out a moan, thrashing against the belt as the metal stud of his tongue ring knocks against my skin. When I open my eyes, he's sitting back again. This time, he unzips his pants, reaching out and freeing his giant, thick cock. I begin to tremble with anticipation as I watch him stroke it.

He knocks my legs apart with his knee, causing me to gasp as he lowers himself on top of me, the heavy weight of his body against my chest. I feel the tip of his shaft against my opening—feel the warmth there. My eyes meet his, and I take in his tanned skin, his clear, blue eyes that look indigo in the dark chapel. He swallows, and his throat bobs—the only sign of nervousness he shows before thrusting into me.

Something splinters apart as he drives into me, and I scream, both in pain and pleasure. We've had sex before, but I was much more warmed up last time—had four guys fawning over me. This feels...different. Softer, somehow. *Reverent.* My eyes don't leave Ledger's as he drives into me again, and this time, I hiss.

"Am I hurting you?" he asks, his gaze fierce.

I shake my head, and the belt buckle clicks against the wooden floor of the altar. Ledger whispers something, but it's unintelligible. It sounds like some sort of prayer, and the thought spurs me on. I throw my head back, close my eyes, and arch my back as he drives into me—the pain surrendering to pleasure that seeps into every pore, every crevice deep inside of me.

When I snap my eyes open, his face is flushed, his mouth pulled tight. Reaching up to one of my breasts, he twists my nipple—roughly—driving into me with such force that I gasp.

"Is that too much?" he whispers, his voice frenetic. He's completely overtaken with something primal—his pupils are dilated all the way, and he's panting.

"No," I breath, swallowing. "I like it."

He gives me a lecherous smile then, and clamps his fingers on both nipples, twisting viciously. He's thrusting into me with such force now that I can feel my body squeeze him, tightening with every movement.

I scream—and then I unexpectantly come apart.

Gasping for air, my orgasm rips through me—every taut muscle releasing in wave after wave of pleasure so potent and strong that I buck against the belt. The clanking permeates the silence of the chapel, and I feel my body completely succumb to his as he roars, his climax sliding through him just as quickly as mine did.

"Holy fuck," he pants, pulsing inside of me.

Our breathing slows as we both still, and he drops his head to mine, kissing me softly—first on my lips, and then on each cheek, and then my eyelids. It feels intimate, and I swallow as he looks down at me.

"Wow," I whisper, and he unbuckles my wrists. They spring free, and I shake them out. I see red marks on them, and I try to hide my smile.

He said I would be sore tomorrow, and I have to wonder if he was rough on purpose.

Neither of us says anything for several minutes as he collapses beside me on the altar. I assume there are more partygoers upstairs, considering the music and voices have gotten progressively louder over the last minute or two. Ledger faces me, smiling, then gestures the sign of the cross.

I swat his arm playfully, and we both laugh for what feels like hours. Finally, he helps clean me up, holding me as I slip back into my dress and shoes, and we head upstairs to the party.

62

BRIAR

I spend the next morning recounting my night with my mom and Andrew. My mom is totally freaked out about Cam, but Andrew reassures her that he'll help bolster police activity in the area to keep an eye out. After a late breakfast, I tell them I'm headed to Jack's house.

A few minutes later, I pull behind Jack's BMW i3. I look down at the directions on my phone, squinting against the bright autumn sun as I compare the address on the school roster with the address on my phone. Is it a requirement that every person in Greythorn have luxury cars and pretentious houses? I lock the Subaru, walking up to the ornate front door and knocking. A couple of minutes and two knocks later, I'm just about to turn around when a woman opens the door, and I know instantly that she's Jack's mother.

"Hi," I say, my voice uncertain. "I'm Briar. I'm here to see Jack?"

She gives me a warm smile. Beautiful—younger than I

imagined, with porcelain skin and bright red hair, the exact shade of Jack's.

"He's actually with Scarlett," she says, her voice throaty and low. "He should be home soon if you want to come inside." Studying me, she tilts her head to the side. "You're Andrew's stepdaughter, right? I think he mentioned your name to me." She must see my look of confusion because she continues. "I work as an attorney, and we recently updated some documents for the Academy," she explains. "How are you finding Greythorn? I hope it's not too soul-sucking," she jokes.

I huff a laugh. "It's fine."

She seems nice, and I feel at ease. And it seems that she has Jack's sense of humor.

"We must have you all over for dinner sometime—"

"Briar?"

I twist around, and Jack is standing there with Scarlett. They're watching me with careful concern—they don't know why I'm here.

"You're welcome to come in with Jack if you want. I think I hear my phone ringing. So wonderful to meet you, Briar," Jack's mom says politely before turning and walking away.

I'm left with the two of them, and neither of them move.

"I was hoping we could talk," I say quietly.

"Briar—"

"No," I interrupt Scarlett, holding a hand out. "I really need to talk to you. There are things you don't know about me, and—"

Jack pulls Scarlett past me. By the time I turn to face them, Jack has a hand on his front door, ready to slam in my face. "You made your choice, Briar. We get it. But it's not like we can change your mind."

He moves to shut the door, but just before it clicks shut, I call out— "I was raped!"

The door pauses.

"In California. He was my mom's boyfriend at the time, and he... he raped me. There was a trial, and he was sentenced to thirteen years."

The door slowly opens again, and they both watch me with crossed arms.

"None of them are like their reputations. They're caring, compassionate, kind. That day in a quad? I said something about men raping women, remember? And they stopped. They *stopped*. None of them ever tried anything shady, despite being jerks the first few days. And they...they look out for me. Because Cam—the man who raped me—escaped prison three and a half weeks ago."

I leave out the part about Cam being in Greythorn. The authorities know, my mom and Andrew know, and there's no reason to worry anyone else.

Scarlett's throat bobs. "I'm sorry about what happened to you. I didn't realize..." She trails off. "And you're...sleeping with all of them?"

I nod. "It just sort of happened."

Jack looks at me, standing up straighter. "How does that work, exactly?" His voice is still a bit skeptical, but there's also a hint of curiosity.

I shrug. "I don't know. They all offer something different. And they aren't planning on making me choose one of them to be exclusive with. We're just kind of having fun," I explain. "It feels normal. Natural. Like this was always meant to happen."

"They never really publicly dated anyone," Scarlett adds, dropping her hands to her side. "I mean, I'm sure they messed around. Girls threw themselves at the Kings every single day. And of course Samson dated Micah, and Ash fooled around with Jack—"

"Hey," Jack whines.

"Sorry, Ash *dated* Jack," she clarifies.

"It was three months," he says defensively.

"My point is," I start, trying not to smile as they both lower their arms. "They've been wonderful. I'm not saying you have to forgive them, Samson especially. But he loved Micah—he told me they were in love, and that everything was a misunderstanding."

They look at each other before looking at me. "And Medford?" Scarlett asks.

I tilt my head. "It was Ash's idea, because his father abuses him. He wanted to send a message."

"I knew it," Jack hisses, his voice cruel. "He used to have bruises on his ribs. "But every time I asked, he'd change the subject."

"Is that why Christopher is in prison?" Scarlett asks.

I nod. "Ash recorded the last time it happened and sent it to the police."

They look between themselves, and then at the ground. Scarlett looks up at me through her lashes.

"Are you happy?" she asks.

I swallow. "Happier than I've ever been."

"I still don't trust them," she murmurs. "But I trust you." And then she hugs me, and I sag with relief.

I've missed them—and even though the Kings are fine friends, sometimes I just need a break from the angst.

I put my arms around them as we head inside, and Jack's mom makes us a delicious meal. I learn that both his parents are attorneys, and, like most of the kids here, Jack and his family come from old money. When we finish eating, we head up to Jack's room, which is filled with paperbacks of his favorite books—mostly paranormal romance. As we catch up on life, I tell them a bit about the guys. When I finish giving them a very brief overview of our camping trip, Scarlett gasps.

"I'm, like, jealous in a weird way?"

I snort. "I thought you didn't like men."

She shrugs. "I don't—but who wouldn't love being worshipped like that?" she squeals.

"Scarlett is right," Jack muses, his handsome face stoic and serious. "I am definitely jealous."

"And Ash?" I ask, my real question unspoken.

He gives me a small smile. "Ash is...*was*...the love of my life. But it was always unrequited."

I swallow.

Ash—the brooding bad boy with skeletons in his closet and a heart of gold.

Every time I think about which one I would choose if I had to, it's impossible.

"Real question though..." Scarlett says, her voice soft. "How does this end?"

I look at them, crossing my arms. "I have no idea."

We're quiet for several seconds until my phone beeps, and when I look down, my pulse quickens.

"Oh, my god," I whisper, a smile playing at my lips. "They released Hannah Greythorn."

❦ 63 ❧

BRIAR

I'm restless as I pace our large living room, waiting for Hunter to get home. He'd gone with Ash to pick Hannah up, and I swallow when I think about what Ash must be going through right now—to be reunited with his mother, to see her outside the sterile walls of the psychiatric hospital. The complicated, *loving* relationship they had—regardless of Hannah's affair, the pregnancy, and ultimately having to choose his father over his mother. He was a kid—a *child*. How was he supposed to choose? Especially with Christopher Greythorn whispering horrible things in his ear.

It was no wonder Ash turned out the way he did—sometimes crass and insecure, but loyal as all get out. He'd had his mother ripped from him, had his family torn apart. He lashed out—made a show of being strong, unbreakable.

But maybe he was the one who needed the most care.

Hunter pulls into the driveway, and I throw the door open. I'll never get over his refined, effortless style and moody disposition. He might as well have been straight out of my fantasies—dark, brooding, dangerous.

"Is Ash okay?" I get out, crossing my arms as he walks into the study.

Hunter nods, leaning against the desk. "Yeah, he seemed okay. Hannah looks exactly the same, too—so whatever she had to endure in that place didn't break her spirit."

"That's good, right?"

He shrugs. "I think only time will tell. But they both seemed happy. Christopher had fortunately kept her things— so she doesn't really have to settle in all that much. And her friends are bringing them dinner for the next week or so. They're going to need to learn how to live with each other again. So much has changed..."

I look down for a few seconds before I respond. "What will happen to Christopher?"

Hunter's dark eyes find mine. There's a hint of sadness in them. The media speculates he'll remain in jail, bit I want to hear it from Hunter. "Christopher will be in jail for a long time." Something about the way he says it—full of conviction —sends chills down my body. He continues. "Ash caught him on camera. Even though Ash is eighteen, it ruined his career. There were...other things...Ash may have secured him a spot at MCI-Norfolk for many years to come."

I'm quiet as I look out the window, taking in his words. How strange must it be to walk back into your house after five years... I'm about to reach for him when he tugs me into his hard body.

"Where are you going in that tight, little outfit?" he growls, trailing a finger down my chest, down the Lycra fabric of my sports bra. His fingers slip into the waistband of my leggings, and he lets out a low snarl.

I twist my lips to the side, pushing him away playfully. "I was going to go on a jog."

He smiles down at me. "Briar Monroe jogs?"

I laugh. "I don't know. I was so on edge last weekend after that car followed us... I thought maybe it would be a good way to dispel some of the tension—the nervous energy."

"There are other ways to dispel nervous energy," he states, his voice gravelly.

"Oh really?" I tease, blinking a couple times as his fingers move against my clit. My breath catches when he moves my underwear to the side, thrumming my nub with two fingers. I throw my head back, and his teeth find my neck, biting gently.

"It's going to be a problem if I keep having to refer to you as my sister," he growls, his hot breath against my skin.

I open my eyes and look up at him. Something soft— something profound—passes across his face. He places a gentle kiss on my lips, and at the same time, he thrusts two fingers deep inside of me.

I gasp. "Fuck," I breathe, feathering my tongue along his. I don't even know if we're home alone. What would happen if someone were home? If my mom or Andrew heard us...saw us?

"I'm sick of pretending you don't mean anything to me." He pulls my hips into his. I groan into his mouth as his erection presses against me. "Fuck, Briar," he whispers, his voice shaky. "You drive me fucking wild."

I remove his hand and pivot, hopping onto his large desk. "Show me."

His lips are wet and red from kissing me. His brows furrow slightly as he takes me in. Without breaking eye contact, he unbuttons his jeans, stepping out of them completely as he pulls his Henley over his head.

"What if your—"

"I don't give a shit anymore," he growls, stroking his

mammoth cock. "I'm going to go crazy if I don't fuck you right now."

His words send a bolt of electricity through me. The need is evident on his face, the animalistic urge to take me in a place that either of our parents could walk into...

I swallow as I pull my bra off and then my leggings.

There's no foreplay, nothing to indicate he's about to drive into me, until he places one hand on my throat and grabs my hips with the other, moving me onto his cock in one swift motion. I cry out.

"Fuck," he shatters, his mouth open in an 'O'. Plunging into me, he takes me differently today—needy, hungry, greedy. I ignore the heavy ache in my chest as his eyes bore into mine —as his warm hands grip me, as I squeeze my eyes shut.

I'm falling for my stepbrother.

I'm not sure I'm ready for what that means.

Holding me by my neck, he groans with every push into me, the crescendo of our voices getting louder. I open my eyes, and a piece of hair has fallen in front of his face, his eyes narrowed, studying me.

I'm sick of pretending you don't mean anything to me.

I clench around him, my muscles taut and ready to spring free. Hunter circles his hips as he quickens his tempo, his nostrils flaring as he breathes heavily. I meet every thrust, moving my hips with his so that he fills me to the hilt over and over. I expect the motion to start my climax, but it's not his cock inside of me—it's the way his eyes find mine, the way they're completely open, the way he almost looks as emotional as I am... A half-sob, half-moan escapes my lips as I study Hunter—who's eyes are on my face, so fervently tender.

"Look at me. You are mine," he hisses, and then he lets out a roar so loud, it shakes the desk.

Shakes me to the core, like an earthquake.

Something molten breaks free from inside of me.

I'm speechless as the lightest, sweetest climax rips through me unexpectedly, caressing every pore, every molecule. I feel myself soak him, feel it hit the desk, feel him pulse and empty inside of me.

After a few ragged breathes, he helps clean me up. I reach for my clothes, but he grabs my arm and pulls me into him—our naked bodies pressed against each other. His heart is thundering—I can feel it. Our breathing is still irregular, and his fingers contract around my flesh, squeezing me tight, pulling me impossibly close. He kisses the top of my forehead.

"Do you think it was fate? Your mom, my dad..." He runs a hand through his wavy hair.

I pull back and smile up at him. "Maybe. Or maybe it was random, and it could've been any guy with a hot son," I joke, sticking my tongue out.

He laughs, nipping my lower lip with his teeth. Pulling away, he helps me into my clothes, and we walk into the kitchen, grabbing some food and sitting at the breakfast nook together. It's nice—and it feels like...*home.* I wonder how the future will unfold with him, because I sure as hell don't want to let whatever we have go. I never want to stop. The problem is, I can't give up his friends, either. How will this all play out?

I give him a quick goodbye kiss a half an hour later, pulling on my shoes and heading out for a quick jog. As I run down the driveway, the same six words continue running through my mind.

It could always be like this.

It could always be like this.

64

LEDGER

I drive left onto the main road, and when I stop at the intersection, I think I'm hallucinating when I see a figure run into the park—a figure that looks a hell of a lot like Briar. But I know her, and I know she'd never be running—for fun, at least. I circle the park, and when I get to the other side, I grin when I see her jogging home, red-faced and looking hot as fuck in her running outfit. I pull next to her, and when she sees me, she rolls her eyes, turning in the other direction to avoid me.

I honk, and she flips me off. I chuckle as I park and get out of the car, jogging up to her.

"Hey," I call out, and she turns to face me.

Wiping her brow, she sighs. "Great. The last person I want to see."

I flick my eyes up and down her body, taking in her curves, the sweat making her cleavage gleam in the sun, the way her dark, curly tendrils are sticking to her hairline... I want to lick it off.

I want to lick every inch of her.

I have a sudden urge to paint her—something that surprises me—to remember her this way forever.

"Why?" I ask, cocking my head.

"Because. You're just going to make fun of that fact that I'm running wrong or something," She shields her eyes from the sun.

"Why would I do that?" I ask, my voice quieter than I intended. "I'm surprised, but I'd never make fun of you."

She growls and throws her arms to the side. "Because, in P.E. that day, you told me how to run correctly. And you made a couple other smartass comments about how hard I was working."

I feel my lips twitch with a smile, but I keep my composure. "And? Is today easier than that day?"

She shrugs, and I can tell she's thinking my words over. "Yeah."

I walk up to her. "I didn't mean for it to sound like I was making fun of you." I smile as I run a finger down her damp arm. Something jumps inside of me at the contact—the feel of her warm, soft skin. The scent of her sweat hitting my nostrils. "I didn't know you ran recreationally," I say, my voice soft. "I'd love to go with you—"

"No," she insists, shaking her head. "You're, like, really good. And I suck."

I laugh. "Briar—"

She turns and jogs away.

"Hey!" I catch up with her and spin her around.

She pulls away from me, and it's then that I see her bottom lip tremble ever so slightly.

"No!" She glares up at me. "I started running last weekend. I had to—I had to burn off some energy. I wasn't sleeping well. I felt like I was hyper-caffeinated all the fucking time. I was going crazy with all that energy." She looks down sheepishly. "I like it, but I'm nowhere near as good as you."

I try to hide my smile as I pull her into me.

"I'll never make fun of someone trying to better their life," I murmur, kissing the top of her head, and she relaxes against me. "If you want, I can help you. If not, that's fine, too." I release her, and she takes a step back, looking at me skeptically.

"I just feel so good after, you know?"

I grin. "I know."

She laughs and shakes her head, looking away. When her eyes find mine again, she looks...relieved. "Fine. I'll let you help me."

I nod. "Okay. Let's start with three days a week. Ease into it a bit. I'll stop by tomorrow morning."

She winces. "What time?"

I walk backwards to my car. "Six."

Sighing, she puts her hands on her hips, and I'm suddenly so acutely aware of how it felt to be inside her Friday night.

"Tomorrow—Monday," I repeat, climbing into my car. "Do you want a ride home?"

She shakes her head. "No. Now I have to get about ten times better before tomorrow, so I should run home."

I laugh. "It doesn't work like that."

She rolls her eyes and turns around. "Goodbye, Ledger," she chirps before jogging off.

I'm still smiling as I drive away, and that's when I realize my mornings are about to get a hell of a lot more interesting.

65

BRIAR

My alarm goes off at five forty-five the next morning, and I groan as I snooze for three minutes. By the time I drag my exhausted body out of bed, I'm already regretting this decision. I pull on a pair of jogging pants, a sports bra, a windbreaker, sneakers, and I put my hair into a ponytail. After I brush my teeth, I head downstairs, rubbing my sleepy eyes. Waking this early, for a night owl like me, feels like pure torture. I was smart enough to make some cold brew with milk yesterday, so I pour a cup, leaning against the counter as I drink it down. When my phone dings, alerting me of Ledger at the front door, I grab my keys, a water bottle, and a granola bar.

Opening the door, I can tell he's trying not to laugh when he takes my appearance in. Instead of teasing me, he just smiles.

"Ready?" he asks, and I drink in his running attire. He's

wearing fitted running pants, a sweatshirt, and his hair is pulled back in a headband.

"No," I groan.

"It gets easier, I promise," he says, his voice clear as if he's been awake for hours.

"Oh god, are you a morning person?" I ask as we walk to the sidewalk. I don't see his car, so he must've run here—but he doesn't look out of breath or sweaty at all.

He bends over, stretching his long, muscular limbs. "I love mornings," he replies, grinning.

"Just my luck," I whisper, mimicking his stretching.

"Come on," he says, turning and jogging away.

"Wait, shouldn't we stretch more?"

He laughs, jogging backward. "Can't forget to warm up!" He squints at me with a hint of a smile.

That's exactly what he said to me a couple weeks ago before we messed around in the shower room...

Smartass.

I sigh and jog after him, already regretting every decision that led me here.

࿇

An hour later, I'm sprawled on the grass in front of his house, gasping for air.

"It's better if you don't sit or lie down when you're cooling off," he chuckles, pulling me up.

"I...can't...breathe..."

We ran from my house to his—only a little over three miles, but it felt like thirty. I'd never run this far. There were a lot of breaks, and I'm sure I was going at a snail's pace the entire time compared to Ledger. But I did it—and he was very patient with me.

He crosses his arms and looks over at me. He's not even sweating.

Asshole.

"You're testing your endurance," he starts, leaning against the side of his house. "It's just as important as strength training, or sprints. It'll get easier with every run. Maybe you'll be able to run marathons with me by this time next year."

I bark out a laugh. "No way. I could never—"

He places his arms on either side of me, pinning me to the side of the house. Kissing me, he sweeps his tongue into my mouth. I groan, kissing him back, but just as quickly as he'd descended on me, he pulls back, looking at me with hooded, dark eyes.

"Stop being so sure you could never do something, Briar." He nips at my bottom lip with his teeth, pulling on my flesh a bit before letting it go. "Just the fact that you took it upon yourself to *want* to get better means you're one thousand percent stronger than everyone else who just thinks about it. The people who accomplish great things aren't the people who get lucky. They're the people who work their ass off, day in and day out."

I swallow and nod. "Yeah. You're right."

"I know I'm right. Besides, you have the best trainer in the world."

I snort. "And so humble, too."

He laughs. "Come on. We have to hurry or we're going to be late for school."

"Where are you taking me?" I ask, smiling.

"I think we both need to shower off, don't you think?" he asks, winking.

My stomach turns over, and I follow him inside.

Unlike last time, when he took his time screwing me, he collides against my sweaty body, peeling my running clothes off as quickly as possible, his lips on mine as he moves us toward the stairs.

"Where are your parents?" I ask, my voice ragged.

"Fuck if I care," he growls.

"Isn't premarital sex a sin?" I laugh, and he bites my lower lip, spurring me on.

"It is," he muses, grabbing me and throwing me over his shoulder as he scoops our clothes up and glides up the stairs. "Why do you think I like to fuck so much? When something is forbidden, it creates an obsession."

There are no formalities—no explanations—as he turns the shower on in his bathroom. I look around briefly, smiling when I see some darker art and a meticulously organized sink area. He pulls me into the shower. As the steam clings to the clean glass, as he drops to his knees and feasts on me as the water runs down my body.

I should be quiet as he licks and devours me, as his mouth cups me at my apex, sucking. His tongue ring knocks against my clit, and I grip the slippery handle of the shower door, throwing my head back and crying out.

"Ledger," I rasp.

Before I can come, he jumps to his feet and pushes me against the marble wall of the shower. He licks my neck, trails it down my back, and then his tongue flicks between my cheeks. I tense, but he doesn't notice. Not as his hands spread me, as his tongue feasts on the other part of me—the part no one has ever tasted with their mouth. It's odd at first, but so intense that my knees begin to quake. A hand moves between my legs, swirling a finger around my clit, causing me to come so hard that the glass shakes with my cries. Pulse after pulse powers through me, more intense with his mouth on my ass.

And then he claims me—thrusting into my pussy, his chest against my back, driving into me so hard that I leave the floor each time. Grunting, he presses me against the cool marble of the shower, biting my neck at the same time. I realize then that this might be my favorite kind of sex—rough, needy, unkind—in a way that is almost animalistic. We moan in unison as we climax together. I grip him with each wave, feel him fill me, and then he pulls out, leaving me a trembling mess of nerves.

I'm about to get out of the shower when he grabs my hand, pulling me directly under the stream. He grabs the soap and slowly, ever so slowly, begins to clean me. First my body, then my hair, his large hands making me groan with pleasure as they massage my scalp. He trails kisses along my collarbone, and I have to squeeze my eyes shut as he takes a comb through my hair—it feels *too* intimate, too intense.

My chest aches as he hands me a towel, pulling me into a tight embrace. The towels are even warm from the heated towel rack. I rest my head against his chest.

These boys—these *Kings*—will be my undoing.

❦ 66 ❦

BRIAR

An hour later, the five of us walk through the gates of Ravenwood Academy together. Unlike before, I feel like I might belong with them—might *actually* be the missing puzzle piece. And the best part is, Scarlett and Jack sheepishly walk over to us, the latter eyeing Ash suspiciously.

"Hey," Ash says, nudging his jaw at Jack.

"Hey, man," Jack answers. "I heard about your mom. I'm glad she's..." he looks down. "You know. I think we're all glad she's out of that place."

Ash swallows and clears his throat. "Thanks."

They begin to walk away, but I lunge forward and grab Scarlett's arm. "You can sit with us."

The silence that follows is uncomfortable for everyone. So many assumptions, so much history, and belief systems that have to be dismantled entirely. But I widen my eyes and look at each of the guys, inferring that this is happening whether they like it or not.

"Um, okay," Scarlett answers, giving Hunter a small smile.

The look he returns is more like a wince, but at least he's trying. I have to give him credit for that.

The seven of us head to the center of the quad, and as Scarlett gives me a silent look of disbelief, the rest of the students at Ravenwood are slightly dumbfounded. Every single person is watching us with bewildered expressions, and I have to bite my tongue to keep from grinning. Even though Samson and I did get crowned homecoming King and Queen, there's still an air of skepticism.

The Kings thought they were getting a Queen, but in actuality, they were getting the woman who would smash their reputations to the ground—the woman who would knock them down from their pedestal, who would humanize them again.

"I think we might be cool again," Samson murmurs into my ear.

I snort. "You guys were always cool. *Too* cool."

When I turn to face him, he's watching me with confusion. "We never thought of ourselves as cool, Briar. We were the outcasts. The people everyone feared, the people no one wanted to associate with." He juts his chin toward Jack and Scarlett, who are seated stiffly next to Ledger. The sight is hilarious. "Why do you think they were so mad at you?"

I shake my head. "Misunderstood, maybe, but everyone came to your parties. You were Homecoming King."

He shakes his head, putting a casual arm over my shoulder. "There's a difference between popularity and coolness, Briar. Dictators are popular. Lizzo is cool. People want to hang around her. People want to *be* her. People hated us because of who we were." I open my mouth to disagree, but he continues. "I'm not trying to play the victim. But let's say you swim in the ocean with other people, and you start to drown...we weren't the kind of people they would want to save."

I look around, and a few people shake their heads and look away, their gazes harsh and heated. Perhaps I was naïve to think one week would be enough to shatter the rumors. One week—when some of these students have known the Kings since Kindergarten. For some, it's a lifetime of mistrust and skepticism. My work didn't end when I was crowned homecoming Queen. I need to keep going, keep reaching out.

"Because of Micah?" I ask, looking back at Samson.

"Yeah." He sighs, sitting down on a step. I sit next to him, and he leans back on his elbows. "After Micah died, people blamed us. And maybe we were at fault. He was the first outsider we'd let in—the first person besides the four of us, since before I can even remember. One day, they started yelling at us—throwing food at us—and the hatred was evident. They thought we caused him to kill himself, Briar," he says, his voice fraught with emotion. "But we didn't. And that day—people really started to push their boundaries with us. A few people shoved us into lockers. One person spilled acid on Ledger in chemistry—he was fine," he interjects when he sees my horrified expression. "So that night, we decided that instead of fighting against the grain, we might as well embrace it."

"So you played the part," I murmur.

He nods. "We got ahead of the curve. They already hated us, so it didn't matter to us if they hated us even more. Quite frankly, we couldn't care less about what they thought. So, the next morning, Hunter picked on another junior—a guy who kept making snide comments about Micah. He tried to shove Hunter against the lockers, but Hunter was too quick, too smart. To this day, we're still not sure what Hunter said to him, but it was enough for him to back off—for them all to back off. Our rite of passage was complete, and our reputations were solidified. We maintained it over the last year, but until you came along, we just tried to live our lives in peace."

I hug my knees and lean back against the concrete of the center of the quad. "You were just trying to survive," I add. "Playing dead, in a way."

He hums in agreement, and then he's quiet as he looks around. Ash is talking to Scarlett and Jack, and Hunter is deep in conversation with Ledger. His eyes find mine briefly, and he gives me a small smile. "If people stopped hating us, it might not be the worst thing. It's lonely on this throne."

"You're going to have to show them," I retort, smirking. "Show them the side of you that I know."

He makes a face, but then he kisses me quickly—before anyone notices.

The bell rings shortly after that, and as we all walk to our separate buildings, and as Scarlett and Jack flank either side of me, I realize that we may be shaking things up at Ravenwood Academy.

Finally.

❦ 67 ❦

HUNTER

"Ready?" Aubrey asks, zipping her fanny pack as the four of us stand around the front door.

"I'm always ready for Halloween festivities," Briar responds, grinning. "It's my favorite holiday."

I didn't know that.

"Oh, you're going to love how they do it up—it's terrifically spooky," my dad adds, putting an arm around Aubrey.

We lock the door and head to the Subaru, and Briar and I have to actively try not to hold hands as my dad starts the engine.

"Briar used to volunteer at the pumpkin patch back in California," Aubrey muses, chuckling. "She made the cutest witch."

Briar groans. "Mom, please."

Aubrey sends her phone back to me, and when I see the screen, I can't help but grin.

"Is this you?" I ask, laughing.

"Yes," Briar mumbles, her face in her hands.

It's a picture of Briar—at maybe thirteen or fourteen—and she's flashing her braces at the camera, clad in a black robe, a black hat, and black lipstick.

"You do make a cute witch," I add, and she swats my shoulder.

Dad puts on some classic rock, and we're silent as we head up to Salem, Massachusetts for their annual Halloween Fair called Haunted Happenings. My mom used to drag us to it every year, but we haven't been since she died. They have a marketplace where people sell all sorts of creepy things, psychic readings, reenactments of the Salem Witch Trials, yoga at the satanic temple...the list goes on. If Briar loves Halloween, she's going to adore the things we can explore in Salem.

Thirty minutes later, Dad parks in one of the paid lots, and we exit the car. Aubrey and my dad offer to walk around with us, but Briar shoos them away, and we agree to meet in two hours at Settler, one of the nicest restaurants in Salem. Briar and I immediately make out in one of the back allies before she drags me to the gift ship, purchasing half of the store's witch paraphernalia. Afterward, we head down the main road to the courthouse, where an interactive reenactment of one of the trials is taking place—and audience members are being chosen as actors.

I laugh when Briar is instantly found guilty by the actor, and she gives me a droll little smile before playing along, claiming her innocence. The judge—an older man with a beard—declares that she is guilty, and to our surprise, several audience members declare she should be hung, and it's hard not to laugh. When the trial is over, Briar takes a picture with Sheriff Corwin and a couple of the Puritan actors, and we get a picture of the two of us in front of the hanging tree. Laughing, we stumble out and meander through the marketplace.

This—this is *fun*. I can't remember the last time I smiled this much. Maybe never? Not since my mom died. And we certainly haven't been back to Salem since her death. Knowing the last time I was here was with my mom stings a little, but Briar is the antidote to that pain. The feeling of being here is different now, but in a good way. Like we're making new memories. I wouldn't want to be here with anyone else.

We meet up with my dad and Aubrey and then eat our weight in bread and seafood. On the way home, Briar naps against my shoulder, and my dad's eyes find mine in the rearview mirror. I look away; I know what he's thinking.

We're not just stepsiblings.

We're more than that, and it's becoming very evident to those around us.

As we pull into Greythorn, I notice my dad's eyes flicking to the rearview mirror every few seconds—only not at me this time. I look behind us, and there is a black SUV tailgating us. I decide not to wake Briar. She's sound asleep on me, and I don't want to worry her. Dread fills me, because I know who might be following us.

"This person is on my ass," my dad growls. Pulling over, he waits for the car to pass—but it doesn't, instead stopping behind us. "What the hell is their deal?"

I swallow and wipe my sweaty palms on my jeans. When my eyes find his, I know we're thinking the same thing.

"Just keep driving," Aubrey chimes in. "They're not going to follow us all the way home," she huffs, laughing.

She has no idea.

We pull onto our street. My dad slowly pulls into the driveway, and the black car slows considerably, nearly stopping, before speeding off.

Just like before.

I give my dad a knowing look before waking Briar, gently

335

nudging her as Dad and Aubrey make small talk about grocery shopping for dinner. Once inside, Briar and I head down to the basement, and when we're out of earshot, I turn to her.

"I think Cam was following us again," I say, taking her hand.

"Just now?" She rubs her eyes. "Did he follow us home?"

"Yes." Her face falls, and I can't stand the worry etching onto her face. I'll do *anything* to make it better. "He's not going to touch you here," I growl, hot, angry heat spreading through my limbs. "If he thinks he can touch you here, he will be sorely mistaken."

She nods. "But he knows. He could follow us anywhere now. I didn't even think... We have the same car. The Subaru. He must've seen it, and started following us..."

"Shh," I whisper, kissing her forehead. "It's okay. You're safe. The police know he's here. Our parents know he's here. We're safe, Briar."

"I can't do this anymore," she says, her voice breaking with a sob. "I'm sick of him ruining my happiness. I earned it, Hunter—I fought for that happiness these last nine months. I just want it over with. I want him back in his prison cell, rotting away forever."

"I know. Me too, baby."

Her head snaps up. "What if we lure him out?"

My heart stutters in my chest. "*Lure* him?"

I let her words roll through me, digesting them. "And then what?" I ask, stepping back and crossing my arms. "We let the authorities take over?"

She shrugs. "Yeah. Maybe. I don't know. I'm just tired of always looking over my shoulder, you know?"

"So, what's the plan?"

She looks down, her arms hanging at her sides. "I just want him gone. This was supposed to be the place I started over—the place my mom and I found some semblance of peace. And now he's here, and he's fucking with us...fucking with the people in our life..." She wipes a tear from her cheek. "He's tainting something that should've been my reprieve."

My jaw ticks as we think. "So, we should lure him out of wherever he's hiding, like you said."

She sniffs. "Yeah. But how? I wish we had something like in Salem...some big carnival or something to intrigue him enough to risk being seen. Like homecoming."

I take her hands. "You forget who you're talking to," I drawl, placing a finger under her jaw. "You want a carnival? I'll give you a carnival."

She swallows, but something behind her eyes lights up. "A Halloween carnival. In the main square. No face masks allowed, obviously, because we need to identify him. And we tell the cops about our plan, so they're ready."

I take a step back, grinning. "We're on it, little lamb." Her eyes darken at the nickname. "Consider it done."

68

BRIAR

Scarlett, Jack, and I all spend the next week prepping for the Halloween Carnival—which is taking place on Halloween night, in Greythorn's town square. Halloween is only two weeks away, so we have a lot of work to do before then— things like music, crafts, furniture rentals, permits, sponsors, marketing, costumes... The list goes on. The first thing we decide is what we're going to do—and after the seven of us talk it over, we decide that we'll have a couple of rides, a showing of the *Halloween* movie, food, and trick-or-treating for the kids. We attempt to cover all age ranges, hoping word will spread far and wide. Scarlett and Jack have no idea *why* we're hosting this carnival—they just think we've been planning it all along.

We meet with the officers at Greythorn police station, and the sheriff elects to send twenty officers to the carnival in disguise. Though he isn't totally on board with the idea of *luring* a convicted rapist out of the woods, he agrees it may be our only shot to get to Cam before Cam gets to us.

The food is the easiest to secure for the carnival. Between Scarlett's parents, who own Romancing the Bean, and Samson, who volunteers at his uncle's restaurant, *Enclave*, we have appetizers, dinner, pastries, alcohol, and dessert. The rides are secured by Andrew after one quick phone call to a friend. Ash's mom and my mom volunteer to spread the word by posting advertisements all around the town square, on the campus of Greythorn, and near all the grocery stores. Hunter gives them specific directions—place these posters anywhere that may be visible to anyone and everyone. We all post on social media—Facebook, Instagram, anywhere that we can get the word out.

I also make sure my name and picture are on the poster, and of course the guys want Samson and me to ride the float we arranged—to bolster the Ravenwood Academy spirit, obviously, since we were homecoming King and Queen.

We wanted to lure him in?

Well, we might as well have gone fishing with his favorite bait...

Ledger gets his brother to recommend a band from Boston, and Ash takes care of getting the permits and securing the furniture. Scarlett and Jack begin organizing the decorations, outsourcing to the middle school. We also borrow a lot of things from various haunted houses in the vicinity.

I guess it helps to have connections.

Hunter is in charge of securing sponsors, and with how well his dad is liked, it's not a hard thing to do. We don't necessarily need the money, but a few hundred bucks makes us feel legitimate, and we create a raffle for people to win a weekend away in Salem, all expenses paid.

In a little over a week, we'd taken care of the big things. It's a flurry of school, jogging with Ledger three mornings a week, dinners with my mom, Hunter, and Andrew, a couple of dates with Samson, and random sexual encounters with Ash, usually when he needs to release some steam—like in a broom closet at Ravenwood Academy a few days ago.

I can hardly keep my eyes open when I collapse into bed each night, so when the day before Halloween approaches, I get up early and go for a jog. It's not my morning to jog with Ledger, but I decide to go on my own anyway. I'm up to nearly two miles without wanting to feel like I'm about to die, and I don't want to lose steam.

I jog down the cool, misty street toward the center of town. It's so cold—autumn is in full swing now, and I have to wear a fleece jacket over my running clothes. My nose is numb as I round the corner into the main square, and just as I'm about to stop and stretch, I see Ash sitting on a bench up ahead, facing the park.

When he sees me, he pulls his AirPods out, smiling.

"Briar," he purrs.

"Why are you just sitting on a random bench at seven in the morning?" I ask, looking around. There are quite a few people out—one of the reasons I'm fine jogging in the mornings by myself.

He shrugs as I take a seat next to him. "I couldn't sleep, so I went on a walk, and then I ended up here."

I nod and cross my arms. I don't even realize I'm not out of breath until I feel a trickle of sweat drip down my back. I'm not running marathons yet, but running consistently for a month has really improved my endurance.

"How's it going with your mom?" I ask, my voice quiet.

He turns to face me. "It's been good. She's exactly the same, like she just stepped back into her old life."

I swallow. I can tell by his tone that this bothers him for some reason. "And?" I ask, placing a hand on his.

He sighs. "And I'm not. Her getting committed was such a

huge part of my life, but it's almost like she thinks she went to go run errands or something." He's quiet for a minute. "It makes me wonder if she even missed me."

Something cleaves in my chest at his words. "She loves you, Ash. She remained strong—for you. Not despite you. *For* you. So that when she was able to come back to you, she could show you what strength looked like—so she could protect you from the things she probably felt and saw."

He puts an arm around me and pulls me close, exhaling loudly. "Yeah. You're probably right."

"My mom is the same way," I add, whispering. "She stays strong in front of me, but growing up, I heard her crying alone in her room plenty of times."

He nods. "My father is an asshole, and I feel ashamed to be related to him."

I put my phone in my pocket, crossing my legs. "Hunter said the Greythorn name is old. Maybe there's someone else who can make you proud to be a Greythorn?"

He's quiet for a minute, eventually pointing to the park. "The mausoleum, Elias Greythorn. He was born in 1702, and he founded this town." He tugs me closer, and I relax against him.

"See? There you go." I look into the park. "That's where you were all drinking that first day—when you called out to me."

I remember that day so clearly. Having just moved to Greythorn—and I hadn't even met the guys yet. Still, they intrigued me even then.

He chuckles. "Yeah. Do you want to see it? I have a key."

Shivers work their way down my spine. "A key? To what?"

He shrugs. "His tomb."

I pull away. "I didn't realize they made keys for tombs."

He gives me a lopsided smile, and in the clear morning light, his eyes are the palest of blue.

"They don't normally. But nothing about Elias Greythorn was normal. He was very eclectic. He was a good guy, when not a lot of men back then were good guys."

Standing, he tugs me along after him. We enter the park, and today it's so much quieter than that first day. Walking toward the thickest part of the park, I gape when I see the large, stone structure come into view. It's not just a mausoleum—it's a small house.

Ash pulls a skeleton key from his pocket, walking to the door. "Wait," I hiss. "Is his...body...in there?"

Ash laughs—tipping his head back as the sound echoes against the trees. "No body. It was just a place he wanted his family to remember him. He's buried in the cemetery just outside of town."

He opens the tomb, and we step inside. It's just four walls with a stone seat built into one of them. There's a small window made of warped glass, and the gas lamp on the wall speaks of another time. Ash closes the door behind him, letting the silence permeate the space. It smells like damp grass, and because of the stone, it's at least ten degrees colder than outside.

"The weight of the Greythorn name is sometimes too heavy to bear," he explains, his voice frayed, uneven. His eyes find mine, the light from the window shining down on him. "I'm supposed to live up to this honored ancestor. I can't wait to leave it all behind. Find a place where no one knows about my father, or my mother, or the Kings."

I take a step toward him. "I wish you could see yourself the way I see you," I mumble, unzipping my jacket and shrugging it off, letting it fall to the floor.

His gaze is blazing now, his eyes two blue flames. "And how do you see me, Briar?"

I lean against the opposite wall, trying not to shiver. "Broken. Beautiful. Cunning. Loyal as fuck. Raunchy."

He laughs. "Raunchy?"

I smile. "Yeah. I mean, you do things to me that no one else dares to do."

Something unleashes from him then, because he walks forward, pressing his lips against mine. His body is hard under his clothes, and I groan as he places two hands on my breasts, squeezing as he moans. Then he drops them, reaching down and pulling my pants off in one frenzied movement. He lifts me up, and I wrap my legs around his waist as he pushes me against the cold, stone wall. Then, he unzips his pants.

I tilt my head back and gasp as he enters me, his head thick as it slides in with ease. He pushes into me, and I buck my hips against his, and then he stops moving as I ride him. He grips my ass, and I undulate my hips back and forth, arching my back as I get closer.

"Fuck," Ash whispers. "Look at how well you ride my cock, Briar." He grabs my chin and forces me to look—to see his wet shaft, so large, he practically hits bone when he's inside me fully...

I move against him, and he growls in response, his hands squeezing my flesh with need.

"I want to make you feel good," I whimper. "I want you, Ash."

He lets out a feral cry as I change my angle a bit, and he slams a hand against the stone near my head, breathing heavily. Watching him come undone like this, unraveling before my eyes as I ride him...

Watching him watch us—his eyes looking down, the way his chest rises and falls unevenly, like he's trying to catch his breath—sets me off. His eyes flick up to my face and he watches me with furrowed concentration, with animalistic need. My climax starts slowly, and I feel myself grip him with every wave, feeling every muscle release inside me in a cacophony of pleasure. I soak his shirt, clawing my fingers down his arms, a whimpering mess.

Feeling me come around him makes him let out a frenzied desperate cry, but he doesn't move as his cock pulses into me —he releases inside of me, his expression intense with disbelief, like he didn't expect to come like that. His shaft rises and falls, his hands gripping me firmly, and then he sags against me as the last of it leaves his body.

"I've fucked a lot of women," he starts, and I bark out a surprised laugh. "But your pussy feels the best. I'll never be able to fuck someone else now."

I snort. "I'm sure you'd be able to find someone—"

His hand comes to my face, and he kisses me roughly, his tongue needy and firm. When he pulls back and lowers me to the ground, he growls as he presses himself against me.

"I'm not joking. I'll never get my fill, and I don't want to be with anyone else."

His words cause my throat to tighten up, my chest to ache. "I feel the same way," I whisper.

"I don't fucking care about my friends, either. I just need you—however I can have you."

I nod and grip the fabric of his shirt. "I'm yours," I answer.

This might be the best thing that ever happened to either of us.

🌿 69 🌾

Aꜱʜ

I walk Briar home, and then I head toward my house a couple miles away. I think about what she said—about my mom hiding the horrors of the hospital from me. I think of the nights we've spent together since she's been home—the meals she's cooked, the floors she's mopped—and I wonder if she goes into her room and cries, like Briar's mom. My heart breaks a little bit just thinking about it.

As I walk through the door, the heaviness in my chest intensifies when I see her sitting at the dining room table. There are two plates.

She made me breakfast.

"Hi," I say, closing the door behind me.

"Hey, sweetie. Where have you been?" It's not accusatory. She knows I'm eighteen, and she's not exactly going to enforce the same rules my father did. If I was one minute past curfew, he'd beat me up.

"I just went on a walk," I explain, sitting down and shoveling eggs and toast in my mouth. I didn't realize how hungry I was. "I needed to clear my head."

About you. About Briar. About Dad. About...everything.

"I see. Well, I put your clean clothes on your bed, and I ordered that shampoo you like, so that should be here tomorrow—"

"Mom." I place my fork down on the table a little too loudly. "You don't have to pretend to be holding it all together. I know you probably had to deal with a lot being in there, and I don't expect you to waltz back here like nothing happened," I add, my voice rough and gritty.

She frowns, and the lines in her forehead deepen. Her pale blue eyes—*my eyes*—soften around the corners. "I didn't expect that, either. I thought I'd be a mess. And it's only been a couple of weeks, but I feel...okay, Ash."

Her words caress some locked-up part inside of me, and I swallow. "I just don't want you to put on a brave face for my benefit, that's all."

She reaches out and takes my hand. "I'm not. I promise. I have my baggage from that place, but do you know what I hoped for, every single day?"

I shake my head. "What?"

"To see you," she answers softly. "To be a part of your life again. I didn't care about anything else. So when I was released, it felt as though my prayers had been answered. Of course there are things I have to deal with, but overall, I feel lucky, grateful, and blessed to be here with you."

I swallow. "I'm glad you're here."

"Me too, sweetie. Me too."

We go back to eating, and I can't help but feel slightly lighter than before.

"I hope he rots in his cell," I add, and I swear I see a hint of a smile on my mother's red lips.

70

BRIAR

The atmosphere at Ravenwood Academy the morning of Halloween is frenzied—and excited. For the last two weeks, Scarlett and Jack have become the plus two to our group. In fact, their seamless integration is so subtle that I don't notice the aftereffects for a few days. Slowly but surely, people begin to smile at us. Instead of fear in their eyes, we are met with a little trepidation, but also a little curiosity. Since Micah—and then me—no one has penetrated the reign of the Kings.

So on the morning of Halloween, a few people take a chance and sit with us in the center of the quad, and no one says anything—not even Ash, who looks slightly suspicious. I know he means well, and he does an excellent job of *not* glaring at people, but it's going to be an adjustment for all of them. Over the course of the day, most of the students slowly walk by and study us. The dictatorship seems to be crumbling with each passing day.

At lunch, a few freshman girls ask me about the

Halloween Carnival tonight. There are flyers all over campus, but I think they want to test the waters to see if the rumors are true. I give them all warm smiles and hand them a few free ride passes. They walk away giggling, and I can't help but smile because it solidifies what I think I've known for a few weeks: the reputation of the Kings is unfounded, and people might finally be starting to realize it.

Costumes aren't allowed at Ravenwood Academy, but I manage to find a badass Edward Scissorhands costume for later, complete with long, silver nails (I opted out of actual scissors for practical reasons), and a leather ensemble. I can't wait to wear it. The guys opted out of wearing costumes, and I try not to laugh at their lack of Halloween spirit. But then I remember, not everyone is obsessed with All Hallows Eve like me.

Scarlett and Jack opt to go as the Wicked Witch of the West and the Wizard of Oz. After school, Scarlett, Jack, Hunter, and I all head back to the house to get ready for the carnival. My nerves are shot the minute we leave school, because I know tonight might be the night we catch Cam. I've made a conscious effort not to think about it too much, because every time I do, I want to back out.

But then I remember that I have four guys who have vowed to protect me, my mom and Andrew, Scarlett and Jack, and the security of twenty police officers. Tickets are sold out, and Andrew suspects the vast majority of Greythorn residents will be present. Plus, the authorities have been trained for this. They have regimented plans, foolproof strategies. This may have been our idea, but they'll take over from here. If Cam shows up, they will find him.

"This is gorgeous," Scarlett croons, running a hand down the black leather bodice of my costume.

"Thanks," I muse, looking at myself in the large mirror in my bedroom.

"It enhances certain aspects," Jack muses, joking.

He's referring to the low-cut neckline. He's donning a dark green tuxedo, and his hair is slicked back.

As Scarlett and I fix our hair in my mirror, I can't help but smile. Even though parts of tonight might be daunting—and I have no idea how it will all go down, so the unpredictability is nauseating—at least Scarlett and Jack don't hate me anymore.

Scarlett's black cloak and green makeup is exquisite. She's added black lipstick and thick, black eyelashes, while also accentuating her eyebrow arches. Just as we pull our shoes on, Hunter walks in, taking in all our costumes. Jack and Scarlett make a great pair, and Scarlett picks up her broom, grinning. I see Hunter try to hide his smile as he turns to me.

I have on a leather bodice and matching leather pants with multiple belts around my middle, and black combat boots. I teased my hair so that it's wild, and I hold my hands out, showing him my long nails.

"Damn, Ravenwood," Jack taunts. "Do you hate Halloween or something?" He's referring to the lack of costume.

"It's not really my thing," he muses, giving us all a small smile. He bends down to kiss me, and Scarlett clears her throat. She's been a little more reserved with the guys—especially Samson. I don't blame her. Everyone is getting used to things being different, getting used to each other. We all head downstairs.

My mom takes a million pictures. Andrew and my mom are Dumbledore and Hagrid from Harry Potter—my mom being Hagrid. Her fake beard is endearing, and I can't help but snort when they kiss each other and their beards get tangled. Wiping my sweaty palms on my costume, I feel my pulse tick up with each passing minute.

We'd discussed what would happen at the carnival, how

five officers in disguise would take a place on each corner of the town square. The nine of us—including my parents—are supposed to go about their nights as usual.

I just have to hope beyond belief that one, he comes, and two, the authorities are able to arrest him.

"Okay, how is everyone getting there?" Andrew muses.

"I can take Jack," Scarlett volunteers.

"I'll ride with Briar and our parents," Hunter adds.

"That works!" My mom grabs her purse, and then she, Andrew, and my friends file outside.

Hunter turns to face me. "Ready?"

I swallow.

Am I ready?

To what—capture my rapist? Hope he walks into the trap we set? A lot is riding on tonight. If he doesn't come, or if he gets away again...

I shake my head. "Why don't I drive separately? I... I need a bit of space."

His brows furrow. "Briar, I really don't think you should be alone tonight." Pulling me into him, he kisses my brow. "Let me wait with you," he suggests.

I give him a long, slow kiss—my hands getting tangled in his thick, dark hair as I run my fingers through it. Pulling away, I touch my lips.

"I think I'm going to text Sonya. I just need...reassurance, I guess." He looks at me skeptically, so I offer him an olive branch. "What if we walk out together? I'll look my car doors, call Sonya, and meet you there in five?"

He watches me for a second, his pupils darkening. "Are you sure?"

I smile. "You go with the bearded lizards," I joke, referring to my mom and Andrew. "I'll be right behind you."

He nods. "Alright. If you insist. I'll let our parents know."

I grab my purse as we walk out together. I see my mom

and Andrew waiting in Andrew's Lexus. Hunter leans down, giving me a kiss on the forehead.

"I'll see you in a few," he murmurs.

I wave to them and walk to the Subaru. They watch me get in, and once it's locked, they give me a thumbs up and drive away. I lean against my seat, taking a few deep breaths.

I'm fine. Everything is fine. I am safe.

I pick my phone up and text Sonya, and while I don't go into explicit detail, I just tell her that I'm nervous with Cam having escaped prison. I leave out the part about him swarming us—*me*—like a shark.

But I fought back last time, and I will fight back this time —by beating him at his own game. By outsmarting him. By ensuring I'm never in that position again. We have so many people watching out for him tonight, and he has no idea. If we'd had someone watching for him at homecoming...

I push the thought away.

He was so close—and yet, we weren't prepared.

But we *are* prepared tonight.

Sonya's text comes through just as I'm about to start the car, so I relax against my seat and read it.

Evaluate your surroundings. Listen to your gut. Apply common sense. These three things will almost never fail you. Be smart, but you also need to live your life. The chances of Cam being anywhere near Greythorn are so small. Enjoy your night, and Happy Halloween!

I try to find comfort in her words, but I can't—not right now. Because he is in Greythorn—and I've seen him.

And now it's time to take him down—once and for all.

I toss my phone into my purse, and then I quickly pull the mirror down to check that my black eyeliner hasn't smudged. I stare at my reflection. My face is calm. Serene. Despite the upheaval, despite my past coming back and haunting me, I know that whatever I'm doing right now is good for my soul.

Hunter, Ash, Ledger, and Samson...they are my saviors.

They are good for my soul.

Smiling, I close the mirror, and my eyes catch on the movement in front of my car. My stomach bottoms out, and my veins pulse painfully beneath my flesh.

I am frozen—paralyzed. And my heart pounds against my ribs painfully.

"Hello, Briar," Cam says loudly enough for me to hear. He's in a white shirt and jeans, and I can see the thick, dark scar running down his neck from here. I frantically fish for my keys, my phone, *anything*—but he growls and throws my door open, grabbing me underneath my arms and dragging me out of my car.

My door. I forgot to lock my door, like I promised Hunter.

My pulse is rushing in my ears. I kick against the driveway, screaming, but he's too strong, too big. "Open the door," he commands, throwing my purse at me as I scramble away from him. We're a few feet from the front door. "And turn the camera off."

He must know about the smart camera, then.

"Fuck you," I hiss, grabbing my purse and hunting for my phone.

"You looking for this?" he asks, smirking. He has my phone in his hand, and he crouches down to where I'm sitting. "Don't even think of running away, Briar. Or calling one of your boyfriends. Turn. The. Camera. Off," he growls, handing my phone to me.

My lips tremble slightly as I unlock my phone, and he watches my every move as I open the app and disable everything.

"Good girl." In one swift motion, he yanks my phone out

of my hands—my last lifeline—and throws it against the driveway.

It shatters, and my heart sinks.

Before I can react, scream, anything—he grabs my hair and drags me to the door. With a foot on my stomach, he empties my purse and finds the keys, unlocking the door. I try not to panic, instead pounding against his thick calf. It's no use. He's like a stone statue. I scream one more time before he drags me inside and slams the door shut.

Picking me up, he throws me against the foyer wall, my face smashed against the drywall. He comes up behind me, and his breath is hot and sticky on my exposed neck. I feel hands roam to my ass, gripping it roughly as he sniffs my hair.

Just like ten months ago.

Just like before.

No.

"I think we need to have a little chat," he says, fisting my hair and dragging me away.

71

SAMSON

I keep waiting for her green Subaru to drive into the parking lot, and every SUV that could be hers sends me craning my neck over the fence I'm standing by. When I met up with Hunter, he told me she would be here in a minute, and our float ride is in less than an hour. I check my watch—it's been twenty-six minutes. No sign of Cam, but also no sign of Briar.

Pulling out my phone, I text her, and the message stays on delivered—no read receipt like usual I glance around at the carnival goers, ensuring none of them look like the tall, muscular guy I saw in the grocery store a few weeks ago...

My uncle is working kitchen setup outside his restaurant on the perimeter of the square. I see Ledger with his brother, who came in from Boston to see his friends play. I know they plan to start soon. Hunter is by the raffle, encouraging everyone to enter—but I see the way his eyes scan the crowd. Aubrey and Andrew are sitting near the food, enjoying funnel cakes—though Aubrey checks her phone nearly as much as I do. Ash is talking to the furniture rental company, and Scarlett and Jack are on the other ride—a small rollercoaster—completely oblivious to the fact that Briar's rapist could be here.

Could be.

I swallow and push my glasses up. What if he doesn't show up? What if he sees through our plan? There are a few officers stationed at other points in Greythorn, in disguise. I just have to hope that one of them finds him if he chooses not to come here.

I check my phone again a few minutes later, and it's still on delivered.

Fuck.

It's been thirty minutes, and she's barely a five-minute drive away.

She should be here by now.

I jog over to Ash, but he tells me he hasn't seen Briar. I find Hunter next.

"Hey man, where is she? We have to be on the float in like ten minutes."

Hunter glances down at his phone. "She's not answering my texts."

I fidget with the hem on my shirt, trying not to think of the reason she could be late. "Try calling her. Maybe she got distracted—"

He already has the phone up to his ear. "Fuck," he hisses, looking at his screen. "It went straight to voicemail. Maybe she's talking to her therapist." He tries again and lets out an exasperated breath. "Hold on, Aubrey has her location on her phone. Let's go check where she is."

We head over to where Aubrey and Andrew are laughing with beards full of powdered sugar, and Hunter asks her if he can check on Briar. A hint of worry passes over her face.

"It says 'Location Not Available.' Looking at me, her lips

thin. "Maybe she turned her phone off, but I think one of us should check on her."

I nod. "I'm on it, Mrs. Monroe." We walk back to the front gate.

Hunter shrugs. "Maybe she lost track of time talking to Sonya?"

I chew on the inside of my cheek. "I don't buy it. She'd be talking on her phone, and she would've seen our notifications. It seems like her phone is off." I look up at him. "She was in her car, right?"

His brows knit together. "Yeah. She said she would be leaving in a minute."

I grab my phone and text Ledger and Ash. "Something's not right. Come on, let's go."

Hunter gestures to Aubrey, who jumps up and follows us, and he gives them the key to his car.

"You guys drive separately. I'm parked two blocks that way," he says, gesturing toward the park. "I'll ride with the guys."

By the time Hunter and I make it to my car in the lot, Ledger and Ash are right behind us.

We all share a look—the same dark, agitated expressions.

Please be okay.

She has to be okay.

BRIAR

My screams are muffled as he ties me up to one of the dining room chairs. He's so cliché—using duct tape. I would laugh if I could, but he placed a piece of tape over my mouth first thing. The motherfucker didn't enjoy me hurling insults at him as he carried me over his shoulder. I *did* manage to bite a chunk of flesh off his arm, and his rage and subsequent bellow caused him to throw me against the hard floor. I'm pretty sure he broke one of my ribs, but I'm trying not to think about it.

"Your whore mother thinks she leveled up, huh?" he asks, his voice slightly slurred as he takes in the mansion. *Ahh, nothing like a psycho rapist...especially a* drunk *psycho rapist.* I glare at him as he circles me. "My, my, Briar," he purrs. "You've really filled out this year." His eyes flick to my chest.

My heart clenches when I think of him—of all the guys. If something happens to me...*to them*...

"You were so fucking easy to find," he adds, smiling as he

swings his arms. "And it was simple enough to get here by car from California. Of course, I knew what to watch out for, being a cop once upon a time. But I'm honestly surprised you didn't try to hide your whereabouts a bit better," he muses.

I want to scream, but my throat is already raw.

I kick my feet out at him, my tongue tasting the bitter glue of the duct tape, and he snarls. "You've turned into such a feisty bitch, pretty girl."

That nickname makes me want to vomit. The whole night begins to flash through my mind, and even though Sonya and I have worked through it, seeing Cam here, hearing those words...

I remember the fear of his body overpowering mine. The pain, the violation of the rape. And then the shock at having stabbed him. The cold when I ran out the back door. The way the mud and twigs caught on my bare feet, how my feet were cut up for weeks. I remember the panic rising in my throat like bile, making me spit every few steps, making me feel feral and wild, like an animal. I remember my dress, plastered to my body from the wet, windy mist. I remember the anger.

The soul-wrenching, burning *anger*.

At what he'd done.

I'd trusted him.

And he'd betrayed me in the worst way possible.

I dig my nails into my palm, my tears sliding down my cheeks as Cam paces the dining room.

"I'm going to make sure that if and when I'm caught, at least the smug, little cunt who ruined my life will be dead. What do you think, pretty girl?"

I begin to shake, my eyelashes wet against my face. *I am strong. I survived. I fought back—I really fucking fought back.*

I did everything right.

He's in the wrong.

I need to fight back.

Narrowing my eyes at him, I force my body to still. Being scared won't do me any good right now. I refuse to let him hurt me again. I refuse to become another statistic. I did not go through what I went through just to have my rapist kill me after everything. This is not going to be the end of my story.

Cam walks over and stares down at me. My chest is rising and falling, and I will myself to be calm. *Think, Briar. Think.* His nostrils flare as I narrow my eyes and give him a hateful expression. *I will win this fight.*

Reaching down, he rips the tape off my mouth, and my eyes water as I bare my teeth at him.

"What do you want, Cam? You want me dead? What does that accomplish? I don't want to die, and you don't want to go to jail for life."

He chuckles, running a hand over his lips. "So? I didn't want to go to jail for thirteen years. Sometimes life's not fair."

I start to respond, but then he pulls a knife out of his waistband. My whole body runs cold, and I feel a trickle of sweat run down my back underneath the leather costume. He tips my chin up with the point of the knife, and I glare at him.

I won't die this way.

"I'm going to kill you the same way you almost killed me. Nothing you say will change my mind, pretty girl. I didn't formulate an escape plan and put three of my friends in danger for nothing. I didn't drive across the country for *nothing,*" he spits, digging the point into my skin. I feel the blood begin to pool in that spot, and I hold back a whimper. "I've already accepted my fate, Briar. Have you?"

Before I can say anything, he drops to his knees.

No.

Grinning maniacally, he pulls my pants off, sitting back on his haunches as he stares at the bareness between my legs.

I'm not wearing undies.

It was supposed to be a treat for Samson.

"You fucking slut," he snarls, running the smooth back of the knife along my leg. "Did you do this for me? You think I didn't know you were hoping to turn me in tonight? You think I didn't know the fucking posters with your face were for me? Or the way you stayed behind tonight? Can't you admit you did it all for me?"

No.

Never.

But...

This is my chance.

My chance to get revenge.

My chance to take him down.

Play this right, Briar.

"Yes," I say softly, faking a sob. "Yes. Okay? Are you happy now?"

He stills, and his eyes find mine, searching for the lie. But I let my lip wobble slightly, shrugging as much as I can all tied up.

"I didn't think you'd attack me like this," I add. "Not after what happened. I knew you escaped for me, Cam. I hoped you would. I made a mistake that night," I finish, sobbing. "I was young and confused. I had such a crush on you—" His eyebrows shoot up, and I continue, feigning shyness. "I haven't been the same since everything happened."

"I don't believe you," he muses, taking the hilt of the knife and caressing the inside of my thigh, getting closer to... "If you wanted me to badly, why did I see all four of your worthless boyfriends fucking you at once?"

Squeezing my eyes shut, I breathe heavily, the bile beginning to creep up my esophagus.

My god, he saw everything.

I shake my head back and forth violently, trying to clear

my mind of the idea that Cam was watching—that he was there. That he saw everything. It makes me gag, and Cam chuckles.

"Oh, you didn't know I saw you guys up there in the woods? I was so close at one point, I could've touched you." He clucks his tongue. "I almost killed you all then and there. I was so angry, Briar. So angry that you would so willingly spread your legs for them and not for me. But it would've been too obvious. Plus, I don't care enough about those pricks to kill them. Only you. I needed you alone, so I could finish what I started."

Snapping my eyes open, I sob again. "I'm sorry, okay? I thought... I thought they could be like you. I didn't know what else to do. You awakened something in me that night, Cam."

Believe me.

Believe me.

"They seem to really like you," he starts, placing the dull hilt against my opening. *No.* "They seem to love fucking you," he growls. "Just like I did."

Panic floods me, but I get a grip on it before it takes over.

Swallowing thickly, I nod. "You're right. I can't deny that what you're doing feels good," I groan, bucking my hips once. "I was so young before. But now? I've fucked most of the senior class just trying to get over you."

He gives me a monstrous smile. "Oh, really?"

He's buying it. Keep going.

I grin. "Of course." I look down, furrowing my brows. "I still don't understand why you attacked me, though. Couldn't you tell that I was waiting for you?"

Something moves behind his eyes—and he gives me a lecherous smile. "I know you so well, baby. You fucking whore."

No, you don't.

I give him a small smile. "Knife play is one of my kinks. I like it dirty—bloody. Just like that night. Keep going," I moan.

His eyes flash with something that makes me want to hide under my bed forever. But I can't—I have to play this *just right*.

"You're such a slut," he grunts, scooting closer. Swirling the knife around my opening, I close my mouth to keep from screaming—from roaring with fury.

I throw my head back in an exaggerated show, spreading my legs slightly so he has better access. I swallow the vomit working its way up my throat.

"Keep going then," I demand, biting my lower lip.

Keep going—a challenge.

Cam unbuckles his belt, and it takes every ounce of resolve not to head butt him—not to scream and claw my way out of this. But I don't know what else to do. I have to work him into a frenzy, and then I have to attack.

I look away as he pulls his cock out, feigning arousal as I squeeze my eyes shut. Thrusting upwards, I moan again, and this time, he lets out a low groan. I hear him spit into his hand and begin to stroke himself.

"I need better access," I whine, snapping my eyes open. "Untie my feet. Please." He hesitates, but I bite my lower lip again. "I want my legs over your shoulder."

He growls as he tears at the tape, but it doesn't budge.

"Spread your legs," he commands.

"What?"

"Your legs. Open your knees and the tape will tear with enough force from all sides."

I do as I'm told, and then Cam slams a hand down, effectively breaking through the layers of tape.

Interesting.

"The couch," I mumble. "You can keep my hands tied. I want them above my head."

He mumbles something, but he's not really paying attention —he's jacking himself off. In one swift movement, he picks me up and carries me to the couch in the living room across the hallway, and as my body hits the cushions, I cry out—faking it.

Even with a plan to murder me, even with all the power, he's still so, *so* stupid. He has no idea that with each request, I'm grabbing my power back.

"Yes," I whimper, spreading myself before him. I move my hands above my head as he lowers himself on top of me.

I can't breathe...

Gasping, I feel him trying to maneuver into me. While he's distracted, I rear my tied hands back farther, spreading them as wide as I can against the plastic.

One chance.

I have one chance.

I close my eyes and pray to whoever will listen that this works.

I have the upper hand.

I win this war.

In one fell swoop, I force my joined hands downward as hard as I can, and the tape breaks against Cam's skull before he realizes what's happening. I slam a knee into his groin, and we both roll off the couch. I scramble up and run for the knife in the other room.

"Briar!"

I twist just in time to see Hunter, Ash, Ledger, and Samson running toward me, and Cam coming from the other room.

"Watch out!" I scream, and instead of coming for me, Cam rushes to the guys.

Idiot.

Ash roars and unleashes upon him, punching him in the face with such force that I hear a crack. Cam stumbles backwards, and I slide the knife over to them.

Samson looks down at it, and then his eyes meet mine as he slides it back with his foot.

"All you, little lamb."

"Fucking finish what you started," Ledger growls.

Hunter nods, looking down at the knife and then at me. "Do it."

"If you don't, I fucking will," Ash snarls.

"Briar—please—" Cam rasps, stumbling as he tries to get up. He begins to crawl to me—his face red and pained, his nose pouring blood.

Cracking a smile, I cock my head as I rush over.

And I stab him in the chest—once.

Twice.

Three times.

When he falls onto his stomach, prone and unmoving, I wait until I don't feel a pulse before standing. The knife clatters to the ground.

He didn't finish what he started.

I did.

73

BRIAR

The world tilts a bit, and Samson rushes over just as I faint. When I come to, the police are checking Cam's pulse, and my mom and Andrew are speaking to them. Someone must've pulled my pants back on because they're loose and around my waist. I tie them tighter, sitting up as a couple of cops notice my movements. My mom rushes over to me.

"Briar, oh honey," my mom sobs, pulling me close. We hold each other, swaying in place, for what feels like forever. Andrew puts a warm hand on my shoulder. I relax fully for the first time in weeks. "I'm so sorry," she whispers, hugging me tightly.

"It's okay. I'm okay," I murmur.

I'm not sure if I'm trying to reassure her, or myself.

"Ms. Monroe? We have a few questions for you," the sheriff asks, his face apologetic.

"Of course."

I am hounded with questions, and I answer them all truthfully.

He attacked me.

I stabbed him.

The guys walked in just before I killed him.

It was self-defense.

After a few minutes of additional questioning, they're satisfied with my answers, and then they move onto the guys as I sag against my mom on the couch. I don't look as they wheel Cam away.

"Ma'am," one of the officers says, walking over to me with a piece of paper. "We still need you to answer some additional questions, but you can come into the station tomorrow."

I nod. "Sure. Whatever I can do to put this behind me," I respond.

Once and for all…

He nods and gives me a sympathetic look. "Get some rest tonight." He walks away slowly, looking down at his phone.

"Wait!" I cry. He turns, eyebrows raised. "He said three friends helped him escape in California. You might want to make sure the Marin City police department knows."

He gives me a small smile. "Do you have any names, or any other information you could give me?"

I shrug. "No. He just said three people helped him escape San Quentin."

He nods solemnly. "Thank you. I'll put in a call to his old station tonight."

And then he's gone, leaving me alone with my family— and the guys.

"Someone should tell Scarlett and Jack," I murmur.

"I'm on it," Andrew offers, grabbing his phone and texting them.

I turn to my mom. "I think I'm going to go upstairs and clean up," I say quietly, the shock still numbing me. "I—I have his blood all over me," I say quietly, looking down at myself.

"Do whatever you need to do. How about I make you some tea?" Her eyes flick to the guys briefly.

I nod. "Sure. Thanks, mom."

She gives me a small smile, kissing my forehead. "Just come down whenever you're ready." Her and Andrew walk to the kitchen, leaving the five of us alone.

I turn to face the guys, and none of them say anything. For whatever reason, I feel the need to explain.

"I didn't realize he would be—"

"Briar," Hunter commands, crossing his arms. "There is no excuse for what he did."

"I know, but I should have—"

"What? Anticipated that your rapist would be waiting for the second you were all alone?" Ash adds, his voice tight.

I shrug. "My therapist taught me how to evaluate if a situation is safe. Evaluate your surroundings. Listen to your gut. Apply common sense."

Ledger shakes his head and looks away, and Samson walks up to me, taking my hands.

"Those are great parameters to abide by, but this was... different. Okay? Nothing you could've done would've stopped him. If it wasn't tonight, it would've been in a week, or a month, or..." he trails off, closing his eyes briefly as his jaw ticks. "He would've slipped past your self-imposed guards somehow. I don't think your therapist accounted for a situation like this."

"He's right," Ledger says, rubbing his mouth with his hand. "And I'm not discrediting her wisdom, because it's good advice. But someone you're close to who rapes you? And the same guy who attacks you when you're alone? What could you have done differently?"

They're right, of course.

The three rules that Sonya taught me will only get me so far. People know how to slip past the warning signs—people can follow all the rules until it really matters. For example, getting close to your girlfriend's daughter so that she trusts you. Or waiting until she's alone to attack her with a knife. The three rules couldn't have saved me in either scenario.

They couldn't save me, but I saved myself both times.

And that must count for something.

Swallowing, I look down. "He saw us. He was there—the night we were camping."

Hunter's eyebrows come together, and I see him ball his fists. Ash swears and turns away, kicking something invisible. Ledger just crosses his arms and frowns, and Samson is schooling his face into neutrality—but I see the way his jaw ticks.

"I swear to God, if that motherfucker wasn't already dead," Ash hisses, placing a hand over his mouth.

"He's dead, man," Ledger says quietly. "He lost. We won."

Hunter is quiet as he fidgets with his jaw, his feet tapping on the floor. "I think I can speak for all of us when I say, I'm glad you're safe, Briar."

I swallow and I glance at each of them. "I was sure he was going to kill me. I just want it all behind me." My voice catches on the last word, and I look down at my hands, which are still stained with blood. I clench my fists at my sides as I shake my head. "I thought it would be easy—seeing him again. *Facing* him again. But it was just as hard as the first time."

Ash takes my hand. "Come on. Let's get you cleaned up." I pull away, opening my mouth to protest, but he interrupts me. "We couldn't help you. We got here too late. So let us at least take care of you now."

"Ash—"

"He's right," Hunter ponders with a scowl. "You fought back, and that's fucking badass."

I give him a grateful smile.

"Briar, would you rather be by yourself?" Samson asks, glancing at Ash with annoyance.

I love that they look out for me—that each of them is in tune with a specific part of me, that they can each figure me out in their own ways.

I shake my head. "No. I don't want to be alone."

Ledger walks to the stairs. "Come on. Let's get you cleaned up."

I follow him upstairs—the other guys close behind.

❧ 74 ❧

HUNTER

I kneel on the floor of Briar's bathroom, helping her step out of her shoes. Ash takes her costume off, Samson starts the bath, and Ledger stands next to her, wiping her arms with a washcloth—ensuring all the dried blood is gone. It hits me then—how alike these things are with relation to her.

Me at her feet, worshipping her strength, her soul.

Ash helping her out of her clothes, worshipping her body.

Ledger cleaning her up, worshipping her physical health, ensuring she's fully taken care of in that department.

And Samson pouring bath salts into her bath, worshipping her mental health—checking in, going slow, thinking about what will make her comfortable.

I swallow as I stand, and Ash helps her into the bath. None of us crosses that boundary. I think we're all under the assumption that she doesn't want to be touched—doesn't want *that* aspect of her relationship with us right now. Which is why her next words stun me—stun *us*.

"Which one of you is getting in with me?" she purrs, bringing her knees up and resting her cheek on them.

"Briar, maybe you should just sleep tonight," Samson offers, and a very, very small part of me wants to tell him to shut his fucking mouth.

But the bigger part of me agrees.

"No," she whispers. "I'm done being afraid," she starts, sniffing. "He ruined my junior year in California. Ruined men for me for a long time. Ruined homecoming, and Halloween..." Swallowing, she looks down at the water as her hands trail through the soapy liquid. "I feel good when I'm with you guys, and right now, I really, *really* need to feel good. I want to salvage the night. I want to remember being with you. Not—not him."

We all watch her for a beat. "I'll get in with you," Ash offers quickly, already removing his clothes.

Samson snorts, leaning against the door, and I sit on the counter, trying not to smile. Ledger leans against the glass of the shower. We all share a look, but they don't ask us to leave.

Ash climbs in behind her, and Samson's gaze heats when he notices Ash's erection. He clears his throat.

"I can go—" I offer, pointing to the door with my thumb.

Briar looks over her shoulder at me. "Stay."

A command—not a question.

Our Queen.

Oh, how the tables have turned—and I wouldn't have it any other way.

She leans back against Ash, who cups her breasts in his large hands. I shift, wondering if I should acknowledge my hard on, or ignore it like Ledger and Samson seem to be doing.

Ash's hands trail down her stomach, water pooling in her belly button. She moans, closing her eyes as she arches her back slightly. Suddenly, the physical need to be inside her is all consuming. Ash groans, and his hand finds its way between her legs. I crane my neck to see, but it's covered with cloudy water. Still, my cock pulses inside my pants when I see Ash's fingers working her.

"Does murder make you wet, little lamb?" Ash croons, bucking his hips against hers.

"No. You do." Opening her eyes, she meets our gazes. "All of you," she clarifies.

It makes me happy to see her enjoying this after tonight's nightmare. I can't wait to make her feel good—can't wait for each of us to make her feel good.

If she said jump, we would jump.

I pull my shirt over my head, and Samson and Ledger do the same. Stepping out of my pants, I stroke my throbbing shaft. Ash's tempo gets quicker, and Briar writhes against him —her nipples pink and hard. I let out a shaky breath at the sight of her perfect tits bouncing.

"You're so fucking beautiful," Ash whispers. He removes his hand from between her legs maneuvers his cock there instead. Her sharp inhale lets me know he's inside her, and he moves underneath her, gripping her side as he thrusts deep. The water threatens to spill over the edge of the clawfoot tub.

"Oh, God," she whimpers, squeezing her eyes shut.

I wasn't sure if I'd enjoy seeing someone else fuck her. Last time we all did this, I was behind her, fucking her ass. But this is *hot*. Especially as I glance at my other friends, who have the same heated expressions—their cocks in their hands.

"Ash," she groans. "Harder. I want you to fuck the thought of him out of me."

"Fuck," Ash rasps. "Happy to oblige, my Queen."

And then he pushes her forward onto her knees, slamming into her from behind.

She screams, and the sound reverberates around the small room.

"Yes, Ash, yes," she cries. "Deeper. I want to feel you everywhere."

"Holy shit," I utter, my knees going weak. I hold on to the counter, steadying myself. *This is so fucking hot.* Everything about her—every single imperfection, every single personality trait—is perfect. *This* is perfect.

"Come for me, Briar," Ash growls.

She looks over her shoulder at me furtively before flicking her eyes to Ledger and Samson. Arching her back and gripping the edge of the tub, she pants.

"Oh, fuck," she says quietly, and I see the crescendo of muscles contracting from her core to the rest of her limbs. Shaking, she bellows as she explodes, twitching with every wave, her eyes fluttering closed.

"Holy shit," Ash whispers. "I'm coming."

He fills her, grunting and grabbing the flesh of her ass, pulling her onto his cock forcefully as the last of it leaves him. They both collapse against the edge of the tub.

I slow my hand. "Briar, go to your bedroom."

She obeys, and the other guys follow me.

"I want you," she starts, looking at me. Then her eyes find Ledger. "And you."

I'm not sure when it's agreed that I'll take her pussy this time, but soon she's climbing on top of me. I look over at Ash, who is on his knees before Samson.

Fuck, if I weren't straight...

"Relax, Briar," Ledger growls as she lowers herself onto me. He has a bottle of lube in his hands.

"Fuck," I hiss. "You're so fucking wet."

"You're welcome," Ash says, and we all laugh.

Briar closes her eyes as she takes me in fully, and we both hiss.

"Open your eyes," I say. When she looks at me, straight fire shines through her pupils. Her chest is flushed, and she shudders when I run my finger down her abdomen.

"Please," she pleads, her eyes hooded as she looks back at Ledger.

He spreads her ass, and her eyes widen a bit as he slowly moves inside her. Like before, I feel his cock slide against mine through her thin wall.

Holy fucking shit.

She reaches down and plays with herself, and I throw my head back at the double sensations. We both cry out as I quickly drive into her, more stars exploding before me. As she moves on top of me, her pussy milking my cock with each movement, I look over at Samson just as he groans and spills into Ash's mouth.

Fuck.

Fuck.

My climax builds quicker than I expected, my shaft beginning to throb inside her. She's close, too, because she grabs my hand and moves it to her clit. I swirl my thumb around, using her wetness or Ash's cum or my pre-cum—whatever it is—and that thought pushes me over the edge.

"Holy fuck." My voice breaks. Her breathing is labored, and her eyes don't leave mine. Her warm pussy, swollen with need, contracts tightly around me, setting me off at the same time. Waves of pleasure shoot through me as I watch her come on top of me. My eyes stay locked on her as I pour into her.

She is mine—and I am hers. *We* are hers.

"I'm coming," Ledger says, hissing as he jerks. Briar's mouth pops open, and her hand goes back around to him. Biting her lower lip, she turns back to me, smiling.

Samson is cleaning himself up when Ledger pulls out, and Briar climbs off me.

"I'll never get enough of you," Ledger murmurs into her ear while cleaning her up.

"Thank you," she replies, looking at each of us with such openness, such vulnerability, that something in my chest cleaves in half. "All of you."

"Get some sleep," Ash says, pulling his clothes back on. Turning to Samson and Ledger, he gestures to the door. "Come on. She needs sleep now."

They each give her a kiss, and soon it's just the two of us.

She changes into pajamas, using the restroom and washing her face. I sit on the edge of her bed and rub my temples, waiting to tuck her in. She climbs into the flannel sheets, sighing contentedly.

She's content—*we* did that.

Even though we weren't there until the very end—a fact that bothers me to no end—we were able to help her in other ways. The oath we took doesn't change just because the man we vowed to protect her from is now dead.

I don't think any of us wants to ever give her up.

"Stay with me?" she asks, closing her eyes.

My dad will know—as will Aubrey. They could open her door and see us when they get home. But fuck it. She comes first. I'll explain everything tomorrow.

Pulling my underwear on, I climb in behind her.

"Don't leave, okay?" she asks, her voice already slurred with exhaustion.

"Okay," I whisper. "And Briar?"

"Hmm?"

"I love you." I don't know what else to say. Only those three words can adequately summarize how I feel about her.

"I love you, too," she murmurs.

She has no idea how much I worship her, how I would do anything for her. Getting to her tonight... I would've burned the world to the ground to save her.

But she saved herself.
A true Queen.

75

LEDGER
Six Weeks Later

I wait for Briar to answer the door, jogging in place so that the frosty, December morning doesn't freeze up my muscles. When the door swings open, she grins at me.

"You look cute in your hat and scarf," she croons, tying her own scarf around her neck and pulling on a beanie.

I smirk. "I could say the same thing, little lamb." I tickle her playfully.

We start gradually—the cold causing us to go slower than normal until we're fully warmed up, about a mile in.

She doesn't fall behind, doesn't ask to stop, the entire six miles. When we nearly collapse in front of my house—a tradition just to spite my parents—she bends over, gasping for air.

"How much was that? You took a different route, so I know it must be more, right?"

I smile. I'd lied to her. Three miles is our normal distance.

I doubled it today—she was ready.

"Six. Congrats, Briar. You just ran your first 10k."

She gapes at me, and then she punches my arm—*hard*.

"You asshole," she growls. "I thought it felt freakishly hard."

I shrug, still grinning. "You did it, didn't you?"

She blows an exasperated breath through her lips. "Barely."

"How shall we celebrate?" I ask, pulling her waist into my torso.

She wiggles her eyebrows, and I laugh as we sneak into my house and down into the chapel.

⚜

After I fuck her on one of the pews, she's quiet as she plays with a piece of hair. I'm stroking her bare stomach, swirling circles around her belly button. She turns her head to the side as her eyes land on random objects in the chapel.

"For so long, I didn't allow myself to think about this— about my future. What it could look like." My fingers still, listening to her words. I could listen to her talk forever. "Samson said something that day, in the woods. Remember? If you have an opportunity to get revenge, wouldn't you?"

I swallow. "And? Did you?" I look at her, fury enveloping me about what was done to her.

She gives me a feline smile. I remember the quad incident —how every interaction with her was met with trepidation. How she recoiled from Hunter the first day I ever laid eyes on her.

"I think so. Now it can all stay in the past. Cam tried so hard to break me that night—both nights. But especially after he escaped. I couldn't breathe. It wasn't until the night he died that I took my first full breath. And guess what?" She smiles as she turns to face me. "I fucking won. He's dead, and I'm alive. I guess that's the best revenge, huh?"

I place her hand on my chest so that she can feel how fast my heart is beating. "You won," I repeat. "That's the *best* revenge."

"You all made it possible," she says quietly.

I shake my head. "No. You did it on your own, baby."

"But you all gave me the courage to believe I could do it myself. Don't you see?"

I pull her on top of me, inhaling the scent of vanilla and honey. I make a promise then and there to show her just how strong she is for the rest of my life. Little does she know, she saved me, too. Gave me the courage to buck my family's history, and consider what I really want to do with my life. I love track, but the more I think about it, the more I want something different for myself. Maybe art school—maybe Boston, to be closer to Silas. Or maybe nothing at all while I figure myself out.

She changed *my* life, too.

I kiss her forehead. "Are you excited for the trip next week?" I ask. The sixty-four students enrolled in senior French are going to Paris for a week—including the five of us.

"So excited." She grins, and her eyes light up. *That* look— her excitement for the future—burns away all the shadows of her past.

She won.

She fucking won.

76

BRIAR

"Give me all the deets," I say, grinning as Jack rolls his eyes. We're all seated on the quad...along with a good chunk of the school population.

Jack sighs. "I met him at Romancing the Bean. Who knew I'd find someone in Greythorn I *hadn't* ever met. He's new—he moved this summer from Georgia. A junior. Into anime," he explains, shrugging. "He's really nice."

"Is Jack Dormand in love?" Ash croons, walking past us.

"Fuck off, Greythorn," Jack says, but they both smile as Ash continues over to a group of students, telling them about a party at his house tonight.

It's as if nothing—and everything—has changed at Ravenwood. Instead of the Kings being hated by everyone, they kind of...blend in now. No one moves when they walk down the hall. No one averts their eyes. It's like the whole thing was a fever dream, and everyone seems to love the newfound lack of hierarchy at Ravenwood.

"That's wonderful. I can't wait to meet him."

"Oh, my god," Scarlett says, laughing from next to me. She points to a group of three guys walking through the gate. "Look at them."

They must be freshmen. I don't think I've ever seen them before, but as they stalk through the quad with menacing expressions, it's clear they want people to know who they are. A few people look at them skeptically.

"Who are they?" I ask as one of them gives me a hard stare.

"The next generation," Hunter muses, putting an arm around me. "I told you. Once our reign fell, someone else would want to swoop in to claim that power."

I twist around and kiss him. When I pull away, I'm nearly laughing. "You poor, poor little dethroned boy."

He shakes his head and looks away.

"I'm going to have to keep an eye on them," Ledger muses, crossing his arms.

"They're just walking. Calm down, everyone." Samson gives me a half smile.

⚜

The party that night is different than my first Ravenwood party. Ash especially seems lighter, more himself. He gets people drinks, shows off the art his mother has picked out— thanks to my mom—and he doesn't seem to want to get away from the crowd like he did that first night. Still, I keep my eye on them all as the party wears on. Jack and I dance to the music before he slinks off with his new endeavor, and Scarlett is making eyes at some junior girl with long, blonde hair.

As the music dies down, and people begin leaving, I say goodbye to Scarlett and Jack. Hunter offers to drive everyone home, since he stayed sober. I walk them out, and then I turn back to help Ash clean up. Instead, he's grinning at me with my jacket in my arms.

"Let's go."

I roll my eyes and take my jacket as he locks up, leaving the horrifically messy house behind. Thankfully, Ash's mom is on a girl's weekend with my mom. It's sweet—they've really bonded these last few weeks. I'm temporarily breathless as the cold, winter air slams into me. I'll never get used to that feeling. It's like an invisible weight being pressed into my chest. Though I'd never admit that to the guys.

They'd never let me live it down.

"Where are we going this time?" I ask.

"You'll see."

We're quiet as we drive through Greythorn. No music, no talking. It's nearly two in the morning, and the mist is thick against the Edwardian architecture. He pulls into a reserve, driving down a dirt path a couple of miles before coming up to a small shack. It looks abandoned, but the way my skin tingles tells me it was recently occupied.

"Ash," I warn.

He doesn't answer me. Instead, he stops right in front of the dilapidated front door. His eyes find mine a second later.

"Cam lived here."

I grip the edge of my seat. "I don't want to be here—"

"I think you need to let it all out, Briar. This isn't revenge for me, or Hunter, Ledger, or Samson. This—this is for you."

I give him a warning look, and he laugh. "I know, I know. If you go over there and kick rocks for ten minutes, so be it. But every person needs a chance to get revenge. Do whatever you need to."

Hopping out of the car, I slam the door shut and walk to the front door. At first, I just stand there, jaw clenched. But then something strange happens, and I begin to feel the fury roll through me. The frustration that he took so much of my life, that he violated me, that he betrayed my trust.

But I'm here, and he's not.

I lift my face to the sky, and I scream.

When I'm done, Ash exits the car and walks up to me. He's holding a box of matches and some gasoline.

He grins. "Let's fuck some shit up."

77

BRIAR

Paris is everything I hoped for, and more. Though we're chaperoned, Samson manages to cut away from the tour group on our second day. He pulls me into an alley, and I'm breathless with excitement. We emerge onto another street, and throngs of people pass us. The colorful awnings are bright against the grey and white sky, the trees dark and bare from winter.

Everything—I love *everything* about Paris.

The artists along the Seine. The European cars that zoom by on the street. The scent of crepes and falafel. The diversity, the art, the culture...

This is home.

"Where are we going?" I ask, laughing as Samson drags me across the river to Notre-Dame. I pull my jacket close, even though it's warmer here than it is in Massachusetts right now. I look up at the massive stone structure. "I thought it was closed all week?"

"I pulled some strings," he says, smiling. Taking his phone out of his pocket, he speaks to someone in French on the other end.

"Of course you did," I say, feigning annoyance. I am giddy with excitement.

We walk up to the gate, and it's swarming with tourists. Before I realize what's happening, Samson is pulling me through one of the doors to the gothic cathedral.

A security guard nods once, gesturing to a staircase to his right. "You have an hour."

"Thanks, Tom."

Samson pulls me behind him as we ascend a stone staircase. "Who the hell was that and how did you know his name?"

He laughs, tugging me after him—which is good, because despite running three mornings a week, I'm still struggling for air two stories up.

"My uncle knows a lot of people in Paris. He went to culinary school here."

"Ah."

I'm pretty sure all the Kings could pull strings in every city around the world.

We continue to climb, and I have to sit every couple of stories. My legs are burning. Ledger is always talking about cross training, and in this moment, I hate him for being right.

By the time we get to the roof, I nearly collapse.

"Samson," I gasp, but before I have a chance to sling an insult his way, he points to the view.

Every atom in my body stills. Even my breathing regulates in the presence of the magnificent city below me. Not just below me, but out—spreading as far as I can see. The Seine snakes through the center of the city, and I admire the Edwardian buildings, the white stone gleaming in the winter light.

Samson comes behind me, pressing his body into my back. Kissing my head, he holds me. "Beautiful," he says quietly.

"It really is."

"I was talking about you, Briar."

I twist around and wrap my arms around his neck. All the other guys have said *I love you*—except Samson.

I know a part of it is because of Micah.

"This might be the best date you've dragged me on, Samson Hall."

We have a standing date night every weekend, and this one is, by far, the best one yet.

"Which is why I wanted to wait to tell you that I was in love with you. Until I could tell you here, in a place like this."

My breathing hitches as his eyes crinkle around the edges. *God, he's stunning.* And so romantic it sometimes physically hurts.

"I'm in love with you, too," I say quietly, using my tiptoes to kiss his soft lips.

His hands rove down to my jacket, and he unbuttons it one button at a time. I pull away and raise my eyebrows.

"What?" he asks, grinning. "Tell me this wouldn't be the most fun place to have sex."

All the other guys say fuck—but Samson can hardly ever bring himself to say it. I cock my head as I unzip my pants.

"It's cold, so I'm keeping my clothes on."

He growls as he unzips his pants and presses me against the plastic—the only thing between me and my death hundreds of feet below. I swallow.

"Look," he instructs, pointing to the city.

"Fine, you win," I joke, and then I gasp when he enters me, my whole body contracting against him.

"I better win," he rasps, taking my hands and entwining his fingers with mine.

He thrusts into me in a skilled manner—not rough, but enough to pull an orgasm out of me quickly. Undulating against him, he groans as he explodes inside of me, panting as we remain joined together—with Paris spread out below us.

After he cleans me up, we sit and watch the city. I know we'll probably be in a lot of trouble when we rejoin the group, but this was so, so worth it.

"What's going to happen when you go to school here and I'll be in Massachusetts?" he asks quietly, handing me some chocolate.

I bite into the sweet candy. "I don't know. I haven't really thought about it."

He's quiet for a minute. "Is this—are we—" he stops and looks down. "I would understand if this thing—with all of us —was just a casual fling. Something fun to tell your future boyfriend or something."

I look at him, and his eyes find mine. Taking his hand, I kiss it. "How would I ever be able to go back to one guy? My god, it would never, ever compare."

We both laugh, and as we make our way down a few minutes later, I pull him to me in the dark staircase.

"I don't have an answer to your question, by the way," I murmur. "But I love you all equally, and I don't want to stop what we're doing. Next year may look different, but the five of us didn't get this close for nothing. I think we all share a bond that doesn't come around that often. I'm not going anywhere."

And then I kiss him—deeply. Passionately. Wholly.

The Kings of Ravenwood can have me.

I surrendered a long time ago.

EPILOGUE

Nine Years Later

"Sweetie, that's a little too high," I croon, trying to keep my voice from sounding as panicked as I feel.

"They have to learn some time," my mom mumbles. Beatrice, my eight-year-old half-sister, is walking Easton, my toddler, along the perimeter of a *very* high play structure.

"He could break his neck," I whine, shifting from foot to foot.

She rolls her eyes, and I guess as a seasoned mother of three, she would know. Blake, my half-brother, is sitting contentedly in the sand, his baby cheeks chubby and pink from the heat.

"I don't understand how you had another one," I joke, crossing my arms. "Easton is a handful."

She smiles and shrugs. "I don't know. I guess I wasn't ready to stop."

"You were almost done raising me! And then Bea came along, and she was older, and bam! Then there was Blake."

She laughs. "I'm going to be sixty-three when he graduates high school."

We break into a fit of giggles. My eyes flick back to Easton. "Careful!"

"Bea has him. Don't worry." She tilts his head. "His hair is getting blonder," she muses, smirking.

I roll my eyes. I'm just about to make a snarky comment when another mom walks over to us.

"Your kids are so cute!" She shields her eyes. "Are they all yours?" she asks me.

I laugh. "Nope. Just the toddler boy. This is my mom, and those are her two kids."

I can see her trying to figure it out—the math, the logistics—but she just nods.

"Hey, babe," Samson says, coming up behind me and wrapping his arms around my stomach. I love when he's in a suit.

"Aw, so sweet. Is this the father?"

My lips twitch with a smile. "One of them."

Her eyes widen, and then she half-walks, half-jogs away.

"You really should stop messing with people like that," Samson purrs in my ear.

I laugh, and my mom smiles as she looks away. "It's so much fun, though."

⚜

Two hours later, I hop out of the shower after my run. Checking my phone, I see a picture of Samson and Easton at the museum. I send a quick heart emoji as I pull on a bra and underwear. Slipping into a cocktail dress, I pin my short, light-brown hair up—

my mom 'do, as Ash likes to call it. I step into my pumps and grab my purse, exiting my house and climbing into my Porsche. Easton's music begins to blare through the speakers, and I turn it all the way down and place my hands on the wheel.

Sometimes—every few weeks or so—I wish I knew which partner he belonged to. I'm merely curious—I wouldn't necessarily do anything with the information, since they're all so involved in his life. But my mom's comment earlier—about his hair getting blonder...

Three years ago, I went off birth control, and the five of us decided to have a baby. We all got genetic testing, and nothing crazy came up, so we decided to pursue it naturally. We also decided the baby could take a DNA test at any time if we needed any vital medical history, or if he decides he wants to know when he's older.

I got pregnant the first month, and the guys love to joke it's because there are four of them and one of me...

Everyone in our life has been so supportive of our relationship. We have a good system figured out, too. Mondays are Hunter. Tuesdays are Ash. Wednesdays are a free for all... come one, come all. Thursdays are Ledger. Fridays are Samson. Saturday and Sunday are my days to take alone time, run errands, and I have the option of inviting one or some or all of them over. We split childcare evenly, with a similar, rotating schedule for Easton.

Our only rule is that we have to be open about other relationships. So far, we've all only ever been committed to each other.

The guys each have a separate house in Greythorn—the place we all ended up coming back to. I couldn't imagine leaving my mom, Beatrice, or Andrew, so after four glorious years in Paris, I moved back, got my masters in Boston, and now have my own practice as a therapist. Hunter is working on his sixth book, Ash is the youngest mayor Greythorn has ever had, Ledger is a successful artist, and Samson is an environmental engineer.

I feel lucky most days—overwhelmed, every once in a while—but mostly grateful.

I pull out of my driveway and smile, following directions to a small French place in Boston. Mom life has been a hard adjustment, but having four dads care for our son has helped with *so* much. And it really doesn't matter whose biological son he is. Because really, they all love him equally. I park and walk into the restaurant, excited to see Scarlett and meet her partner. She's in town from New York. Jack is supposed to be here tonight, too. He's in from Miami.

I push the door open, and before I can register what's happening, a bunch of people are shouting at me.

"Surprise!"

"Happy Birthday!"

I nearly fall over and cup my mouth as Hunter descends from the crowd, carrying Easton.

"Hi, sweetie!" I squeal, taking him. It's only been two hours since Samson picked him up, but reuniting with him is my favorite thing in the whole world.

"Mama," he mumbles, wrapping his soft, little arms around my neck. "Ma miss you."

"He did," Hunter muses. "Wouldn't stop saying mama on the car ride home."

I laugh and give him a kiss. "This is incredible," I say, looking around. "Did you plan it?"

"Please," Scarlett interjects, raising her perfectly arched eyebrows. "This was all me."

Hunter chuckles. "It's true." He takes Easton. "Go mingle. Happy Birthday, love."

Scarlett introduces me to her partner, Victoria. They're both chefs in New York. Jack saunters up and kisses me on both cheeks. Though he's still single, he's doing fabulously as a literary agent in Miami. I continue around the room, saying hi to my mom, Andrew, Beatrice, and Blake. I make sure to squeeze Blake as much as I can. The baby chunk gets me every time.

My eyes flit to Ash, who is drinking a beer and talking to Samson. His hair is a bit longer, but the most notable difference is how much muscle he's put on in the last nine years. All the guys really grew into themselves—but Ash especially. Being mayor really had him growing up quickly, and as he smirks at me, I swear I can still see the mischievous glint in his eyes from when we were teenagers. And Ledger, who now has hair tied up into a bun, bends down to kiss me and present me with a bouquet of flowers.

"This is beautiful," I remark, looking around.

"Of course. Did you think we'd forget?"

I laugh. "No, I just—"

"You look beautiful, Briar." Kissing my lips, he trails his finger down my jaw.

"Thank you."

I walk over to Samson, wrapping my arms around his neck. He doesn't need his glasses anymore thanks to Lasik, but I do miss them from time to time. His hair is cut shorter now, and he's always dressed in suits.

"Happy Birthday, little lamb," he whispers.

I give him a peck before walking back to Hunter. Really, I just want to hold my baby.

Hunter gives me a knowing smile as he hands Easton over. He's changed the least—still longer, wavy hair, and stubble. He pulls off the melancholy, tortured writer look very well. It suits him.

"Miss, it's time to be seated," the hostess says, ushering us to a large table. "I wasn't sure which one is your husband, so I—"

I place a hand on her arm. "They all are." Giving her a

warm smile, I leave her stunned as I take a seat at the head of the table. I give my mom and Andrew a warm smile, and then I sigh contentedly. On nights like tonight, it's so hard to remember the scared, little girl that first day at Ravenwood. Because without that catalyst—without everything happening the way that it did—my life would be so different now.

Hunter, Ash, Ledger, and Samson all sit surrounding me, with Easton in my lap.

It doesn't matter who is where.

Because they're all here.

And they're all mine.

❦

Thank you so much for reading Ruthless Queen! I truly hope you enjoyed this world and the four Kings. If you want to read all about Ledger's brother, Silas, grab the first book in the Savage Hearts series! It's a completed reverse harem trilogy set in Greythorn.

Savage Hate
Savage Gods
Savage Reign

BONUS EPILOGUE

Briar

Halloween, Freshman Year of College

I pace back and forth in my tiny dorm room, wiping my palms on my tweed skirt. I check my blouse buttons and sit on my bed, legs crossed, admiring my knee-high boots that Emilie, my roommate, picked out for me. My phone dings and I jump, standing and trying to quell my shaking hands as I lift my screen to my face.

Be there in 5. ;)

I swallow and sit back down, clutching my phone tightly.

Five minutes.

Five minutes until I see my boyfriends—all four of them.

Five minutes until we reunite after two months apart.

And now they're here—in Paris. For *two* weeks.

Hunter is taking a gap year, and until last week, had been living in a shoebox in Brooklyn. Ledger is also taking a gap year and living with his brother, Silas, in Boston. Samson is at MIT, and Ash is at Yale.

I miss them—so much. Most nights, I wake up gasping for air, wishing they were here to warm my sheets. Emilie knows about the situation, and has gracefully given us this weekend alone to spend time at her family's beachfront condo in Cannes. She's an amazing roommate, albeit adorably insufferable, seeing as she scattered condoms all over the floor before she left.

I play with the hem of my skirt, and my legs begin to tingle as I hear footsteps and wished voices in the hallway. It's nearly ten at night. Their flight didn't get in until seven, and because of customs, the train ride to Paris, and walking to the Sorbonne, I'm sure they're exhausted. I glance at the food and wine I have laid out, wiping my hands on my skirt again.

There's a loud knock at the door, and I take a calming breath before I throw it open.

There they are.

I grin as we all hug, and then I usher them inside, closing the door before quickly glancing into the hallway. Luckily, most people seem to be gone for the weekend, but I probably should keep quiet when we...

The thought makes me blush, and Hunter walks up to me, running a finger down my cheek.

"Hi, little lamb," he murmurs, placing a finger under my chin and giving me a gentle kiss. He looks the same—they all do. Not much has changed in the two months since I've seen them.

Ash kisses me next, then Ledger, then Samson. Each of them hugs me tightly, and then I point to the food, and we all resort to our usual camaraderie as they eat and drink straight from the wine bottle. I smile as I watch them, feeling more shy than normal. It's only been two months, but I've changed, and I'm sure they have, too.

I end up putting on some music as I catch them up on my life here, my psychology courses, and life in Paris. The wine begins to loosen my nerves, and after an hour of catching up as we all sit on my small twin bed, I kick my shoes off and lean back. A soft, indie rock song comes on, and immediately, the air changes as silence surrounds us. It has to be past midnight now.

Aren't they tired?

Ash pours everyone a bit more wine from our third bottle, winking at me as he finishes what's in his cup. Samson hums along to the music, looking anywhere but at me, and Ledger is twiddling his thumbs to the beat, pretending to swirl his wine.

Maybe I'm not the only one who is nervous as hell. It's not that I don't want to do what we've done so many times together. It's just that I feel out of practice, and they've all been living in new cities, with new people, and new experiences. I have, too, but I missed them—every single day, I missed them. I can't even look at any of the guys here in Paris. We hadn't really discussed exclusivity, but it was agreed upon that we'd let each other know out of courtesy, so as far as I know, they hadn't been with anyone else, either.

Still... I was so far away, and I was only one person, and none of them had an obligation to stay with me—

"Briar."

Ash's words cut right through me, and I snap my eyes to his.

"Yeah?"

He gives me a lopsided smile as he sets his wine down and crawls over to where I'm seated at the end of the bed. I don't even know if they're in the mood, having travelled for hours. Maybe all of this—the wine, the boots—was presumptuous. They need sleep first and foremost.

But then Ash grins as he pulls me onto him, grabbing my bare thighs and moving one of my legs over his lap roughly, pulling my face down to his. He kisses me—hard, fast, and with fervor. I let out a small moan, and he smiles against my mouth.

"I missed all of the sweet, little noises you make, little lamb."

I'm panting when I pull away, and then I feel Ledger move my hair off of my neck, planting a kiss against the delicate skin behind my ear.

"You're all flushed," he murmurs, gliding his tongue against my hairline. "God, you taste fucking delicious. Just like I remember."

Samson and Hunter watch me from the other end of the bed, and I give them both an indolent smile. They crawl over, and Hunter moves to my other side, reaching for my blouse and beginning to unbutton it.

"Is this—are you—" Samson asks, not touching me.

"Yes," I whisper. "I missed you. All of you."

Ash and Hunter grunt in response, and Ledger scoots over so that Samson can join in. I feel Samson's hands lift my skirt, squeezing my bare ass.

"Fuck," he says, a little unevenly. "I'm already so fucking hard."

"I wasn't sure if—"

"If we'd want you?" Hunter growls, incredulous. "Briar, I think I speak for all of us when I say, tonight will be an unleashing."

An unleashing.

Jesus.

I meet each of these eyes, inhaling the scent of Hunter's cologne, or Ledger's musky shampoo, of Samson's soap and Ash's sweet breath. My sheets are silky, the comforter soft, and I take in the ambient light from the string lights on my wall. I don't remember who, thanks to the wine, but someone must've turned off the main room lights. Swallowing, I shrug my blouse off, climbing off of Ash's lap and off of the bed.

The wine is coursing through me. I feel free, sexy—and ready for whatever's about to happen tonight.

I turn to face all of them as I unzip my skirt and step out of it. I'm not wearing underwear, and I reach behind me to unfasten my bra. One of them inhales sharply, and when I look up, they're all watching me like feral wolves.

Two months.

Two months of built up tension, built up lust. For me, two months of not quite hitting the spot with my vibrator. It wasn't the same. I can only imagine how they feel, seeing as they're all looking at me like a piece of juicy meat after two months of starvation.

They part and give me space in the middle of the small bed. It'll be tight, but Samson motions to Ash, and they scoot off so that Samson's hips are hanging off of the edge of the bed.

Ash falls to his knees, grabbing Samson's hips and unbuckling him roughly.

"I'm going to suck your cock," he murmurs, his voice tight. "But I want you to come in her with me after they're done."

A flash of heat shoots through me, and Hunter grabs me, pulling me on top of him as he removes his shirt. With my thighs on either side of his abdomen, I reach down and unzip his jeans, grinning when I unleash his giant cock. I look over my shoulder, and without asking, Ledger comes up behind me, pulling both Hunter and I to the edge of the bed so that he can stand.

"You're so fucking beautiful," Ledger murmurs, running a hand over my bare ass. I turn to face Hunter below me and I hear Ledger unzip his pants.

"Fuck," Samson hisses, and I look over just as Ash's lips take in Samson's thick shaft. "Your mouth is so fucking warm," he says, his voice hoarse.

My clit throbs as I look down at Hunter and smile.

"Go on," he muses, smirking. Grabbing my hips, he lowers me down until his stiff length is teasing my entrance. "Unless you want me to do it?"

"I—"

Before I can protest, he drives my hips down onto him and enters me fully. I cry out, arching my back, and Ash moans with a mouth full of Samson's cock.

"Why am I always the last one?" Ledger jokes, and I hear him reach into his pocket for lube as Hunter drives into me again. I groan, closing my eyes but also not wanting to close my eyes and miss the show.

"Why are you guys so far away?" Samson asks, his hands over his face as Ash bobs his head up and down on his dick. "Ledger, can I at least eat your ass?"

I feel Ledger stiffen slightly, but then his hands come around to my breasts, and he squeezes them gently.

"By all means," he replies, laughing.

I ride Hunter's cock and let Ledger ease his length into me slowly, and that all-too-familiar stretched feeling gives way to such incredible, full-body pleasure. Ash and Samson move to the ground—Ash laying down and sucking Samson's cock as Samson kneels and takes Ledger's ass in his hands. I feel Ledger twitch the instant Samson's tongue runs around the rim of his ass, and I swear his cock hardens and lengthens even more, his cock piercing massaging my insides.

"Fuck," Ledger cries, his hands squeezing my breasts tighter now.

"Hey," Hunter whispers, trailing his hands up my stomach. It's such a dizzying flurry of feeling—Hunter and Ledger inside of me, feeling the way Ledger's drives become more erratic with Samson at his ass... "This is for you," he says quietly. "Let us give this to you."

I nod and close my eyes, and Hunter slows his pace as Ledger quickens his.

"Holy shit," Ash says roughly, and when I look over my shoulder, he's jacking himself off furiously. "Watching all of you is going to make me come."

"One at a time," I joke, thanking the universe for birth control when I imagine how much they'll fill me tonight.

My whole body begins to twitch. I hear Samson murmur to Ash to stop, and then Ash comes around to my side, grinning before kneeling next to Hunter.

"What are you—"

I gasp when his face goes down on me, his cheek resting on Hunter's abdomen as his tongue flicks against my nub.

It's too much—Ash's face, Hunter's hand gripping his hair as he fucks my pussy, and Ledger behind me, now moaning with every thrust.

Everything begins to blur together as I feel myself beginning to climax. My toes curl and my cries get more desperate, more frantic, as everything winds up and—

I scream as my orgasm slams into me, and Ash groans as I soak his face, each wave unleashing more and more and more.

"That's it, baby," Ash says, licking and slurping. I stop twitching just as Ledger slaps my ass. *Hard.*

"Oh, fuck," Ledger says, his voice hoarse. "I'm coming, I'm—"

He lets go, filling my ass with come, roaring as his hips buck erratically. Samson moans and slurps, and I feel every throb, every pulse of Ledger emptying himself into me as his body convulses against me.

"That was so fucking hot," he says, panting and pulling out of me. I feel his come slip out and onto Hunter's thigh, but I don't care.

"Fuck, Ledger," Hunter growls, baring his teeth as he grabs my hips and slams into me. "You made me fucking come," he says unevenly, closing his eyes and slowing as he pulses into me, some sort of feral sound leaving his lips as he grips me tighter with each wave.

I'm breathing heavily as I look down at Hunter, and I lift myself up as come drips down my thigh.

"Holy shit," I whisper, my legs shaking. I turn to Samson. "You know what to do."

He smirks as Hunter and Ledger clean themselves up, and he comes behind me, stroking his hard cock. Using Ledger's come as lube, he enters my ass and pulls me to a standing position carefully. I'm a little bit sore, but Ledger squirts some actual lube on his shaft, and then it feels really good again.

Ash walks over to my front, kissing me deeply and fisting my hair as he inserts his length into my still-wet pussy.

"Jesus Christ," he rasps. "You're so warm, so *tight*." He looks at Hunter. "So *wet*."

They share a look that I can't handle right now—as if they don't care if they have to share. That it never mattered. That I can be all of theirs at the same time.

I moan as the two of them writhe against me, fucking me at the same time. I lift my chin and kiss Ash as he moves slowly—nothing quick, nothing frantic like before—but with intention. I cry out as his shaft massages the sensitive spot inside of me, and a crescendo of pleasure rains down on me, and I feel myself soak the dorm carpet below me.

Ash pulls out and watches as I twitch in Samson's arms, my eyes squeezed shut as wave after wave rolls through me.

"I love you," Ash murmurs as he thrusts into me again, quickening his pace again. "I haven't let myself come in two months," he says, grinning as I rear my head back in surprise.

"Really?"

"I can't say the same," Hunter jokes, and that's when I

notice he's jerking himself off—both he and Ledger are as they watch us.

"Fuck, Briar," Samson whispers against my ear. He bends down and plants a gentle kiss on my neck, and then he stops thrusting altogether as he comes inside of me. "Fuck, fuck, fuck," he whispers, grabbing my sides and squeezing.

"I'm coming," I reply, feeling my whole body bunch up and then release like a tidal wave, and Ash roars as he comes and fills me, both of us coming at the same time.

Samson and Ash both stay inside of me for a few seconds afterward, and then they pull out at the same time, helping me back onto the bed since my legs are now useless.

Hunter and Ledger kneel on either side of me. I watch as both of their faces contort, and they both spray my breasts with come, groaning loudly and fucking their hands as they do. When they finish, I look around at all of them.

Mine.

They are *mine*.

"Worth the two month wait," Ledger says, chuckling as he hands everyone a wipe. He looks at Samson and winks. "You're good at eating ass."

"He's had a lot of experience," Ash retorts, and we all laugh.

All of them help me clean up, removing my bed sheets and helping me into cozy pajamas. Like always, after being with all of them, I am utterly exhausted. Samson walks me to the bathroom down the hall, and when we get back, the other guys have made up the room by placing all of the blankets on the floor and forming one giant bed.

For all of us to sleep together.

I smile as Samson tucks me in, and a few seconds later, I feel the others climb in on both sides of me. Closing my eyes, I sigh contentedly as we all fall asleep together.

ACKNOWLEDGMENTS

Thank you to my husband, Peter. Your comments and advice helped shape a lot of this story, and I'm grateful you took the time to read it (twice!) I'm sorry my screen is so bright when you're trying to sleep, lol.

To my Dark Hearts—thank you for encouraging me to write something outside of my comfort zone. I know how excited you are for this story, and it was your excitement that got me through those moments that had me second guessing myself.

To Traci Finlay, for the diligent editing. As always with you, this story is ten times better now thanks to your suggestions, edits, and comments.

To my author friends, specifically the ones who helped shape this story in some way, even if you didn't know it—R Holmes, Brianna Hale, Sara Cate, Hollis Wynn, Elizabeth Dear, Kate Farlow, and so many more. Thank you for the DMs, the cover excitement, the blurb critiques, and for letting me vent when I thought this story was the worst thing I've ever written.

To Shelbe, I'm so glad we "met" on TikTok! Thank you for customizing bookmarks for me, for taking the time to make incredible teasers and graphics, and for generally being so supportive of me and my writing.

To my boys, for being adorable menaces. Where would I be without you? More rested, probably, but I cannot imagine doing this life without your cute, little faces by my side.

And last but not least, my readers. Whether you found me from a silly TikTok video or you've been here since Evi and Nick... whew! It's been a wild ride. Thank you so much for being here. I would not be doing this without your comments, messages, and emails.

ABOUT THE AUTHOR

Amanda Richardson writes from her chaotic dining room table in Yorkshire, England, often distracted by her husband and two adorable sons. When she's not writing contemporary and dark, twisted romance, she enjoys coffee (a little too much) and collecting house plants like they're going out of style.

You can visit my website here: **www.authoramandarichardson.com**

Printed in Great Britain
by Amazon